I0634808

Generations of the Eagle

ThunderSongs presents:

Generations Of the Eagle

a novel

by Pete Jorgensen

Generations of the Eagle © 2010 Peter Jorgensen. All rights reserved. No part of this book may be used or reproduced in any manner whatsoever without written permission except in the case of brief quotations used in critical articles and reviews. For information, address ThunderSongs, P.O. Box 783, Isle of Palms, SC 29451.

First Edition

ISBN 978-0-578-00431-0

TABLE OF CONTENTS

PROLOGUE: THE ANIKUTANI.. 1

1: A NEW WORLD 8

2: THE FRONTIER.. 24

3: THE GAWONISGI NVYA 33

4: GATHERING STORM 50

5: FOOTSTEPS OF THE EAGLE... 71

6: GHOST DANCE 86

7: SEQUOYAH SCHOOL.. 95

8: THE STORY TRUNK.. 108

9: PINE RIDGE.. 116

10: EAGLE DANCE... 126

11: A SACRED WAY... 131

12: A SON OF THUNDER.. 141

13: A PARTING 154

14: A NEW TOMORROW.. 163

15: THE SONG OF SHOUTING CROW... 169

16: DISTANT THUNDER.. 180

17: THE ROCK... 185

18: DEATH AND LIFE... 199

19: BURY MY HEART 209

20: ANCIENT FIRE 217

21: FLYING FREE... 222

22: NEW THUNDER 228

23: ENDINGS AND BEGINNINGS... 238

24: THE TOWERS... 247

25: LIVE TO FORGIVE.. 261

26: HOMECOMING.. 274

EPILOGUE: A STORY TO BE TOLD... 286

ACKNOWLEDGEMENTS

I first thank my God, the Creator of the Universe and all that is, whom the Cherokee know as Unetlanvhi. I also thank His Son Jesus the Christ whom the Cherokee know as Tsisa. I thank my wife Terri who gave me the space to write this book and the accompanying music of The Trail of Tears Suite. She gave many valuable suggestions and input that helped to shape both. I thank my elder daughter Rachel for diligent proofreading and precise creative suggestions. I thank my youngest daughter Melody for her unflagging interest and excitement in this project. Her enthusiasm always helped take the work forward.

I thank my lifelong friend Monty Pierce for a creative suggestion that sparked and molded the character of Phillip Shouting Crow. I especially thank my friend Mike Florio for his focused suggestions and his excellent vocal work in The Trail of Tears Suite. Mike has become the singing voice of the Suite and his musical contributions have helped to mold this book. I also thank the other collaborators of Vertical Alignment whose musical offerings took the story to a new level: Randy George, Dan Lile, David "Shreddy" Wallimann, and Kevin Thomas. I also thank all the encouraging brothers and sisters of CPR. A special thanks to the late Ross Rorie for his narrative contribution to The Trail of Tears Suite. I will see you again my brother when we sit together in the true council of Elders.

I give a special thank you to Robert Whitlow who took time from his own writing schedule to read the first part of this book. His suggestions and praise helped to focus this work and prepare it for publication. Extra thanks go to Bart Boge for his comprehensive and notated proofreading. A huge thank you goes to Eddie Jerlin who carefully ferreted out typos and made awesome creative suggestions.

I would like to thank my growing circle of Cherokee

friends. To Frankie Sue Gilliam I give special thanks. She has been the Cherokee Grandmother of this project and a source of information, insight, and true encouragement. I want to thank Peggy Tiger for graciously allowing the use of her late husband Jerome's poignant artwork. Thank you to John Ross for his sage advice. I give over the top and overflowing thanks to Lisa LaRue who has become the single most important source of information for this project. Lisa has closely proofread the manuscript and offered a wealth of suggestions to make the book true to the Cherokees. As Acting Historian for the Keetoowah Band of the Cherokees, she has given me access to rare one-of-a-kind documents that have allowed me to paint a historically accurate picture. She also assisted in creating the Glossary for this book. I also thank Durbin Feeling for valuable advice on Cherokee spelling and pronunciation.

–Pete Jorgensen
Mt. Pleasant, SC
May 30, 2010

GLOSSARY

Cherokee

Word	Pronunciation	Meaning
Ameliquo	uh-MEH-lee-quo	America
Anigiduwagi	a-KNEWW-gih-doo-WAHG	Keetoowah people
Anikutani	a-KNEE-koo-TAH-knee	Legendary ancient Cherokee priest order
Aniyuntikwalaski	a-knee-tuhn-TEE-qua-LAHS-gi	Thunder Beings
Aniyvwiya	a-KNEE-yuh-WEE-yah	The People
Awohali Ganohili	a-wo-HA-li gah-no-HEE-lee	Eagle flying, Soaring Eagle
Chooch	chooch	fond slang for "boy"
Dohi kununawa	doe-HEE glkoo-new-NAH-wa	a peaceful pipe
Duda	DOO-da	Dad
Edudi	eh-DOOD	Grandpa
Elisi	eh-LEES-si	Grandma
Gawonisgi Nvya	GAH-woe-KNEES-skey NUH-ya	Speaking Stone
Geyhutsa	geh-HYOU-jah	Girl
Osiyo	oh-see-YO	Hello
Siyo	S'yo	Hi
Tookah	TOO-kah	a woman's name
Tsalagi	jah-lah-GEE	Cherokee
Tsisa	JEE-sah	Jesus
Uktena	OOK-tain	legendary creature with spiritual powers
Unetlanvhi	oo-NEH-tla-NUH	God, the Creator
Wado	wah-DOE	Thank you
Yvwi Tsunsdi	YUH-wee Junes-DEE	Little People

Lakota

Hechetu aloh	HEY-che-tu YAY-lo	So it is
Hey-hey	HEY HEY	Look here
Hoka hey	HO-ka HEY	Onward, or, It is a good day to die
Tatanka	ta-TAAN-ka	Buffalo
Waken Tanka	WAA-ken TAAN-ka	God, the Great Mystery
Wanekia	WAN-e-KEY-a	Savior, One Who Makes Live
Wasichu	wah-SEE-choo	White People
Turtle Island		Lakota name for North America

Catawba

Manatou	MAN-a-too	God, The Creator

Cover Illustrations:

"The Last Journey"

and

"Devotion"

by Jerome Tiger

© 2008 Peggy Tiger

used by permission

golden eagle © 2007 Paul Moore

Vertical Alignment and ThunderSongs logos © 2010 ThunderSongs

In every truly life-changing story is a mountain that rises to the heavens.
But before the mountain is a valley that descends into the depths.

-Ted Dekker

PROLOGUE: THE ANIKUTANI

1194 AD
AMELIQUO

The smoke of a terrible burning floated across the inland sky like a mortal wound. Overhead the sun shone and the sparkling reflections of life flared in the faces of two Aniyvwiya beneath the palm tree near the ocean's edge. The two were friends but the Rebellion had ended all such friendships.

One named Star Rider lay gasping for breath in the arms of his friend, Two Turtles. A broken off lance protruded from his midsection, the point buried deep in his bowels. Blood seeped continuously from the wound as Star Rider clung desperately to the cord of life.

Two Turtles cradled his friend in his lap as the blood flowed freely over his bare legs. "I will light a pipe for you and all will be well."

"No, no; there is no escaping this death. The Anikutani have brought this upon all of us. Those who would oppress all Aniyvwiya with a poisoned religion have wrought their own fate. I am one of them; I must share their end." The wounded Anikutani priest shuddered as the lance wound wracked his body. "You must take this." He reached into a pouch at his side and extracted a strange object. He pressed it into the hands of his friend.

Two Turtles saw a holy intensity flare briefly in his eyes. He looked at the artifact in wonder. It was roughly a square with sides a little longer than a hand span. Its thickness was less than that of a man's hand, its surface covered in intricate figures punctuated by raised bumps or studs. Star Rider pressed a stud near the bottom and spoke. "This is for Two Turtles. Use this to remember the stories of my people."

He then pressed a stud next to that and a voice sounded from the air around them, "This is for Two Turtles. Use this to remember the stories of my people."

Two Turtles recoiled and held forth a hand palm outward in defensive posture. He looked around them for the unknown intruder that had approached so closely but saw no one.

Star Rider laughed but that quickly descended into a deep coughing spell that ended with blood trickling from the corner of his mouth. He closed his eyes briefly then reopened them and stared at Two Turtles with great intensity. "It has been said that we can record the words of the people upon the wind. This is true." He spoke softly so that Two Turtles leaned closer and hung onto every word. "Many summers ago in the time beyond times, the Yvwi Tsunsdi brought us these Gawonisgi Nvya's. We have never known how they work; only what they do." Star Rider proceeded to show Two Turtles the operation of the ancient device. Finally, he pressed it into his friend's hand. "The Anikutani will all die. This is the last Gawonisgi Nvya. Use it well. Don't let the story of our people die."

Two Turtles shook his head as he tried to absorb what his friend was saying. *The Anikutani could catch words from the wind!* Perhaps more of the stories of the priests were true than he had expected. He looked down at his dying friend. "Can the priests also capture thoughts on tablets? Can they be saved to be repeated to others?"

The holy man held onto his friend's words as a last thread to an existence that was surely slipping from him. His voice faded to a whisper. "Far from here there are mountains that rise up and blot out the sky."

Two Turtles nodded. "I have heard of these things my friend."

"There are caves in those mountains where my brothers find the yellow metal that we can beat with shaping stones. It is soft and easily formed into thin sheets; thin like the hide of a deer." Star Rider coughed and doubled up with the pain. More blood trickled from his mouth. "We can use stone styli to inscribe the holy characters upon them, the characters that talk." He pointed to the Gawonisgi Nvya. "Those are some of the characters. These too are a gift of the Yvwi Tsunsdi." He closed his eyes and winced with the pain. "There are sheets in the Temple hidden in the Holy of Holies that tell the meaning of all these characters. We call them the Talking Leaves." He reached out and grasped his friend's arm with the desperate strength of a dying man. "Find the Talking Leaves, Two Turtles. Save them."

Two Turtles looked in amazement at his friend. "What do the Talking Leaves say?"

Star Rider leaned his head back further into his friend's arm. "They do not talk like this stone." He nodded almost imperceptibly at the device that Two Turtles held. "When you perceive the meaning of these symbols, you can follow them on the sheet and hear them in your mind."

Two Turtles' brow knitted as he grappled with this foreign concept. "I do not understand."

Star Rider motioned for the Gawonisgi Nvya and pointed at the characters under the bumps that they had used. "This one says 'hear.'" He pressed it and they heard again Star Rider's voice admonishing to remember the stories of my people. "This one says 'speak.' You press it to remember what you speak." He closed his eyes then reopened them to stare at his friend intently. "Remember the stories of my people. Find the Talking Leaves." Star Rider closed his eyes for the last time and slipped away to join his elders. The last thing that Two Turtles heard from his lips was, "Tsisa!" His mouth formed a smile and then he was gone.

Two Turtles gently laid the now lifeless body onto the sand. He looked inland and saw that the smoke of the burning had increased. If he was to save these Talking Leaves, he had to hurry. "I will leave you here by the ocean you loved, my brother." He said a prayer of protection for the body until he could get back and give a proper burial. He quickly gathered palm fronds and covered his friend's remains. There was madness in this Rebellion and a young brave would quickly mutilate the body of a priest. The covering and his prayers would keep Star Rider safe.

He slipped the Gawonisgi Nvya into his belt pouch and set off at a loping run on the path that led to the Temple. Two Turtles heard shouts and screams as he drew near. The front half of the building was engulfed in flame. No matter, the Holy of Holies was in the back section. He ran to the secret entrance that his priestly friend had shown him many moons ago and stopped briefly to look around. No one was near so he slipped inside.

A layer of smoke hugged the floor as he burst into the secret room. He had never before seen this place; none of the braves had. Only the High Priest could enter here and only then once in a summer. At least that was what the priests told the rest of the Aniyvwiya. Two Turtles was stunned to see a large box in the center of the room with two winged warriors on the top that appeared to be a lid for the container. It was partially slid off the box as if someone had reached inside in great haste and hadn't closed it. The warriors on the lid were facing each other with the whole of it covered in that mysterious yellow metal that never lost its sparkle. One warrior held a bow and a lance; the other held a thin tablet inscribed with the strange characters. On the floor next to the box lay the body of a dead priest.

Two Turtles stepped gingerly over the body. *What was your sin, holy man?* One arm lay propped against the mysterious box. *Maybe it killed him.* He shook his head at this mystery and then looked around the room.

Where could these Talking Leaves be hidden? He quickly felt around the walls for any hidden compartments and found nothing. He got down on his hands and knees and felt along the floor. There beneath the low stand on which the golden box rested he found a secret panel. He lifted it away and was rewarded with an open space. There he found a large bag of deer skin that he lifted out of the cavity. His eyes became round with wonderment as he gazed inside. In the bag were several of the golden sheets that Star Rider had described to him. He pulled one out and found it covered in small and precise characters. Knowing that his quest was achieved he slipped it back into the bag and secured it with the covering flap.

As he stood, he saw the first flames licking up the wall. He turned to find himself next to the mysterious golden box. Two Turtles peered inside where the lid was pushed away. He could see some pieces of stone but nothing more. *The thieving priests have taken the treasure that was here. They probably killed this one.* He looked again at the dead priest, and then reached out to touch the golden box. He felt a sudden warning tingle in his hand and stopped. There was no time. Some of the mysteries of the Anikutani must die with them. Two Turtles slipped back out of the secret entrance just in time to see the whole of the Temple now engulfed in flame. He ran on the path back toward the beach and heard jeering yells over the demise of the great center of the priest's powers. He quickly returned to the place by the tree where he had left his friend's body.

This was the exact spot and there was no sign of the body or the leaves with which he had covered it. He crouched down and looked closely at the sand around the area. He could only see his movements to and from the spot. No one had been here and yet the body had vanished. As he stood, he thought he heard faint high-pitched laughter from amid the trees further down the beach.

1976 AD
OZARK MOUNTAINS SOUTHEAST OF TAHLEQUAH, OK

Phillip Wilson sat cross-legged under the great Texas Live Oak that had once guarded the old dirt road that ran from the Arkansas River up to Tahlequah. The asphalt ribbons that now connected all of southeast Oklahoma had bypassed the old thoroughfare many decades ago, but the ancient oak tree had continued to thrive. A new Cherokee ceremonial center that hosted Native gatherings and festivals had surrounded the old tree in recent years. Storytelling was always a traditional part of these gatherings. At such get-togethers, Wilson could always be found under the old tree with his Story Trunk beside him. The mysterious dusky wood and shiny brass latches of the diminutive chest never failed to attract a crowd of curious children.

Wilson's expression was dark, portraying the story that he told. "Star Rider was the last true priest of the Anikutani. All the rest of that priest clan had become evil. They stole from the rest of the Cherokees. They took mothers away from their children. They kept the best of the food for themselves and let the people starve. They lied to the people and told them that Creator had told them to do this."

Wilson paused, raised a river cane flute to his lips, and played a lonesome melody that punctuated the story. The Cherokee flute is a unique instrument that has two distinct air chambers. The player blows into the mouthpiece and the air passes through a decorative whistle block, moving from the first to the second chamber where the finger holes control the pitch. It has a remarkably beautiful earthy round tone that no other instrument shares. Wilson used it to great effect, punctuating and emphasizing the story that he was telling.

Wilson lowered the flute but kept it poised. "One day, all of the Cherokees rose up against the Anikutani. They killed them in a terrible slaughter." He quickly raised the flute and played a dramatic trill. "Star Rider had a friend among the Cherokee named Two Turtles. That man tried to save his friend after he was wounded. He left him to get help and when he returned, Star Rider was gone. He heard high-pitched laughter and looked and behold, the Little People were bearing Star Rider to safety. Two Turtles laughed because he knew his friend would be safe. The Little People were the friends of all true Cherokee." Wilson again played the melody that had begun this story, and then he leaned forward. "The Cherokee vowed to never again have a priest clan. They decided that each man and woman needed to speak to Creator on their own. The people became stronger for this."

Wilson reprised the lonesome melody on the flute, letting that note trail off mysteriously. "But who were these Little People?

They came from a distant time and only showed themselves to those who were true. They were helpers to the Cherokee, but they also liked to play tricks on us. From beyond our oldest memory they were known as the Yvwi Tsunsdi, and they even journeyed with the Cherokee people across the Trail Where They Cried." Wilson looked down for a moment, and then scanned across the young faces that were paying close attention. "This thing the Yvwi Tsunsdi always did; they always pointed the way to Creator." Wilson looked up at the mothers and fathers who stood listening too. "This one thing we must also do." He met the eyes of each man listening without flinching, challenging them to a higher path.

Wilson reached to deposit his flute in the Story Trunk and he heard a bold little girl speak out. "Please Mr. Phillip, one more story." He looked up and into the pleading eyes of the little one. She was a beautiful girl dressed in ceremonial garb that her mother had probably spent weeks preparing. She seemed to Wilson in that moment to be a spirit from another time.

Wilson shook his head and smiled. "For Laura Halfmoon, one more." He reached and touched the girl on the head lightly and picked up his flute once again. "Once many years ago when America was young and the Cherokees still owned the hills of Georgia and Tennessee, a man came to this country. He was a great Prince in his homeland of Romania who wanted to make a new life in our territory. He crossed the great ocean and landed on our shores. One of the first people he met here was a wise Cherokee. The intertwining of their lives happened in the strangest fashion. This was the way of it." Wilson put the flute to his lips and produced a new melody, one that expressed hope but intoned a terrible danger...

1: A NEW WORLD

1795 AD
CHARLESTON, SC

"Right this way, Your Majesty. We can be off this frightful vessel in just a moment." The chancellor bowed and spread his hand toward the gangway.

The royal figure standing next to him stretched to his full height and sniffed. He held a handkerchief to his nose. "What is that dreadful smell?" He looked around with narrowed eyes to find the perpetrator of this new crime.

Prince Galen Mondragon stood an imposing six feet two inches. His body was lean and fit, his face framed by dusky longish hair that faded into a luxuriant auburn beard. He wore the trim black traveling outfit he favored topped with his ermine cape. It sported a gold silk lining that would flash and glitter in the wind. He carried an ornate walking stick that concealed a slim and rather deadly sword. He was quite skilled in its use.

The chancellor stopped a crewman who was walking by. "You there, what is that smell?"

The crewman's face split into a grin revealing several missing teeth. "Oh that? Well, guv'ner, that's 'is Royal Majesty's pluff mud. It's all old King Charles has left of this town, God rest 'is soul. Stinks unto heaven at low tide." He bobbed his head once and then continued on his way.

The Prince fixed a sharp gaze on the chancellor. "Lead us off this wretched craft, Lord Banica."

"Yes your Majesty, right this way." The chancellor descended the ramp into the mayhem that was the docks of Charleston, South Carolina. Prince Mondragon followed, being careful not to touch anything. The pair moved quickly through the crowd and onto East Bay St.

The year was 1795 and America was still a brand new nation. Charleston was much older than that, however. Founded as Charles Town in 1670 at a site further up the Ashley River, the city moved to the current site in 1690. Situated on a beautiful harbor, it had become a prosperous center for shipping and commerce. It was also the main port used in the slave trade. African natives stolen from their homes were brought to this place to be sold to planters and businessmen. It had only been a few years ago in 1783 that the city officially changed its name to Charleston.

A Negro servant in impeccable livery hailed them. "Lord Mondragon, I presume?"

The Prince looked right through the underling.

"Yes, this is His Royal Majesty." Banica looked sternly at the servant.

"My apologies your Majesty, I am Francis and I will take you to the plantation." He opened a carriage door and motioned towards the interior. "If your Lordships will make yourselves comfortable, I will fetch your baggage." Francis glanced over at the tangle of shipping at the docks and then back at Banica. "Which vessel did you travel on?"

"It was the Valiant, a name far too noble for such a dismal craft." The chancellor sniffed.

"My apologies sir, I trust your stay in Charleston will be much more pleasant."

"I certainly hope so." Banica sniffed once more and then turned away to help the Prince into the carriage. Francis melted into the crowd.

Prince Mondragon looked around the carriage and a faint look of approval brightened his features. "This will suffice for a short journey."

Banica struggled in behind the Prince. His portly frame made negotiating such narrow entryways quite challenging. He puffed out his cheeks once as he acquired the seat facing his ruler.

Thomas Banica was much shorter than his master's imposing height. Only a mere five feet five inches tall, what he lacked in height, he made up for in girth. His perpetually reddened cheeks contributed to his air of impatience. Always searching for the best for the Prince, he generally presented the worst to those around him, especially underlings. He wore a tan travelling suit with flashy neck and wrist ruffles spilling out of the dull beige background. Even in his dress, Thomas sought to present a contrast to the Prince that cast the latter in the best light.

Mondragon chuckled and allowed the ghost of a smile to drift across his face. "Really Thomas, those pastries will be the death of you."

"Would you take one of the few pleasures an old man can enjoy before he dies?" He looked at the Prince with a wide-eyed innocence that coaxed another chuckle from the stately Romanian. Away from the masses, the two were fast friends. Thomas had served in the court of the Prince for all of the monarch's adult life and they shared a unique bond.

Mondragon glanced across East Bay St. and noted a strangely dressed individual standing stock-still and staring in their direction. "Behold the noble savage."

"Sire?" Thomas looked out the window and saw the Native. "Oh my, Is that an Indian?"

"I don't know Thomas."

He was dressed in clothing fashioned from some kind of animal skin. He wore beads and other primitive decorations. His hair was long, very black, and had feathers attached in some unknown fashion. A strange tuft of some coarse fur-like substance sprouted from the back of his head and formed what appeared to be a low halo from their vantage. A quiver of arrows protruded from his back and he wore a bow carelessly over a shoulder. It was plain that it could be in his hand in less than a heartbeat. A long knife that was almost the size of a small sword was sheathed at his waist. The man was a picture of peaceful menace, a dangerous artifact that was not to be handled casually.

"Oh my," Banica said. "He appears to be watching us."

"I wouldn't worry my old friend. He won't do anything here."

"Will you protect us with your little sword Galen?"

"Take care, Lord Banica. My little sword can still put a hole in you."

They were silent for a moment, and then both broke out into laughter. "Thank you sire, you are my noble protector."

"A prince's work is never done my friend."

They felt the carriage lurch as a trunk was loaded onto the back. Francis peered into the compartment. "The crewmen are loading your baggage now, your Lordships. We will be on the way momentarily."

"Francis, who is that odd individual across the street? He has been staring at us the whole time you were gone." Banica looked nervously across East Bay St.

Francis glanced over and broke into a smile. "Oh him? That's old Tom-Tom. He works for my master. He is our, ah, security."

"But, what is he?"

"Oh, I reckon you gentlemen have never seen an Indian. Tom-Tom is a Cherokee. He comes and stays with us from time to time when he needs work. You couldn't find a more reliable man. When he's here, that is."

Mondragon leaned forward, his curiosity overcoming his royal instincts. "He was watching over us."

"Yes, your Lordship."

Thomas bristled and said, "You will address the Prince as Your Royal Highness, servant."

Mondragon waved his hand. "Pish posh Thomas, this is the New World. We can accept this servant's address." He nodded at Francis who smiled broadly. "Francis, would you call that, um, Tom-Tom over here?"

"Yes Your Highness, just a moment." He turned and made a high sign to the Cherokee who nodded imperceptibly and started across the street. He arrived to stand at the side of the carriage. He folded his arms and watched them impassively.

Mondragon looked at him closely. "Does he speak English, Francis?"

Tom-Tom raised an eyebrow. "I speak English, French, Cherokee and several other Nation's languages."

"Un jour plaisant à vous monsieur." Mondragon lifted his chin and looked the Cherokee in the eye.

"Et pouvez vous avoir beaucoup de demains plaisants." Tom-Tom looked back at the Prince.

"A scholar." Mondragon took the measure of the man and found him formidable. Almost as tall as the Romanian, he was lean and well muscled. The Prince nodded. "I too speak many tongues. Besides English and French, I speak Spanish and my native Romanian as well. I have never heard an Indian tongue, however. Perhaps you could teach me. What is a word in Cherokee?"

"Osiyo."

"Oh see yo? What does that mean?"

"It is a greeting spoken in friendship."

"Oh see yo." Mondragon struggled to grasp the strange word. "Oh see yo Tom-Tom."

Tom-Tom now raised his chin. "Would you be a friend?" His eyes glittered with distrust.

Francis stretched out his hands. "Now Tom-Tom, you must be respectful of His Lordship. He is a Prince in his home country."

"Cherokee do not have princes."

Mondragon inhaled sharply. "I have heard you live in tribes that have princely chiefs."

"The white men would like to think so."

"This is not your way?"

Tom-Tom seemed to consult a source outside of himself. "We travel the pathway together. We walk in agreement. The Creator guides our steps."

"I see." Mondragon's brow knitted in mild confusion. "So your chiefs tell you what to do."

"The Creator tells us the path to travel. It is up to us to come into agreement with the Creator."

Mondragon looked at Francis. "I presume that Tom-Tom will be accompanying us. Have him join us in the compartment. Move over Thomas."

The chancellor looked at his prince with what bordered on panic. "Your Highness? A savage seated with us?"

"Tut-tut Thomas. He won't bite." He looked over at Tom-Tom with an unnatural smile. "Won't you join us?"

Tom-Tom stood stock still for a moment, and then opened the door and slid gracefully into the seat while sweeping his bow and quiver into his lap in one smooth motion. He looked at the prince and said, "Wado."

"What does that mean Tom-Tom?"

"That means thank you."

"Why, you're welcome, I'm sure." Mondragon braced himself as the carriage lurched forward. "Tom-Tom, this is Thomas Banica who is vying for space next to you." The Cherokee nodded sociably to the chancellor. "Thomas, I think a new protocol may be in order in this new America. They have lately freed themselves from royalty and perhaps it would be prudent if we did not insist on such formalities."

"How should I introduce you, Your Highness?" Thomas looked puzzled at this unexpected development.

"Perhaps we should just use my name. Let me earn my titles here and not rest on Romanian tradition." Mondragon stroked his beard absently.

"His name is Red Beard." Tom-Tom folded his arms after his pronouncement. The two Romanians looked in mild astonishment at the Cherokee in their midst.

After a moment of silence, Mondragon started to chuckle. "Well Thomas, I do believe I have my first Indian name."

"It would seem so, your Majesty."

"I think that for everyone else, you can simply introduce me as Galen Mondragon. Let the Americans add titles as they see fit."

"And me?"

"You continue in your formal mode of address, Thomas. If the natives wish to follow, they will, or they will call me Mr. Mondragon. It matters not in this place."

"Why yes Mr. Mondragon."

The Prince glared at his chancellor in mock severity and then chuckled. "Very well Mr. Banica."

They rode in silence as the carriage struggled to break free of the tangle of people and horses that surged through the streets of the seaport. They finally cleared the city's congestion onto a pleasant lane that ran along the Ashley River. Tall stands of palmetto trees interspersed with live oaks weeping Spanish moss lined their passageway. They passed a party of Negro slaves carrying farm implements who walked ahead of a mounted white man who carried a gun.

The Prince cleared his throat. "Thomas, didn't Charles write that Drayton Hall had its own moorage?"

"Yes he did, your Majesty. Our noble captain simply would not avail himself of their docks." Banica sniffed as he looked idly out the window.

"I have corresponded with Charles Drayton for several years. He has told me that it is twelve miles by water from Charleston to Drayton Hall." Mondragon brushed at an insect that had flown into their compartment.

Tom-Tom held up his hand to Mondragon and leaned forward. He deftly captured the small flier in one loose fist. He carefully opened it in front of his own face and looked gently as the insect sat quietly on his hand. He brought his gaze up to meet the Prince's puzzled look. "White men do not understand the importance of all the nations of beings on our Grandmother. The small winged creatures have great importance. The Cherokee and all Indians know to treat them with great respect." Tom-Tom held his hand forward and the insect fluttered his wings but stayed seated. "This one is a healer. If you have the swamp fever, he will sacrifice himself to make you well." He held his hand to the window and blew lightly. The insect took wing and was gone from the compartment. "Would you do the same for him?" Tom-Tom leaned back in his seat.

Banica puffed out his cheeks. "This is absurd. Do you worship bugs, Tom-Tom?"

Mondragon shook his head. "No Thomas, I see a small bit of what our Cherokee friend was saying. His kind have studied this marvelous land and unlocked many secrets that we would do well to learn. Thank you Tom-Tom."

The Indian nodded but remained silent. Banica sighed and looked out the window. They rode in silence for a moment and then Thomas spoke. "I for one am glad that Mr. Drayton sent this carriage for us. I am heartily sick of the rolling seas."

"Indeed, Thomas. You were looking quite green out there."

Tom-Tom looked over at Banica. "White man turned green?" He looked the chancellor over carefully. "He looks white now."

Thomas smiled at Mondragon. "That is an expression, my noble savage," the Prince said. "In this case it means he felt very sick."

"Sick of the rolling sea." Thomas held is hand to his mouth and mimicked stomach illness.

"Ah." Tom-Tom nodded. "That is why Cherokee do not go on white men's boats. They are bad for you."

They felt the carriage turn and looked to behold a large house at the end of a tree-lined lane. Francis called out, "Drayton Hall, your Lordships." In a moment, they rolled up to the door where another finely attired Negro servant opened the compartment. They stepped out of the vehicle and stood. Tom-Tom slipped out behind them and quickly faded into the shadows of the live oaks.

The servant opened the massive door and beckoned to the new visitors. "Right this way, your Lordships. Mr. Drayton is anxious to greet you." He led them to an elegant drawing room where they were offered refreshment. Charles Drayton entered the room with a beaming smile.

"Welcome, my good gentlemen. Welcome to America and welcome to my humble abode." He strode forward and gave a firm handshake to both the Prince and the chancellor. "Lawrence," he motioned to the Negro servant, "Brandy for our guests and one for me too."

"Right away sir." Lawrence bowed slightly and retired to a small bar in the corner of the room. He reappeared quickly with three ornate glasses on a tray that he distributed to the three men.

Drayton lifted his glass. "To a pleasant future for you here in America, your Majesty."

Banica looked meaningfully at the Prince as he lifted his glass.

Mondragon smiled ever so slightly. "A pleasant future," the chancellor and the Prince echoed.

"Let us enjoy this brief libation and then my servant will show you to your suite. By then your baggage will have been delivered and you can rest and refresh yourselves."

"Thank you Mr. Drayton. Your hospitality is exceeded only by your graciousness." The Prince dipped his head toward his host.

"Thank you your Majesty. Please, call me Charles."

"Why yes, Charles. I would likewise be delighted if you addressed me as Galen. After our many letters, I feel as if I know you already."

"Yes Galen, thank you for that honor."

They continued in genial small talk for several minutes as the brandy was finished. The two Romanians then retired to their rooms, but not before promising to join Drayton and his family for dinner.

"I think we're off to a smashing start, Thomas." Mondragon walked down the upstairs hallway behind Lawrence, who opened the door to their suite.

"Oh yes your Majesty." Banica shut the door softly behind him and lowered his voice to just above a whisper. "I think your place in this new America is assured."

The Prince looked over at his chancellor and raised an eyebrow. "Quite."

Thunder Walking strode silently over the narrow woodland trail that led to his camp. He was careful never to disclose its location to the white men with whom he associated while staying in the Lowcountry of South Carolina. The events of the day had left him troubled. He needed time alone; time to think, time to pray to Creator, and time to sleep and perhaps dream.

He had never met a man like the Romanian Prince. His flashy cape, red beard, and walking stick, (obviously a disguised weapon,) had made a deep impression on the Cherokee. He felt a dangerous evil in the man with naught but a veneer of civilization keeping him from dealing death and destruction. That he held himself tightly in check was plain to Thunder

Walking. He was amazed that neither the white men nor black men that had met the Prince seemed to notice.

As he rounded a bend in the trail, he heard his horse nicker softly. He whistled the call of the whippoorwill and the horse suddenly appeared on the trail in front of him. Thunder Walking reached up to stroke the horse's neck. "Hello my pony." The horse snorted in reply. "Have you come to ride me back to camp, Trail Blossom?" The horse nodded her head knowingly as the Cherokee slipped onto her back. "Take us home, geyhutsa."

Trail Blossom started at a fast walk towards the hidden camp. It would have taken the Cherokee two hours to traverse the distance on foot. Riding Trail Blossom, he made it in half the time. She seemed to know when he was coming and would usually meet him halfway. Creator had blessed him in the friendship he had with this fine member of the Horse Nation.

Thunder Walking had acquired her from a wandering band of Dakota. Recently displaced from their Minnesota woodland homes, many Dakota were wandering far in search of new homes. This group had obtained horses in a running battle with the Ojibwa. Although they lost ground, they made the Ojibwa pay in mares and stallions that they stole from their camps. Among those were several that were spotted like leopards. These were exceptional animals and Thunder Walking was able to trade for one. He named her Trail Blossom and she became a fast friend.

Safe on the back of his steed, the Cherokee reached into his buckskin pouch and extracted the Gawonisgi Nvya. He shook his head as he gazed in wonder at the strange object. His Grandfather had passed in on to him many years ago before he died. "Remember the stories of my people," he had admonished. *I remember, my Grandfather.*

He pressed a stud near the bottom and the rolling tones of Prince Mondragon sounded in the air around him. "No Thomas, I see a small bit of what our Cherokee friend was saying. His kind have studied this marvelous land and unlocked many secrets that we would do well to learn. Thank you Tom-Tom."

Thunder Walking pressed the stud to turn off the voice. *No white man has seen such things so easily. This one walks in two* worlds and is not what he seems. He took a deep breath and exhaled slowly. *O Creator, give me Your wisdom to know the truth of this man.*

He closed his eyes and felt the cool wind of the Spirit. A voice whispered quietly within him. *Is he a man?* Thunder Walking's eyes flew open as he apprehended the question. Could Red Beard be something far more than he appeared?

Trail Blossom snorted and shook her head in response. The four leggeds were always quick to understand such things; it was the two leggeds that had become dull and dense. Thunder Walking patted the neck of his beautiful spotted pony. "Thank you Trail Blossom. You are right, I must learn more."

They rounded a final bend and his camp lay before him. A Cherokee brave melted from the shadows and spoke. "Siyo Duda, has your day been well?"

"Yes my son, it has been most enlightening. I met a most unusual man today."

"Who is he?"

"He is a Prince from a land named Romania. I have never met the like."

The brave reached out to stroke Trail Blossom's neck and was rewarded with a nicker. "Your pony went after you so I have been expecting you."

Thunder Walking chuckled. "She is a most amazing horse. She tries to speak to me, you know."

"If only we could understand, Duda." The young brave held the horse as his father slipped off her back.

"Your Great Grandfather could, you know." Thunder Walking looked at his son with a twinkle in his eye.

The brave made a face. "That was the story you told me when I was a small one."

Thunder Walking laughed. "That's the story he told me, my son. He would tell me when the horses wanted me to feed them."

"That's one way to get you to do that job." They looked at each other with straight faces that dissolved into shared laughter.

Standing Oak was the tall lean son of Thunder Walking. He

had spent his fifteen summers as the generations before him, learning hunting and horse riding at an early age. He was a fiercely competitive stickball player and an excellent swimmer. His aquiline features gave him a predatory appearance that was belied by his easy smile. He was already taller than his father was and wore his hair long and free.

Thunder Walking led his pony to the creek next to their campsite and into the water. She drank deeply as he splashed the cooling liquid on her flanks. Satisfied that she was comfortable, he returned to the camp.

"I caught some fine bass fish today Duda. Are you hungry?"

"I am very hungry."

"Good. I can have them ready soon if I use the white man's frying pan." The younger Cherokee reached into a bundle near the fire and pulled out a large cast iron pan.

Thunder Walking shook his head. "How can so much good and so much bad come from the same race? The white man has forever changed how we do things."

"Sometimes we must take the good and leave the bad."

"May we have the wisdom to know the difference."

"The fish is exquisite, Charles. What species graces your table?" Prince Mondragon dabbed his lips with a linen napkin and smiled graciously at his host.

"Tonight we are enjoying striped bass prepared by Chef Marcus. The fish were harvested upstream from us in our own Ashley River." Drayton smiled and leaned forward. "Although, Galen, the river dwindles sharply as you travel inland. We have one of the last deep water moorages. Beyond here, it's not much of a river."

"It sounds like the British won't be attacking from upstream then."

Drayton laughed and nodded. "I don't think we will have to worry about that again."

Mondragon leaned back in his chair. "You and your countrymen must remain vigilant Charles. The Crown remains most displeased with the outcome of their adventure."

Drayton stiffened. "What have you heard Galen?"

"Nothing more than you already know my friend. The British

wish to rule the world and thirteen upstart colonies will not thwart that desire."

Drayton leaned back in his seat and raised his eyebrows. "America will have no part in that plan."

"Yes, I'm sure." Mondragon's tone sounded conciliatory. "You know that you have become a beacon of freedom for many peoples. For that beacon to remain bright requires eternal vigilance." Mondragon sipped the delicate Chardonnay served with the repast. He looked briefly at the crystal stemware glass that he held, and then returned his gaze to Drayton. "This means that you must control the forces on your own soil."

Drayton pursed his lips. "You speak of the Indians."

"Indeed, Charles."

"Those that are enemies, we defeat. Those that are friends, we employ."

"Such as your friend Tom-Tom?"

"You have met our Cherokee guardian." Drayton motioned discreetly and a servant appeared to refill his wine glass. "He is a fine example of what friendship can accomplish."

"Perhaps." Mondragon left the word hanging as he addressed the final piece of bass on his plate.

Father and son relaxed by the fire after a delicious dinner of striped bass supplemented with wild roots and vegetables. They had chosen their campsite well, inland and away from the swampy areas that dotted the coast. The capricious biting gnats that populated coastal areas at dusk were nonexistent.

Standing Oak leaned forward as he gazed into the fire. "Perhaps we should share the pipe and seek the wisdom of Creator." He glanced over at his father. "About this prince from... where did you say?"

Thunder Walking nodded. "From Romania. As I understand it, the country is in the far eastern part of Europe." He rose and walked to their lean-to and reached inside, extracting a long deer hide bundle. He returned to his seat and reverently unwrapped the two parts of the pipe. Fitting the bowl onto the stem, he reached into his pouch and pulled out a pinch of the tobacco and herb mix that the Cherokee used on such occasions. He loaded the pipe and then lifted his face once to Creator. He then reached for a burning stick. After lighting the pipe, he took the seven ritual puffs. There was one for each of the cardinal directions, one for the sky, one for the earth, and one for himself. He passed the pipe to his son who duplicated the ritual.

Standing Oak produced a small drum and began beating a steady rhythm. They began to sing and went on for sometime, being careful to keep the volume down. They had no wish to invite any white intruders to their campsite.

The singing ended but Standing Oak kept a soft beat going. Thunder Walking looked up into the darkening sky. The first star was out and he smiled at the timing. "Oh Unetlanvhi, You are so great! You make the sky and set the stars in it. You make the sun and the moon to chase one another across that sky. You have made the four legged and two legged nations and You have made me and my son. We thank You Creator."

"Thank You Unetlanvhi," echoed Standing Oak.

Thunder Walking took a breath and continued. "Unetlanvhi, give us wisdom and show us the truth of this man called Red Beard. Teach us to stay on Your sacred path and not be fooled."

Standing Oak suddenly stopped drumming and cried out as if in pain. He leaned forward, doubling over so his body touched the earth. He stayed prostrate in this fashion for several moments before sitting up with a dazed expression.

Thunder Walking allowed him to reorient himself before he spoke. He then quietly reached into his pouch and activated the Gawonisgi Nvya. "You have had a great vision, my son."

"Yes Duda." Standing Oak shivered despite the warmth of the night. "I saw the man you call Red Beard. He looked across the land now called America and was filled with covetousness. As I watched, he began to laugh and then he turned into a giant bat like creature. He flew to Washington and sat on a father's shoulder. It was a President, of that I am sure, yet I have never seen him before. He had a long and sallow face. He coughed continually. The bat creature whispered in his ear and he seemed to take strength and the cough receded. He stood and pointed a finger to the west, beyond the Mississippi. I then saw untold numbers of Cherokees on a bitter winter trail. Many of them died there. That was the end of it."

As Standing Oak finished, a bat swooped low over the fire. It circled and crossed over the fire three more times and then vanished. Thunder Walking raised his chin and spoke. "Creator has sent a sign with your vision, the sign of the bat. This is powerful medicine. It is plain that Red Beard is no good."

"Yes Father, it is plain. But what do we do?"

"I do not yet know, chooch."

"Yes Charles, I keep a supply of Spanish cigars. I have heard of the cigars from Cuba but never have tried one." The Prince lit the hand made Havana with a candle left burning for that purpose. He looked up at the ceiling as he puffed it several times. "Yes, yes, this is excellent. Very smooth."

Drayton beamed at his distinguished guest. "I am glad you approve, Galen. Lawrence, fetch a box of these Havana cigars for His Majesty."

"Really Charles, you needn't do that."

Drayton held up his hand. "I insist. I will also put you in touch with the importer who brings these fine cigars into the country."

"Very well, I accept. Thank you Charles."

"Not at all, Galen." Drayton sipped from his after dinner brandy and took another draw from his cigar. "As I was saying, Georgia is a new frontier. Now that the Tories have been expelled, there are many opportunities there. I think it would be a fine place for you to settle."

"I'm glad you feel that way. With your permission, we will stay with you for a few days while we make our travel plans."

Drayton leaned back in his chair. "You will need a guide. May I recommend our Cherokee friend Tom-Tom?"

"Excellent idea Charles. I deem him a trustworthy fellow."

"He will be back in the morning." Drayton looked over as Lawrence re-entered the room with a wooden box. "Ah, your parcel from Havana." Lawrence handed the box to Mondragon's chancellor. He was a servant who understood protocol. "Thank you again, Charles," Mondragon said.

"Lawrence, would you call Francis in here?" Lawrence nodded and slipped out of the room. He reappeared in a moment with Francis in tow.

"How may I be of service, sir?" Francis looked expectantly at his master.

"When Tom-Tom returns in the morning, would you make arrangements with him to guide our Romanian friends to the wilds of Georgia?"

"Yes sir, I would be happy to be of service. I believe most of Tom-Tom's family lives in northern Georgia. He would probably enjoy such a trip." Francis bowed toward Drayton and then toward Mondragon. He turned on his heel and left the room.

Mondragon nodded and looked at Drayton. "Your staff is most efficient, Charles."

Drayton beamed at his guest. "I am glad you are pleased."

2: THE FRONTIER

1795 AD
UPSTATE SOUTH CAROLINA

A sturdy dray horse plodded ahead of the stout wagon that Prince Mondragon had purchased for the trip. Upon Thunder Walking's advice, he had also hired six additional Cherokees including Tom-Tom's son Standing Oak. The land they traveled into was fraught with peril, as much from bands of white robbers as from rogue Indian groups. Two Cherokees ranged on ahead and reported back from time to time. In this way, they were able to avoid pitfalls on the trail such as felled trees blocking the path. More importantly, the scouting Cherokees were an early warning system that was invaluable against attack.

Drayton had exerted his considerable influence and before they left, the party was outfitted with brand new Springfield rifles. They all spent a day in training with the new weapons under the tutelage of a crusty Sergeant. Even the Prince submitted to this training. This gained him a degree of grudging respect from the Indians. The Cherokees had a difficult time with the session because Thunder Walking had to interpret the sometimes profane orders from the soldier. At the end of the day, however, they were all competent with the flintlock.

Thunder Walking and Standing Oak rode just ahead of the wagon which was ably piloted by Thomas. The elder Cherokee dropped back beside the wagon when the trail permitted. He enjoyed chatting with Banica. The portly Romanian was a storehouse of information about his homeland.

Prince Mondragon rode ahead mostly by himself. He sat astride a magnificent black stallion he had purchased from Drayton before leaving Charleston. He would drop back to ask pertinent questions of Thunder Walking or Standing Oak but he was not interested in chitchat. Thomas more than made up for it with his happy ramblings. Thunder Walking suspected that the Prince ranged on ahead to escape his chancellor's voice.

"So your proper Cherokee name is Thunder Walking. Is that what I should call you?" Banica looked quizzically at the Indian riding beside the wagon.

"I am used to white men calling me Tom-Tom." Thunder Walking glanced at Thomas. "You can still call me by that name. I will not be offended."

"Thunder Walking; such a noble yet menacing name."

"The Aniyuntikwalaski are noble and menacing. They are the Thunder Beings after whom I am named."

"Are they your gods Tom-Tom?"

Thunder Walking was silent for a moment as he considered the question. "There is only one God, He is the Creator, Unetlanvhi. There are other beings that He has created and some of these are greater than man in power and wisdom. That does not make them gods." He looked over at Thomas. "Even as you give homage to your Prince, so do the Cherokee to these great beings. But neither your Prince nor these beings are gods."

Banica looked at him with a wide-eyed expression. "Well put sir! You have made me understand." Thomas called a quick encouragement to his horse before continuing. "You know that there were times in history when great rulers claimed to be gods."

"I have heard of these things. They all died like men."

The trail narrowed as it climbed a low hill. Thunder Walking moved ahead of the wagon, cutting off their conversation for the moment. He felt rather than saw the Prince ease back beside him. "How do you know that I am not a god, Thunder

Walking?"

The Cherokee fixed a piercing gaze on the Prince and their eyes joined in challenge. "Galen Mondragon is many things and none of them are God." Thunder Walking strengthened his stare and beheld a smoldering in Mondragon's look unlike any he had seen in even the fiercest enemy. Distant stars swirled in the Prince's eyes and threatened to swallow even the faintest memory of one noble Cherokee. He sat erect upon Trail Blossom and spoke. "I am Thunder Walking of the Aniyvwiya and my fathers walked this land before your Romania existed. I bear the power of the Aniyuntikwalaski and I acknowledge no God but Unetlanvhi, the Creator."

Mondragon hooded his gaze as one discovered. "My apologies Tom-Tom. I am still becoming adjusted to life in this new land. I meant no offense."

The Cherokee stared at the Romanian for a long moment. "None taken, your Majesty."

The Prince nodded and then urged his mount on ahead. He rode silent and alone for the remainder of the day.

"Louisville up ahead, your Majesty! We have finally arrived." Banica stood in the wagon as he pointed to the buildings now coming into view.

Mondragon glanced over to his Cherokee guide. "Tom-Tom?"

"Yes, your Majesty, we have reached Louisville, Georgia." Thunder Walking urged his spotted mount ahead and called out to the forward scouts. In a moment, they joined him as the group entered town together.

They pulled into the one dusty lane that was this small outpost town. Banica guided the wagon to what appeared to be an inn and dismounted. "Tom-Tom, will you and your Cherokee compatriots stay with the wagon until we make arrangements and return? You can assist then in any offloading. After that, I will discharge you according to our agreement."

Thunder Walking nodded silently. Banica and the Prince strolled into the structure and returned within several minutes. Banica hopped into the wagon and pointed down the lane.

"There is a stable and storage there. Let us put this wagon to rest and then you gentlemen can depart." The group moved down to the stable and the Cherokees quickly had the horse unhitched and the goods offloaded. "Excellent work. I will distribute your pay now. In addition, the Prince has informed me that he would like you each to keep the Springfield rifles that we provided."

Thunder Walking quickly translated and the group broke out into smiles. The rifles meant far more than the gold they received. Banica shook each of their hands and bid them farewell.

Thunder Walking lingered as the rest departed. "Will you stay in this place Thomas?"

"For now, Tom-Tom. The Prince has not revealed his long range plans to me."

"Perhaps I will see you again." The Cherokee and the Romanian shook hands and then Thunder Walking departed.

1804 AD
LOUISVILLE, GA

"Well Galen, it's a new century filled with new opportunities. With Louisville as the Georgia state capitol, we can move beyond that Yazoo fiasco." Governor James Jackson leaned back in his chair and took a draw from the fine Havana cigar that Mondragon had provided. "The Federal funds that paid for all that land were a great boon to the Georgia economy."

"The public burning of those land documents was a stroke of genius. That event began to turn the whole land fraud from a liability to an asset. You have been a hero ever since James." Mondragon tipped the ash from his cigar into the ashtray.

Jackson leaned forward and adopted a conspiratorial tone. "I've been told that Patrick Henry turned a fine shade of purple when his involvement was exposed."

"His Virginia Yazoo Company was as valuable as the worthless notes he tried to pay with." Mondragon sniffed. "This much good has come of it: the Federal government is now committed to extinguishing all land claims of the Cherokee and

Creek Indians in Georgia."

Jackson thumped his desk with a fist. "And that we must do posthaste. As long as those savages dwell in our land, no good Georgia citizen is safe."

Mondragon leaned forward. "Perhaps the officials in far away Washington need to be confronted face to face."

Jackson gazed out his window. It was a fine spring day and the air was clear. He noted an Indian family coming down the street, the woman seated on a horse and a Cherokee warrior leading them. She was great with child. "Yes Galen, perhaps." The Cherokee family moved out of view and he turned his full attention to Mondragon. "You have been a faithful and valuable advisor in my government, Galen. I believe you may be best suited to represent our desires to the President and Congress."

Mondragon smiled thinly. "Thank you for your trust, James. Thomas Jefferson is a proponent of Indian removal. He just needs to be nudged more firmly in that direction."

"Yes, send them all west of the Mississippi."

"Precisely. There are, however, many who favor assimilation."

"They can not become like us. An Indian will always be an Indian."

"Agreed." Mondragon revived his cigar, which had almost gone out. "James, I am at your service. What would you like me to do?"

The Governor tapped his desktop absently and took a deep breath. "Let us commission you as special envoy of the State of Georgia. In that way, you can represent our interests without the worry of being voted out of office. We will have to introduce legislation to that effect to make it official, but I foresee no difficulties."

"Very well Governor, I will have my chancellor begin to put our affairs in order in preparation for a move to Washington."

Jackson rose and extended a hand to Mondragon who grasped it warmly. "I will be in touch soon with all the details, Galen. Your service to the State of Georgia will not be forgotten."

"Thank you James, it is my pleasure." Mondragon turned for

the door and allowed himself a small smile of triumph. As he exited the building, he noted a Cherokee leading a horse bearing a pregnant Cherokee woman. They came close and the Prince raised his eyebrows in recognition. "Greetings Standing Oak. Is this your wife?"

Standing Oak looked suspiciously at the Prince. He had not seen Red Beard since they left him in this dusty town so many years ago. He still remembered the protocol. "Yes, your Majesty, this is my wife Deer in Water." He looked at his wife and said, "This is Prince Galen Mondragon whom I have told you about."

She glanced at the Prince in curiosity and then quickly lowered her eyes. She remembered the vision of Red Beard that her husband had related years ago. She felt apprehensive but hid it well.

"How is your father?" Mondragon was being polite.

"Thunder Walking is well. His spirit is strong and he still walks the land in the grace of Creator."

Mondragon sniffed. "Quite. Give him my best when you see him." He moved to go but Standing Oak stepped in front of him. He looked at the Cherokee in mild shock.

"You are going now to the Great Father in Washington."

Mondragon blinked. For once, he was caught off guard. "How did you know?"

"I have seen you in the spirit world. You are not a friend to the Cherokee."

Mondragon laughed and shook his head. "I would not harm you."

"There are those among us who are strong and will meet you in the spirit world."

Mondragon narrowed his eyes and ever so briefly let something out that he had kept under lock and key for all the years that he had been in America. He watched as Standing Oak crumbled onto the dust of the street.

Standing Oak looked at the wavering landscape of the spirit world as he stood on his feet. Far away, he saw his brothers, too far to help. Before him stood Red Beard. As he watched, the Prince morphed into a hideous creature, half man, half bat. He-it let out a piercing yell and Standing Oak fell onto the spirit plain. He looked weakly towards his distant brothers and saw that they too had fallen. He closed his eyes and remembered no more.

Deer in Water screamed and slid off the horse. As she leaned down to her husband, a crowd gathered. "The poor boy simply fell over," the Prince explained to those around him. "Most unfortunate."

After a moment, Standing Oak revived. He looked up at Mondragon with a fiery expression but said nothing. "There, he seems to be better now. Take good care of your husband, Deer in Water." He nodded at the Cherokee woman. "Farewell Standing Oak," he said as he turned and walked away. He could feel the burning gaze of the Cherokee on his back. "Until we meet again in my world," the Prince murmured.

1816 AD
NEW ECHOTA, GA

With a great final effort, he was born into the day. Deer in Water collapsed onto the bedding as the mid-wife held the newborn and massaged his chest. The newborn took his first breath and began to cry heartily. She cut the umbilical cord and rubbed the baby's body down. She then nestled him into his mother's arms where he found his first warm mother's milk.

"Standing Oak, come in here," called the mid-wife. "You have a son!"

As Standing Oak turned to enter the longhouse, he heard the cry of a great raptor in the clouds. He looked up to behold a Golden Eagle circling directly overhead. The great bird of prey was close enough that he could see her turn her head directly towards him. As he watched, she continued to circle as she called out to Standing Oak. She then looked up and sped away.

Standing Oak quickly entered and knelt by his wife and son. "Are you well?"

She smiled a dreamy and exhausted smile. "I am fine. Behold our son!" She looked down with a tender smile at the

infant.

Standing Oak reached out and tenderly stroked his head. "An eagle came and told me about you, little warrior." He glanced at his wife and then back to the baby. "I know what the Elisi will name you for she told me." He looked again at Deer in Water. "It was a powerful sign. She called out to me four times."

"We must let Elisi Wind in the Reeds speak over our son. It is our way."

"I know, but I just know what she will say." Standing Oak turned as he heard someone enter. "Elisi! Come and see our son."

Wind in the Reeds moved slowly to their side. She was an ancient woman who had seen over a hundred summers. Her wisdom was legend among the north Georgia Cherokees. "I would hold the child." Her voice, though cracked with age, brooked no delay or compromise. Standing Oak tenderly handed the baby to the ancient woman. She smiled at the little one as he lay silent in her arms. "The naming ceremony is in four days, but I think we can do things differently with this one. He comes with powerful medicine and I think his father already knows his name." She looked at Standing Oak who remained impassive. "Tell us, o reader of thoughts, the name that Unetlanvhi has put in my spirit for this one. If you are right, he will grow with you and your wife. If you are wrong, I will take him for myself." She looked from Standing Oak to Deer in Water with narrowing eyes.

"Standing Oak, don't. She is trying to trick us." Deer in Water looked at her husband with panic in her eyes.

"No, my wife, she is trying to bless us. She is just making it interesting." Standing Oak fixed a piercing gaze on the old one. "I know his name for a great eagle came and told me. She flew in the sky at his birth and called out that name four times before flying away."

The old woman raised her chin. "Four is a holy number. That is strong medicine. But when did Standing Oak learn to speak the Winged Nation's language?"

"I heard her in my own tongue; in Tsalagi."

The old woman edged closer and she clutched the infant.

"Speak it boy!"

Standing Oak took a deep breath and glanced at his wife. She shook her head no, her eyes wide. He looked directly into Wind in the Reeds face. "His name is Awohali Ganohili."

The room was silent as the old woman looked from father to mother and then to the baby. Her voice became very soft. "I heard the eagle speak those words too, my son." She looked into his eyes. "He is Awohali Ganohili, and like the Soaring Eagle that is his name, he will be a great leader of our people, but it will be in a place we do not know." A look of sorrow engulfed her aged features. "On a Trail where we are all herded like cattle we will cry. Beaten down until there is no hope left, the fathers and mothers will weep. In the midst of that sorrow, Soaring Eagle will keep the flame of hope alive through the dark years, for we will rise again. The Cherokee people will rise again." She stood silently holding the infant for another moment, and then gently handed him back to his mother. She turned and slowly left the longhouse.

3: The Gawonisgi Nvya

1832 AD
North of New Echota, GA

T he young brave approached the entryway boldly. He had fulfilled the traditions. He had gone on the hunt and returned with the best cut of meat. Soaring Eagle only hoped that Yellow Dawn would accept his offering. He stopped at the entrance and called out, "Yellow Dawn, I have come with a gift." An impossibly tall Cherokee brave stepped into the light and crossed his arms, effectively blocking the only way into the dwelling. Soaring Eagle grimaced and held out the suddenly scrawny gift. "For Yellow Dawn?" The Cherokee maiden's father looked menacingly at the young brave for a few moments. When Soaring Eagle stood his ground and met the elder eye to eye, the old brave nodded and moved aside, still expressionless. Soaring Eagle inhaled and blinked, then stepped inside. The friendly smile of Yellow Dawn's mother met him as the maiden shyly took the gift.

Yellow Dawn's father stepped over and took a seat by the fire. He motioned for Soaring Eagle to join him. When he sat down they both remained silent for several moments.

The father's name was Red Bear. He was a warrior of renown among their people. Red Bear reached behind him and brought

forth a deerskin wrapped bundle. He held it reverently for a moment with closed eyes. He then pulled forth a ceremonial pipe. He assembled it and filled the pipe with the tobacco and sweet herb mixture used in the ceremony. "It is said that Uktena gave the first pipe to Arrow Woman on the shores of the sacred lake Atagahi." He reached for the cool end of a burning stick and lit the pipe, which he puffed several times to light. He then took the seven ceremonial draws from the holy instrument: for the North, the South, the East, and the West. He then took one for the Sky, one for the Earth and a final one for himself before passing it to Soaring Eagle. "It is also said that Uwohali brought the pipe to a woman of the Aniyvwiya as a sign to end their warfare. Whatever is true, this remains: we smoke the pipe together in peace."

Soaring Eagle puffed the dohi kununawa seven times before handing it back to Red Bear, who held it up towards the open sky peeping through the smoke hole. "We thank you, Unetlanvhi, that we can live in Your peace." He then cradled the pipe silently for several moments. He stared intently into the fire and spoke. "I am a man of war. I have killed both white man and Catawba. I have always fulfilled the blood oath for my household." He stopped and looked over at the young Cherokee. "You are a man of peace. I want you and my daughter to live in that peace. That is all I have to say."

Soaring Eagle knew that a reply was neither required nor desired so he hid the words of Red Bear in his heart. They felt very warm and comfortable in that place.

Kindled long ago in years beyond memory, The Sacred Fire burned in the center of the clearing. The seven clans assembled in that holy place to witness the union of the two young Cherokees. Each clan stood in one of seven arbors positioned equally around the fire. At a sign from the leader of the ceremony, the young couple circled the fire and stopped in front of the Clan Mother of each group. Each woman scrutinized them carefully and then nodded. When they reached the Paint Clan, the daughter of old Wind in the Reeds looked at them carefully and then turned to Soaring Eagle. "My mother told me

of you, Awohali Ganohili." She stretched forth her hand and closed her eyes. "You have a strong destiny and are in need of strong medicine. Walk the Trail that Unetlanvhi will put before you in power and might, for He will go before you." She opened her eyes and looked piercingly at Yellow Dawn. "Hold tightly to your husband and be his strong right arm, child." She nodded once and fell silent.

The couple completed the circle and received the endorsement of all seven Clan Mothers. Before Unetlanvhi and all the Cherokee, they were now married. Through the entire wedding Red Bear never smiled.

1833 AD
WASHINGTON, DC

Silently he flew into dreams. His black leathery wings afforded little purchase for the noise of passage and thus he remained undetected. He soared over Tennessee hills where one man trod. He was tall and sad and walked alone. The bat conjured and behold, fierce Cherokee braves erupted from the ground like stones displaced by fearsome tremors. They appeared all around the man and his expression became panicked. The bat conjured and a fearsome weapon from the future appeared in the man's hands. He looked at it in stark amaze but quickly apprehended its operation. He began to crank the handle that projected from the side and a fierce spray of bullets streamed into the Indians. The man began to scream with manic joy as he pivoted around while spraying fiery death. In a few seconds, it was over. All the Cherokees lay lifeless. The man dropped the smoking weapon and walked over to the nearest brave. A gold ingot projected from his mouth. He grabbed it and then saw the same in each Indian. He began to build a glorious golden pile as he robbed the dead. The bat flew higher, ever undetected.

"Is it the dreams again, Mr. President?" Special Envoy Mondragon sat in a plush chair in the President's office. It was a quiet and bright day, the kind favored by poets and songwriters. The cheerful calls of songbirds sounded in the air.

The White House stood firm, largely rebuilt since the British had set it afire during the War of 1812. On damp days, a faint smell of smoke still lingered in the older areas of the structure. This did not serve to dim the prospects of an ever-advancing nation. The ashes of that dark day had given way to a brighter present.

President Andrew Jackson coughed deeply and then took a ragged breath. "Yes Galen, but the dreams hold promise." His eyes glinted as he stared back at the Romanian. "The Cherokee put great stock in their dreams. They think that they are sent to guide them." He stood at the window overlooking the garden. It was one of the few peaceful places in the President's demanding life. He moved over to his chair and seated himself. He leaned forward with his hands clasped atop the oak desk in an iron grip. "The air is rich with rumor from Georgia. Perhaps you can tell me the truth of the matter."

"As always, you choose your words carefully, Mr. President. Indeed, one could even say that there is a wealth of promise in the air." Mondragon smiled ever so slightly as he raised his chin.

The President chuckled and again began to cough, but quickly regained his breath. "Do tell, Galen." He looked impassively at his guest.

"To be plain, sir, there have been isolated discoveries of gold in north Georgia. We have so far been able to contain the news, but this will not last much longer." Mondragon shifted his weight and looked at Jackson.

The President's eyes narrowed. "Perhaps this will give the citizenry impetus to immigrate to the area." He sighed and steepled his fingers as he looked up at the ceiling. "Of course, our poor Cherokee children will have to give way before the weight of civilization."

Galen Mondragon ever twisted and pushed to arrange events into compliance with his goals. Nevertheless, he avoided misrepresenting the plain truth of a matter. He always felt that the truth was much easier to twist to his purposes. In this way, he built credibility with his allies and struck fear into the hearts of his foes. "They have built a substantial civilization where

they are. Some of them live as kings with estates and slaves. They have made truly remarkable progress in this century."

Jackson looked at the Prince keenly. "I know this well, my friend. Some of whom you speak served under me at the Battle of Horseshoe Bend."

"The Cherokee defeated the Creek for you. That was a bitter irony for the bold victor."

Jackson briefly held a hand to his mouth. "Nevertheless, the floodgates will open when the news of this gold becomes known. The Cherokees must go west. It is the only way."

The room was silent as both men regarded this prospect. Mondragon leaned forward and spoke in a low voice. "We must prepare the way, sir. Allow me to send my chancellor Banica to New Echota to determine the situation in person. That way, we can make more enlightened decisions."

Jackson's face brightened at the prospect. "Yes, the Cherokee capitol in Georgia would be the ideal place to feel the pulse of the Cherokee people." Jackson nodded and reached for pen and paper. "And how is Thomas these days?"

"He is old and cranky, Mr. President. He never seems to run out of energy, though. Thomas has been a faithful friend and companion and you could entrust this mission to no one more capable."

Jackson finished writing and blew on the sheet to dry the ink. "There, executive orders granting Thomas Banica the highest level of access." He handed the sheet to Mondragon.

"Thank you sir, he will not let you down."

"Very well, Galen. Your services are, as always, quite invaluable. You have my gratitude, sir." The President rose in dismissal and extended his hand.

Mondragon rose and shook Jackson's hand. "Thank you, Mr. President." He turned with military precision and swept from the room.

The President of the United States stepped to the window and looked out over the garden. He inhaled a fragrance drifting by and immediately fell into a fit of coughing. He withdrew a handkerchief and placed it over his mouth as he collapsed into his chair. The coughing passed and he removed the handkerchief. A small pool of blood dampened the center of the handkerchief. A small pool of blood dampened the center of the cloth.

1833 AD
NEW ECHOTA, GA

"I am old, Awohali Ganohili. I think that Unetlanvhi has just a few small things for me to do before I cross the Milky Way." Thunder Walking sat in his home in New Echota along with his grandson. Everyone else was out on various errands so they were quite alone. The elder Cherokee leaned forward and fixed a piercing gaze on Soaring Eagle. "It is time to reveal a secret purpose that is for you alone, although you will eventually share it with your wife, too." He reached into his pocket and withdrew a strange artifact. "Come sit by me, my grandson."

The younger Cherokee pulled a chair over next to his grandfather and looked in curiosity at the strange object the elder held. "What is that, Grandfather? I have never seen the like." Thunder Walking smiled mysteriously and pressed on one of the studs that lined the face of the object. The rolling tones of Major Ridge speaking in Cherokee appeared in the air around them. Soaring Eagle jumped up. "Aii! That is The Ridge. Where is he hiding?"

Thunder Walking pressed another stud and the voice stopped in mid-word. Soaring Eagle sank slowly back into his chair. "What medicine is this, Grandfather?"

"You are right, that was The Ridge. Those were the words he spoke at the last council." The old man held the stone forth, inviting closer inspection. "You have heard the tales of the ancient ones, the Anikutani."

"The old Cherokee priest clan. They were all put to death."

"Yes, our people rose up when their rape and robbery of all Cherokees became intolerable." He looked down at the device. "This is the Gawonisgi Nvya, the Speaking Stone. The last priest gave it to Two Turtles before he died. It was said that the priests could capture words on the wind. This was how they did that feat. It has been passed down, usually from grandfather to grandson, in an unbroken line from that time."

Thunder Walking stood and moved over to the fire. He pressed a series of studs on the device and a new voice appeared. "This is for Two Turtles. Use this to remember the stories of my people." Soaring Eagle's mouth dropped open in amazement.

The old man smiled. "Those were the words spoken by Star Rider, the priest, when he gave the stone to Two Turtles. He told him to use this to remember the stories of my people. Each Keeper of the Stone since has spoken those same words." He walked over to his grandson and held forth the stone in two cupped hands. "And so I say to you today. You are the next Keeper. Remember the stories of my people."

Soaring Eagle pushed back his chair as he stood. The thought of refusing such an honor did not occur to him. He reached out and gently took the stone, examining it closely. He looked up from the device into his grandfather's eyes. "These markings by each little stick, this is in the Cherokee Syllabary. How can this be, Grandfather? It was only recently that Sequoyah invented these figures."

The grandfather's eyes twinkled. "Did he invent them or rediscover something far more ancient? Either way, the man is a genius, of that there is no doubt." The elder took a breath. "Two Turtles also recovered something called the Talking Leaves but they later vanished."

"Sequoyah calls the syllabary the talking leaves."

Thunder Walking gazed silently at his grandson for a moment with a half smile on his face. He turned and walked again to his chair and sat down. "It is a remarkable and poetic name, don't you agree? Whatever the fact of the matter may be, you have a new tool that no other Keeper ever had available in the time since the Anikutani. You have become well versed in the syllabary. You can read and comprehend the legends on the stone. Those that have gone before you learned by trial and error and passed on that knowledge to their heir. You, my grandson, will be able to teach me some things about this stone before I go to be with the Creator." The old man rubbed his face. "You must keep this secret. Every Keeper eventually tells his wife and this is good and proper, for she can see to its safety if harm should come to you. But no one else must know, not even your children." He motioned the young Cherokee to his side and showed him the basic operation of the stone. He successfully tested both the record and playback functions. The elder then looked up at the young brave standing before him. "Take this now, Soaring Eagle. The Creator has shown me that the stories that you remember will be the most important in our long history. We will speak again after you have made some discoveries. That is all I have to say." The old man leaned his head back in the chair and promptly fell asleep.

Soaring Eagle brought a blanket to cover his grandfather and quietly left him. He secreted the stone in a buckskin pouch he was wearing and walked outside into the back yard. There was much to think about, much to understand.

Thomas Banica descended from the coach into the town square of New Echota. His hair was gray but his vigor unabated. He strode swiftly to the makeshift claims office on the corner opposite from where his transport had come to rest. Throwing the door open, he entered imperiously. He glared in all directions until his piercing gaze rested upon a lone clerk behind an imposing counter. Scales and other paraphernalia littered the untidy surface. "You there, under whose authority are you operating this office?"

The clerk looked up from beneath his green visor. Plainly, he was not impressed. "Well mister, I'm here on behalf of the sovereign state of Georgia."

"Sovereign? No state of the Union is sovereign, sir."

"Well mister, I reckon you'd better take that up with the Governor."

"I most certainly will. I am here on the authority of the President of the United States and on his orders I must ask you to suspend your operations." Banica slapped down the executive orders that he had carried so far for just such an occasion.

"Well, them's mighty impressive mister, but I ain't closing." He withdrew a cocked and loaded pistol from beneath the counter. "I reckon you'd better leave. And take yer fancy paper with you."

Thomas Banica drew to his full five feet five inches and snatched the paper from the counter. "You haven't heard the last of this." He spun around and stalked from the room, a small smile of triumph on his face.

He returned to the coach to find his luggage offloaded onto the boardwalk. He fished out a coin from his pocket and tipped the driver who boarded the carriage and took off down the street. Behind him was a general store where he entered to gain his bearings. "You there, storekeeper, where is the town inn?"

An elder Cherokee stood with his back to the chancellor in conversation with the shop owner. As the storekeeper looked over at Thomas, the Cherokee turned his head and spoke. "I have not heard that voice in many summers, yet I cannot forget that bullying tone. Thomas, is that you?"

Banica's mouth dropped open as he realized who spoke to him. He was now very old with gray hair and deep wrinkles that told a tale of joy rather than sorrow. Two eagle feathers hung from his hair and an ancient Springfield flintlock hung from his shoulder. "Thunder Walking, is that you?" He stepped quickly to the ancient Indian and extended his hand. The Cherokee grasped it with both of his, his face wreathed in smiles. "I never thought I would see you again in this place." Banica grasped with his other hand as Thunder Walking nodded. Banica released his grip and reached to touch the Springfield. "Is this what I think?"

"The rifle that Red Beard gave me? Yes my friend. It has served me well." Thunder Walking looked Thomas up and down. "Your years with the Great Father have treated you kindly." He reached out and touched the lapel of the chancellor's finely tailored jacket. "Is this what they wear in Washington these days?"

Banica grinned. "This is just what the servants wear. You should see the Prince when he attends a great function." Thomas rolled his eyes. "Military chic is the dress of Washington. The clattering of swords drowns out the orchestra." The chancellor glanced at the storekeeper and back at the Cherokee. "I was going to ask the location of the Inn."

Thunder Walking kept a straight face. "We don't have one." He looked at Banica. "Did you bring your tipi?" The Cherokee paused and then looked over at the storekeeper. Both broke into laughter.

Banica smiled. "That is fine, I will sleep here."

Thunder Walking looked seriously at Banica. "No, my old friend, you will stay with me. Then you can tell the Great Father how his savage children are living." The elder sighed deeply. "My wife has gone to be with the Creator so my son and his family share my house. It is a two story colonial style at the edge of town. We have a spare bedroom."

Banica looked undecided. He felt unsure what message staying with a Cherokee would send. Upon quick reflection, he saw the good of it. Both the Prince and the President would be cast as friends of the Cherokee by his action. "Very well Tom-Tom. Do you have a wagon that can transport my luggage?"

"Yes I do. It is tied up out back. Follow me." The Indian turned and headed out the back door with Banica in tow. They climbed aboard his flat wagon and drove around front where they picked up the chancellor's baggage. The elder looked over at his old friend. "Welcome to New Echota, Thomas. Here you will see what a Nation can do."

Banica nodded but kept silent. What a Nation could do was irrelevant. The will of the Great Father was inexorable and unchangeable. He lowered his head and softly sighed.

The trip to the house was short and uneventful. They pulled into a carriage house behind an imposing two-story brick colonial home. "Whoa," Thunder Walking called to the horse. "Joshua, would you unhitch old Del for me? We have a guest."

A Negro dressed in frontier style buckskins appeared from a stall. "Oh, yes sir, Mr. Thunder." He looked curiously at Banica. "Who is our guest, sir?"

"Joshua, this is my old friend Thomas Banica who is here all the way from Washington. Thomas, this is our right hand man, Joshua."

Banica looked from Joshua to Thunder Walking. "A slave, Tom-Tom? I am impressed."

Joshua smiled infectiously. "Oh no sir, I'm a freedman. Mr. Thunder saw to that a long time ago."

Banica's eyebrows rose. "Really? Why do you stay?"

"I stay 'cause Mr. Thunder and his family treat me right. They love the Lord and I do too."

Thunder Walking turned toward Banica. "We have heard the teaching of the Moravians and we understand that they too worship Unetlanvhi." The Cherokee shrugged. "We walk the same path."

Banica blinked rapidly. This was an entirely unexpected development. He had heard of some inroads of Georgia missionaries into Cherokee culture, but he did not expect a wholesale acceptance. "Are there many Cherokees who feel as you do, Tom-Tom?"

"Yes Thomas, there are many. You will meet them." He picked up one of Banica's bags. "Come. Let me show you your room." He turned towards the Negro. "Joshua, would you bring the rest of Mr. Banica's luggage when you are done?"

"Yes sir." Joshua watched the two old friends walk into the house. He turned and unhitched the horse. "Such an important visitor, Del." The horse raised its head and snorted. "And all the way from Washington." He looked at the closing door at the rear of the dwelling. "I sure hope Mr. Thunder tells that man the right things." Del nodded his great head and whinnied in affirmation.

1833 AD
WASHINGTON, DC

The strange engine that he piloted could scoop out a grave in one stroke. Willing helpers waited to plant the dread seed of tomorrow. Into each hole, they threw the dead body of a Cherokee warrior. The piled dirt fell in upon the dead as quickly as they were planted. A golden gravestone grew from the head of each burial site. Inscribed on the face of each gold stone was In God We Trust. He waved his hand and the stones flew from their Georgia home to encircle Washington. Over the gold encircled capitol of white America, the bat flew in silent spirals.

"Senator Forsythe is a formidable proponent of your cause, Mr.

President. Nevertheless, what Thomas did is proper in these circumstances. By his declarations in the claims office he has established that your administration has no ties to the current Georgia gold rush." Special Envoy Mondragon crossed his legs and flicked off an offending piece of lint from his trousers. "To the common man this says that Andrew Jackson isn't in it for the money."

The President nodded with dour expression. "Perhaps, Galen, you can reassure the esteemed Senator of Georgia that the Federal government has no intention of nationalizing any gold claims."

"The Senator can be very literal in his interpretation of events. I believe, sir, that I can help him to, ah, read between the lines." Mondragon tapped on the arm of his chair. "Before he makes it a national issue, of course."

Relief washed some of the tension from the President's face. "Thank you once again for your assistance, Galen. You have served your adopted country well." Jackson looked down at the letter laid before him on his desk. "As I read between the lines of Thomas's report, I detect quite a fondness for the Cherokee people, and especially for his friend Thunder Walking."

Mondragon nodded. "I am not surprised. Thomas and Tom-Tom became quite close on our first trip to Georgia."

"Tom-Tom?" Jackson looked quizzically at Mondragon.

"That was the name he was called by the white men in Charleston." Mondragon shrugged. "It stuck and he didn't seem to mind. It was easier than saying Thunder Walking."

The President smiled. "The chancellor's affections notwithstanding, Indian removal will proceed. The groundwork is laid in Congress. It is just a matter of time."

Mondragon uncrossed his legs and leaned forward. "Yes, that is well understood." The Special Envoy watched the President for a moment. It was time to speak as a friend. "Andrew, this whole affair has been taxing on your health. Yet I can't help but notice an improvement in you today."

Jackson reached into a drawer and withdrew a small buckskin bundle. "I owe thanks to Thomas for this improvement." He opened the bundle on his polished oak desktop revealing a mixture of dried herbs. "It would seem that in conversation with your Tom-Tom, he happened to mention the Great Father's terrible cough. The next day, Tom-Tom handed him this bundle." The President took a small pinch of the mixture and placed it under his tongue. "It seems that Tom-Tom consulted a Cherokee healer who prescribed this medicine. Thomas sent the package with instructions to use it several times daily. It has served to quiet the burning in my lungs considerably."

Mondragon raised his eyebrows. "Really? That is quite amazing." The Special Envoy cleared his throat. "Does this serve to soften your feeling for your Cherokee children?"

Jackson's expression hardened. "Not in the least. I will instruct Thomas to have the healer stockpile seeds of these herbs in anticipation of a move. I'm told the soil is quite fertile in Indian Territory."

1833 AD
NEW ECHOTA, GA

Standing Oak had avoided Thomas Banica in the months he stayed at his father's house. The son of Thunder Walking and his family occupied a suite in the corner of the home and it was easy to stay cut off from general household activities. The memory of Red Beard in the spirit world was still strong and consequently he felt that Banica did not have their interests at heart. He was still Red Beard's chancellor. However, the occasional casual contacts and the family meal times served to soften his view of the man. There was something likeable in the old fellow. He could be cranky and kind in the same moment and Standing Oak understood his father's attachment to the Romanian.

As he sat on the front porch cleaning his rifle one sunny afternoon, Banica rode up on the bay horse his father had loaned him while he was in New Echota. He tied off the pony and climbed the porch stairs. He found a seat in a rocking chair next to Standing Oak. "Good afternoon, Standing Oak. Wonderful day, isn't it?" He shaded his eyes and squinted into the bright blue sky. A light wind played in the treetops around the house.

Standing Oak kept his eyes on his work and nodded. "Um hmm."

Banica began to rock slowly. The chair creaked softly at the motion. "I enjoy these hot July days. Romania is always so cold." He glanced briefly at the Cherokee. "I have not seen Soaring Eagle or his wife for several days. Have they gone somewhere?"

The Cherokee continued to focus on the firearm. "They have gone to Tennessee to visit some friends." He picked up a lightly oiled cloth and began to rub down the gun barrel. The wind died away completely leaving only the swish of cloth on metal.

Banica leaned his head back and sighed. "Standing Oak, I know you don't like the Prince and can barely tolerate me. I also know something happened between you and the one you call Red Beard." Banica stopped at the end of a forward rock and put his forearms on his knees, looking over at the Cherokee. "I saw you fall in the street that day. I was just coming out of the General Store when it happened. Although he never touched you, I could feel the pressure that Galen was exerting." The Romanian leaned back and continued to rock. "The Prince has been a mentor and a friend to me for my entire life. Yet, there are large areas of his existence that he keeps hidden from me. I do know this." He ran a hand through his gray shock of hair. "I am now old and gray and Galen is still hale. He is still Red Beard."

Standing Oak looked over at Banica and searched his eyes. He saw trustworthiness there. The Romanian stopped rocking as he held the Cherokee's gaze. Standing Oak silently prayed to Creator and felt the liberty to speak what he had never spoken to anyone. "Perhaps he is not a man." He held Banica's gaze as the other's eyes darted back and forth, searching both of Standing Oak's eyes. The Cherokee then turned back to his rifle.

The old rocker started its musical creaking once again. Standing Oak glanced over to see Banica staring into the sky as he rocked, his brow furrowed in concentration. He turned his attention back to the rifle, squinting down the bore to check for any wayward debris. "Do you ever dream of bats, Thomas?"

Banica stopped and looked sharply at the Cherokee. "Why,

do you?"

Standing Oak looked down at his rifle. "After Red Beard met me in the spirit world, I was plagued with dreams of bats for quite some time. Now I don't have those dreams much any more."

"The spirit world? What are you saying, Standing Oak?"

The Cherokee laid the rifle across his knees. "He drew me there back on that day. Unlike him, I was not strong enough to stay conscious in both places, so I passed out in the street." Standing Oak looked at Banica. "I saw Red Beard there. He turned into a giant bat and screamed so terribly that I was thrown from that place."

Banica stared at Standing Oak silently for a long moment, and then lowered his head. He looked out again at the blue Georgia sky and resumed rocking. He closed his eyes and rubbed them with thumb and forefinger. "I have just realized that this is the first time in my work with the Prince that I have been away from him for so long. I had come to accept dreams of bats as normal." He looked over at the Cherokee. "I haven't dreamed of bats in my whole time here." He drummed his fingers on the arm of the rocker. "Prince Galen Mondragon has a proud heritage. He is directly descended from Vlad III, a king of Romania."

"Vlad the Impaler."

Banica looked open-mouthed at his companion. "You astound me, sir. Are you a student of Romanian history?"

Standing Oak looked over and smiled shyly at the chancellor, the first smile that he had granted the Romanian during his stay in New Echota. "After my incident with your boss, I made it a point to study your land. You have a bloody history." He looked down briefly. "Then again, so do the Cherokee."

"Surely you had no one as cruel as the Impaler."

"Many summers ago, long before the white man came, we had a priest clan. They were so cruel that my people rose up and killed them all."

Banica formed an o with his lips. "I suppose every culture has its dirty little secrets."

"Even America, Thomas?"

Banica looked over at the Indian. "I think we are writing those dirty little secrets now, Standing Oak."

The Cherokee leaned his rifle against the porch railing, reached to a table, and picked up a publication. "Have you seen our newspaper?"

Banica peered over at the periodical in Standing Oak's hands. "Ah yes, The Cherokee Phoenix. I was talking to the editor, Mr. Boudinot, just the other day. His paper is well known in Washington."

"This is a special extra edition that just came out. It includes a transcript of an address to the people of the United States from the Cherokee Council." Standing Oak opened the paper and thumbed to a page. "It says, in part, 'We wish to remain on the land of our fathers. We have a perfect and original right to remain without interruption or molestation. The treaties with us, and laws of the United States made in pursuance of treaties, guaranty our residence and our privileges and secure us against intruders. Our only request is that these treaties may be fulfilled, and these laws executed.'"

The Cherokee folded the paper in his lap. "I think that neither you nor I know the extent of dirty little secrets that are now being written, Thomas."

1833 AD
WASHINGTON, DC

The Prince sat in his Washington townhouse with a letter from Thomas Banica in his lap. His cat rubbed against his legs and purred, stopping to look up at him in that directly disarming way of felines. The Prince smiled faintly. "Yes Pasha, I do believe Thomas is showing signs of going native." The cat sat down and meowed once. "No, I wouldn't have believed it myself, but then again, look at me. Once a Romanian, now an American and no one suspects a thing." The cat lay down, rolled on its side, and meowed in agreement.

The Prince reached down and rubbed Pasha under his chin. He then stood and walked to the window, carrying the offending document. He held it in the light and said, "Just listen to this. 'Your Highness, I perceive a grave injustice is being done to the Cherokee Nation. These people are more civilized than the frontier white settlers, yet they are termed savages.'"

The Prince walked back to his chair, affording Pasha an opportunity to jump into his lap. Mondragon stroked him absently as he looked out the window. "Perhaps this is better, Pasha. Thomas is no fool; he surely notices my absence of aging." He lifted Pasha into his arms and rose again to walk to the window. "It will be better for the plan if he stays with his Cherokee friends."

Mondragon sighed and returned to his chair. "Too long have I held this form, Pasha. I have to remember that Thomas is only human." The cat meowed in question and looked up at his master. The Prince chuckled and rubbed his head. "I was starting to worry about him, Pasha. Can you imagine that?" Mondragon's eyes became dark and remote. Pasha meowed in alarm and jumped from his arms to land on the floor and dart into the next room.

4: GATHERING STORM

1833 AD
NEW ECHOTA, GA

T he midwife looked out of the back door and motioned to the group of men standing under the tree. "Soaring Eagle, come over here and meet your new daughter."

The young Cherokee broke out into a huge smile and let out a whoop. He ran to the door and into the house as the men chuckled. He reappeared a moment later with a tiny bundle in his arms. "Father, Grandfather, Thomas, look! I have a daughter!" The Cherokee men broke out into whoops as Banica applauded. They rushed over to meet the new infant. As they approached, the cry of an eagle was heard overhead. All looked up to see the great raptor circle once and depart. As they watched, a single feather floated down and circled lazily until it landed at the new father's feet.

Thunder Walking reached down and picked it up. He straightened and held it forth silently. All looked at the unprecedented signpost from the sky with wide eyes. The old grandfather motioned to Soaring Eagle to take the feather. "Grandfather Eagle, lord of the Winged Nation, has sent your new daughter a gift." Soaring Eagle nodded mutely. "We will seek Unetlanvhi for her name and pray that He gives it to old

Raven Head for the time of naming."

Soaring Eagle looked intently at his grandfather. "The eagle spoke to me, Grandfather. He spoke her name."

Banica ran his hand through his hair. "All I heard was screeching."

Standing Oak looked at Banica. "The eagle spoke to me at the birth of this, my son." He spread a hand towards Soaring Eagle. "Thomas, if Creator wills, He can give us ears to hear. He did this for ancient Balaam that he might hear the donkey's rebuke. Cannot the One Who is the same yesterday, today, and forever do the same for one Cherokee today?" He turned toward his son. "Do not speak it chooch. Hide it in your heart until the naming. Then you will know the truth of it."

1834 AD
NEW ECHOTA, GA

The changing modern lifestyle of New Echota left few moments for cherished pastimes. The daily household chores along with tending to the family fields at the edge of town kept both the relatives and staff of Thunder Walking quite busy.

Thomas Banica had become a valued part of that Cherokee family. With his years of experience managing Prince Mondragon's estate, he was able to impart profound financial wisdom that allowed them to prosper.

Banica was sitting at his desk by the window of a morning when he felt a tug at his shirtsleeve. He looked down to see a Cherokee toddler beaming up at him. "Why, good morning Feather. I didn't hear you enter."

"You weren't supposed to," said a voice from the door. "We teach them very early."

Banica turned to see Standing Oak leaning against his door. He smiled at the grandfather of the little one. "The word of the eagle was true. She Who Floats on the Wind lives up to her given name."

"Grandfather Eagle seems to know what he's talking about."

"Where are my manners? Come in, Standing Oak. I have a fresh pot of tea here. Would you join me in a cup?"

The Cherokee smiled and walked to a chair by Banica's desk. He took the proffered cup of tea and sat.

Banica looked at him with an eyebrow raised. "I do have a price, however."

Standing Oak adopted a mock severity. "What is that, white man?"

Banica reached and grabbed Feather who laughed with glee. He raised her to his knee and looked at her grandfather. "I would hold your granddaughter on my lap while we talk."

Standing Oak broke into a smile. "As long as she wills it, my friend."

Feather cooed and snuggled back into Banica's ample belly. "You see? None of you can offer her such comfort."

Standing Oak sighed. "Sadly true, Thomas. Our bellies are like iron from the hard life of a Cherokee."

"While mine is soft from sitting here and making you all more profitable." Banica pushed an open ledger back as Feather reached for the book.

Standing Oak simply nodded as he took a sip of tea. "My son and his wife have taken the wagon into town for supplies. I have been assigned a task. What do you white folks call it?"

"A nanny?"

Standing Oak nodded. "That is it, although it seems to refer to a female." The two men laughed.

"I am glad to share the joy of raising this child with you."

"We all share that joy in the house of Thunder Walking."

A new voice sounded from the doorway. "Is someone speaking of me?"

Banica beamed, his face wreathed in a smile. "Tom-Tom, please join us. I believe there's some tea left."

The elder Cherokee sat and poured himself a cup. "I am glad to see my great granddaughter so well entertained."

Feather laughed and held out her arms to Thunder Walking. "A-dood," she sounded out.

Standing Oak chuckled. "She can almost speak Tsalagi, Edudi."

Banica lifted Feather across and she wiggled into Thunder Walking's arms. She leaned back into his belly, then sat up straight again.

"Not as soft," Standing Oak deadpanned.

"No, hard as that old flintlock he carries."

The three men enjoyed a quiet moment with their tea while Feather played with the beaded decorations on her great grandfather's shirt.

Standing Oak became serious. "I'm glad you're here too, Edudi. I need to speak of something."

Thunder Walking nodded and focused grave attention on his son. Banica carefully set down his cup of tea and looked over.

"I had a dream last night. It will not leave me and I know it is important." Standing Oak drained his cup and set it down. "In my dream I saw the spirit form of Red Beard. I saw the great bat circling over our house here in New Echota. Then I rose into the air and he beckoned me to follow. He flew to the north and we were at Ross's Landing. He pointed and a great fire streamed from his finger. He then pointed west and the fire scorched a path on the earth over the horizon. I rose up to escape him and kept rising until the whole land was laid out beneath me." Standing Oak shook his head. "Our homeland is so beautiful from high in the sky. I saw the flaming trail that Red Beard had made. It went far to the west beyond a great river. That river was amazing. It was the largest I have ever seen."

"The Mississippi," Banica said.

"Yes." Thunder Walking stroked Feather's head briefly. "It is beyond that mighty river that many of our people have gone. They hope to escape the wrath of the Great Father."

Banica shook his head. "I fear it will catch up to them."

Standing Oak closed his eyes, straining out the last details of his dream. "The flaming trail ended far west of the river in a green and beautiful land."

"Indian Territory," Banica whispered.

Standing Oak nodded. "So I suppose." He was silent for a moment, then continued. "I then flew back to New Echota. All of our beautiful Cherokee houses were filled with white men. I did not see an Indian anywhere. I sank down in the field behind our house and wept. I awoke with those tears." He looked at Banica with a tortured expression. "Thomas, does Mondragon hold such power over these things? Is he preparing our destruction from far away Washington?"

Banica rubbed the bridge of his nose. "Galen has no power of himself. However, he has become the trusted advisor of presidents and statesmen. His influence on them cannot be underestimated."

Thunder Walking's expression darkened. "He has power beyond mere influence. He almost revealed it to me once and he did reveal it to my son."

"Ah, the incident in the street."

Standing Oak inhaled sharply. "Yes and the creature in my dreams was the same as the one I saw on the spirit plain that day. I believe it is the true form of Red Beard."

"Then he is an agent of our worst enemy."

"Without a doubt."

1838 AD
NEW ECHOTA, GA

The five-year-old girl was brimming with life. She ran through the field towards a cold creek, following the old dog. "Wait for me Tookah!" The dog barked in reply without slowing.

Yellow Dawn looked at her companion as they strode behind the two runners. "Did the dog speak to you my husband?"

Soaring Eagle looked at her and grinned. "No, actually he spoke to Feather. He said, 'Catch me if you can, She Who Floats on the Wind.'" He shifted the bundle on his back as they vainly tried to keep up with their daughter.

"She will reach our favorite place and climb the old oak so she can jump down and surprise us."

"No, I think she will hide in the brush by the stream." The couple laughed as they tried to predict their daughter's antics.

They were almost to the creek when they heard Feather scream. Soaring Eagle dropped the bundle and ran like a streak towards the sound. As he approached, he heard the dog barking loudly. A shot rang out and Tookah let out a yelp and was still. He ran into the clearing to see three armed white men with the old dog lying in a pool of blood before them. Feather stood across the clearing with her hands over her face only showing her stricken eyes. He ran and scooped his daughter into his arms as Yellow Dawn burst into the clearing.

She stood stock-still and looked in fury, first at the dead dog, and then at the three intruders. She spoke clearly and with a quiet menace that made the men grip their guns more tightly. "What have you done?"

"Now missy, the old dog was a fixin' to tear into us. It was self defense, I tell ya."

Yellow Dawn walked over and wordlessly picked up the body of her pet. She turned on her heel and walked from the clearing with her husband following. Little Feather burst into tears as they walked the path. Soaring Eagle paused to scoop up the bundle he had dropped and they continued towards the house. Behind them, they could hear a heated argument among the three white men. Soaring Eagle hurried his family towards safety. In another moment, they were in the yard and saw both Standing Oak and Thunder Walking rushing towards them with guns in hand.

"Get behind us my children," the grandfather called out. Just then, the three men broke into the clearing at a run to find several Cherokees with guns leveled at them. They skidded to a halt in confusion while Yellow Dawn laid the body of Tookah by the porch steps and grabbed the rifle that her mother-in-law tossed to her. She aimed at the men and walked slowly forward.

"You men are on my property," Thunder Walking called out. "I suggest you leave."

One man spread out an open hand as he firmly gripped his rifle in the other. "Now mister, we was just worried about the little girl, see? Wanted to make sure she was okay."

Soaring Eagle still held his frightened daughter in his arms. "She is fine," he called out.

Standing Oak kept his aim as he spoke. "Leave."

The white men milled about and then backed out of the yard. Standing Oak kept his rifle at the ready and followed them to the edge of the property. He watched carefully as they headed down the path to the creek and disappeared. Satisfied, he lowered the weapon and turned back toward his family.

Feather slipped out of her father's arms and ran towards her grandfather. Just as she reached him, a shot rang out and he fell at her feet. "Grandpa," Feather screamed.

From down by the creek a voice called out, "Aw Zeb, what'd ya go and do that for?"

The family rushed to their fallen one. Deer in Water dropped next to her husband and cried out, "Standing Oak, Standing Oak, do not leave me!" Soaring Eagle kneeled and gently rolled his father onto Deer in Water's lap. A crimson stain that quickly darkened to black spread across the plain gray dress she was wearing.

Standing Oak gasped and clenched his teeth as he held his eyes closed. Slowly he relaxed and his eyes drifted open. He looked at his wife and son and his gaze drifted into the sky. "Look! The Elders are waiting for me."

"No Standing Oak. Don't go!" His wife bowed her head over him as her tears freely spattered his chest.

The stricken Cherokee strained to refocus on his wife. "It's okay Deer in Water. It is a good day to die. The Elders have brought a fine pony for me to ride across the Milky Way." He squeezed his eyes shut in a grimace of pain. He opened them and looked upon Soaring Eagle. "Take care of the family my son. Take care of your mother." He looked over at Thunder Walking. "I think I will see you soon, my Father. You will not have to walk on the terrible Trail that is coming, for you will be with all your relatives and the Lord Tsisa." He closed his eyes slowly, and then reopened them to look upon his wife. "Don't grieve. I go to be with all my grandfathers." His eyes stayed open as the life drained out of them.

"Aii!" Deer in Water leaned back her head in a sorrowful scream.

1838 AD
NEW ECHOTA, GA

"We gather to say farewell to Standing Oak. He was a true son to his father and a true father to his son. He was a faithful husband to his wife Deer in Water. He was always truthful and he treated all men fairly, Cherokee and white man alike. His death was untimely and his murderer remains unpunished."

The young missionary looked out over the sizable crowd at the gravesite. They were mostly Cherokee, but a few white people braved the scorn of their peers to pay their respects to the fallen brave. He knew that he took a risk in pointing to the perpetrator of this atrocity, but his conscience would allow no other course. "I stand by this grave and call to account the one named Zeb who killed this man. His name was clearly heard by the family of this man as the one who had done the deed."

Others standing nearby muttered their assent as Soaring Eagle nodded from the crowd, his face grave and laced with anger.

"And now we commit these earthly remains to the ground. Ashes to ashes, dust to dust." The young minister paused and closed his eyes. "I thank you Lord that Your servant has found his way Home. I thank You that he now sits in Your great council. I pray that You will comfort those that he has left behind. Amen."

The crowd uttered agreement and the coffin was let down into the grave. Deer in Water watched with tear filled eyes but Soaring Eagle remained stern and aloof.

Zeb Fuller was brought to trial for the murder of Standing Oak. The proceedings were a travesty. The defense introduced complex testimony about the dangerous dog that attacked the party of white men. The witnesses lied about what had happened and painted a totally false picture.

The defense was not allowed to bring key witnesses to the stand. All of their arguments were discredited. In the end, Zeb Fuller got off scot-free.

Banica had been away from the Prince for several years and to see him again in New Echota was startling. He had received the letter that he was coming only days earlier. "Your Highness, it is good to see you." The words felt dry in his mouth.

"Hello Thomas. You are looking well. Life with the Cherokee is agreeing with you."

"And you, your Majesty. I have many friends here, sire. I have brought some with me."

Mondragon surveyed the two mounted Indians with Banica.

One was very old and carried a vaguely familiar flintlock on his shoulder. "Tom-Tom, is that you?"

The Cherokee lifted his chin slightly. "It is I, Prince Mondragon." He swept his hand towards the young brave beside him. "And this is my grandson, Soaring Eagle." The younger Indian nodded ever so slightly.

Galen Mondragon had taken some care to present an appearance of aging. He had procured some of the new chemical Hydrogen Peroxide from his contacts in France and had used it to streak some gray into his beard and hair. Applied gradually and regularly over the last few years, it had mimicked the sudden progression of age. His associates in Washington knew that he had been in America for over forty years, so it was not unexpected. To Banica it was startling and surreal.

"I have heard of the loss of your son from Thomas. My condolences, Thunder Walking." The Prince dipped his head slightly.

"You honor me with my true name. Thank you for your sympathies, Your Highness."

"Not at all." The Prince peered at the firearm on the old Cherokee's shoulder. "Tell me, is that the rifle I gave you so long ago?"

"Yes it is. I used it to chase away the white men who killed my son."

Banica looked away as the Prince lowered his head and cleared his throat. "I'm glad you still find it, ah, useful." He looked up and smiled thinly. "I must repair to my room at the Inn. Thomas, will you accompany me?"

"Yes sire." Banica glanced at the two Cherokees.

The Prince nodded at the elder Indian. "Good to see you again, Tom-Tom. Un jour plaisant à vous monsieur."

"And you, Prince. Un beau jour à vous, votre Majesté."

Mondragon smiled briefly and nodded once at Soaring Eagle as he wheeled his steed away and up the lane. Banica waved at his friends and fell in behind the Prince. A few moments later, they tied up the horses in front of the lodging. The Prince motioned to a Negro waiting by the door. "Porter, would you be so kind as to tend to our steeds?" He motioned to the two horses.

"Oh, yes sir, be happy to, sir. They'll be fed and watered and resting in the stable out back."

The Prince nodded. "Good man." He reached into his pocket a pulled out a coin that he pressed into the man's hand.

"Oh, thank you sir!"

Mondragon and Banica swept into the lobby and climbed the stairs. The old chancellor chuckled as they reached the second floor. "Have you found a new kindness for the servants, sire?"

The Prince smiled at his old friend. Of a truth, it was good to see him again. He had missed his dry wit. "Washington has taught me many things my old friend. Among them is the power of gold. A very small investment always smoothes the way." He walked to a nearby door and entered with Banica in tow. "Besides, you were no longer around to handle such sundry details. I had to develop a new approach, more in tune with these enlightened times in which we live." He swept his hand toward a comfortable looking nook by a window. "Have a seat Thomas, we have much to discuss."

The chancellor nodded and found a comfortable chair where Mondragon had indicated as the Prince shed his outer jacket and loosened his neckwear. "Damned hot in Georgia this time of year."

"I've become accustomed to it." He leaned forward and lowered his voice. "Frankly, I prefer it to the cold stone castles of Romania."

Mondragon laughed and walked over to his chancellor. "You know, I think the heat is better than those drafty old relics too. I've simply forgotten what it's like to be so damned cold all the time."

Banica peered closely at the Prince. "Have you adopted the American penchant for colorful metaphors, Galen?"

Mondragon looked at the chancellor and sighed. "It does seem to be the preferred communication of Washington." He sat down in the other chair be the window. "You protest that such is not worthy of Romanian royalty?"

Thomas pursed his lips and raised his chin slightly. "You once held yourself to a higher standard."

Mondragon looked out the window and tapped his nose

pensively. "Perhaps I am no longer Romanian."

Banica leaned forward. "But you are still royalty."

The Prince felt a warm flush of friendship that was starkly human. Were all of the long years effecting a change that was more profound than he realized? He briefly consulted deep within himself and found comfort in the ever-present darkness. No, it was a brief emotion, method acting controlling his character and molding the Galen Mondragon persona. It convinced even him. He smiled disarmingly at his chancellor. "I have revealed my poverty in your absence." He bowed his head slightly and briefly lowered his eyes. "I will henceforth keep your example before me and attend to these important details."

Banica smiled broadly. "I am honored, sire."

"It is nothing." Mondragon stood and looked out on the street. He clasped his hands behind his back and raised his chin. "You know that Congress has passed the Indian Removal bill."

"Many Cherokee think that it is a bark without a bite."

The Prince sighed. "Would that it was so, Thomas. I have been recalled here by the Governor of Georgia to quietly prepare for what is coming." He strolled to the center of the room, keeping his back to the chancellor. "The President is preparing to order troops into Georgia. They will detain all Cherokees in preparation for a forced move to Indian Territory." He turned to face Banica. "This will happen very soon, within the next two months."

Banica rode to his feet with a look of shock on his face. "Galen, no! What have these people done? A finer race I have never known."

Mondragon looked at him with a hint of sadness in his eyes. "Their crime is simply this. They are where white men need to be. They are the gypsies of America, Thomas. Even as we rejected those people in our homeland, so America rejects these Indians." The Prince smiled inwardly. He played this role exceedingly well.

Banica reddened and lowered his head as he remembered his own racial intolerance for the strange nomadic people of Romania. "We made them slaves just as the Americans have done to the Negro."

"Each race has its own dirty little secrets."

Banica looked sharply at the Prince and briefly held his gaze. He turned and looked out the window and spoke quietly. "They are my friends, Galen."

"Then you have a chance to prepare them, Thomas." Mondragon approached his old friend closely. "Your heart has become divided. I was going to ask you to return to Washington with me when this business is done, but I now question the prudence of that course."

Banica lowered his head and then looked up with tortured eyes. "So do I, Galen."

Mondragon stood still for a moment, and then reached into his pocket. "Take this, old friend." He handed him a slim folder. "These are special credentials for you from President Van Buren. Perhaps they will help ease the way for Tom-Tom and his family."

Banica pulled a paper from the folder and unfolded it, briefly scanning the document. He glanced up at Mondragon, and then peered again at the paper. "Thomas Banica is given the charge of Presidential Special Attaché to the Cherokee Nation." He looked up again with open mouth. "Signed by Martin Van Buren, President of the United States."

"You cannot change the Removal, Thomas, but you now have extraordinary discretionary power to ease the way for many of your friends. Use it wisely."

"Yes I will." The hand holding the paper dropped to his side as he looked at his old friend in appreciation. "Thank you, Galen."

The Prince walked back to the window, waving his hand dismissively. "It is nothing Thomas." He looked back at Banica and smiled. "I knew that if I didn't do something, you'd end up in the stockade when all this happened, and how would that look, hmm? I can't have my chancellor playing the criminal, can I?" It was truly a move of enlightened self-interest on the part of the Prince. That it served the chancellor too was good but inconsequential to the bigger picture.

"Then, this is goodbye, Galen." Banica looked sadly at the Prince.

"Not quite yet, Thomas. I must stay here for some time, probably until spring."

Banica visibly brightened at the prospect. "That is good news. Allow me to take my leave of you now. I have new and important things I must accomplish."

The Prince raised his chin slightly. "Indeed you do." They both walked toward the door. "Would you join me for dinner later? This small establishment serves excellent fare."

"I would be delighted."

"Six o'clock?"

"I will return then." Banica reached out and gripped Mondragon's hand. "And thank you, Galen."

Mondragon smiled silently as he closed the door. This was going well. Any entanglements with Banica were being eliminated. Soon it would be time for the next step.

That night Banica dreamed of bats.

"My time is very short, grandson. My son's prophecy to me before he died was true. A Trail is coming but I will not walk upon it." The old Cherokee lifted up on one elbow in the bed. "You must remember the stories of my people, Soaring Eagle."

The young man at the bedside smiled. "I have been doing that, Grandfather, and I have discovered much more about the Stone." The two were alone in the house and Soaring Eagle reached into the deerskin pouch that he now always wore. He extracted the strange device and pressed an unfamiliar series of studs.

"I have never done that, grandson."

"I know. Watch this." He pressed one more stud and suddenly the image of Galen Mondragon and Thomas Banica astride their horses filled the bedroom. Mondragon's black stallion snorted and nodded his head.

Thunder Walking recoiled involuntarily. "What have you done chooch?" The old man sat up on the edge of the bed and reached up to the horse. His hand passed through the image.

The ghostly likeness of the Prince spoke. "I must repair to my room at the Inn. Thomas, will you accompany me?"

Banica answered dutifully, "Yes sire."

The Prince looked eerily right at the old Cherokee seated on the bed. "Good to see you again, Tom-Tom. Un jour plaisant à vous monsieur."

Even as he heard his own voice, Thunder Walking silently mouthed the words. "And you, Prince. Un beau jour à vous, votre Majesté."

Soaring Eagle grinned as he pressed another series of studs and the image dissolved. "There is much more to this Gawonisgi Nvya than you realize, Edudi. I am just beginning to comprehend some of its capabilities."

The old man lay back down very slowly with a sharp inhale as he reached the surface of the bed. He closed his eyes briefly and then opened them and looked at his grandson. "You will be great in the story of the Keepers, Grandson." He looked at him softly with a hint of a smile on his lips. "There is an ancient prophecy in the Stone. You will find it if you look carefully. It says that one day there will be a great Keeper. He will begin to unlock the true power of the Stone, the power only known to the most ancient of the Anikutani. You are that Keeper, Soaring Eagle."

The young man looked solemnly at the elder. "I will follow the path that Unetlanvhi unfolds, Edudi."

The old Cherokee patted his grandson's hand. "That is as it should be, Grandson." He slowly closed his eyes and drifted off to sleep. Soaring Eagle made sure he was covered and slipped out of the room, quietly closing the door behind him.

1838 AD
THE EDGE OF ETERNITY

The old man awoke with a start. It was a pitch-black middle of the night. Over his head, a swirl of light suddenly appeared and expanded until it stretched far beyond the confines of his small room. He looked and, behold, the stars of the Milky Way were strewn before him, a roadway that swept across the universe toward an incredibly bright pulsating star. He looked again and saw a runner approaching at impossible speed. He was clothed in beautiful white skins that seemed to conform to both the outline and motion of his body. As he came near, he recognized his son Standing Oak as he called out, "My Father, arise! Run with me."

The old Cherokee stood and looked down in amaze. He was floating in the air several feet above the bed. The bed. It looked so confining and finite. He ran his hand across his chest to feel the fine white skin in which he was now clothed. He reached and touched a strand of his long hair that was falling across his shoulder. It was a luxuriant glossy black, the hair of his youth. He looked up to see Standing Oak standing before him. "My son!" They fell into an embrace which neither wanted to break. Finally, the elder who was now young held his son at arm's length. "Standing Oak, are you well?"

The young warrior broke away from his father and laughed. It was a laugh that was as deep as the ocean and high as the sky. It burst in upon Thunder Walking with such joyous power that he recoiled, but then spread his arms to receive the delight that was emanating from his son. "My Father, I am better than well, I am Recreated." With that, he took off like a streak. He called over his shoulder, "Come Father, we go to see the Lord Tsisa!"

Thunder Walking did not see his bedroom fade away as he leapt with a shout after his son. He stretched and stretched until his legs and body were a multi-dimensional blur of faster-than-light rainbow speed. In an eternity or just a moment, they stood before a wondrous golden portal. A lone glowing figure lingered just inside and slowly spread his arms towards Thunder Walking. "Well done, my good and faithful servant. Enter into the joy of your Lord." The elder who was young again fell into the arms of Tsisa.

1838 AD
NEW ECHOTA, GA

The explosive climate of northern Georgia made the appearance by the Moravian missionary dangerous. Oblivious to the fact, Franklin Carter felt it was imperative to give old Thunder Walking the most evangelistic funeral seen in recent times. Both Cherokee elders and Georgia politicians were affected by the life of this great man, and he was determined to honor him no matter what the personal cost. He was well aware that Georgia authorities had imprisoned other dedicated missionaries.

He took a deep breath as he looked around the New Echota town hall, which had been prepared for this solemn occasion. He held his Bible closely and whispered, "Lord, let the words of my mouth and the thoughts of my heart be pleasing in Your sight this day. Even as You brought Thunder Walking and his household unto Yourself, I pray that You will use this memorial to bring others unto You." He sighed before he continued. "Forgive, O Lord, the sins of me and my brethren in being stiff-necked and unyielding to the Cherokee. I pray that You soften my heart and the hearts of the Cherokees that have resisted You. This is my fault, Lord, not Yours. Show me how to show the Indian Your love for him rather than my unreasoning judgment." He paused and bowed his head further, squeezing his eyes together tightly in holy supplication. "Thank You Lord for the wisdom that You will show me today. I pray all this in the precious Name of our Savior, Jesus Christ, amen."

Carter opened his eyes and looked over at the Cherokee in his coffin. Decorated with a single eagle feather, he was as unassuming in death as he had been in life. The Moravian walked by the coffin and gazed at the elder briefly, then took his seat on the low platform. As if on cue, people began slowly filing in.

Quatie Ross entered and sat at the far right in the front. Her husband John was away in Washington attempting to put a halt to the Removal. The Principal Chief was an active and vocal advocate of the Cherokee Nation and many felt his presence in the white capitol was their only hope, particularly after the Ridge Party had signed the Treaty of New Echota.

Galen Mondragon and Thomas Banica slipped in and sat near the back of the already full room. The Prince nudged the chancellor and motioned with his head towards Quatie Ross. "The sons of Uwatie are not here to oppose her husband," he whispered.

"They have sold their people into an unknown future, your Majesty. They are considered traitors." Banica inhaled and shook his head as he kept his voice low. "I have heard much talk of fulfillment of the blood debt. Even out beyond the bounds of America in Indian Territory, Stand Watie, Elias Boudinot, and Major Ridge have a sentence of death upon them. Thunder Walking and his grandson were among the few voices of reason counseling against such final action."

Mondragon looked at his chancellor appraisingly. "Perhaps their early move beyond the Mississippi has given them a stay of execution."

"It has indeed, sire." Banica fell silent as the Moravian minister rose and walked to the pulpit.

Franklin Carter surveyed the crowd before him, struggling to feel the pulse of a group that he largely did not know. There was undeniable tension in the room. A terrible decree had been pronounced against the Cherokees and it showed in their expressions and their very carriage. An awful doom was upon them and they were powerless before the storm. Carter bowed his head. "O Lord our God, we come before You this day as we remember our brother Thunder Walking. We thank You that he is already standing in Your presence, for this You have promised to all who profess their faith in You. From the times before the white man came to this wide land, the Cherokees have worshipped the Creator. I thank You that Thunder Walking understood Who that Creator truly was, and that he freely gave that knowledge to his entire family."

Carter briefly opened his eyes and saw that Soaring Eagle was watching him closely. Cherokees could still be unnerving for they did not blindly follow the religious traditions of the white missionaries. Soaring Eagle never closed his eyes when praying, yet Carter felt that no one prayed more fervently. He closed his eyes again. "Lord, we thank You for the life and example of this man. Comfort now his family in their loss we pray in Jesus' Name, amen.

Carter's wife began to play the strains of *Amazing Grace* on the upright piano in the corner of the hall. It had not been tuned in years and the humid north Georgia air had wreaked havoc with the soundboard. Carter played the role of song leader and signaled the start of the first verse with a down stroke of his right arm. The mostly Cherokee congregation came in with surprising gusto. They sang in their own tongue as if they owned this song and perhaps they did. The Cherokee had found their own lyrics for the familiar melody. It was a song that would travel with them into another time. The fervor of the crowd swelled over the piano's loss of intonation.

Banica knew this version of the song well and understood enough Tsalagi to interpret the words in his mind as he sang along with the Cherokees.

God's Son
Paid for us
Then to Heaven He went
After paying for us

Galen Mondragon had a pained expression on his face as he turned to his chancellor. "I could never stand this song Thomas. Give my respects to the family." He slipped out and away as Banica stared after him. The old Romanian joined in the second verse.

But He said
When He rose
"I'll come again"
He said when He spoke

All the earth will end
When He comes
All will see Him
All over the earth

All the good people living
He will come after
In Heaven always
In peace they will live

The song concluded and Carter gripped the sides of the lectern. "Friends, we gather today to celebrate the life of Thunder Walking, an elder of renown among his people." More that a few Cherokees in the room nodded at these words. "He was a tireless servant of his people and his family. He will be remembered as a father and grandfather that was always there when his children needed him." Carter leaned forward as his gaze hardened. "More than that, he was a servant of the Most High God. When he committed his life to the Lord, he was diligent to be sure that every member of his extended family did also." Carter looked across the first row with the descendents of the dead elder and their wives and children, all of them listening attentively. "Every member." He paused briefly. "Today, each of you has a chance to join in that legacy. I can say with confidence that Thunder Walking would will that it were so. I know this from my conversations with him."

He paused again and looked out over the room. He was quietly pleased that all were giving him their full attention. He noted that the distinguished Romanian Special Envoy had exited the room and wondered at his passage. The missionary went on to introduce several Cherokees who eulogized the elder who had moved beyond this Momentary into true Reality. The last to speak was Soaring Eagle who gave a moving account of the deep relationship he enjoyed with his Grandfather. Finally, a Cherokee singer presented a song to ease the departed on his way and fulfill the traditional rites of passage.

Carter returned to the pulpit and leaned forward, again gripping the sides. He briefly recounted his friendship with Thunder Walking and the Indian's humble leadership of his family. He highlighted his service by noting how that Cherokee had purchased the freedom of several slaves. More than a few Indians looked uncomfortable during this part. The Cherokees had so absorbed the white civilization that many had become slaveholders.

"Thunder Walking stood for peace under the great Cherokee leader Attakullakulla. Even when Dragging Canoe took his band to war against the whites, Thunder Walking remained a voice for peace. When he first heard the good news of Jesus Christ, he recognized that it was good news of peace. Thus, he came to know the only Son of the Creator, who was always a Man of peace."

Carter paused and sent up a brief prayer. He stepped back,

looking high over the crowd. "There is a path beyond this temporary world over the great Milky Way. It is a path of peace that leads to a place of peace where One who is known as the Prince of Peace dwells. In the Cherokee tongue, He is called Tsisa. In my language, He is known as Jesus. It is this Man who knew and loved Thunder Walking so much that He was willing to die for him."

Carter again grabbed the lectern with white-knuckled intensity. "This thing Jesus did almost two thousand years ago, the totally righteous Man dying for the sins of Thunder Walking. He did this once for all, one time for every one of us. Each of you can participate in the peace that Thunder Walking knew, a peace that is held by the Lord Tsisa for each one of you."

Thomas Banica was suddenly gripped with the story of Tsisa. He had heard it before from Tom-Tom, but it suddenly had an urgency that he could not deny. He saw an answer there that went far beyond the old Eastern Orthodox traditions he had known in Romania. This was not ritual, this was personal.

"I want each of you to now remember the heart of the great Cherokee Thunder Walking as we now pray. I want you to remember the path of peace."

Banica leaned forward and bowed his head, squeezing his eyes tightly shut. As the missionary prayed, he could feel the presence of something far beyond himself, something that was wooing him to the path of peace. He felt an urgency to find this path but he did not know the way.

As Carter finished the prayer, he looked up at the congregation. "If any of you felt something calling you as we prayed, you must answer that call. Please come and see me at the close of this service. He motioned to the Cherokee pallbearers who sat ready on the front row. They rose up, lifted the earthly remains of Thunder Walking onto their shoulders, and bore him from the room.

The crowd exited behind the pallbearers and they all walked down the street to a quiet graveyard. There, Thunder Walking was placed in the ground and the people paid their final respects and gave their final handshake as they tossed a handful of earth into the grave.

Banica walked hesitantly up to Carter after the last words

were spoken. He introduced himself and Carter smiled. "Yes, aren't you the assistant to the Special Envoy?"

Banica nodded. "I have served Prince Mondragon all my life but now I feel that I have become a part of the Cherokees. I have told the Prince that I plan to stay with the Indians. I will do this even if they are driven beyond the Mississippi."

"They need more people like you." The missionary looked closely at Banica. "What can I do for you my friend?"

Thomas looked down, suddenly unsure of himself. "You spoke of feeling something calling to you at the end of your sermon." He looked up and into Carter's eyes. "I felt that something. I want that path of peace but I don't know the way."

The missionary nodded solemnly. "What you felt was the Holy Spirit, that part of God which touches us directly in our hearts. He is calling you Thomas; the Lord Jesus is calling you."

"How do I answer?"

Carter looked over at the fresh grave and then up into the blue Georgia sky. "I used to have a nice doctrinal answer to that question, a checklist of things for you to do. My long years with the Cherokee have changed all that and I have turned to the Bible for the answer. The place to start is believing in Jesus." The missionary proceeded to tell the greatest story ever told, the story of the life, death, burial, and resurrection of Jesus. At the end of it all, Banica knew he could follow such a Master.

Carter and Banica prayed together and the Romanian walked away from that encounter as a new man. He returned to what was now the household of Soaring Eagle and told them what had happened. All rejoiced and Soaring Eagle gave Banica his Grandfather's old Bible. "Start with the book of John," he counseled.

That night Banica prayed and felt the warmth of acknowledgement. He went peacefully to sleep and did not dream of bats.

5: FOOTSTEPS OF THE EAGLE

1838 AD
ROSS'S LANDING, TN

Banica sat astride his horse on the banks of the Tennessee River at Ross's Landing. Soaring Eagle was beside him on his horse and a U.S. Army Captain stood facing them. Banica's face was tense with ill-concealed anger. "You have kept this people in stockades for months on end and you expect them to have strength to travel? My own friends among the Cherokee would not have eaten in this time were it not for the supplies I had regularly delivered to the fort where they were prisoners."

"Guests, Mr. Banica, guests. We were merely ensuring their safety." The Captain was impeccably uniformed; his blues pressed to razor sharpness, his brass polished to shine like the sun. He rested his hand casually on the hilt of his sword as he answered his questioner. "We also regularly supplied food for these poor souls."

Banica looked over at Soaring Eagle who was shaking his head. "Food that was eaten by worms or rancid. The food Congress gave us, the white men ate."

The Captain bristled. "The hell you say! I inspected shipments myself and they were perfectly fine."

Soaring Eagle stared at the officer. "What happened after

your inspection? How long did it take for the food to reach us?"

Banica raised his hands. "Such discussion is fruitless for it does not answer the need of today. If I am to lead this band into the wilderness, we need supplies, Captain. I have done all that I am able."

"You are scheduled to depart tomorrow. I will requisition what I can to add to your store." The Captain spread his arms apologetically. "That is all I can do, Mr. Banica."

"Very well Captain, I appreciate your help. Until the morning, then."

"Until the morning." The officer executed a precision about face and walked toward a group of Bluecoats.

A cloud of dust up the road announced the approach of a rider. The two men watched as the distant person appeared with his horse at a brisk canter. Soaring Eagle recognized him first and he pointed in his direction. "Red Beard."

Banica sat forward in his saddle and gaped at the rider. "It is the Prince, indeed." He raised his hand in a hail and the rider responded in kind. In a moment, he pulled up by them, his horse snorting.

"Greetings Thomas, hello Soaring Eagle."

"Hello your Majesty. I did not expect to see you here." Banica held onto his saddle horn and made no move to dismount.

Mondragon's black horse stamped one foot and whinnied. "The Governor has asked me to oversee the departures from Ross's Landing. When I looked over the list, I was surprised to see your name, Thomas. Are you planning to move to Indian Territory with these people?"

Banica sighed and looked sadly at his old friend. "Yes Galen, I will stay with my new family. Soaring Eagle here has taken me as his elder brother." He reached behind him and pulled forward the feather that now dangled from his hair and smiled shyly. "I guess I'm the first Romanian Cherokee."

Soaring Eagle nodded. "We have given my brother a new name. He is Leaving Europe." He looked at Mondragon with a deadpan expression and then over at Banica. The two held their gaze for a moment until Banica burst out laughing. Soaring

Eagle chuckled.

Mondragon smiled wanly. "I came right away when I saw you were departing tomorrow. You can expect two extra wagons of supplies for your group, Thomas. It is the most I can do under these trying circumstances."

Banica's eyes widened. "Thank you, your Majesty! Would you also be so kind as to inform the Captain over there that you are sending them? Many shipments such as these have disappeared."

"I am aware of these difficulties, Thomas. My shipment is coming with a security detachment." The Prince paused and took a deep breath. "This is farewell then. I wish you a good life in the great West."

"Thank you, sire." Banica nudged his mount closer and extended his hand. The Prince shook it briefly. "Galen, I wanted you to know. I am now a follower of the One whom the Cherokee call Tsisa. I follow the Jesus Way."

The Prince withdrew his hand quickly. "Indeed?" Banica saw his expression darken. The large black stallion did a stamping back step away from Banica. "We shall not see each other again. Goodbye Thomas." He wheeled his horse and galloped away down the dusty lane on which he had arrived.

Soaring Eagle leaned forward on his saddle horn as he observed the departing Romanian. He looked over at his companion. "That went well."

Banica slowly looked at the Cherokee. His eyes were wide and he shuddered involuntarily. "That man is far more evil than I have ever seen. The Lord has opened my eyes."

Soaring Eagle nodded as the dust of Mondragon's passing settled. "You have told me that my father once said something about him."

"Yes. He said, 'Perhaps he is not a man.'" Banica shook his head as the words out of the past took on new import.

1838 AD
ON THE TRAIL OF TEARS

"The winter has become very hard my husband. Feather is

getting worse." Yellow Dawn looked at Soaring Eagle with a pleading desperation. They walked along a snowy trail amidst the thousand or so Cherokees of the band being led west by Thomas Banica. The Cherokee maiden of seven summers sat astride their only horse as her parents walked beside her.

Soaring Eagle shook his head. "The Bluecoats force Thomas to continue when he wants to stop and give us all a rest. Our daughter suffers to keep the white man's schedule." He looked beside them where they walked. "The healer has given her the last of her herbs and there are no more to be had along this trail. The groups before us have scoured the land clean."

Word came down the line that they would be pulling off to camp just ahead. The wagons, horses, and walking people all clustered into a large clearing and set up camp. Soaring Eagle erected the makeshift lean-to that he had packed on the sides of the horse below where Feather sat. Yellow Dawn quickly gathered some firewood from a nearby copse of trees and shortly had a merry blaze kindled.

The wagons that Mondragon provided would have supplied them well with food; however, a band of unknown Indian raiders had stolen one in the night several days earlier. The bandits sent a diversionary attack to draw away the soldiers while the rest accomplished their true purpose. Banica had to set up strict rationing so that all would have a share in what was left. There would not be enough to get them through the winter so they began scavenging what they could as they walked. Cherokee hunters ranged to the sides of the march but had little to show for their efforts.

Soaring Eagle looked around and was satisfied that his family was secure. He then walked to the supply wagons to withdraw their meager share of food for the night. At least they were able to eat that evening. After dinner, the family relaxed by the fire. Feather snuggled close to her mother as her father idly threw small bits of wood into the warm blaze.

A Bluecoat walked towards the family and suddenly came into view in the ring of firelight. Soaring Eagle tensed and reached for the long dagger he kept secreted under his clothing. Even a man of peace must be prepared to defend his household.

The soldier stopped near their fire and looked right into Soaring Eagle's eyes. "Sir, I haven't come to hurt you." The words puffed out into the frigid night as a procession of small white clouds. "I heard your daughter's sick and, well, I wanted you to have this." He thrust the small bundle that he was carrying towards the startled family.

Soaring Eagle and Yellow Dawn exchanged wary glances. He reached to touch a series of studs on the ancient Stone that lay beside him as he rose to face the man. He reached forward and the Bluecoat dropped the bundle into his hands. "I'm Private Burnett, sir. If there's anything special you need for her, just ask me." He looked over and smiled at Feather.

Soaring Eagle opened the bundle enough to see that it was a warm Army issue blanket. He looked in wonder at the soldier. "Thank you, Private Burnett," he said. "We would share our fire with you." The Cherokee indicated a place beside the blaze.

"Why, yes sir, I'll sit with you folk for awhile." Burnett sat down close to the blaze. He shared the warm silence with the family as Yellow Dawn wrapped the new treasure around Feather. She looked at the Bluecoat with grateful eyes.

"You Cherokee folk have another name for yourselves, don't you?" Burnett looked at Soaring Eagle with the question in his eyes.

The Cherokee was silent for a moment, and then he looked over at the Bluecoat. "The name given to the Cherokee at the dawn of time was Anigiduwagi. We were given that name by the Creator." Soaring Eagle looked into the fire as an exploding cache of tree sap released a shower of sparks that strained to reach the sky. He looked back at the Bluecoat. "There is another name that you have probably heard. We call ourselves Aniyvwiya which in your tongue is the Principal People."

Burnett was nodding as Feather added, "It could also be translated the People of God." She looked boldly at the Private. He waited patiently for a correction from her father but it never came.

Private Burnett quickly inhaled and then told them of how he remembered the Trail's beginning. He spoke for some time of being an unwilling participant in a military action against a peaceful people. He then concluded his narrative. "Chief John

Ross led in prayer and when the bugle sounded and the wagons started rolling, many of the Cherokee children rose to their feet and waved their little hands goodbye to their mountain homes, knowing they were leaving them forever."

"I was one of those sad ones, Private Burnett," said Feather.

Burnett looked at Feather briefly then lowered his head in silence. After a moment he said, "I best be going. You folks have a good night." He stood and put forth a hand to Soaring Eagle.

The Cherokee grasped Burnett's proffered hand. "Wado, Burnett." The private looked over at Yellow Dawn and said, "Ma'am." The private smiled again at Feather, bobbed his head once, and then turned away into the chill night. Soaring Eagle reached down and touched another stud on the stone that had lain unobserved during the whole exchange.

Yellow Dawn encircled his arm with hers and leaned against Soaring Eagle. "Words on the wind, my husband?"

Soaring Eagle reached to stroke her black hair. "More than words now my wife." He looked at her quizzically. "Haven't I told you?" Yellow Dawn shook her head. "Sequoyah's Syllabary has recovered the full understanding of the Talking Leaves and has unlocked the meanings of the legends on the Stone. I have been studying those legends and have come to understand there is much more to this object." He stopped and looked over at Feather. "It will also record a speaking image." He pushed a combination of two studs on the stone and a ghostly image of Private Burnett appeared over the fire. He smiled at Feather, bobbed his head once, and then seemed to turn and disappear into the night.

Feather clapped in excitement and began to laugh. This brought on a fit of coughing which left her drained under her new blanket. "That was wonderful Father." She smiled weakly.

"It is only for our family to know, Feather. Tell this thing to no one." Her eyes got large and round in the firelight as she nodded solemnly.

Soaring Eagle had contrived a pony drag to carry Feather's weakened body as they pressed forward. Yellow Dawn rode their last remaining horse, pulling the drag behind her. Soaring Eagle walked beside his only daughter.

Even in her weakened state, Feather remained alert. She lay snuggled under all the blankets and bedding that they owned. Private Burnett's gift was close to her body, hidden under the lesser blankets on top. "Father, are we really going to a new land and a new home?" She spoke with clarity far beyond her seven summers.

Soaring Eagle looked at her with tender compassion. "Feather Who Floats on the Wind, you are still young. Know that the Lord is the Heaven Dweller, and it is He Who will bear us on eagle's wings to a land beyond this white man's trap. If we come to our new land, so be it. Yet, there is still a better country. In this, we all can hope."

The girl looked up at her father. The single eagle feather protruding from the turban on his head was ruffling in the breeze. The sadness of years of oppression lay etched into his noble face. With the stoicism common to his people, he faced the frigid wind with head held high.

"Father," she said. He turned to her. "Father, I do believe. Thank for your gift of hope."

He laid a trail-hardened hand on his only daughter's head. "Feather, you are precious to me, but there is One to whom you are even more precious. Our people live anew beyond the stars. One day we will rise again and live forever with them and our Eldest Brother!"

She rose up on one elbow on the pony drag. She took her father's hand as he walked beside her. A melody seized her and she sang in reply to him, "We endure this icy passage to stand with them forevermore!"

He laid a trail-hardened hand on his only daughter's head. He smiled at her, masking the gnawing empty pit behind his eyes.

That night Feather died of the pneumonia that had been wasting her young body. Soaring Eagle and Yellow Dawn buried her and marked the grave as best as they could with a flat stone. It was a spot on the downwind side of a low slope near an ice-laden Mississippi River. Soaring Eagle also left a marking of stones at the top of the windy rise. The new blowing snow drifted over the site as the brutal march took them onward into Arkansas. In later years, they searched for the grave but could never find it.

Heartbroken, the couple began again in the Indian Territory that would become the state of Oklahoma in the next century. There they had a son and two more daughters. The young family helped Soaring Eagle build a log cabin on a bluff near the Arkansas River about fifty miles west of Fort Smith. He only cut the trees that he needed for the walls of their new dwelling. This was unlike the white men who would clear-cut a huge field around their houses. Soaring Eagle was sorry for the loss of the trees and he thanked the Creator that they would live on as their family dwelling.

A small settlement grew up in the beautiful spot by the river. Fish and game were plentiful and the soil was fertile for the growing of crops. Soaring Eagle helped Yellow Dawn till a large field very near their house and then Yellow Dawn took over, planting crops that came forth in abundance. To the Cherokee, women were the bringers of life. They always did a better job at planting and harvesting than men did.

Soaring Eagle found the hunting rewarding around their homestead. He would take his sons and go on a hunting trip in the Month of the Nut Moon. Until the time of the Civil War, they would always return with meat for the winter season and hides to trade at Fort Smith.

1842 AD
EAST OF NASHVILLE, TN

Galen Mondragon stepped from the coach and gazed up at the imposing facade. The two story tall Doric columns flanking the entrance leered down at him haughtily. A servant approached him and asked, "Prince Mondragon?" He nodded once. "Welcome to the Hermitage sir. President Jackson is anxious to see you. I understand you worked closely with him in the old days in Washington. He is looking forward to your visit. Right this way, sir."

The Prince followed silently, taking in his surroundings. The house had the feel of a monument to things gone by that could never be recovered. There was a lingering sadness about the place.

He stopped briefly before a large portrait of a stately woman. The servant turned to see him gaze at the painting. "That was Miss Rachel, sir, the President's wife. She died two weeks after he first took office." The man shook his head. "He never got over that, sir."

Mondragon looked sharply at the man and noted he was older than he thought. "You were with him then?"

"Oh yes sir. I've been with the President a long time, since before he was President."

The Prince looked back at the painting. "What was she like?"

"She was a sad lady at the end, sir. The press falsely accused her of adultery and the President says that she died of a broken heart." He looked down momentarily. "I think he was right."

Mondragon pursed his lips and turned away from the sad portrait. The servant walked ahead to a set of double doors and opened them. "Right in here, sir." He looked into the room and called out, "Mr. President, presenting Prince Mondragon."

"Call him your Majesty, James. He would be a king in his own country." Andrew Jackson's familiar voice rolled out the door.

The servant turned to Mondragon with a stricken look on his face. "My apologies, your Majesty."

"Quite all right my good fellow," Mondragon said as he walked through the entryway. "Andrew should have better schooled you in the intricacies of Romanian protocol."

The old President smiled at his guest. "Galen, it is good to see you. Welcome to my humble abode. Forgive me if I don't rise." He coughed deeply and then caught his breath, motioning to a chair beside him.

The Prince seated himself and looked over at Jackson. "Has the Cherokee healer not sent you any of his new crops from Indian Territory?'

The President shook his head. "I received a cordial letter from the man a year ago. He informed me that none of the seeds he brought from Georgia would grow properly in the soil out there. It is fertile, yet they would not grow to maturity. He was unable to harvest any with medicinal properties." Jackson held his hand over his mouth as he coughed again. "He said that he was looking for new herbs native to that area but it would take some time." The President closed his eyes as he rubbed the bridge of his nose. "Funny, isn't it? My actions have brought me harm."

"That is sad news Andrew." Mondragon leaned forward. "Are you comfortable here?"

Jackson smiled. "James takes excellent care of this old man. I want for nothing, Galen."

"Except those Cherokee herbs?"

"Except the herbs, Galen." Jackson crossed his legs and stretched his back. "How is our friend Thomas?"

Mondragon's expression darkened. "He has gone native Andrew. He was adopted by a Cherokee family and he actually led a group out to Indian Territory. I have not spoken with him since he left Ross's Landing."

Jackson looked thoughtful for a moment. "Relationships are often seasonal, particularly political ones. Fortunate is the man who has a friend for life."

Mondragon nodded. "Speaking of political friends, I bring you greetings from President Van Buren."

"And how is Martin these days? I haven't seen him in years but we still correspond."

"He is well, sir, and wishes you the best."

Jackson leaned forward and coughed. "Galen, you will stay for a few days and keep an old man company, won't you?"

"Why certainly sir, that was my plan in coming here."

"Excellent. It will be like the old days."

"Yes sir, like the old days."

1844 AD
INDIAN TERRITORY

Soaring Eagle sat on the porch of the snug house he and his family had built. It was a cool and clear day. Large storms had passed through the previous night leaving a bright morning in their wake. The Cherokee was reading his Bible when a familiar person rode up and dismounted. Soaring Eagle broke into a smile. "Harold Red Stone, osiyo! How are you this fine day?"

Red Stone tied his horse at the hitching post and climbed the stairs to the porch. "I am well, my friend. I bring news." He sat down next to Soaring Eagle and pulled a letter from his pocket. "I thought you'd like to know."

"Speak, my friend."

"I received this letter yesterday. It is from James, the personal servant of Andrew Jackson." Red Stone stopped to pull out a pair of reading glasses and put them on.

Soaring Eagle chuckled. "A healer that wears the white man's glasses?"

Red Stone frowned at his friend. "There is nothing wrong with my eyes. These just make it easier to see."

Soaring Eagle grinned. "Now you speak like a white politician."

Red Stone looked heavenward for mercy and found only grace. "Okay, I admit it. I'm having trouble seeing things that are close. These help." He adjusted the spectacles and then turned to the letter.

"James wrote, 'Dear Mr. Red Stone, I know that you have helped the President in the past with your wonderful herbs. He was always grateful for that help and it made his last days in Washington easier. I write to inform you that President Jackson has died. He left peacefully and I'm sure he's in a better place. I thought you would want to know.'" Red Stone looked up at his friend. "This was dated less than two weeks ago."

"The author of our troubles has gone on to his reward." Soaring Eagle shook his head and looked at Red Stone. "You know that Chief Ross saw him recently at The Hermitage." The healer nodded. "John said he was very sickly, more so than when he was in Washington. This is not surprising." Soaring Eagle leaned back in his chair. "Unfortunately, Jackson's Indian policies did not die with him."

Red Stone shook his head. He removed his glasses and slipped them into his pocket. The two friends sat in silence.

1845 AD
NASHVILLE, TN

The spectacled lawyer looked down his nose at the document. "It seems that this was the final provision of the will, written only days before his death." He glanced up sharply at the man sitting across the desk from him, and then back at the paper. "It is properly witnessed and signed; therefore I must honor his wishes." He pulled the spectacles off as he set the paper on the desk before him. His visitor shifted uncomfortably in his seat. "Normally I would request an investigation into this matter, but as James himself has vouched for you, I will make this disbursement."

The elderly attorney turned to an open safe behind him and pulled out five tidy bags. He turned and set them on the desk. "The President never trusted banks or bank notes. He kept his liquid assets in gold." The man pushed the bags across the desk and then set a paper beside them. "Please sign here to indicate that you received the amount." He pushed an inkpot towards the man and handed him a quill. As the visitor leaned over the paper and penned his name with a flourish, the lawyer laid his hand over the bags of gold. "I do not like this, sir, but I must abide the final wishes of my client. This was money that had been designated to go to the Cherokee people. It was one final thing he wanted to do for them after their terrible Relocation. You, sir, have robbed them of this gift."

Galen Mondragon held his lips in grim compress. He pushed the signed document towards the old lawyer. "May I now take what is rightfully mine?" The lawyer withdrew his hand and Mondragon quickly grabbed the heavy sacks and distributed them into the pockets of his greatcoat. He stood and looked at the old man with a gaze filled with the frost of the wintry day that waited to receive him. "Good day, sir." He turned on his heel and swept from the room.

The old lawyer shivered at the departure.

1846 AD
INDIAN TERRITORY

"The Prince has retired?" Thomas Banica quickly perched his spectacles on his nose as Soaring Eagle handed him a newspaper. "When did you read this, Daniel?" Banica called him by his adopted name with which the Moravian missionaries had christened him

Soaring Eagle consented to the name and added the last name of Porter. It was easier to deal with the whites this way. He took quiet pleasure in his new name for the Daniel of the Bible was a seeker of visions. A Cherokee understood the power of such visions.

"It was just yesterday that I received the Washington newspaper," the one called Daniel said. "The article is on page fourteen." The Cherokee sat down next to his Romanian friend.

Banica quickly thumbed to the page. "Advisor to four Presidents retires." He quickly scanned the article and then looked at Soaring Eagle. "He has no plans to return to Romania."

"How old is he now?"

Banica did a quick mental calculation. "He would be in his mid-eighties."

Soaring Eagle nodded towards the picture of Mondragon shaking the hands of President Tyler. "He ages better than an Indian."

Banica looked intently at Soaring Eagle. "You were with me the last time I saw him, Daniel. Although his hair was grayed, there was still not a line on his face."

"I noticed that." The Cherokee leaned back in his chair. "To me, the hair looked like it was painted, like what some of the Western tribes do to their hair for special dances."

Banica raised his chin and his gaze became thoughtful. "Painted, yes."

"Maybe he's not a man."

Banica smiled grimly. "We've had this discussion before, Daniel. If not a man, what is he?"

Soaring Eagle inhaled deeply once, his chest rising and

falling. "Far to the west live a mysterious tribe named the Hopi. It is said that they dwell atop desert mountains." Soaring Eagle looked beyond Banica with a gaze that seemed intent on penetrating all mysteries. "They believe that there are spirits who oversee the things of this world. They are called kachinas." A look of profound insight crossed his face. "Perhaps he is a kachina of gold, a spirit who oversees the lust of that yellow metal."

"There are no kachinas in the Bible, Daniel." Banica leaned forward. "But there are fallen angels." He paused for a moment. "Galen was always involved with the politics of gold. The gold drew him to Georgia so many years ago." Banica shook his head and puffed out his cheeks. "Such talk is absurd. Galen Mondragon is simply a well preserved old Romanian."

"As you say, Thomas." Soaring Eagle nodded expressionlessly.

1847 AD
NEW YORK, NY

"Galen, you old monster, what are you doing in New York?"

"Palak, you ancient scoundrel, it's good to see you. I thought I needed to take a break for a few years."

"A few decades, you mean! You have been living a rather high profile existence since you left your lovely Transylvania."

Mondragon chuckled in contentment. "It was quite a ride my old friend. How many of us have had four Presidents in their pocket, hmm?"

The one called Palak bowed in mock formality. "Your achievements are legend in our ranks. Would you like your crown now or later?" The two looked at each other for a moment, and then broke out into loud guffaws.

Palak draped his arm around his companion. "I have a little place you can hide away until you're forgotten. I can even provide some, uh, friends for you. You know, of the female persuasion."

Mondragon lifted an eyebrow. "This human form does have some distinct advantages." He looked seriously at his companion. "Before I disappear, I have some ill-gotten gains that I must invest." He reached into his pocket, withdrew a small but heavy cloth bag, and threw it to Palak.

The other creature deftly caught the bag and hefted it up and down. "Ah, the spoils from the Cherokees that I've heard about. I think my friend Mr. Morgan can look after this nicely. A few decades in his care and you will have enough for several lifetimes on this dismal planet."

Mondragon smiled broadly. "Excellent! Keep one of those lifetimes for yourself." He leaned forward. "I know that Palak still has much to accomplish." He reached into his pocket and withdrew the four remaining bags. He handed them to Palak with a grimace.

"Can't stand to part with it, eh? You old monster. As greedy as ever."

Mondragon shrugged. "Hey, it's what I do. Besides, my greed supplies your need."

Palak poured two stiff drinks as his friend spoke and then handed him a glass. "Into obscurity?"

"Into obscurity." The two glasses clinked together and then the pair drained them.

6: GHOST DANCE

1850 AD
INDIAN TERRITORY

Soaring Eagle became a trusted leader of his people. He was elected as Principal Chief of the Arkansas River Band. He had a wonderful way of melding important traditions and his faith in the Creator and His Son. Regular events of the Nation, such as the Green Corn Dance, became expressions of ultimate praise to the One who was older than the universe.

Their eldest daughter, Morning Fawn, grew to be a beautiful young maiden. Her father's heart swelled at the sight of her as he remembered his beloved Feather. Morning Fawn was as beautiful as Feather would have been had she grown to maturity.

One day a handsome brave from the Wolf Clan appeared at the door of the family house bearing the ceremonial meat to be cooked. He handed it to Morning Fawn, indicating his desire. Soaring Eagle raised his chin in approval. He was glad that the old traditions were coming alive again in this Indian Territory. He was even gladder that Morning Fawn had found such a fine brave. The young man was Wild Paw, a respected member of his clan and a fitting mate for his daughter. Yellow Dawn tittered behind her hand as her daughter prepared the meat.

Wild Paw became the devoted husband of Morning Fawn.

Just as they began their life together, the Civil War descended on America and the Cherokee Nation like a blanket of choking smoke. Wild Paw joined the Cherokee Mounted Rifles under the Cherokee Confederate Colonel Stand Watie and fought valiantly at the Battle of Pea Ridge. He took the last name of Winchester in the time of enrollment for the white man's endless records. He thought it appropriate to be named after the rifle that was to remain in his hands for the next several years. Morning Fawn stayed with her parents in that dark time and they became war refugees in their own country. They remained separated from Wild Paw until after the war's end.

Thomas Banica died shortly before that start of the war. He had lived to see the rebirth of the Cherokee Nation and he died happy and fulfilled. He was buried at the new cemetery in Park Hill and given the highest Cherokee honors. It was the mercy of the Lord that he did not have to live through the terrible reshaping of the Civil War.

1862 AD
PEA RIDGE, AR

Wild Paw held tightly to his mount with his legs as he took careful aim. The horse hurled headlong towards the advancing Union line as deafening cannon fire expelled death in their direction. Wild Paw picked off a key lead man who fell from his horse, causing it to stumble. The stricken animal tumbled sideways, bringing down three more horses who were galloping headlong behind. A Cherokee war cry rose up in victorious declaration as the Mounted Rifles swept through the Northern cavalry unimpeded. They rushed upon the Union gun emplacements that were behind the horsemen in such fury that the gun crews fled in terror. They were cut down mercilessly as the Cherokees surrounded the Union engines of war. Wild Paw and another half a dozen of his comrades quickly dismounted and wheeled the great 20-pounder Parrott rifles around to face their owners. They began loading and firing the big guns. An unrelenting cycle of fiery destruction descended upon the surprised Northern aggressors. The Bluecoats began to fall back from the determined rear action that had caught them totally off guard.

Colonel Watie raised his sword and a group of mounted Cherokees followed him in a devastating sortie against the retreating Northern troops. They quickly withdrew like a great warrior bee content to leave its stinger of death in the enemy. Unlike that doomed bee, they lived to deliver several more quick blows until the Bluecoats were beyond the range of the great guns.

Behind the Cherokee Mounted Rifles, scores of Confederate troops broke from cover and began to hurry southward away from their terrible defeat. The Cherokee action against the Union forces continued as hundreds streamed to safety.

Wild Paw had the crews quickly hitch the guns to the waiting horse teams and hurried them forward until they were once again in range. They reopened their bombardment of the Northern forces, effectively keeping them at bay for hours. At dusk they melted away southward and the Bluecoats could find no trace of them.

1866 AD
INDIAN TERRITORY

The Cherokee people were devastated in the aftermath of the Civil War. All of their work in building a new civilization after the Trail was totally destroyed. Making this desperate situation almost untenable were the demands of the government decreed at Fort Smith, Arkansas. A large number of Cherokees had sided with the Confederacy, so all treaties were considered null and void. New efforts began to steal from them the land that had been "given forever" west of the Mississippi. Some six million acres were taken from the Nation and opened for settlement. The Cherokee Strip that had produced grazing income for the Nation was suddenly beyond their grasp.

Soaring Eagle and Wild Paw worked together to secure a small corner of Indian Territory for them and their children. They were able to rebuild at the very spot they had lived upon for years. With careful work, the remainder of the Arkansas

River Band was able to acquire adjoining properties and a semblance of their pre-war life emerged. As their town was rebuilt, the Clan traditions faded into the reality of Reconstruction. The family unity engendered by Soaring Eagle and nurtured by Yellow Dawn kept at least a shadow of the old ways alive in their rebuilt houses.

The time came when Morning Fawn gave birth to a beautiful baby girl. Ever looking for a better day, she named her Sunrise. The little girl grew through the uncertain days of the latter nineteenth century and became even more beautiful than her mother.

1880 AD
INDIAN TERRITORY

Soaring Eagle was now an old man, a respected elder. He had resisted the Moravian missionary's attempts to integrate him into their society, preferring to find his way with the Lord among his own people. He was an early and strong proponent of worshipping the Lord in the solemn Cherokee traditions and he took considerable heat from the Moravians over his stance. As he held firm and a group of sincere Cherokee believers banded together with him, the missionaries began to give grudging acceptance to this unorthodox style of worship.

Rev. Steadman would visit them from time to time and spend hours in conversation with his friend Daniel. He would travel for a day on horseback from the New Springplace Mission north of Tahlequah and spend the night with the Porter family when he came. Soaring Eagle liked the white holy man and appreciated his acceptance of the anointed dreams and visions of his people. He had taken to interpreting these events in the way of old Cherokee holy men. He understood the source of the visions and knew they were far removed from any pagan traditions. When questioned of these things by his Moravian peers he always had the same reply. "A tree is known by its fruit."

1890 AD
INDIAN TERRITORY

The years after the Battle of Little Big Horn were terrible with uncertainty for all Native peoples living in their land now called America. Custer's death cast suspicion on every Chief, every brave. It was late in 1890 amid that climate of doubt and fear that a Lakota Sioux of the Oglala Band appeared in their midst. He was a warrior covered with the dust of a hundred trails and the foggy mist of dozens of battles. His name was Shouting Crow. He had evaded all of the Long Knives in the last battle of which he was a part. Alone in the Dakota Badlands he kept vigil in the night for the warriors who had fallen by his side. Waken Tanka had given him a vision, a vision to take the Ghost Dance to the Nations far to his south. If he did this, the vision told him, they would give him something even greater.

The Ghost Dance had swept the Plains Indians like wildfire. The notion that a dance could bring about the end of the white man and a return of their relatives and the bison was heady. The idea grew even greater with the introduction of Ghost Shirts, said to be invincible against white man's bullets. Shouting Crow had already seen warriors fall who wore the Ghost Shirt. Their heart must not have been pure. His Ghost Shirt had always protected him.

Soaring Eagle quietly called a council and Cherokees from surrounding towns came and assembled in the great community hall of the Arkansas River Band. Shouting Crow stood and addressed the people. He was a friend of the Cherokee. He knew them and spoke their language. "I am Shouting Crow of the Oglala, friend of Gray Raven of the Oglala and Standing Bear of the Minneconjou." Several around the fire gave assents of recognition. Even the Cherokees knew the great holy man Gray Raven of the Oglala Sioux. "Some summers ago Wovoka of the Paiute prophesied that the time of the Wasichus would end and our relatives and the tatanka would return. This would happen when we all performed the Ghost Dance. Hechetu aloh!"

In the open center of the hall, Shouting Crow demonstrated the Ghost Dance for the people. He directed the drummers into new rhythms and several young braves jumped up and joined him in the solemn movements. Shouting Crow sang as he danced: "There is the Father coming, the Father says this as He comes. 'You shall live,' He says as He comes!"

The Cherokee that had joined the dance sang in response, echoing the words. This had gone on for some time when Soaring Eagle shook his aged head and stood. The dance slowed and stopped as all attention turned to the old Chief.

He stood silent as stone for a moment, then looked directly at Shouting Crow. "You speak words of great power and bring a dance of great authority. I hear your words, my brother. A great many moons ago, before the Trail Where We Cried, our fathers heard these words. We had a dance very like your Ghost Dance and believed that it would bring the end of the whites. It did not. The Ghost Dance came among us and never took us home."

As the words echoed in the chill December air, a running messenger appeared in the community hall. "Speak, brother," said Soaring Eagle.

"I bring word of terrible tragedy. Soldiers murdered some three-hundred Lakota who were on a mission of peace under Chief Bigfoot only a day ago. There were largely unarmed and camped by Wounded Knee creek when this happened. They are almost all dead, including women and children."

Shouting Crow sank to his knees and let out a mournful cry. "Hey-hey! The Long Knives have murdered my people!" He put his hands over his head and wept openly. The Cherokee people around the fire were riveted by the sadness and drama of the moment. Many also wept.

After the first exclamations of grief were expended, Wild Paw stood and fixed his piercing gaze upon Shouting Crow. "I was a soldier of the Confederacy in the Civil War and I too fought these Bluecoats. Many of them were without honor, but the killing of women and children is beyond even that." He walked out into the center of the community hall. "General Watie led us on many missions of which I am not proud. It seemed that Stand Alone was often more interested in obtaining revenge against Chief Ross than in winning the war against the North." Wild Paw looked across the gathered people. "I do not see the reason or wisdom of killing unarmed women and children. That is all I have to say." He shook his head and returned to his seat.

Old Chief Soaring Eagle lowered his head as a tear crept down his face. He walked over to Shouting Crow and said, "We all share your grief, my brother." He stood silently for several long moments. "We have found another way, my son."

The warrior lifted his tear stained face to the old Chief. Standing Eagle took a breath and fixed a piercing gaze on the Sioux warrior. "It is a truth proclaimed by some white men, but it is true far beyond both red and white men. It is the Jesus Way, the way of the Creator's Son. We know Him as our Eldest Brother Tsisa and the truth of His ways is beyond all reckoning."

Shouting Crow stood. "I have heard of this, my grandfather. The Black Robes speak of this one as suffering on a cross. How can a warrior serve one who hangs between land and sky, neither dead nor alive?"

"That is only part of the story. He died on that Cross and was buried. The third day he rose again and later ascended unto the Creator, His Father and your Grandfather. He lives today and sometimes He walks among us."

A light came into Shouting Crow's eyes at these words. "Does He come as a warrior, grandfather?"

"No, my son; He comes as a Man of peace."

"Bigfoot was a man of peace and he lies dead in the snow of Dakota."

"Tsisa is a Man of peace and He is alive forevermore."

"I would hear more, my grandfather."

Soaring Eagle sat once again in the circle. The air was crisp with a fresh winter not yet ready to unleash its worst. The old chief began to tell the stories, the wondrous stories of a Man who once walked the earth; who conquered disease and hypocrites with just a word. They then danced in memory of Tsisa, an excited dance where they threw their hands in the air and shouted. Morning found them still lost in praise to Unetlanvhi and His Son.

Shouting Crow stayed with the Cherokee for there was nothing to which he could return. His entire family had perished in the unrelenting attacks of the Long Knives and only he remained. Although he accepted Cherokee ways and took the name Samuel Wilson, he was forever a wild Oglala. He continued to wear modified traditional garb well into the twentieth century. This one thing he did that forever changed him: he embraced the Jesus Way. The wild Oglala became a man of peace.

Learning the Cherokee way of courting, Samuel one day appeared at the door of the house of Sunrise. Wild Paw met him with stern countenance and folded arms. Samuel held up the prime cut of meat. "A gift for Sunrise," he said. Morning Fawn pushed around her husband and ushered the young warrior inside. Wild Paw hid a smile.

Samuel Shouting Crow Wilson and Sunrise were married with great ceremony in the Cherokee town. Morning Fawn could not remember a more beautiful gathering. Each of the Clan Mothers had a blessing for the young Oglala.

Samuel Shouting Crow had the deep spirituality of his people and he brought a holy solemnity to the ceremony. Everyone there knew that he had given all of himself to Sunrise.

The family of Soaring Eagle went through the trials of Senator Dawes and Oklahoma statehood. When the land apportionment was decreed, the old man fasted and prayed for several days. He then met with his family and the Wilson and Winchester families in council. "We will each take the apportionment and trust the Creator to grant us this land in the new Oklahoma." When they submitted their claims, they were granted the amount of contiguous land that they had dwelt upon for over sixty years. It was a miracle; many Cherokee did not do as well. "The smile of Tsisa is upon us," said Soaring Eagle.

They moved along with their people into the twentieth century. Unlike most of the Cherokee, they were blessed with electricity and telephones. Samuel and Sunrise had three daughters together and then finally, a son. He was born in 1918; half Cherokee, half Sioux, and no white blood at all.

1918 AD
SOARING EAGLE, OK

The family had named the old Arkansas River homestead after its founder several years earlier. Soaring Eagle was over a hundred years old, one of the very last living survivors of the Trail. Yellow Dawn had left this life over ten years ago and he was alone, yet remained surrounded by generations of his family. His mind remained sharp and his speech firm, though he had the tendency to fall asleep for short periods when talking.

In the year of 1918, Sunrise gave birth to a little boy. Shouting Crow was pleased to have a son. When Soaring Eagle heard of the birth of his great-grandson, he asked that they bring the child to him. Sunrise appeared with the little papoose and Samuel trailed behind.

Sunrise placed the little one in her grandfather's lap, hovering nearby in case he couldn't hold on to her son. Soaring Eagle gave her a piercing glare. "I held you at this age granddaughter." She lowered her head and backed away. The old chief stared at the baby and a light of recognition flared in his eyes. "His name is Phillip, like the evangelist in the Bible. He will take the Good News to many nations."

Sunrise and Samuel looked at each other with wondering smiles. "That is the very name we were talking about, grandfather," said Samuel. "Your words are true. The Eldest Brother has shown us that he will be a Storyteller."

Soaring Eagle smiled knowingly.

7: Sequoyah School

1925 AD
Tahlequah, OK

It was about thirty miles from the family homestead on the Arkansas River up to Tahlequah. If you had a Ford Model A you could make it over the dirt roads in less than two hours. When the best you could do was a horse and buggy, it took all day. Samuel and Phillip were dusty and tired by the time they made it to the gates of the school just south of the old Cherokee Nation capitol. Sunrise was not feeling well and had decided to stay home. She had said her tearful goodbyes to her son that morning.

A prim and severe white woman met Samuel and Phillip at the gate. Samuel handed her the papers that they had filled out which she reviewed briefly. She leveled a stern gaze on the boy. "Do you speak English, Phillip?"

"Yes ma'am," he replied as he glanced helplessly at his father. Philip felt a tight knot grow in his stomach in that first moment which would stay with him for many years.

"That's good, boy. You will not speak a word of Cherokee when you are in this place, do you understand?"

Phillip gulped. "Yes ma'am."

She put a firm hand on his shoulder and began to pull him

into the school grounds. She looked up in shock as Samuel placed a restraining hand on hers. "You will wait a moment, madam. I would say farewell to my son." His hand on hers tightened imperceptibly into a threat.

She withdrew her hand, momentarily flustered. "You will say your goodbyes here. Parents are not allowed onto school grounds."

Samuel fixed a piercing silent gaze on her for a moment. "We shall see." He knelt down and laid a hand on his son's head. He spoke a prayer intentionally in Cherokee. He prayed for God's protection over his son in this hostile place. His hand slipped down onto his son's shoulder and he then spoke a blessing in Oglala. "May Waken Tanka who makes our pathways straight always set your foot on the path of peace, on the good red road. You are Phillip Shouting Crow, a son of the Ozarks and a son of the Plains. May you have the strength of the tatanka and the wisdom of Soaring Eagle and may you walk in a sacred manner. Hechetu aloh!" Phillip spoke both Cherokee and the Lakota dialect of his father. He understood every word and hid them in his heart.

Samuel rose and leveled a stern gaze at the woman. The fire of an Oglala warrior of another time flared briefly in his eyes and she took a step backward. "You will take good care of my son." He looked down at the boy who stood bravely facing the unknown. "Farewell Phillip."

"Farewell Father." Phillip wiped a tear away as his father turned towards the family carriage. It would be many years before he would see him again.

Phillip heard a quick sigh behind him and turned to face the new unknown. "My name is Miss Stillborn. Follow me young man." Phillip picked up the cardboard suitcase he had brought with him and followed her into the school grounds. The gate closing behind him had a sound of eerie finality.

Phillip crawled into the hidden attic holding a kerosene lantern. His three friends came behind him, one of them also carrying a lamp. They moved quickly to a far corner where they found the space that they had furnished with blankets and pillows. It was a comfortable and secure hiding place and as long as they remained careful, Miss Stillborn would never know of its existence.

The four boys gathered in a loose circle, placing the lamps in the center. Phillip took a deep breath and said in clear Cherokee, "Let us all speak only in our own tongue in this place. The whites do not bother to learn it and what we say here will remain secret." His three companions nodded solemnly. Phillip closed his eyes briefly, and then stared at each boy in turn. "Grandfather told me many stories when I was young. I will tell you one tonight."

The shadows from the lamps flickered behind the boys and transformed the spot into something that was not quite of this world. It seemed to each boy that, for a moment, they were no longer dressed in the dour clothes that the whites had forced upon them. Instead, they each wore the deerskin of a Cherokee warrior. In the dim light, it seemed that they grew eagle feathers of honor falling from intricate porcupine roaches woven into their long black hair. The kerosene lanterns became a crackling campfire and one boy fancied that he heard a wolf howl in the distance.

Phillip leaned forward. "In the time of my grandfather, the Cherokee people were forced to leave their beloved ancestral homelands. Bluecoats with guns and bayonets herded them like cattle into stockades. Many sickened and died there. Those that remained were forced onto the Trail Where They Cried."

There were murmurs of sadness from the other boys. "What happened on that Trail, Phillip Shouting Crow?" one asked.

"There were many things that happened but tonight I will tell you one of those things. My grandfather was in a band led by a kind white Romanian named Thomas Banica who was a true friend of our people. Both Banica and my grandfather saw and heard these things with their own eyes and ears. It is because of this that I know them to be true." Phillip closed his eyes and took a breath. When he reopened them, his demeanor had changed. He had stepped fully into his calling as Storyteller.

Phillip began. "The Trail to the west was hard and long. It grew very cold and the people's hearts were heavy with sadness. Their tears fell and dried in the hard ground over which they walked. The women cried most of all, and many began to fear for their lives and the lives of their children. The Elders of the group knew that the survival of the children depended on the strength of the women and so they met together to see what must be done. As they sat in council around an evening campfire, Edudi rose to speak. 'We must all call upon Unetlanvhi,' he said. 'He alone has the power to help us.' The Elders then joined in prayer unto the One who sits beyond this earthly existence. They cried out to Him of the people's suffering. They told the almighty Heaven Dweller that if the women and children died, they would not be able to rebuild their Nation in the Indian Territory beyond the Mississippi."

Phillip paused and looked at each boy present. "Unetlanvhi then spoke to them. All the Elders in that council clearly heard His voice. That Voice seemed to come from everywhere at once. Thomas Banica was also a part of that council. The Creator said, 'I will show you how much I care and by this sign you will all gain new strength. In the morning, look back upon the Trail and behold! From every place a mother's tear has fallen will spring a new plant. It will have seven leaves for the seven clans of the Cherokee. A beautiful white rose will spring from its center. The flower will have five petals that represent My grace which is upon you. It will have a golden center to remind the Cherokees of the white man's lust for gold that drove you from your homeland. The plant will be sturdy and strong with stickers on the stems. It will totally defy anything that tries to destroy its life. Look upon this plant and know the strength that I have put into My Cherokee people.'"

Phillip looked down briefly and then gazed up over the heads of the three boys. "In the morning the people gathered. Edudi spoke and told the mothers to look back over the Trail upon which they had walked. Before everyone's wondering eyes, plants had sprung forth and were growing in their sight. As they all watched, beautiful white blossoms emerged and slowly opened. As the women beheld this marvel, they forgot their sadness and began to feel strong and beautiful like the amazing plants. They saw how the plant protected the blossom. In that signpost, they gained new strength and knew that they would have the courage to take their children into the West and there begin a new Nation."

Phillip looked again at his three friends. "Along the whole length of the Trail Where They Cried, that wonderful plant sprang up behind them. It even defied the bitter snows of winter. They named the plant the Cherokee Rose and so it is unto this day." Phillip fell silent as the boys absorbed the story.

They sat silently around the lamps for some time. Finally, Phillip rose and spoke. "Come brothers, we must return to our beds before we are missed."

One boy rose and looked at Phillip. "Thank you for the story, Phillip Shouting Crow. You have given us all hope." The other boys nodded as they rose. The group carefully and quietly returned to their dorm room and slipped into their beds. Miss Stillborn never knew that they were gone.

1936 AD
SOARING EAGLE, OK

"Mama, they took me in a room and cut off all my hair. They burned all the beautiful clothes you made me and gave me this." Phillip swept his hands down over the severe shirt and pants he wore. He shook his head before raising it again to look at his mother. "Children died there mother and if it were not for my Eldest Brother Tsisa I would have died too."

Phillip had left his parents as a frightened boy and returned eight years later as a bitter young man. Samuel inhaled sharply as he listened to his son's story. His words brought back distant visions of wild and angry young warriors wearing Ghost Shirts. So many of them fell in battle and in the end, it made no difference at all.

"They would beat us for not pronouncing a word correctly." Phillip puffed out his cheeks and looked at Samuel. "They beat us Father!"

Samuel nodded as he looked at his son. "They beat you but they did not kill you. In this you may be glad my son." He paused and raised his head as he remembered the deaths of so many of his friends. "You have not resisted unto blood my son.

You have not seen warriors fall in battle from the guns of the Bluecoats. You are still alive. I think that you now have a story to tell." Samuel leaned forward and looked intently into Phillips's eyes. "You have a choice. You can bring either life or death to our people. Death comes when you speak of hopelessness. Life comes when you dream of hope."

"Father, there are some who died. The whites do not speak of this yet it is so. There were those that I called friend who simply vanished."

Silence enveloped the room like choking gauze. Samuel looked heavenward. *O Creator, can this be so?* His son had insisted on this earlier. Phillip would not lie. "Phillip, this may be so. I do not doubt you. The point is that you are alive and it is your life with which we are concerned. You can waste it and be killed in an impossible resistance like my Oglala brothers or you can step beyond this into a new tomorrow. Your school is gone; look to the future. Let our Creator guide you into true paths. Learn to walk in a sacred manner my son."

Phillip dropped his head and the combative earnestness that had buoyed him seemed to drain out like old dishwater. He looked at Samuel. "I have missed your wisdom my father. Too many years have I heard the folly of white men. It is good to be home."

Sunrise sat next to her son and put an arm around him. "It is good to have you back Phillip."

Phillip slipped an arm around his mother and laid his head on her shoulder. "It is good to be home Mother."

The doorbell rang and Phillip straightened in surprise. "Who could that be in the evening?"

Samuel rose with a twinkle in his eye. "We shall see."

He walked to the door and let in three familiar voices. Phillip jumped up and ran to see the new guests. "Rosie, Sarah; my sisters... and Grandfather!" He stopped and looked back and forth, not knowing who to go to first. They all broke into laughter as they converged on the young man and enveloped him in one great group hug. "Oh, it is so good to see all of you! I have missed you so much. Grandfather, you look great! Look at you walking like a young brave."

Soaring Eagle slapped his great grandson on the back and laughed. "Yes my son, the holy fire still burns within me. It seems that the Creator still has a few chores for me to do here on old Earth before I go home."

Phillip looked around the group and got a puzzled expression. "Hey, where's Laura?"

"He remembers how many sisters he has," Rosie deadpanned.

"She is in Washington harassing the Great White Father," Samuel said. "We're all hoping that he gets so tired of her that he'll do something about his poor Cherokee children."

Sarah patted Phillip's arm. "She sends her love brother. I'm sure you'll see her soon."

Samuel put his hands on the happily entangled group and began ushering them into the living room. He first seated Soaring Eagle in his own easy chair where he promptly fell asleep. "I know we're all excited but let's keep it down. The old grandfather needs every moment of rest the Creator gives him."

"How old is he now Father?" Phillip looked at Samuel with happy surprise on his face.

"Sit, sit, everyone sit." Samuel pulled in extra chairs from the dining room and finally followed his own directive. "Grandfather is a walking miracle Phillip. He was born in 1816 and he and Yellow Dawn were still a young couple with their first child when they went on the Trail."

"She Who Floats on the Wind," said Rosie.

Samuel looked over at his daughter. "Yes Rosie, the one we have never met."

Phillip was doing some quick math in his head and asked, "Is Grandfather 120 years old?"

"Not quite. His birthday is next month." Samuel stopped and looked down momentarily. "If he makes it that far... our people are known for long life but he is extraordinary. I know the Creator has a special reason for keeping him here."

"Is he sick Father?" Sarah looked over at her great grandfather in concern.

"There is no disease in his body; it's just so old that things are not all working. I am glad that he got to see Phillip."

Soaring Eagle stamped his foot. "Are you talking about me

again Shouting Crow? I am right here."

Everyone tried to hide their giggles. "I am sorry my Edudi. I thought you had left the room." Samuel looked appropriately penitent.

Soaring Eagle looked satisfied. He looked over at Phillip. "I must speak with you my grandson. There are important things for you to know. This is why Creator has kept me here for this long." The ancient Chief sighed deeply. "The veil is thin and my time is spent. Sometimes I can see my brothers beckoning to me and calling, 'Come Home soon!' My daughter Feather awaits me there along with her mother and my wife Yellow Dawn. It will be good to be with them again." He closed his eyes for a long moment until all thought he had fallen asleep once more. He suddenly spoke without opening his eyes. "We will Sing the Song of Life that has no beginning or ending." His eyes suddenly opened and looked again with a youthful intensity at Phillip. "We must speak now my grandson." He looked around the room imperiously. "We must speak alone."

Samuel stood up and said, "Why don't you girls help your mother get us all something special to eat? You know, one of Grandfather's favorites?"

Sunrise stood and bustled into the kitchen with her daughters in tow. "Grandfather, you must excuse me. I need to get more firewood in for the night." Samuel strode purposefully to the back door where he grabbed an ax and stepped outside. The comfortable sound of wood being split underscored the noise of the new work in the kitchen.

Soaring Eagle nodded with a half smile on his face. Years seemed to drop away as he inspected Phillip. "You wear the white man's clothes Phillip. Do you also think the white man's thoughts?"

Up until now, they had all been speaking in English. Their native tongue had been relegated to second place in communication and in many families, it had disappeared completely. Phillip now shifted into Cherokee. "No my Grandfather; my thoughts still travel the southward path to the place of peace."

Soaring Eagle nodded again with a full smile. He replied in

Cherokee, "You still remember how to speak. That is good. I cannot give what I have to a man that is mute."

The conversation now stayed in Cherokee. It was good for Phillip to again speak his native tongue openly. "Even a mute man has hands, Grandfather."

"Hands can hurt but from the tongue can flow rivers of living water."

"I would speak of this living water Grandfather."

"And you will Phillip Shouting Crow. Come and sit near to me grandson."

Phillip dragged one of the dining room chairs over by the old man and sat. Soaring Eagle grabbed his hands in a surprisingly tight grip. "Your spirit is strong. You will need that strength. The evil one has tried to destroy our people and he is doing so again now. This dust bowl time in Oklahoma is dissipating my people. Many of the mixed-bloods are going to California where they will be consumed by the white man's culture." The old man closed his eyes and continued. "I am to give you a precious gift. It is for this that I am still here." Soaring Eagle dropped Phillip's hands and reached into his pocket to extract an odd square stone covered with small studs and matching legends. He held it up once and smiled. He pressed a series of studs in a rapid sequence that Phillip could not quite follow. Suddenly an image appeared in the air next to them.

Phillip sharply inhaled. "What is this Grandfather?"

The aged Chief chuckled. "You don't recognize your old Grandfather?" The image showed a Cherokee couple in traditional garb by a campfire. On one side of them lay a little girl swaddled in blankets and on the other sat what looked like a soldier of a distant era. The image was still like a photograph but translucent as it floated in the air. Soaring Eagle pressed another stud and the image came to life like a talkie, except in full color.

The soldier was speaking. "Chief John Ross led in prayer and when the bugle sounded and the wagons started rolling many of the Cherokee children rose to their feet and waved their little hands goodbye to their mountain homes, knowing they were leaving them forever."

Soaring Eagle pressed another stud and the scene froze once

again. Phillip's eyes never left the image. "I have read those words. They were by an Army Private about the Trail of Tears." He looked at his grandfather with open mouth. "What am I seeing Grandfather?"

"You are seeing young Soaring Eagle and his wife Yellow Dawn. Beside them is their daughter She Who Floats on the Wind. The soldier is Private Burnett, a kind Bluecoat who made Feather's last days a little warmer with the gift of a blanket. We are all sitting at a fire in the midst of the Trail of Tears." The old man pressed another stud and lowered the device to his lap as the image faded into mist and disappeared. He nodded in the direction of the stone. "This Gawonisgi Nvya has been handed down through many generations since the time of the Anikutani."

Phillip's head was spinning with this new knowledge. "You mean the Priest Clan? Many now think that was just a legend; a story like the ones about the animals."

"Most legends begin with truth Phillip. Some three hundred years before white man ever walked upon this Ameliquo, the priests were overthrown. They allowed knowledge to puff them up and became terribly corrupt. They did awful things to our people until one day everyone rose up and killed them. This stone was held by the last true hearted priest who gave it to your grandfather and my grandfather who was alive then." Soaring Eagle paused and closed his eyes while he breathed deeply.

"The whites do not like it when we call North America by the old name of Ameliquo. I was beaten for saying that once."

The aged Cherokee opened his eyes and shook his head. "The whites have given us much, both good and bad. We have given them some things too but the Cherokee have so much more to give." He closed his eyes again. "So much more." He reopened his eyes and leaned forward. "My time is short and there is much for you to know. You comprehend the syllabary so you will be able to decipher the operation of the stone. There are many ways in which it works and it never forgets. You will find voice recordings from the very time of the Anikutani here. If you look very hard, you will even find a conversation with the Yvwi Tsunsdi."

Phillip's eyebrows shot up in amazement. "The Little People?" He nodded at the ancient Elder. "Mother told me stories of the Yvwi Tsunsdi when I was very little. I was sure they were real then, but now I don't know."

A smile played across Soaring Eagle's face. "Angels come in many sizes Phillip."

"Edudi, my head is spinning!"

"Hold it still for a moment grandson. You must know this: this Speaking Stone is a family secret only known to two or three persons at any time. The eldest grandfather is to pass it on to the youngest son who is of an accountable age. You are now given this charge. Take this stone and remember the stories of my people. That is your charge Phillip. Remember the stories of my people. When you reach your final maturity, Unetlanvhi will show you who to give the stone to next. That is all." With that, the old grandfather leaned back in the comfortable chair and promptly fell asleep.

A speaking stone? Anikutani? Little People? It was almost too much for Phillip to fathom all at once. He ran a hand through his hair and looked at the unknowably ancient stone in his hands. How would he hide this from everyone? As if in answer, there was a quick rapping on the front door. His mother's voice floated in from the kitchen. "Could you get that Phillip?"

"Sure Ma." He walked to the door and looked outside. The new electric porch light revealed nothing but a small ornate trunk by the steps. Phillip stepped out and looked around. "Hello?"

He leaned down and saw a tag attached to the trunk. On it was written, "For Phillip: in this you can keep the stories of your people." It was made of a rich dark wood and had beautiful brass hinges and a brass latch. He opened the latch and the top sprang up with a soft sigh. The rich smell of cedar filled his nostrils. Under the lid a small compartment fell open. It was just the size of the Gawonisgi Nvya. Phillip instinctively fitted the stone inside and shut the inner lid. He felt again and found a stud that released the inner door which opened to reveal the stone. If he pressed it twice, it retracted so as to render the control inaccessible. He quickly found that two quick presses would expand the stud. Satisfied, he closed it and the lid, fastening the brass latch. The trunk fit comfortably under his arm. He rose clutching the new treasure and thought he saw movement at the edge of the clearing. He distinctly heard high-pitched laughter in the trees tinkling like delicate glass bells.

"Phillip, who was it?" His mother stood in the doorway holding a towel. "What is that?"

He looked down. "It's a gift for me Mother."

"Well bring it in, let's see."

He brought it to the living room, relieved that he had found concealment for the stone. "It was on the front porch." He looked at the gift tag but it had changed somehow. It now said, "For my Great Grandson Phillip: A place to keep your memories. From Grandfather Soaring Eagle." *That wasn't there before.* Along the bottom was printed "Tulsa Wood Works."

"Ah, they got my gift here in time." Soaring Eagle was wide-awake again. "Welcome home Grandson. I sent all the way to Tulsa for this."

Phillip looked at his grandfather and the old man winked. "Well, uh, yes. I mean, I don't know what to say."

"Say thank you, son." Samuel leaned against the doorjamb smiling.

"Thank you Grandfather! Thank you all!" The room dissolved into laughing and happy chatter as the small trunk was passed around and admired. Phillip never took his eyes from it the whole time.

1936 AD
THE EDGE OF ETERNITY

Soaring Eagle lay down with a deep sigh. The bedroom in Laura's house had been a blessing to him. He smiled when he thought of his granddaughter's mildly obsessive care for her old relative. *"Grandfather, you must get to bed earlier. A man of your years needs extra rest."*

Since you are in Washington, I can stay up late and sleep late. He smiled to himself. The bed was so comfortable, a luxury unheard of in the time after the Trail. He reached over and turned out the light. *Phillip is such an earnest young man. He will be a fitting steward of the stone. Lord Tsisa, please bless my grandson on his life's journey and, if it be Your will, reveal to him the true purpose of the stone.*

"I will do all this and more, Daniel Soaring Eagle." The ancient man suddenly beheld the very form of his Lord. The Eldest Brother extended his arms toward Soaring Eagle. "Your path is complete, my old friend. Enter now into the joy of the Lord."

Soaring Eagle arose with sudden vigor. He looked down at himself and spread his arms. He was dressed in beautiful white buckskin like none he had ever seen. He looked up at the Lord Tsisa and suddenly broke into a run. The Lord turned and broke into a sprint ahead of the Recreated Cherokee. As Soaring Eagle followed Him, he reveled in his renewed youthful vigor. He looked down and it seemed that they were giants running across the Milky Way. A gleaming portal beckoned him ahead and the Lord stopped there and turned to face him. "Welcome Home, my son." Soaring Eagle fell into the arms of his Lord Tsisa.

8: THE STORY TRUNK

1936 AD
SOARING EAGLE, OK

P hillip tightened the straps that secured the load to the back of the mule. He had packed the vegetables carefully into burlap sacks and stacked them high. At the very top rested a familiar dark wood trunk with brass latches. The mule stamped and snorted under the load. "Easy Tommy," Phillip said. It was a heavy load but Tommy was still young and strong. Everyone had to do his part.

It was a minor miracle that they had any produce at all. The Arkansas River had dwindled to a trickle after years of drought. If it weren't for the spring of clear fresh water near the fields, the plants would all be dead dust like the rest of Oklahoma. The produce he was taking to Tahlequah was a treasure in these times.

Phillip heard a keening call overhead and looked up to see an eagle circle once and then fly towards the east. Phillip nodded. "Thank you my friend," he whispered to the receding raptor. Ever since Grandfather had died, the great eagle came to remind Phillip of important things. Today it reminded him to pray. "O Unetlanvhi, please guard me and Tommy on this long road today. These are bad times so keep us from bad men of the road.

Get us safely to Tahlequah and I thank You for granting me a good sale of the produce." He halted for a moment and reached up to touch the trunk. "And Father, give me someone to tell a story to. Let the rivers of living water flow in this dry place, in the Name of Your Son Tsisa." Tommy snorted an amen and Phillip laughed. "Let's go to Tahlequah old friend."

Phillip led and Tommy obediently followed as they walked north from the old homestead. If they hurried, they could make one of Phillip's favorite camping spots near a spring before nightfall. It was about fifteen miles away and that was as far as he could take Tommy today.

It was unfortunate that the wheel on the buckboard was broken. With big Chester pulling, he could have made this trip in a day. Phillip had the dimensions for a new wheel, which he would buy in Tahlequah. Too bad he couldn't buy an auto instead. One of those new Chrysler Town Cars would be nice. *In your dreams, Phillip.*

He patted the faithful mule that walked beside him. "Just be glad you don't have to do this every week Tommy." The mule snorted in agreement.

They had walked into midday and Phillip spied a familiar stopping place up ahead. The old Texas Live Oak had been there longer than even Grandfather could remember when he still walked this road. Its roots went so deep that the drought couldn't kill it. Somewhere way down in the earth the old tree found water and stayed green. He and Tommy could rest a spell under those friendly branches.

As he approached, he saw a young fellow lounging against the tree. The noise of their arrival roused him from his nap. "Osiyo," Phillip called out.

The young man returned the Cherokee greeting in its shortened form. "Siyo." He hopped up and strode over. "Let me help you with that mule."

"Thanks brother. I've got to give him a rest. Here, if we unload the worst of it old Tommy will get a break." He reached for the water container and poured some in a bucket for the mule. "Here you go fella." Tommy slurped loudly and appreciatively. Phillip looked over at his new friend. "Name's Phillip."

"Robert." The young man nodded in his direction. "Hey." He tilted his head at the small dark trunk that he had set by the tree. "What do you keep in there?"

Phillip stood straight and smiled. "That's a special little box. It was the last present my Grandpa got for me before he died. He was a hundred and nineteen when he went Home."

Robert whistled and shook his head. "Must have been old Soaring Eagle." Phillip nodded. "I met your grandpa once a few years ago. He was really sharp for such an old man."

"He stayed sharp like that 'till he left." Phillip reached in his back pocket for a bandanna and mopped his brow. He then scooped out some feed for the mule. He put a healthy portion in the now empty bucket and Tommy grunted as he chewed his first mouthful. Phillip looked down and said, "You're welcome." He looked over at his new friend. "That's what I like, a mule with manners." They both laughed. "Have you had lunch Robert?"

Robert looked down in obvious embarrassment. "Not really hungry."

"Too bad." Phillip pulled an oversize lunch basket from Tommy's back. "My ma usually packs more 'n I can eat in a week." He set it down in a shady spot and opened the lid. "Mm mm, she baked some fresh bread too. Robert, you got to help me with this food."

"Well, okay."

They sat down and Phillip passed around bread, dried meat, and fruit. Phillip watched from the corner of his eye as Robert wolfed down a man size portion in nothing flat. He probably hadn't eaten in days. Phillip filled two large tumblers with water and passed one to Robert. He gulped it thirstily. Phillip reached for it and Robert surrendered without looking. Phillip refilled it and the young Cherokee drained half of the second cup. Phillip ate a few bites and then passed more food to Robert. He didn't say anything. In a moment, the second portion was gone too along with the rest of the water. "We've got a spring that goes real deep," said Phillip as he reached again for the tumbler. "The water's always cold and there's none of that old dust in it."

Robert kept his head down as Phillip saw tears roll down his cheek. He looked up with wet eyes. "Thank you Phillip. That's the first meal I've had in almost a week. Thank you."

"Pshaw. Twern't nothing brother. Here, have some more." Robert gratefully accepted a third portion. By now he was slowing down some and actually chewing his food. "Tell ya what Robert. I've got to walk to Tahlequah and sell this produce then pick up a wheel for our buckboard. Why don't you come along? There's plenty of food for us both." Morning Fawn knew her son's big heart and always packed way more food than he could eat. She knew he would find the person with which the Creator sent to share the food.

Robert looked down again and said nothing. Phillip waited patiently. Finally, Robert spoke in a barely audible voice. "My pa went out hunting. When he didn't come back, my ma sent me after him. I looked for a week but couldn't find him. Don't know but that a mountain lion got him." Robert rubbed his nose with the back of his hand. "When I got back ma was dead." Tears sprinkled the dirt at his feet. "I got no where to go."

Phillip exhaled slowly through his nose. As if the Depression wasn't hard enough. "Robert?"

Robert wiped his eyes before looking up. He mustered his best brave face for Phillip. "Yeah?"

"Come with me. We can go to Tahlequah and then come back to our homestead on the River. We've got room; you can stay with us until you get on your feet."

Robert looked down again and brushed a spider from his pant leg. "Go home little sister." Phillip laughed. Robert inhaled and nodded. He looked up and said, "That's mighty kind of you Phillip, especially in these times. Sure, I'll go with you." He folded his hands together. "There's one thing I've got to do, though."

"What's that?"

"I've got to find my pa. If he's dead I have to bury him with ma."

"Sure Robert. I'll help you. We have an old hound dog that's great at picking up old trails. We'll find your pa."

Robert looked at him with grateful eyes. Phillip nodded with a smile and handed his new friend another hunk of bread.

They ate in silence and Phillip watched Robert noticeably relax. It seemed that a weight had been lifted from his young shoulders. Robert wiped his mouth with the back of his hand and said, "So you were going to tell me about that little trunk of yours."

Phillip leaned back against the tree and yawned. "Yep, I call it my Story Trunk. I've been collecting the stories of my people and I keep 'em in there." He lifted his chin in the direction of the trunk. "The old grandfathers kept 'em in their heads, you know. I wanted to keep 'em more permanent like." He reached over and popped open the trunk. It was filled with scraps of paper and a couple of small composition books. "When a grandfather tells me a story, I write it down, see?"

Robert nodded but his brow was furrowed. "Do you have one that tells why the white man took our land away?"

"There's different stories 'bout that Robert; all the meetings and treaties filled with lies." Phillip fished out one sheet of paper from the bottom of the trunk. "But this one is my favorite. An old grandfather told it to me but I always thought he made it up on the spot."

"Did he?"

"You know how them old Indians are; he wouldn't tell me nothing after the story." Phillip looked at the sheet and closed his eyes. When he reopened them he seemed much older. The magical persona of a Cherokee Storyteller had taken over and Phillip was fully in the center of his calling. He took a deep breath and began.

"One day Wolf walked in the fields to where Lamb was grazing. He said to Lamb, 'I have come to eat you for I hunger.'

"Lamb replied, 'Where are your brothers? For wolf always runs with his family and never alone.'

"'I am alone because my family is sleeping,' Wolf replied. 'I have come to bring them food.'

"'Then you must not eat me, but rather take me to your family,' said Lamb.

"And then Wolf stood on his two legs and took off his mask and, behold, it was White Man. 'No, but I will bring my family here for your field is fair and fruitful.'

"Lamb also stood on his two legs and took off his mask and behold, it was Cherokee Man. 'We would gladly share it with you but I perceive your greed. You are not like wolf; you would take this field for your own.'

"'Yes we would,' said White Man."

Phillip closed his eyes briefly, and then slipped the paper back in the trunk. He looked over at his new friend. "I think the grandfather knew more than he told me."

Robert was silent for a long moment. "I have an uncle who's a Storyteller. He's a lot like you." Robert grinned at Phillip. "His stories leave you with more questions than answers."

"Sometimes that's the purpose of a story; to cause you to find the true meaning of something." Phillip brushed a fly from his face. "At least that's what old Soaring Eagle used to tell me." Phillip pushed back from the tree, slid to the ground and pulled his hat over his face. "Lemme catch a few winks and then we'll hit the road."

"Sure thing Phillip." Robert stayed leaning against the tree. His eyes kept a distant look as if he were walking again with his father in a far-off field.

1936 AD
NEW YORK, NY

Bartholomew Sterling sat at the ornate desk in his office. The room was on the top floor of the massive skyscraper located on Wall Street in New York City. The Sterling Building had briefly held the title as the tallest building in the world but was quickly surpassed by a structure in Chicago. Sterling sat as lord of a financial empire that could not have been imagined in the previous century.

A soft buzz sounded on his desk and he reached to press the intercom button. "Yes?"

An efficient female voice came from the speaker. "Mr. Monroe is here, sir."

"Send him in, Catherine." Sterling took a breath and carefully placed his hands on the desk in a manner that looked casual but ready for action. The large engraved door swept open with his secretary holding the knob. She gestured into the room and a tall and imposing man entered. She shut the door behind him.

Sterling gestured towards a chair in front of his desk. "Mr. Monroe, please make yourself comfortable. Coffee?"

The man crossed the rather large room in long strides. He wore a distinguished suit in the latest New York style. His hair was a deep auburn that shifted into red when struck with direct light. He wore a neatly trimmed goatee that was made of the same deceptive auburn hair. His eyes were dark and his complexion was an unlined olive, betraying an indistinct European heritage. As he reached his seat, he answered, "Only if you will join me, Mr. Sterling."

The older man chuckled. "Galen, you are always such a charmer." He pressed the intercom button. "Catherine, two coffees, please." He looked questioningly at Monroe.

"Black," said the new visitor to the most important financial office in New York.

Catherine's voice was thinned by the intercom system. "Yes sir, I heard."

Sterling leaned back. "That's what I like, an efficient secretary." He was a striking individual with white hair and piercing blue eyes. He was shorter than Monroe, but that did not diminish his presence. When he spoke, his hands were always in motion. It was like he was creating the thing of which he spoke out of thin air. Many said that was exactly what he had done. A poor Midwestern boy, he had come to New York in his youth and built an empire.

Catherine entered carrying a tray with two steaming cups. She served Monroe and then slipped a cup and saucer beside her boss's hand. She swept from the room, her high heels clicking on the hardwood floor that Sterling favored.

Monroe looked appreciatively after her. "Efficient and beautiful."

Sterling allowed a small smile. "I prefer to be surrounded by beautiful things, Galen."

Monroe sipped his coffee and then looked up at Sterling. He waited silently for he knew that the man would clearly speak his mind when ready. He did not have long to wait.

"Galen, your service to the bank has been exemplary. You seem to have a Midas touch, young man. More importantly, your work with the Council has placed us in the halls of power." Sterling carefully laid his arms on the desk, his hands poised to construct the next statement. "The Council on Foreign Relations wants you to be our man in Washington." Monroe's eyebrows raised and his eyes widened. "We will have full time advisors to the President of the United States that live and work in D.C. You will be the first." Sterling took a breath as Monroe inclined his head graciously. "If you accept this post, you will relocate to Washington. You will retain your post at the bank, but that will be largely ceremonial. Your real work will be with the Council."

Monroe lowered his head momentarily, and then leaned forward to look intently at Sterling. "I accept your offer, sir, and look forward to serving the Council and our country in this difficult time. I thank you for the trust that you have placed in me."

Sterling rose to his feet and extended his hand across the desk. He beamed as he shook hands with Monroe. "Excellent choice, Galen." He withdrew his hand and then poised it on the desktop next to the other one, both standing at attention on their fingertips. "See Catherine on your way out. She has a package prepared with all the details."

"Thank you, sir." Monroe turned and strode towards the door.

9: PINE RIDGE

1936 AD
SOARING EAGLE, OK

"I'm just glad we found Robert's father." Phillip sat around the table with his family as they shared supper. The bounty of their spring fed field filled their plates.

Samuel paused with his fork in midair. "It was a close thing son. If it had been anyone but Orson Big Acorn, he probably wouldn't have made it." The old Sioux brought the fork to his mouth and chewed thoughtfully. "I reckon if he didn't have his gun, the canteen, and all that papa in his pouch when that great branch fell and pinned him, he would've died. It had to be more'n two weeks he was there."

"We Cherokee don't call it papa, just dried meat."

"You're half Oglala son; you know what I mean."

"Well, I half know." Phillip grinned at his dad as laughter floated over the dinner table.

"Poor man." Sunrise looked at Phillip with gratitude in her eyes. "You did a good thing by taking Robert under your wing, Little Crow."

"C'mon ma, no baby Indian names." Phillip's three sisters giggled. "I'm glad that Orson and Robert were able to go home. You helped mend him with your great cooking ma."

Sunrise smiled at her son and then looked over at Samuel. "Have you seen today's mail Sam? There's a package and a letter for you."

Samuel raised an eyebrow as he swallowed. "Where from?"

"The return address on both is from Pine Ridge, South Dakota."

Phillip broke into a great smile. "Uncle Rick!"

Samuel adopted a stern demeanor with his son. "There's a time when Gray Raven would have your scalp for such insolence, young one."

The sisters were excited too. "Will you read us Gray Raven's letter father?" Rosie asked.

Samuel let out an exaggerated sigh. "The council of the elders is not for everyone, daughter Little Crow." Phillip whooped at the turnaround on his sister. Rosie pouted. "Let me read it alone first, my family. Then I will share it." He pushed his chair away from the table and stood. "You all help your mother clear the table. I will tend to my reading." Samuel retired to the living room and picked up his mail from the table. He opened the letter and scanned for the signature. Sure enough, there was Gray Raven's mark at the bottom. *Rachel must have written it for him.* He then opened the package and slipped out a thin book. *"Spirit of the Raven,"* he said out loud. His old friend had told him of the Wasichu and his daughter who had spent so much time with him as he told the story of the old days. Rick was not entirely pleased with his portrayal in the volume. It told the story of his vision and the time of the Ghost Dance well, but it left it there. It was only half a life. Still, Samuel had wanted to read it and had asked Rick for a copy. He was glad to receive it. The book had been out for a few years but had met with little notice.

Samuel turned back to the letter. He read it through quickly wanting to hear any news his old friend had brought him. Rick wrote of his work with the Jesuits. He told how he was able to help his people in this way. He no longer spoke scornfully of the Black Robes for he was now one of them, a trusted leader and a catechist in the Catholic community within the Pine Ridge reservation. Samuel shook his head as he remembered the Black Robes. He never understood Roman church doctrine. He then got to the last paragraphs and stood to his feet in excitement. He strode into the kitchen where the family kitchen crew was making short work of the aftermath of dinner. Phillip turned to him expectantly.

Samuel put a hand on Phillip's shoulder. "My son, we must go soon and visit my old friend Rick. He writes that he wants to see you this summer."

Phillip beamed at his father. "We could pack two horses for the trail. It would be just like the olden times!"

Samuel turned to his wife with a serious expression. "Sunrise, I must do this. The crops are in and there are still two moons to the harvest. We could be there and back in that time."

Sunrise looked doubtful and Phillip chimed in. "I'll ride to Robert's house tomorrow ma. I'm sure he would be able to come over once or twice a week to help you and the girls."

Sunrise shook her head. "You are getting too old for this kind of thing Shouting Crow. It's a thousand miles to South Dakota."

"You're right Sunrise. It could take a month to get there on horseback. I have a different idea."

Several voices spoke in chorus. "What?"

Samuel got a shrewd smile on his face. "I've been working on a deal with old farmer Mullins. You know that old Model A he has?"

"Pa, you didn't!" Phillip almost dropped the dishes he was holding.

"Well, it was gonna be a surprise, but I've been doing some special work for him. You know, repairing his barn and fences. Stuff like that. I know he didn't have any money but he does have two cars. I've got one more thing to finish tomorrow afternoon and I'll be driving home!"

Walter Mullins' descendants had come to America and carved out an existence in the great West. After Oklahoma statehood, his father had moved to the eastern part of the new state. There they began a farming operation. Mullins helped his family establish that farm and when his father died, he took over the operation. Mullins had been distressed as a boy over the treatment that he saw afforded to the Cherokees and other Indian Territory tribes. He had befriended the Cherokees of the

Arkansas River Band who were his neighbors and took every chance to better their lot.

The kitchen erupted into cheers. This would be the first car that the family had owned.

That night Samuel read the thin volume that Rick had sent him. Some of the old memories ran along his spine like coyotes in the night. "The nation's hoop is broken," he murmured before turning off the bedside lamp. As he lay in bed, the shadows of the branches in the light of the moon came alive on his wall. He saw his brothers again perform the Ghost Dance as he drifted into a slumber populated by Bluecoats and Oglala warriors.

1936 AD
PINE RIDGE, SD

The trip was long and hard and ranged from dusty and miserable to exhilarating. When they finally stood face to face with Richard Gray Raven, the old man's face showed a hint of a smile. He looked at Phillip. "So this is the one who would be my nephew?"

"This is my son Phillip," Samuel said.

Phillip and Gray Raven had never met, yet he said, "I have seen you before Phillip."

Phillip was awed to be in his presence and remained mute.

The smile that had longed for release now flooded Gray Raven's face. "I think that I can call you nephew, Phillip. Hoka Hey! Come and sit with me, my brother and my nephew."

Although he wore short hair and was dressed in very conservative and current clothing, Gray Raven exuded the spirit of Sioux who were now legend. His face was thin and deeply lined with the years. He spoke in the voice of another time.

They spent hours together as Gray Raven filled in the details of his years as a catechist in the Roman Catholic mission. These were stories he had never told to the man named Borden. The story that that man presented in *Spirit of the Raven* was very focused on the past. Gray Raven lived in a very different present.

Finally, Gray Raven stopped and looked at Phillip. "I have seen you in many visions my nephew. You have many difficult tasks facing you but you must soon take the wings of your great grandfather. Did you bring the stone?"

Samuel looked at his son in surprise. "Have you been speaking to Gray Raven in the spirit world? What is this stone?"

Phillip looked down. Although he had kept the Gawonisgi Nvya secreted in his pocket, he had pressed the voice record command shortly before they had met Uncle Rick. He had obeyed Soaring Eagle and had never told anyone of the stone, not even his parents. Perhaps the Creator had a different idea now, however. Phillip looked up nervously at his father, and then to Gray Raven. "I have never spoken of this thing Uncle."

"I think that Waken Tanka would have you speak now."

Samuel looked over at Rick. "You still use the old name?"

Gray Raven leveled his gaze at Samuel. "The Bible says that God is the same yesterday, today, and forever. I don't think He minds being called by His old name Great Mystery."

Samuel nodded and remained silent. He looked over at his son.

Phillip felt betrayed. He had been diligent to guard the stone and now this old Indian whisked away the cover of silence. *O Creator, what am I to do?* He communed in his spirit for a moment before he felt release to respond to Gray Raven. He slowly withdrew the Gawonisgi Nvya from his pocket and suddenly felt a powerful anointing from above. "Behold the stories of my people!" he exclaimed. As Gray Raven nodded, he heard the quick intake of his father's breath.

Gray Raven reached and he felt impelled to deposit the stone in his hands. "Mm," he said.

The old Oglala's fingers flew over the studs and suddenly an image appeared in their midst. Impossibly ancient Aniyvwiya sat by a campfire across from a coterie of what appeared to be miniature human beings. One of these was saying, "Even now He is upon a terrible Roman cross. He will die there but He will rise again. Remember these words." The image faded.

"The Yvwi Tsunsdi!" Samuel's face was filled with awe.

"I have never seen that Uncle," Phillip exclaimed.

Gray Raven quietly handed the stone back to Phillip. "There is much in this stone that you have not seen." He looked over at Samuel and proceeded to give a concise and accurate overview of the history and operation of the stone. "Grandfather Soaring Eagle was being true to the traditions handed to him but times have changed. The Wasichus make time go faster." He looked at Phillip. "A great war is brewing; a war like old Earth has never seen. An amount equal to five times of all the Native peoples of old Turtle Island will die in this war. It has already begun with Japan's occupation of China. It will be recognized to begin from Germany and end when the power of the sun is released." Gray Raven leaned forward intently and focused all his energy on Phillip. "You will be the eagle of freedom in this war nephew." He closed his eyes and leaned back. "The Bible says that we are surrounded by a great cloud of witnesses. Your great grandfather is one of them. He has asked Waken Tanka to send the great eagle with you into battle. Hechetu aloh! Look for this eagle my son."

Gray Raven seemed to suddenly deflate as if his purpose was complete and there was no reason to go further. "I am weary. Walter will show you to your place. Walter?" Gray Raven said the last loudly and a kind Indian appeared in the doorway. "Would you take my brother and nephew to a place of rest?" The large Oglala man nodded. Samuel and Phillip rose to their feet. The audience was over for today.

There were no priests coming on Sunday so Gray Raven conducted the mass at the chapel. Several sympathetic white homesteaders came to those meetings from time to time and today there were half a dozen white families present. Gray Raven was an accomplished student of the Bible and an experienced orator.

"You white people," he said. "You came to our country. You came to this country, which was ours in the first place. We were the only ones here. There was room to share the land but you did not want to share." Gray Raven spoke without rancor. A couple of the white ranchers lowered their eyes at his frank appraisal. "But you spoke some good things to us and after we listened to you, we settled down." The room was as silent as night in the Badlands. "You're not doing what you're supposed to do; what the Bible teaches us to do. I know this. The blessed Son of Waken Tanka, our Lord Jesus, proclaimed that we must love our neighbors as ourselves. Do unto others as you would have others do unto you. Esteem others better than yourselves. This is the truth."

Phillip glanced over at his father to see that his head was bowed. Uncle Rick's words were challenging to both of them and they reached across the divide between Catholic and Protestant. They spoke of the true mission of all believers on planet Earth.

Gray Raven leaned forward. "Hey-hey! Jesus said to love God and love your neighbor as yourself. This you should do because Jesus is the true Wanekia. He is the One who can save you." The old holy man looked once around the room. Satisfied that all were listening, he said, "That is all I have to say," and turned away from the lectern.

They spent two weeks with Gray Raven. In that time, he took them to visit his Arapaho friends to the west and the Brule Sioux who lived much closer. Meeting these plains Indians was a profound experience for Phillip and it brought him into close touch with the other side of his heritage.

One day Uncle Rick took them to Wounded Knee. As they stood upon the site of one of the most disastrously ill-conceived military actions in American history, the old Oglala was silent for some time. In front of them lay a crooked gulch bounded by a low ridge that defined the horizon. "The blood still cries out," he whispered. Gray Raven then pointed towards the rise and said, "I rode over that hill with my brothers. My face was painted red and I wore my Ghost Shirt. The Bluecoat's bullets did not touch me." He rubbed his temple as if physically pained by the memories. "Most of Bigfoot's band were dead by that time." He turned to Phillip. "Waken Tanka protected me that day my nephew. The Ghost Shirt had no power, this I know."

The old man began to sing softly. "Hey ya, hey yo, Hey ya." The song suddenly resolved into a melody that Samuel remembered. It was the same song he sang to the Cherokees the first time he met them in their town house. The same, except Gray Raven had changed the words. "Lord Jesus You are coming, Lord Jesus You are coming. The Lord says this as He comes, You shall live, He says as He comes!" He danced a slow solemn step as he sang the words and Phillip joined in behind him with Samuel following. This went on for several minutes until Rick stopped and rubbed his temple again. "I am greatly tired."

Samuel strode to Rick and gently gripped his arm. "Come brother, I'll take you to the car." Gray Raven seemed to diminish in stature as he leaned against Samuel. "Yes Shouting Crow, take the old grandfather home."

Parting was emotional as Rick and his son Ron and daughter Katy all said their farewells. Gray Raven's wife Rachel hugged Phillip and whispered thank you in his ear. She had seen years fall from her husband in the time he spent with Phillip. She held him at arm's length and said, "Rick sees something special in you Phillip Shouting Crow. You be sure to write your uncle and tell him your adventures. You don't know how much it would mean to him."

Phillip nodded solemnly and looked over at Uncle Rick. "Don't worry, young Shouting Crow, I will find someone to read your Wasichu scratching to me." He smiled at Phillip and added, "And remember the stories of our peoples." Phillip nodded again and then he and Samuel climbed into the Model A for the long trek home.

1938 AD
WASHINGTON, DC

Galen Monroe sat at his polished mahogany desk. It was trimmed with ornate ivory inlays and was as heavy as a small car. The office that he occupied was large and the desk dominated the room. The floor to ceiling windows behind him gave a panoramic view of Washington, DC. He held a fine gold plated fountain pen poised over a lined yellow pad. As he searched his mind, he found another important item to add to today's list. He had just finished when a soft buzzer sounded. "Yes Elizabeth?"

"Mr. Sterling is on the line for you, sir."

"Thank you." He picked up the ornate French style hand piece and lifted it to his ear. "Hello Bartholomew, how is old New York today?"

A voice of great authority was thinned by the low fidelity connection. "Raining and miserable, Galen."

"Sorry to hear that, sir. It's sunny and clear here."

"Send some my way."

"I will have the President order it up immediately."

Sterling chuckled. "You have become very well connected, my friend."

Monroe leaned back in his chair and swiveled to view the city outside his window. "Yes, but international pressures make it increasingly difficult to properly exploit that connection."

Sterling snorted over the line. "That idiot Chamberlin is trying to play in the sandbox with Hitler."

Monroe nodded in the unconscious fashion of telephone talkers. "He does not know his peril."

"Sometimes I think that only we of the Council can see the true danger." Sterling sniffed before continuing. "Our man in Switzerland is continuing to make preparations."

"The inevitable is coming. We must be prepared."

Sterling sighed. "First a Kaiser, now a Fuehrer."

"Germany has been a problem."

"What of our domestic schedule?"

Monroe paused to properly frame his words. "Indian Relocation is progressing nicely. I estimate that a third of the Cherokees have been dispersed to major metropolitan areas. The Depression worked to accelerate that movement. The numbers of other tribes are similar."

"That is good. To achieve the social goals that we have set, we must achieve full integration of the American population."

"Yes sir, however the coming years introduce an element of uncertainty. The President persists in his policy of isolation."

"I fear that will blow up in Roosevelt's face."

Monroe paused again to more carefully frame his next words.

"I feel, sir, that it must."

There was a pause on the line and then Sterling made an audible sign of thinking. "Hmm." Sterling again briefly paused and then continued, "Arrange a meeting of the inner council."

Monroe pulled his desk calendar into close view. "Friday at two o'clock?"

Pages rustled in New York. "Yes, that's good. I'll see you then, Galen."

"Until Friday, Bartholomew." Monroe hung up the phone and pursed his lips. He turned again to view Washington, searching the city for the answers he needed.

10: Eagle Dance

1941AD
SOARING EAGLE, OK

W ar had burst upon Europe with the violent suddenness of *blitzkrieg*. Less than a year after British Prime Minister Neville Chamberlain had declared "Peace for our time" to a delighted crowd at Heston Aerodrome, Poland lay in ruins and the foundations of Auschwitz were laid. The beginning of Gray Raven's prophecy came true with eerie accuracy.

The Wilson family listened every night to the newscasts on their new radio. It was an amazing thing to snatch voices and music from the air. With growing dismay, they followed Germany's violent expansion. France had fallen and England now felt the full fury of the Luftwaffe and the deadly V-1 rocket planes. Phillip listened with amazement to the accounts of the brave Spitfire pilots who would dive on a V-1 to gain a speed equal to the primitive rocket, slip their wing under the V-1 wing, and do a sudden roll to flip the rocket off course. It would then crash harmlessly in the countryside and not rain destruction on London. Later, they would be defenseless against the supersonic V-2 rockets.

Then, on a chill December day, the voice of Franklin Roosevelt was heard through their small speaker declaring "A day that will live in infamy." On December 7, 1941, the American fleet at Pearl Harbor, Hawaii was decimated by a sneak Japanese attack. America was no longer neutral.

Phillip had learned to fly in the last few years. Mr. Mullins was more than a farmer these days. He had used an inheritance to leverage himself into the flying business. The old backfield of his farm was now a rural airport and he ran a courier service and a crop dusting business from there. He had taken Phillip under his tutelage and taught him to fly. Two days a week Phillip ran the courier route, sometimes to Houston, sometimes over to Little Rock. He once flew all the way to Indianapolis. He always carried the Story Trunk on these trips.

The Wilson family huddled around their radio to hear the President's address. Phillip leaned forward and looked at his mother after Roosevelt finished. "I wanna sign up, Ma. I'd like to fly against those Nazis."

Sunrise frowned. "Oh Phillip, this is no game. You could get killed."

Samuel leaned back in his chair. "Look at it this way. Phillip can sign up today and make his own place, or he can wait for a letter from the Great Father in Washington who will tell him where to go."

Sunrise's face fell as she grasped the dread destiny of the day. Phillip must go to war. "Son, let's all pray together. This is too big for us alone. We need our Brother Tsisa."

The family joined hands and began to cry out to the One Who may always be found. By the end of the evening their hearts were settled.

1942 AD
LONDON, ENGLAND

London looked like a scene from Dante. Everywhere one turned were ruins and empty eyed people. A pall of smoke hung in the air. Firemen continually battled blazes that threatened to overwhelm the little that was left.

Phillip was transported through this desperate scene to an airfield out in the countryside. Here were secreted some of the few advanced P-39 fighter planes that Phillip had been trained to fly. In an era of singularly awkward looking American fighters, the Airacobra was a true thing of beauty. She bore striking similarity to the legendary British Spitfires. The Brits had snubbed the P-39 due to the lack of a turbocharger and many of them ended up in the hands of the Soviet allies. The Airacobras at this base were special, however, and were retrofitted with advanced superchargers. They were secret weapons that could equal or exceed the performance of the Spitfires and Hurricanes.

The trucks pulled to a stop near the camouflaged hangers. Phillip and his fellow pilots jumped out and lined up in loose formation. A dour British officer strode over and snapped to attention. "Glad you chaps made it. Welcome to Croydon Field. My adjunct will show you to your quarters. There will be a briefing in the morning at 0700." He rendered a snappy salute and turned on his heel to walk away.

The young officer accompanying him was more personable. "I'm Lieutenant Reynolds. You're all officers so call me Hank. You Yanks follow me and we'll see if we can't find someone to fluff your pillows."

The pilot next to Phillip lifted his chin at the rapidly departing officer. "Didn't even tell us his name."

Reynolds turned to the young officer. "Colonel Wiggins. He's a good man, just has a bit of the stiff upper lip." The Lieutenant smiled and headed towards the barracks.

Flying the P-39 was exhilarating. The turbocharger gave it power to spare for steep climbs and loops. It would be a formidable opponent against the current German aircraft, which were consistently outclassed by the Spitfires.

Phillip brought the sleek craft back into Croydon after a brief training run decreed by Colonel Wiggins. As he pulled into the line, he saw his fellow pilots busy personalizing their planes. Different imaginative names were being painted on the front panels along with logos ranging from pinup girls to ferocious lions. The Cherokee pilot jumped out and called to a fellow pilot, "Hey Jonesy, where can I get some of that paint?"

Jones tossed a thumb over his shoulder. "Over in the hanger Wilson. That Reynolds guy brought us a few gallons, er, liters of all different colors. Said he knew us Yanks liked being gaudy and apologized for not supplying any chrome bumpers."

Phillip and Jones shared a good laugh and Phillip said, "Lemme mosey over and get some before you guys waste it all."

Phillip returned shortly with a selection of colors and a few brushes. He looked over at his pilot friend. "Hey Jonesy, got my war paint."

"Go get 'em Geronimo," Jones called back.

Phillip spent the rest of the afternoon creating a fearsome image of an eagle's head on either side of the aircraft. Beneath that, he painted the new name of his plane, "Soaring Eagle."

Something extraordinary happened the first time Phillip flew a mission. As he took off from Croydon, a great eagle appeared in the sky next to him near enough for Phillip to take note. When he spotted the raptor, Phillip executed a sharp turn. The eagle paced him in a circle across from the plane's position. He did one full flat loop and then the eagle broke away and Phillip continued on to a fiery rendezvous with The Luftwaffe. When he returned, everyone marveled at the encounter with the eagle.

For as long as Phillip flew in the war, the eagle would reappear at the start of each mission. Each time the plane and the great bird would do a brief aerial ballet before continuing. Phillip's P-39 and his later P-51, (which he also named Soaring Eagle,) were never shot down and always inflicted damage on the enemy.

Phillip's pilot comrades called it the Eagle Dance and esteemed the bird as a good luck token for the whole fighter wing. Indeed, the group's losses were amazingly low. Phillip treasured these things in his heart and remembered Gray Raven's words: *You will be the eagle of freedom in this war nephew.*

1944 AD
SOMEWHERE OVER GERMANY

"Red Leader to Eagle, you've got a tail."

Phillip jammed the stick hard to port and forward, sending the Mustang into a fast downward spiral. "Roger Leader." He glanced over his shoulder to see a Bf 109 diving straight down after him. *Just what I wanted you to do.* Phillip smiled grimly and quickly pulled up on the stick, bringing the nimble P-51 through a fast inside loop. He closed in on the tail of his former attacker and opened fire. The starboard fuel tank exploded, shearing off the wing of the Messerschmitt. It whirled away, narrowly missed Soaring Eagle. The Bf 109 did a crazy looping dance toward the ground. Phillip noted that the pilot ejected safely with seconds to spare. The remains of the plane blasted a crater into the pocked German landscape. The Cherokee circled once to cover the German pilot's landing. He had no more desire for the death of the men, only the destruction of their dread weapons of war.

His headphones crackled with a burst of static and then resolved into a voice. "Geronimo, I need some help. At your ten o'clock." Phillip looked up to see two Messerschmitts closing on Jonesy's P-51. He pulled back the stick and immediately acquired the first target. He opened fire and a stream of smoke erupted from the nearest plane. It rolled its belly to the sky and arced toward the ground. *He's not gonna get out.* Phillip briefly closed his eyes. He opened them to find the next target filling his sights. He opened fire once again and there was a quick explosion. The wounded Messerschmitt drifted towards the ground as the pilot ejected. Jonesy's voice crackled in the headphones. "Thanks buddy."

Phillip nodded as he circled to cover the German pilot's parachute descent while Jonesy flew cover over his head. "No problem, Jonesy," he spoke into the throat mic. They then joined together to fly after the retreating German fighters. It was plain they had lost their taste for combat. "Red Leader to Red Wing, let's head home. Phillip and Jonesy banked away from the fleeing Messerschmitts and set a course of England.

11: A Sacred Way

1945 AD
Soaring Eagle, OK

"I wrote to Uncle Rick every month or two while I was overseas. Katy always wrote back and told me what he said." Phillip tapped on the new table in the family kitchen. Samuel and Sunrise sat with him, the first time they had all been together in four years. "This table is great Duda. Where'd you get it?"

Samuel Shouting Crow looked noticeably older. His hair was once jet-black. Now the gray invaders were counting coup. His eyes were strong and piercing, however, and the Oglala fire was still smoldering. "I made this over at Wally Mullins' wood shop. It took some time but it was worth the effort." He gazed briefly at the glossy wooden surface as he ran his hand over the finish. A smile tugged at his lips.

"It's good to have you home safe Phillip." Sunrise looked at him with the special love that could only come from a mother.

"Ma, it's great to be home." Phillip looked down at his hands. "I'm sick of war and killing. I shot down so many Nazi's that I had to stop painting them on my plane." Phillip shook his head. "329 kills. They gave me this medal." He held up a Medal of Honor. "Only the German Hartman had more than me."

Samuel could feel the bitter regret flow from his son in a wave. "You helped save our country Phillip. You helped save the world."

Phillip was silent for a moment. When he looked at his father, there were tears in his eyes. "Most of those Germans had wives and children Pa." He lowered his head again. "I did a lot of praying to the Creator about that."

Sunrise laid her hand over Phillip's. "What did He tell you?"

"That what Germany had done was irrevocable. There was no other choice." Phillip sighed. "It didn't make it any easier."

They were all silent for a time. How does a mere person answer something of the magnitude of World War II? The ringing of the doorbell interrupted their ruminations. Samuel looked over and said, "Phillip, why don't you get that?"

He strode to the door and opened it to find three happy couples outside. "Hey Pa," he called back over his shoulder, "It's my sisters with three strange men."

Rosie pouted under the porch light. "Well let us in and we'll introduce you to our new husbands."

Phillip flung the door wide and his three sisters surrounded him in embrace. Yes, it was good to be home.

She happened to be in Tahlequah on business when Phillip met her. The maiden was a beautiful Sac and Fox woman who lived in Kansas but frequently came to Oklahoma. Her name was Dorothy Running Water. Phillip invited her to lunch and they spent the rest of the afternoon at a small restaurant. His war tales fascinated her. He was entranced with her stories of wide ranging ministry work helping the desperately poor people of her tribe.

Phillip had always been reserved with girls. He held them in awe and did not want to intrude into someone's life for base personal reasons. Besides, he had never experienced the attraction to a woman as he did with Dorothy. She felt like a perfect fit.

They began seeing each other regularly. Phillip would borrow one of the war surplus Navy trainers that Mr. Mullins had purchased and fly up to her small village to visit. He made quite a stir landing the SNJ-5 amid the Kansas cornfields. The Sac and Fox named him Spirit Hawk.

Tribal traditions had faded so Phillip just asked Dorothy to marry him. When she said yes, the family planned a great ceremony. The Sac and Fox village descended on Samuel's riverfront homestead like a prairie whirlwind. They set up an old-fashioned camp and stayed a month. There were many wonderful nights in the community hall where the grand traditions of Cherokee, Oglala, and Sac and Fox all intermingled into a pulsing display of feathered regalia. Cherokees from all over that part of Oklahoma came to witness and take part in the glorious melding of Native traditions into a fellowship that transcended them all.

On the day of the wedding, Phillip was feeling nervous. "Ma, did I get this porcupine roach right? I never wear all this traditional stuff."

"Come here and turn around." Sunrise reached up and adjusted the ornate hair device. Made from the guard hair of the porcupine, the roach was a distinctively Cherokee headdress. "There, even the old grandfather would approve."

Phillip turned around to face his mother. "I think Soaring Eagle would have loved this gathering."

"He would have loved Dorothy too." Sunrise smiled at her only son. "Time for the wedding, Phillip."

"Yep." Phillip straightened his head and then mother and son walked to the community hall.

"The blessings of the Clan Mothers was beautiful, Hawk." Dorothy leaned her head against her new husband. "The Sac and Fox don't have a tradition like that."

Phillip looked over at his wife. "What is your people's tradition?"

A young Sac and Fox brave overheard the question and said, "We send the groom out after a buffalo. No buffalo, no wife!" The part of the wedding feast that was in hearing of the exchange dissolved into laughter.

Dorothy looked down. "It was a simple ceremony. Most of us don't remember too well. Our tribe was always small and now the elders are few." She looked up into Phillip's eyes. "It is said among our people that if we knew what Lewis and Clark would do after they met us, we would have shot them on sight." She shook her head and briefly closed her eyes.

Phillip sighed and slipped his arm around Dorothy. Such stories were deeply disturbing to him. It was difficult to reconcile the red white and blue post-war America with the deadly behavior of her forbears. "We will do what we can to help your people my little Dove. We Cherokee are losing our traditions too. I think I am the first of my bloodline to not adhere to the clan traditions."

Sunrise leaned forward from a few seats down. "I've been thinking about that son. Perhaps there is a way to honor the old ways at least a little." She looked over at the bride. "Dorothy Running Water, now you are a part of our family. You have taken Phillip as a husband and I have gained you as a daughter."

Dorothy broke into a smile and nodded her head. "I would be a Sac and Fox Cherokee then, right?"

"Yes my daughter. Welcome to the family."

From that day sprang a strong alliance between the Cherokee families of Soaring Eagle and the Sac and Fox Running Water family. There were always reasons to visit one another and Samuel said that they were wearing a rut in the road between Oklahoma and Kansas.

1948 AD
TULSA, OK

Phillip had continued his flying work for Walter Mullins after his return from the war. The old farmer had expanded in the post-war boom economy and had started a regional passenger service. They had been flying out of a small airport in Muskogee until Mullins bought out a failing local carrier. The base of operations moved to Tulsa where the modest fleet of old Navy trainers and a few Lockheed L-10 Electra's suddenly expanded with over two dozen DC-3's. Phillip was a quick study on the big Douglas aircraft and before long he was flying all over the Southwest. Within another year, Mullins promoted him to

Director of Operations and suddenly he had twenty-five pilots working for him. He was even able to locate his old war buddy Jonesy and hire him on.

Jones hurried across the tarmac at Tulsa International Airport. "Hey Wilson, wait up!"

Phillip turned when he heard the call behind him. "Siyo Jonesy! Where are you flying today?"

Jones slowed to Phillip's walking pace as he came up beside him. "Well, I'm supposed to fly out to Phoenix but the DC-3 that was being prepped has hydraulic failure. The grease monkeys say it'll be two days before they can get the parts and finish the job."

"Can we pull another plane from the hanger for the run?" The flight to Phoenix was an important leg and they had many regular passengers.

"The only thing left is an Electra."

"Will it hold the passengers?"

"Yeah, this run is light so they'd fit in the old crate."

Phillip glanced at his old friend. He had the same look that he used to get when they'd fly into Germany. "Hey, I sent the fighter escort on ahead and they already knocked out all the flak guns."

Jones looked over with a lop-sided grin. "It ain't that Geronimo. I don't want to fly Amelia's plane." In 1937 on a highly publicized round the world flight, aviatrix Amelia Earhart disappeared while flying a highly modified L-10 Electra. Many pilots avoided the aircraft like the plague.

Phillip stopped and faced Jones. "Buddy, I can guarantee that Amelia never even saw this Electra. The boss bought the L-10's over in Europe before the war really broke loose." Phillip shaded his eyes and watched one of his DC-3's take off smoothly. "Now that's the way to take off." Jones nodded, his features still grim. "Jonesy, we got to do this run. You want me to co-pilot?"

Jones shook his head. "No boss man, Frank is a great co-pilot."

Phillip looked up at the swiftly departing DC-3. He seemed to close his eyes momentarily, and then he returned his gaze to

Jones. "How long before you go aboard?"

"About an hour."

"Come to my office." Phillip turned on his heel and strode quickly to the side entrance of the hanger. In a moment, they both sat in a quiet office.

"Jonesy, there's two things you know about me. One, I'm an Indian and two, I believe in the Creator. I also know that He is the Lord. I know you don't believe, but I want to do something. I want to pray for you my friend. I believe the Creator can keep you safe."

Jones put his head down and mumbled, "Well, okay Wilson."

Phillip stretched out his hand towards Jones. "O Creator, my Grandfather, I ask You now to grant safety and wisdom to Jonesy. Keep the Elektra flying and keep my friend alive. And Lord, when You've done that, remind him that it was You."

Jones kept his head bowed for a moment before speaking. He spoke in a small voice. "Thanks Geronimo." He looked up at his friend. "You know, I've never told you, but it always helped when you did that in England before we flew a mission." He stood and smiled. "See you when I get back from Phoenix."

"Yeah Jonesy, and don't forget to bring the Electra."

Phillip took the steps up to the tower two at a time and burst into the control room. Several flight controllers were huddled around the radio monitoring communications. "What's the status on flight 640?"

A controller looked around. "Unchanged sir. Port engine has failed and they continue to lose altitude."

"Position?"

"Somewhere over the Arizona state line." The controller turned to Phillip. "Over the Sonoran Desert."

"Can you raise him?"

"Yes sir."

"Let me talk to him." The controller handed him a mic. "Jonesy this is Wilson, do you read?"

A burst of static came from the speaker followed by a familiar voice. "Gotcha five by five Geronimo." The controllers smiled at one another.

"What's your status Jonesy?"

"Port engine out, starboard engine losing power. Unable to maintain altitude. We're going down."

"Jonesy, stand by."

"Roger."

Phillip grabbed a phone and dialed the operator. "Yeah, get me the number of Joe Talking Grass in Show Low, Arizona. This is an emergency." He tapped his foot as he picked up a pencil. He jotted a number down and said, "Thanks." He quickly redialed. "Chief Talking Grass? This is Phillip Shouting Crow in Tulsa." He nodded impatiently at the reply. "Yes, Samuel's son." He nodded again. "Yes sir. Please, I have an emergency. Yes, thank you sir." Phillip quickly outlined the emergency and asked if the Pima tribe could help. "Yes sir, I'll tell the pilot. Can you stand by sir?"

Phillip picked up the mic. "Jonesy come in."

"Roger boss. We still have about five thousand feet underneath us."

"Okay Jonesy, I've contacted the Pima in Arizona. They are lighting a signal fire that will send up a great smoke column. Stand by.

Phillip picked up the phone. "Chief Talking Grass? Yes sir. The fire is lit? Hold on again sir."

Phillip closed his eyes briefly and then picked up the mic. "Jonesy?"

"Yeah Wilson, there's a plume of smoke up ahead."

"Okay, start your descent. Aim for the base of the smoke. The Pima are clearing an emergency runway now. It will be rough but you should make it."

"Roger boss, starting descent." There were several tense minutes before Jonesy came back on the radio. "Boss, we landed. We're all safe." A great whoop went up and the control tower broke into applause.

"The Creator watched over you Jonesy."

"Yeah I guess so."

Phillip picked up the phone again. "Chief? Yes sir, they're all safe. Thank you sir. One day soon I'll fly out there and thank you in person. That pilot is a friend of mine. Yes sir. Goodbye Chief Talking Grass."

The Jones that sat across from Phillip was greatly subdued. He had been sure that the Electra was going down in the desert but somehow they were saved. He remembered his friend's prayer. "Wilson, I guess I owe you my life." He took a deep breath and exhaled through his nose. "Did you pray for me back in the war too?" Phillip nodded. "I guess your Creator was watching out for me."

"You don't owe me anything Jonesy. You do owe Someone greater than me everything." Phillip pulled a small ornate trunk from under his desk and set it on top. As he opened the lid he said, "I call this my Story Trunk. In here I keep the stories of my people." Phillip slipped out a thin volume. "I also have a story which is for all peoples. Many call it the greatest story ever told." He proceeded to open the New Testament and tell him of his Eldest Brother Tsisa. He told him how He died and rose again and how Jones could too.

The crusty old pilot looked at him with clear eyes. "That makes sense Wilson. I believe. What do I need to do?"

Phillip told him of repentance and salvation and the world to come. "You will come to a new way of living. The Sioux call it walking in a waken way. That means to walk in a sacred way; the way of holiness." A short time later, Jones walked out of the office as a new creation.

1948 AD
WASHINGTON, DC

Bartholomew Sterling was still a vigorous man. He strode briskly beside Galen Monroe as they walked around the great reflecting pool in the nation's capitol. They briefly passed into the shadow of the Washington Monument and then returned to sunshine. Sterling looked sideways at his companion. "With VJ day behind us, we can again concentrate on more national issues."

Monroe nodded. "Yes, and thanks to your foresight, Switzerland protected our European assets."

"It was distasteful dealing with the Nazis, but it had to be done. That problem is now behind us." Sterling glanced up to watch a flight of birds sweep over the great pool. "Your words to President Truman were most helpful in bringing an end to the Japanese unpleasantness."

Monroe compressed his lips. "He understood that he had to use all advantages that were at his disposal."

"He used them well." The pair rounded the corner of the pool and crossed the plaza in front of the Lincoln Memorial. Sterling motioned towards a bench and the two men sat down. Neither man was visibly winded.

Monroe crossed his legs and looked over at Sterling. "I am beginning a draft of a new recommendation for the Council. I believe that it is in the best interests of our nation that a policy be put in place that will dissolve the Indian tribes that remain. As long as America remains divided, progress towards a world unity will be hindered."

"Agreed. When will your draft be ready?"

Monroe put a hand to his face and tapped his cheek as he stared out over the pool. "Including the interviews and research, I will need at least a month to present a comprehensive plan."

"Very well, Galen, proceed. Use whatever resources of the Council that you need. You have my full authority."

Monroe nodded and dropped his hand to the bench's armrest. He looked over at the huge statue of Abraham Lincoln and then back to Sterling. "I fancy that Abe likes the springtime best. I know he enjoys the brown turning green and the blossoms springing forth."

Sterling glanced over at the statue. "I've always thought that his eyes were closed all winter, like he was napping. Yes, springtime definitely wakes up the old man." The two shared a laugh and then Sterling stood. "I must get back to New York this afternoon, Galen."

Monroe stood and they began walking to the street behind the Lincoln Memorial. "Is your driver waiting?"

"Yes, I instructed him to be here." Sterling motioned towards the road. "There he is, right on time." He looked at Monroe. "Have I ever thanked you for sending me that Cherokee? He is the most punctual driver that I have ever employed."

"They are an extraordinary race and America is richer for their contribution to our gene pool." The two stopped in front of the car as the Indian driver who stood by reached for the rear door. "Hello Tom, good to see you again." Monroe smiled pleasantly.

The Cherokee nodded. "Hello Mr. Monroe, good to see you sir." His face remained expressionless.

Sterling smiled at Monroe and said, "Have I told you never to play poker with this man? He is the best and most dangerous bluffer the game has known."

"I'll remember that sir. I am very glad that Tom is being of good service to you." Monroe reached out his hand and Sterling grasped it in a brief but strong grip. "I'll talk to you soon, Bartholomew."

"Farewell, Galen." The old man slipped into the cool leather seats of the Cadillac limousine and Tom shut the door. He nodded once to Monroe and walked around to quickly slide into the driver's seat. The car purred to life and rapidly motored away. Monroe watched the car disappear into the traffic of Washington before he hailed a cab.

12: A Son of Thunder

1950 AD
Tulsa, OK

Walter Mullins had looked forward to this moment. Ever since Wilson had returned from the war, he had been on this search and now it had paid off. The Cherokee had been central to the success of Oklahoma Air and he was glad to do this special thing. The intercom on his desk beeped. "Yes?"

"Mr. Jones to see you sir."

"Send him in."

The grizzled veteran pilot walked into the office with the ever-present hint of swagger. "Sit down Jones." He took a chair with a puzzled look on his face. "I've got a special assignment for you."

"Sir?"

Mullins handed him a pouch. He was thoroughly enjoying the mystery of the moment. "In there you'll find directions and tickets to get to an airfield in France. There you'll pick up a very special aircraft. You'll find that it's been fitted with auxiliary fuel tanks. You're to fly this bird back to the States. The cockpit has also been modified to accommodate your needs on a long flight." Jones reddened as he realized the scope of such modifications. "You'll land at New York and refuel. After a layover you'll proceed to Tulsa."

"If I may ask sir, what is this aircraft? Am I qualified on the bird?"

Mullins leaned back in his chair. "Uniquely qualified." He let a small smile play over his face. "This is a very special P-51 named Soaring Eagle."

Jones let out a whoop. "Geronimo's plane! How'd you find it sir?"

"I've been looking for years. I followed a number of tips that were always dead ends. Then I got a letter from a Frenchman that said he had an old fighter with an eagle painted on the sides. I had him send me some photos and I was convinced." Mullins leaned forward and adopted a stern demeanor. "This is not to get out Jones. I want the first time that Wilson learns of this to be when he sets eyes on it right here."

"Yes sir!"

"You leave tonight. As far as everyone else is concerned, you are on special assignment. I have so noted on the duty roster." Mullins stood. "Go rope us a Mustang, cowboy!"

"Yes sir, and thank you Mr. Mullins. You don't know what this'll mean to Wilson."

The intercom on Phillip's desk chirped once and a voice came on. "Mr. Wilson, you better come and see this. Out on the tarmac by the hanger."

"Roger." Phillip jumped up and hurried out the side door. As he rounded the corner he stopped dead in his tracks. Mr. Mullins stood on the tarmac next to a plane. Jones was just jumping out of the cockpit. Phillip's jaw dropped and then he hurried forward. "My old Mustang!" The painted eagle was faded and peeling and the scores of enemy kills stretched back across the fuselage to where he had stopped counting. He reached to touch the eagle.

"I wouldn't do that Geronimo. Engine gets pretty hot after flying all the way from New York City." Jones jumped the rest of the way to earth.

Mullins cleared his throat. "I thought you needed a private executive transport so I found this old crate over in France."

Phillip looked at Mullins and then back to the plane and then to Mullins again. "I don't know what to say sir. I never thought I'd see the old Mustang again. Oh, thank you sir!"

"You deserve it son. Here's the deal: the plane will remain the property of Oklahoma Air. That way you don't worry about taxes and such. Beyond that, it's yours to use whenever you want. I will have some assignments for you with which you can use this plane. In fact, the first is to fly out and properly thank the Pima Indians for helping us out with the Electra." He looked over at Jones. "Before that, maybe this pilot can help you restore this baby."

The two spoke as one. "Yes sir!"

"This is fantastic, Hawk! I think I now understand your descriptions of this plane. It has a life of its own." Dorothy smiled at the sun from the rear seat that Phillip and Jonesy had added.

"Are you comfortable back there?"

"Oh yes, this is wonderful."

"Jonesy was worried about the two seat conversion until he saw the plans for the USAF Mustang trainers. I think it works well." Phillip kept a steady hand on the stick. He knew that Dorothy didn't have the stomach for wartime combat maneuvers.

"Phillip, I have something special to tell you." Phillip glanced over his shoulder. "I was waiting for the right time and I think this is it." She paused and looked him in the eye. "I'm pregnant!"

Phillip let out a warrior whoop and pulled back on the stick. The P-51 rose through the clouds in joyous response.

"It's a son, Phillip Shouting Crow." The Sac and Fox midwife beamed up at the happy father. "Congratulations!"

"Thank you Mary! Will she be okay?" He looked away from the new human bundle to his wife.

"I am fine Hawk." Dorothy's voice was weak but her smile was sure. "Thank you Mary. I don't think I could bear the white man's hospital."

"And you don't need to, Running Water. We have a better

way."

Dorothy nestled the newborn to her breast and looked up again at Phillip. "A son!"

The old man's voice was weak but the Oglala words came over the line with perfect clarity. "You must bring your son to see me, nephew, while there is still time." He coughed weakly. "I would meet this beautiful wife I've been hearing about, too. Oh, and that old father of yours; is he still getting around?"

"Dad's still hard to keep up with, Uncle. We all would love to see you." Phillip smiled into the receiver.

"And your mother?"

Phillip's head dropped and he was silent for a moment. "Ma hasn't been feeling too good lately Uncle Rick. I doubt she will make it."

"I'm sorry to hear that nephew. I will pray for her."

"That would be wonderful."

"So, should we build you a runway like the Pima, young Shouting Crow?"

"If you can build it, I can land on it."

"We will have one ready."

"Let me call you when we make all the arrangements. Give me a few days."

"A few days it is nephew."

"Goodbye Uncle Rick."

The connection clicked and went dead. Phillip turned toward his wife who was holding the baby. "How'd you like to meet Gray Raven?"

Dorothy's eyes danced at the prospect. "He's a living legend! I would be thrilled to meet him."

1950 AD
PINE RIDGE, SD

It took several days to work out the schedule and free up a plane. They flew up in the last remaining Electra. Oklahoma Air had cannibalized the other two to keep this one in tiptop shape. She still flew like a new aircraft. Phillip had mounted auxiliary fuel tanks so they wouldn't worry about refueling. There was enough for there and back again with plenty to spare.

A front had just pushed east so they had clear flying up to Pine Ridge. True to his word, Gray Raven had mobilized the community as only he could and they had cleared a respectable runway. The old Electra easily found the glide path onto the Sioux reservation.

Warriors in full regalia led them to the humble dwelling of Gray Raven. The old man stayed seated when they entered. Gray Raven's face looked more ancient than time itself. "Samuel, Phillip, it does an old Indian's heart good to see your faces one more time here on Grandother Earth."

Samuel rushed to his old friend and knelt in front of him while grasping his hands. "My brother, I am blessed by Waken Tanka to behold your face once again. Soon we will move beyond this Momentary into Reality. For the sake of our children, I am glad we could be together before then."

Gray Raven gripped his old friend's hand. "You are still Shouting Crow. Your eyes betray you."

"And you are and always will be Gray Raven, great in wisdom and teacher of the waken way."

Phillip joined his father. "Uncle Rick, I have missed you. It is good to see you again."

Gray Raven smiled warmly at Phillip and reached for his hand. "My nephew, it has been many years and a great and terrible war since I have beheld your face."

Phillip knelt beside his father. Uncle Rick looked so frail, so far away from the years of riding against Bluecoats. "The power of the sun ended the war just as you had said Uncle."

A shadow fell on the old man's face. "The Great Father in Washington made the sun shine so brightly on Japan that two cities died." He lowered his head and shook it ever so slightly. "If there had only been another way."

Phillip spoke softly. "Japan and Germany were implacable foes who had done unspeakable things." Phillip rocked back on his heels. "It is said the Adolph Hitler studied the Indian Removal policies of Andrew Jackson as he formulated his 'Final Solution.' Tojo was no better."

"I know these things my nephew but it does not lessen the

pain in my heart."

Phillip stood and lightly laid a hand on Uncle Rick's shoulder. "But I think there are some here who would meet you Uncle."

Gray Raven brightened and looked to the group at the door. "And who is this fair maiden? Sac and Fox by the look of her."

Phillip stepped over to Dorothy. "This is my wife, Uncle. She is Dorothy Running Water and yes, she is Sac and Fox. But you cannot fool us old grandfather. You knew that already."

Gray Raven's face creased into a broad grin. "Yes my nephew, I cannot fool you. But I see a baby. Bring the child here."

At Gray Raven's request, they had not told him the child's name. Dorothy brought the baby to the elder and sat him in his lap. Gray Raven looked down at the young one as Dorothy hovered nearby. Gray Raven looked up at her and said, "I have held many little ones, child. I will not drop him." Dorothy lowered her gaze and backed away as Samuel smiled in the strangest fashion.

The old Oglala looked at the baby and the little one looked up into the holy man's eyes. Gray Raven's eyes widened and he said, "His name is James. He is one of the Sons of Thunder. Jesus called the brothers James and John 'Boanerges' which means Sons of Thunder. This is a child of the Thunder Beings. He will bring forth a sound that will turn the hearts of the children to the Father. This sound will shatter the strongholds of the evil one." Gray Raven closed his eyes as he gently laid a hand on James' head.

Suddenly Phillip's sight swirled into a vision. He saw a James who was grown. His hair was long and he wore what looked like a Ghost Shirt, except that the symbols were different. They were depictions of the Holy Spirit. A strange stringed instrument hung around his neck and he stood in front of a microphone. Before him was an endless crowd, most with their hands raised. James spoke into the mic. "I say unto you in the name of the Lord Tsisa, be saved!" A huge number of this group fell to the ground at these words. James then burst into a song of praise unto the Creator unlike any that Phillip had heard, yet with an eerie familiarity.

Phillip awoke to see his wife's concerned face hovering overhead. He heard Uncle Rick speak as if from a great distance. "He has had a powerful vision. Be patient daughter, he will be fine." Phillip saw a gnarled hand laid on his wife's shoulders. Gray Raven appeared behind her as if from another epoch. His stern lined face was crowned with a full Sioux eagle headdress. Phillip shook his head and saw gentle face of Uncle Rick once again.

Phillip sat up to a cross-legged position and looked at Gray Raven. "I saw you just now as a warrior, and then I saw you as yourself." Gray Raven nodded and waited for more. "I saw James as a grown man. He was in a great theater, bigger than any I've seen. It was totally filled with people and there were even people standing in the aisles. He wore a Ghost Shirt uncle! It had symbols which represented the Holy Spirit."

Samuel nodded and spoke. "A Holy Ghost Shirt."

Phillip looked at his father with raised eyebrows, and then continued. "He had a strange flat stringed instrument hanging from his neck. I have never seen the like. I saw him step to a microphone and he spoke to the people and told them to be saved. People fell over at his words."

"Just like you fell over, Hawk?"

Phillip grinned at Dorothy. "Did I fall over?"

Several voices answered in unison, "Yes!"

Phillip favored the room with a lop-sided grin and then stood up. "After that he started singing a song to Creator. I have never heard anything with such power."

Gray Raven slowly settled back into his chair. "Waken Tanka has blessed you with a vision of your son's future." He rubbed his eyes with thumb and forefinger. "I have told you once before how the Wasichus have made time go faster. Your son's tomorrow will be so different from this time after the war that you will not even conceive its possibility. Yet it will be so. James has a destiny. May Waken Tanka give him a vision to match that destiny."

"You are also Sioux nephew. From time beyond time our people have readied ourselves for Reality by preparing the song that is a summation of our life; the Death Song." Gray Raven walked slowly with Samuel and Phillip on either side. "It is the final culmination of the waken way."

Phillip's brow was creased. The Cherokee had no tradition like this. "So I must build this song my whole life?"

"The Song is your life, Phillip." Gray Raven looked over at Phillip's face. He realized the man had understood the words but not their deepest import. He stopped and turned to Phillip. "The Song began this old Earth and it is the only thing you will take with you when you leave. All else is dust, young Shouting Crow."

Phillip's brow furrowed. "Do you speak now of my Death Song?"

"In part my son. You will do well to remember that much."

"I will remember and obey your words Uncle." Gray Raven smiled and then drifted into a quiet reverie. "Why have you not told me this, Father?" Phillip looked pointedly at Samuel.

"I have been Cherokee for over half a century my son."

"Will you sing a Death Song?"

"Yes Phillip. Remember that I am also Oglala."

"Then I shall sing one too." They both turned to continue the slow pace on either side of Gray Raven.

They sat at feast together with the better part of the Pine Ridge reservation. Phillip had bought enough food to feed them all for over a month and, in a typically Sioux response, they threw this great event for the last night the Wilson family would be here. It was a celebration of life. Several of the Jesuit priests even joined in the festivities at the insistence of Gray Raven.

An elderly priest strode over to Phillip with surprising agility and extended his hand in greeting. "Richard has told us of your bountiful gift. We have spent our lives caring for these sheep and on their behalf I want to thank you. I'm Father Thomas."

Phillip grasped the friendly extended hand. "Thank you Father Thomas. The Creator has greatly blessed me and it is my duty to bless these good people." He dropped the priest's warm hand and looked around at the sizable crowd seating themselves around hastily contrived outdoor tables. "Washington will not do this for them."

The priest shook his head. "They have proud looks and deaf ears when it comes to the Oglala or any Plains tribe. Even my own Diocese does not do enough."

Phillip looked quizzically at the wiry Jesuit. "You speak like an Indian, Father."

Thomas laughed and said, "I have spent my life among them." He leaned over to Phillip. "Between us, sometimes they make a lot more sense than the rest of the world."

Phillip sensed a purity of purpose in the man. Although he could not reconcile himself to Catholic doctrine, he did know how to recognize a friend. "Thanks Father. I only hope some of that has rubbed off on me."

Suddenly serious, the priest raised an eyebrow and looked squarely at Phillip. "Oh, it has my son." He paused and smiled. "A pleasure meeting you Phillip. I will pray for a safe journey back to Tulsa for you and your family tomorrow."

"Thank you Father." Phillip touched the brim of his hat as the energetic Jesuit strode over to check on one of his parishioners.

"Phillip, come and bless this feast." Samuel waved him over to a table at the head of the assembly where Uncle Rick was already seated. Phillip strode over to the table and turned to face the crowd. "My brothers," he called in a loud voice. The hum of conversation died down as all turned toward him. "Let us thank Creator for His bounty." Heads bowed across the group. "Oh great Grandfather, we thank You! You have created the four legged and the winged nations. You have also created this great Oglala Nation. Bless these brothers and sisters of my blood and my heart, Grandfather. Bless this time together I pray and bless the feast that You have so graciously provided. I pray this all in the blessed name of our Lord Tsisa, amen."

A hearty echo of amen's ensued which melted back into renewed conversations. Phillip sat down at a special place between his father and Uncle Rick, who turned to Phillip and said, "So my nephew, I did not know you came here on a vision quest. I would have prepared a lodge and the pipe."

Phillip laughed. "I did not look for the vision Uncle; the vision simply found me."

"You know that we have a great tradition for important

visions."

Phillip paused and then remembered the scenes in *Spirit of the Raven* where the people acted out the vision. "I think I know what you mean Uncle Rick."

The old man smiled and said, "Good." He took a large bite of food to fend off any questions.

Samuel looked over at Phillip. "Tell Rick about the British man you met in the pub over there during the war. You know, the one you talked with several times?"

It was obvious misdirection but Phillip was happy nevertheless to supply the story. "He was Irish, actually. He had lived in Britain for a long time, though. We pilots used to go to a pub at the edge of London on Saturday nights as long as there was no air raid. It had miraculously escaped destruction from the bombs and rockets. Well, I met a man there who became very interested when I told him my Cherokee and Sioux heritage. He began to question me at length about our ancient stories, which I was happy to share. He particularly wanted to hear the tales of the four leggeds in the time when they talked."

"They still talk nephew. We just can't understand any more." Gray Raven nodded sagely at Phillip with the faintest hint of a twinkle in his eye.

Phillip nodded with a raised eyebrow. "After I had shared many of these tales with him I saw him again one night. He had a folder of papers as he sat with me. He told me that he had been working on a story for children; one in which animals talked. He invented another land that could only be reached through a magical wardrobe. He read me part of the tales about a great lion who was a gentle yet strong leader of his people. His name was Aslan and the kingdom was called Narnia."

"What was the man's name nephew?"

"A strange name, Clive. Clive Lewis. Turns out that he was already a quite famous Christian author."

Gray Raven nodded. "His book *The Screwtape Letters* sits on my shelf, Phillip. Perhaps we will hear more of this Narnia."

Phillip nodded. "It's been five years since the war ended. I hope he has found the time to write of this place."

The dinner continued with many courses and much laughter.

As it drew to a close, a young Oglala in full regalia called for the tables to be cleared and moved to open up a central space. There a great fire was quickly built and many Sioux in full tribal dress assembled. The same young warrior called out, "We would gather here to honor the great Waken Tanka who sent His Son to die on a cross for us all. Give praise to Him!" The warriors around the fire began to cry out and the crowd answered them in a mighty shout. Then the warrior turned towards the head table. "Phillip Shouting Crow, come forth!"

Phillip looked at Gray Raven who shooed him with his hand while his eyes sparkled. "Leave your hat, nephew. Tonight you are Oglala." Phillip laid it on the table.

As he advanced towards the fire, a group of warriors surrounded him. They shielded him from the crowd's sight as they transformed him into a Sioux. He emerged in full regalia with a stunning eagle headdress and what looked like a Ghost Shirt, except it had a large cross painted on the front. The crowd let out a mighty shout as they beheld Phillip, son of Shouting Crow.

A group of women started a driving beat on traditional drums. The master of ceremonies called out, "Phillip Shouting Crow has had a mighty vision!"

A crowd in regalia had gathered on the other side of the fire. "Show us the vision!" they shouted as one.

A warrior brought Phillip a flat drum that he held in front of him. The young Sioux called out, "Behold James, son of Phillip Shouting Crow! Behold, a son of the Thunder Beings!"

Phillip immediately grasped the drama. The Sioux grouped across from him and raised their hands. He called out in a loud voice, "I say unto you in the name of the Lord Tsisa, be saved!" The grouped Sioux all fell to the ground at the words and a great shout went up from the crowd. The Holy Spirit swept in upon Phillip in that moment and he knew exactly what to sing. He remembered Uncle Rick at Wounded Knee and the Ghost Dance. He closed his eyes and sang out, "Lord Jesus You are coming!" The fallen Sioux all jumped to their feet and gave antiphonal response. Again he sang, "Lord Jesus You are coming!" and again they responded. Phillip felt transported to another century as the song welled from his innermost being. "The Lord says this as He comes." The Sioux responded and then they all began to sing together, "You shall live, He says as He comes! You shall live, He says as He comes!" They began to dance around the fire as they sang. The song grew in power and purpose and continued for some time until all the Sioux present were circling the fire and praising Waken Tanka, the One True God.

The first rays of the morning sun saw the dance ending and sleepy-eyed Indians heading to their homes. Phillip dragged back to Uncle Rick's house where he found the rest of his family fast asleep. He quickly joined them.

He felt a gentle hand on his shoulder. "Hawk, it's after noon."
He cocked open one eye to see his beautiful wife with a smile playing across her lips. "Mm," he said as he closed his eyes.
"Dance the night away and leave us all stranded."
He cocked open an eye to see her pouting with arms folded. "Okay, but you'd better give me room. After a night like that I'm bound to have rattlesnake breath." She jumped up in mock horror as he arose and scratched his head. "I suppose you need a pilot, huh?"
"Well, it's a long walk don't you think?"
"Okay, let me get cleaned up and we'll skedaddle." He stood and stretched. "Hoka hey," Phillip said with a yawn.

The flight home was quiet and uneventful and everyone but Phillip caught up on their sleep. They landed safely in Tulsa shortly after sundown. The trip would prove to be the last time they saw Gray Raven alive in this world.

1953 AD
WASHINGTON, DC

"Indian Termination now has the force of law, Bartholomew. The tribes should be effectively dismantled before the end of the decade." Phone voice quality in the 1950's had noticeably increased. Monroe's words coming from Washington sounded clearly triumphant.

Sterling had several members of the CFR sitting in his lofty New York office. He was using his new speakerphone to full advantage. "Good work, Galen." The other men echoed the praise.

"Thank you sir, thank you all. Without your support, it would not have been possible."

One of the men sat in shadow. The others, Sterling included, clearly deferred to him. He spoke in a quiet voice with the hint of a lisp. "You will continue to shepherd this project forward, Mr. Monroe?"

"Oh, yes sir, Mr. Director. I am receiving regular updates from my Congressional attaches and I consistently discuss it in my meetings with the President."

"Good. We wouldn't want to let any thing fall through the cracks, would we?" The Director steepled his fingers.

Monroe's voice hardened with steely resolve. "Oh no sir."

There was silence in the room for a moment, and then Sterling said, "Very good Galen. Continue giving us regular reports. We will sign off now. Goodbye."

"Goodbye sir and good day to you gentlemen."

Murmured assents sounded before Sterling cut the connection.

13: A Parting

1953 AD
Soaring Eagle, OK

Sunrise sat in the wheel chair to which she had been consigned for the last four years. A stroke had partially paralyzed her lower body but spared her mind, which was as keen as ever. "We all have a luxury most Cherokee don't have Phillip. We can afford to ignore the Termination."

"Thank Unetlanvhi for the wisdom that He has imparted to our family." Samuel leaned forward. "Yes, most of our people are not in our position. Nevertheless, my heart tells me you are right, son. The Bureau of Indian Affairs is trying to complete the work begun last century."

"Rosie can't afford to ignore them." Phillip looked pointedly at his father.

Samuel dropped his head briefly, and then looked up into Phillip's eyes. "Rosie has made her choices."

"Would you let them ship her off to California?"

"I have not been master of Rosie's life for many years, my son." Samuel ran a hand through his long gray hair. "She wouldn't hear me anyway."

Phillip sighed. "I know you're right, Pa. I wish she never married that guy."

Sunrise tapped her fingers on the arm of her wheelchair. "He took her down the wrong path and then got killed in a bar fight."

"I spoke with her back then about returning to the sacred way but she would not hear me. She was in so deep with the peyote church that her eyes were blind." Samuel rubbed his forehead briefly. "Her eyes are still blind."

"Did many Sioux get into the peyote thing, Pa?"

"I remember hearing that Lame Deer spent years in that cult but later abandoned it. There were others, too, but here in Oklahoma they made it an official non-profit church."

"And Rosie's a card carrying member." Phillip ran a hand over his face. "The whole Peyote Church thing came out of nowhere. No tribe had a tradition of worship that involved taking that cactus drug. I think some crazy Indians started eating those peyote buttons out in the desert and then invented a church." The young Cherokee shook his head. "They just want to get high, that's all."

"You may be right, son. The scary thing is that they use the Bible in part to give them authority." Samuel raised his chin and then turned his head toward the window.

The gravel crunched outside under the weight of an arriving car. Phillip strode to the window and peeked out. "It's Dorothy," he said with a grin.

"Should one that pregnant be driving?" Sunrise's brow knitted in concern.

"Aw, she's fine, Ma. I'll go help her bring things in."

Phillip sprang for the door and rushed outside. Dorothy had insisted on doing the grocery shopping for the family feast that they had planned for the evening. She carefully slid out from under the wheel and stood, rubbing her lower back. "Hawk, be a dear and bring the stuff in." She threw him the keys. "It's in the trunk. I've gotta go to the bathroom."

"Always a pregnant woman's priority," Phillip called out as she slipped inside. He quickly followed with arms full of groceries.

"Looks like some good eating is coming to visit," said Samuel as Phillip breezed by and on into the kitchen, stepping around James who was playing with Lincoln Logs on the floor.

"More on the way," said Phillip as he rushed back out for a second load.

Dorothy came into the living room and plopped onto the sofa. "I saw a couple of my Sac and Fox friends up in Tahlequah. I invited them over for dinner tonight." She looked over at Sunrise with a concerned expression. "I hope you don't mind."

Sunrise smiled. "Honey, your friends are always welcome here; you know that. Who is it?"

"Franky and Sue Ann."

"I haven't seen them in a while." Samuel pursed his lips and nodded.

"It will be good to see them dear." Sunrise reached over and patted Dorothy's hand.

Phillip swept by with more groceries. "That who all this extra food is for?"

"No, it's for you, Hawk With An Appetite."

Phillip's head popped out from the kitchen. "We'll need it all for the stomp dance later, huh?"

The room echoed with laughter as they planned a pleasant evening. It was a family dinner that Rosie would not be attending.

1953 AD
TULSA, OK

Phillip flew Rosie to California when the time came. The Mustang wouldn't hold her and her luggage so he rolled the Electra out of semi-retirement to make the trip. Jonesy made it his business to oversee the service on the classic aircraft and even offered to co-pilot for the flight. Phillip gratefully accepted.

Samuel relented for Sunrise's sake and drove his wife to Tulsa to see her off. He played the stern Oglala warrior to his wife's sorrowful mother. He stood aloof as daughter broke down in tears in her mother's arms as she leaned over the wheelchair.

"Ma, I don't know what I'll do there. I wish there were another way." She looked pleadingly at her father. Samuel's expression remained stony.

"They have a new Indian Center in San Francisco dear.

People of many Nations are coming there. You will have much help."

Rosie sniffed and stood upright. "Goodbye Mother." She looked at Samuel. "Goodbye Father."

The old Oglala's expression softened ever so slightly. "Go with God, daughter, and may you once again find the sacred path."

Dorothy and young James stood by Phillip. Dorothy held the new baby Sarah gently in her arms. James looked up at his mother. "Why does Aunt Rosie have to go away?"

Rosie dropped on one knee and smiled at the youngster. "Come here little Indian and say goodbye to your Aunt."

James ran into her waiting arms and buried his head in her hair. "I'll miss you Aunt Rosie."

She held him out at arms length. "Don't you worry, little Indian. Aunt Rosie will call you when I'm settled in. Maybe you can come and visit me sometime."

Phillip and Dorothy exchanged nervous glances at the comment. They never let James alone with his sister. It wasn't that she was irresponsible with their child. It was her friends who could drop in unannounced at any time. "When James is older perhaps he and I can fly out in the Mustang to see you, sis."

James eyes lit up at the prospect. "Oh yeah, Daddy!"

Rosie smiled at Phillip and rose to her feet. "I'll hold you to that."

Dorothy stepped over to Rosie and gave her a one-handed hug as she held onto the baby. "Goodbye Rosie." She stepped back and leveled a gaze at her. "Remember your Creator when the times get tough. He is always there for you."

Rosie dropped her head. "Goodbye Dorothy." She turned and boarded the Electra. Phillip and Jonesy followed her on board and the ground crew closed the hatch. In a moment, Phillip leaned out the pilot's window and waved. "Goodbye Dorothy, goodbye James and little Sarah and Ma and Pa." The small family group waved in return.

The plane fired up both engines and a short time later taxied down the runway. A lone feather borne on the plane's backwash flew back at Samuel and stuck to his lapel. It was black. Samuel held it up for Sunrise to see. "A crow feather."

"From your namesake, Shouting Crow."

Samuel shook his head. "I fear that Rosie may not be coming back while we are still alive."

Sunrise stifled a sob.

Phillip sat across from Walter Mullins as the morning Oklahoma sunshine flooded the office. "The Council on Foreign Relations was very emphatic. They want to charter our best plane and they want an Indian pilot. I told them that Oklahoma Air had the best. When they realized you were the famous World War II ace, they offered double." Mullins grinned at the Cherokee. "I'll give you the extra if you fly the stuffed shirts around for a week. What do you say?"

Phillip scratched his head. "Who is the Council on Foreign Relations and why do they want an Indian?"

"Public relations. It's good for their image." Mullins laid his arms on the desk and leaned forward. "Remember a few years back when that big wig from New York was looking for a driver?"

"Oh yeah. We sent Tom to him. He's been there ever since."

"Well, the big wig thinks that Cherokees are the best drivers around. That's why he wanted a Cherokee flier."

Phillip nodded. "So who's the Council on Foreign Relations?"

"It's some New York think tank."

"They sit around and think?"

"Yeah, then they put it all in a tank." The two men laughed.

Phillip stood and said, "Well, tell the Council that I'm their Indian."

Mullins looked down. "I, uh, already did."

Phillip grinned. "Why am I not surprised? When am I due in D.C.?"

"Um, eighteen hundred hours."

Phillip looked at his watch. "Holy mackerel, boss. That's just seven hours. I've gotta scramble a plane."

"It's waiting on the tarmac." Mullins paused for effect. "And Phil, it's a Connie."

Phillip's mouth opened slightly as he absorbed the information. Oklahoma Air had been fortunate to procure several Lockheed Constellation passenger planes about a year ago. They had used them to begin limited service to the West Coast. The route had become successful, as they were able to undercut national carriers who couldn't afford to specialize in a route from Tulsa. The Constellation was lithe and beautiful. The porpoise shaped body and the distinctive triple tail set the aircraft apart. It was sleek and fast and quite expensive to charter. It was also President Eisenhower's aircraft of choice.

Phillip fielded a crooked smile. "I guess these Council fellas are as important as the President."

"Actually, they advise the President on many matters." Mullins shook his head. "Mysterious bunch, though. They seem to make a point of staying out of the news."

"Well, let me call Dorothy. I won't be home for dinner, I expect."

Mullins pushed his phone towards Phillip. "Use mine."

Phillip gave his boss a wry smile as he dialed his home.

1953 AD
WASHINGTON, DC

"Oklahoma Air Flight 114 to Washington National Airport, requesting clearance to land."

A burst of static belched from the speaker and then a gravelly voice responded. "Uh, roger 114, you have been given priority. You are cleared for runway one nineteen."

"Uh, roger National, adjusting heading."

"Proceed directly to hanger L upon landing, 114."

Phillip raised his eyebrows. This was the real VIP treatment. "Roger that tower. Out." There was another burst of static and the radio went silent. Phillip looked over at his co-pilot. "This might be the most important charter we've ever flown, Alex."

"Yes sir. I don't remember getting priority clearance into D.C. before." The co-pilot reached for a control and made a minute adjustment.

"Me either, buddy." The Cherokee found the glide path and

proceeded to an uneventful landing. He taxied to hanger L as instructed where a ground man with signal paddles directed him into the hanger. A man inside motioned for him to power down when he had reached the parking spot. He quickly went through the shut down and hopped out of his seat with Alex right behind him. The ground crew already had a ladder in place and the hatch open.

A ground man stuck his head in the plane as Phillip approached. "Permission to come aboard, sir!"

Phillip grinned and said, "Granted mate." *That was one snappy anachronism.*

"Mr. Shouting Crow?"

"That's me," Phillip said.

"Glad you flew a Connie. A DC-6 won't fit in this old hanger, the tail's too big." The man looked back and forth between Phillip and Alex. "Name's Carl."

"Howdy Carl. This is Alex and I'm Phil." There were quick nods all around.

"Mr. Monroe and his entourage will be arriving by car momentarily. If you follow me, you and Alex can refresh yourselves and catch a bite to eat. Your party is expecting to depart within the half hour."

"Lead the way." The pilots followed Carl to a small but well provisioned cafeteria where they were instructed to eat their fill.

"No problem," Alex commented with a grin.

After a satisfying meal and a quick refreshment in the hanger's facilities, they made their way back aboard.

They found the passenger compartment already peopled with about twenty men and women. Phillip noted a tall man with reddish hair who stood with his back to them, conversing with an associate in the aisle. His companion motioned towards the pilots and the man turned to face them. Time seemed to slow for Phillip as he strode towards them. The hair on the back of his neck stood at attention. He didn't know how he could be here, but the Cherokee knew who was about to stand in front of him.

Phillip had spent much time exploring the Gawonisgi Nvya. There were amazing historical exchanges there, things totally hidden from man's recorded history, things that were more pivotal and important than the big flashy events to which man attached importance, things that changed the world, though the world knew them not. Phillip was deeply impacted by one final meeting that was recorded by his grandfather. The day that Galen Mondragon rode up to Thomas Banica and Soaring Eagle at Ross's Landing, his grandfather had the presence of mind to quickly enter the keystrokes for full recording. When Phillip first discovered the exchange, he had watched it a dozen times in a row, the snorting pawing horses filling his living room. The angle of view made it unmistakable. When Banica had confessed to following Jesus, Mondragon's eyes had darkened in a supernatural fashion. It was riveting and terrifying in an instant.

There was no mistake. The man facing him now was the one that Thunder Walking had named over a hundred and fifty years ago. His goatee was neatly trimmed but was an unmistakable hue. It was Red Beard.

"Captain Shouting Crow?" The tall auburn haired man smiled and extended his hand. "Galen Monroe. It's a pleasure to meet you. Thank you for bringing this fine Constellation on such short notice."

Galen. His name was Galen. Phillip ignored the extended hand. "Yes sir and you can call me Phil. This is my co-pilot Alex." His insides felt caught in some unknown temporal vortex but his face remained impassive in the typical stone like Indian response that he knew white men had come to expect.

Monroe's brow briefly furrowed as he slowly dropped his hand. "This is one of the last of the L-649's, isn't it?"

"You know your planes, sir. Yes, Lockheed is now producing the Super Constellations."

"Ah, the L-1049." Monroe sighed dramatically. "I fear the days of the Connie are numbered. The de Havilland Comet is a dramatic development." He lowered his voice to a conspiratorial tone. "And the new jet that Boeing is building is sure to revolutionize air travel."

Phillip nodded numbly. How does one talk to a man that is over a hundred and fifty years old? He glanced at Alex who seemed to not think anything was amiss.

"Well Phil, we're ready to go when you are." Monroe looked

expectantly at the Cherokee.

"Oh, yes sir. They've probably refueled her and we'll just have to run through the pre-flight. The itinerary I received shows the first stop is Rapid City."

"That's right; we want to visit with some friends on the Pine Ridge Reservation."

"Yes, well, I will notify you and the other passengers when it is time to belt in for take off."

"Very good. A pleasant flight Phil, Alex."

"And to you and your party, sir." Phillip turned quickly and disappeared into the cockpit. He didn't want to shake hands with Red Beard just then.

Phillip's hand shook slightly as he reached for the pre-flight checklist. Alex looked with concern at his friend. "You okay buddy? You look like you've seen a ghost."

Phillip looked at his co-pilot with a blank expression. "Maybe I have, Alex." He rubbed his eyes. "It was just a story my grandfather told me before he died. That man reminded me of someone from the time of the Trail." He looked quickly at Alex. "You know, that Grandfather told me about."

"Monroe? Seems like a nice enough fella. The goatee can look a bit creepy though." Alex sniffed and rubbed his nose. "You okay to fly?"

Phillip's insides had settled down as he came to grips with the situation. His hand was firm as he reached for the first control on the checklist. "Yeah, I'm good." He looked over at Alex. "Thanks for watching out for me."

"Hey, that's what co-pilots do, buddy."

They finished the pre-flight and were airborne shortly. It was the middle of the night when they landed in Rapid City.

14: A New Tomorrow

1953 AD
Soaring Eagle, OK

"**I** flew Monroe around America for a week. We visited the Lakota, the Nez Perce and Salish, the Navajo and Hopi, and the Oklahoma tribes, mostly the Cherokee." Phillip lay in bed next to his wife. It was the first time he had felt relaxed since he left the entourage back in Washington. "I don't know what they were doing, but it didn't feel good."

Dorothy laid her hand on Phillip's chest. "The Principal Chief met with him. He told me that it seemed like the man was searching for weaknesses, things that he could exploit."

Phillip looked at his wife. She knew the stories of the Stone almost as well as he did, and she knew the absolute truth of what he spoke. "That's exactly what Red Beard would do." Phillip looked up again at the ceiling. "All I can do is watch, Dove."

She leaned over and kissed him. "Watch and pray, Hawk." She reached over Phillip and turned off the light. The great shining that was the namesake of the Month of the Planting Moon stole into their room and enveloped them in an ethereal glow. Phillip enfolded Dorothy in a passionate embrace and their lips met.

"Phillip, there's a package for you all the way from England. Who could be sending something from there?" Dorothy handed the parcel to her husband who peered at it closely.

"It's from a publisher in London." He tore it open and a thin volume slid out along with a letter. Phillip quickly scanned the short missive and gasped.

"What is it Hawk?"

Phillip looked up in excitement. "Listen to this! 'Dear Phillip, It took me some time to track you down but at last I've found you. I wanted to share with you the fruit of some wonderful conversations we had together at a certain pub in London during the War. This is the first one I've written in what will be a series of children's books on the subject. Enjoy this and do tell me how you like it. Perhaps you have a young one by now with whom to share this book. Sincerely, C.S. Lewis.'"

Dorothy's mouth opened in astonishment. "The famous author you've told me about?"

Phillip nodded and looked down at the volume. "'The Lion, the Witch and the Wardrobe.'" Phillip looked up. "It's from the Chronicles of Narnia, stories about that land of talking animals he told me of."

James looked up from across the room. "Talking animals, Daddy? Can I talk to them?"

Phillip laughed and sat down. "Come here son. I think we all can." James climbed into his father's lap while Phillip opened to the first chapter. "Okay James, here we go. The first chapter is named 'Lucy Looks Into A Wardrobe.'" Phillip wet his lips and began. "'Once there were four children whose names were Peter, Susan, Edmund, and Lucy...'"

1957 AD
SOMEWHERE OVER ARIZONA

James was nine years old before Phillip could keep his promise. He had already flown many times with his father in the back seat of the Mustang, but now they were en route to California. It was early evening and James was peering intently upward through the clear canopy of the P-51. "Maybe we can see Sputnik from here Dad."

Phillip chuckled and pulled back on the stick. "Let's see if I can get us up higher and maybe we can. You'll need to put on your oxygen mask son."

James whooped as he reached for the mask. "That is cool Dad! Do you really think we can see it?"

Phillip tapped on the headphones he had just donned to remind James to put on his headphones and use the throat mic. "We could very well catch a glimpse if she's going over now." Phillip's voice was thin in the headphones.

James watched the sky overhead darken into evening. The stars began to shine and beckon. Suddenly he noted a small star that was moving rapidly. "Dad, what's that?"

"I think we have acquired the target James."

"You mean that's it? Sputnik?"

"That's the only star I know that could move like that."

"Wow Dad! That is so neat!"

Phillip glanced at the altimeter. "41,000 feet, that's the highest the old Eagle has flown since World War II."

"That is fantastic Dad! Thanks so much for this flight." James shivered as the cabin temperature dropped.

"Glad to do it son. Let's try one more thing before that Russian beach ball gets out of range." Phillip reached for the radio and began tuning. Static in the headphones suddenly resolved into a regular beeping. "That's Russian for, 'Hello imperialistic capitalists.'"

James laughed along with his father. "That's coming from Sputnik? That's amazing Dad."

The fleet star faded into the distance and the transmission became shrouded with static. Phillip tuned the radio back to flight control frequencies. "I guess the show's over, son." He reached into his flight suit and pressed a stud on Soaring Eagle's old Gawonisgi Nvya. *Glad I brought it along for that moment.* Phillip eased the stick forward and the Mustang began a graceful descent. In another hour, they were landing at San Francisco International Airport.

Strolling into the terminal, they looked distinctly out of place in their flight suits. They saw Rosie waving at them from down the corridor and strode briskly to meet her.

Rosie ran into her brother's embrace. "Oh Phillip, it's so good to see you. Thank you for coming!" Then she turned to James. "Who are you? Where is my little Indian?"

James laughed and ran into Rosie's embrace. "Oh Aunt Rosie, you know it's me."

She laughed and tousled his hair. "The Indian's not so little any more." She put an arm around the youngster and turned to Phillip. "My car's outside, come on." They all turned toward an exit and headed for the vehicle.

1957 AD
SAN FRANCISCO, CA

The neighborhood they drove into had a desperate starkness that hit Phillip like a cold fist. Everything was too small and too close together. Dangerous looking young thugs congregated under streetlights. The air was warm and humid. Police sirens sounded in the distance giving an eerie soundtrack to the darkness.

"We're not in Oklahoma anymore," said Phillip as he looked out the window.

James leaned forward from the back seat and spoke softly in his father's ear. "I don't like this place Daddy."

Rosie smiled over at him. "It looks worse in the dark. It's not that bad James, really. I'll show you tomorrow. We can visit the Indian Center. I've been telling my Native friends about you and they are looking forward to meeting you."

"Okay Aunt Rosie." James looked dubious.

They turned through a series of side streets and finally pulled into a driveway next to a small cottage. "Home sweet home. Come on inside guys."

Phillip and James followed her through the glowering humid darkness. They walked through the front door as Rosie flipped on the light. Phillip looked around without comment. The walls were dingy and the ceiling paint was peeling in places. What furniture there was looked thin and threadbare.

Rosie walked quickly into the kitchen. "Would you all like

something to drink? I have some real California orange juice."

James eyes lit up. "Oh yeah Aunt Rosie, I'll have some."

"I'll take an OJ too sis." Phillip sauntered into the kitchen being careful not to trip on the peeling linoleum.

Rosie handed two frosty glasses to the fellows. "There you go men."

James smacked his lips. "Orange juice doesn't taste like this back home."

Rosie laughed. "Well, it seems I have one thing that's better than Oklahoma."

"Yes Rosie, this is beautiful." Phillip nodded in appreciation.

"Fisherman's Wharf is more than just a little pier. How would you like to see the Maritime Museum, little Indian?" Rosie looked at James and cocked an eyebrow in his direction.

"Oh yeah, Aunt Rosie!" James face lit up with excitement.

Phillip extended his arm. "Lead on my sister."

Rosie led them to an odd ship shaped building. Inside were displays on the history of shipping in San Francisco. There was a section that highlighted submarines and Phillip recognized some models that were in service during World War II. "See that one, James?" Phillip pointed at one of the pictured subs. "I once helped one like that out in the English Channel during the war. I got radio traffic that a German destroyer was lobbing tin cans at the sub. I flew over and dropped a few eggs on the boat." Phillip grinned at the memory. "They quit bothering my friend after that."

James nodded. "Wow Dad, you never told me that one."

Phillip sighed and rubbed the back of his neck. "Well son, there's a lot that I'd rather forget. Seeing the old sub reminded me of that one."

"Were you flying the P-51?"

"Yep, old Soaring Eagle flew that mission."

They strolled through the museum's different floors and before they knew it, an hour flew by. "Well men, if we're done here I'd like to show you another sight." Rosie nodded towards the end of the longest nearby pier. "Let's walk out there."

"Okay sis, lead on." Phillip and James fell into step with Rosie as they made their way out over San Francisco Bay. At the end of the pier, she pointed at a lone island out in the water. "There's the most famous prison in America, the island of Alcatraz."

"You mean that's where the Birdman lives, Aunt Rosie?"

"Yep, that's the place, little Indian, and he's still there now."

"Wow, that's amazing."

The wind off the harbor was brisk and Phillip shoved his hands in his pockets. "Even Al Capone spent time in that place."

Rosie nodded. "That's right. Machine Gun Kelly was there too. If they ever abandon the place there are some of my Native friends that want to move in and renovate the old island."

James laughed and said, "Yeah, the real Graybar Hotel."

Phillip felt a cold chill of foreboding as he beheld the storied Rock. "There is great evil in that place." He closed his eyes and leaned his head back slightly. "Some of the worst criminals in history lived there and still do." Phillip was suddenly jarred with a vision of someone leaning against a railing. Behind it was empty black space. The railing gave way and the person plunged screaming into the darkness below. His eyes flew open and he took a step back.

"Dad, are you okay?"

Phillip inhaled sharply and looked at his son. "It's nothing James. I'm fine." He felt warned to not share the vision but seek its true meaning. He said nothing as Rosie gave him a piercing sidelong look.

15: THE SONG OF SHOUTING CROW

1957 AD
TULSA, OK

T he trip back to Oklahoma was quiet as both father and son mulled over the events of their journey. After a short while, James nodded off to sleep and stayed that way until they touched down in Tulsa. As they rolled into the hanger, Jonesy ran to meet them. He waved both hands in an emergency signal. Phillip quickly cut the engine and opened the canopy. "What's up, old friend?"

"You better come in the office right away. It's your ma."

Phillip quickly roused James as Jonesy rolled the portable stairs into place. Phillip and James scrambled down the steps and strode quickly to the office with Jonesy following. A secretary was standing with a phone receiver that she handed to Phillip. "It's for you, Mr. Wilson."

Phillip put it quickly to his ear. "This is Phillip Wilson."

The voice was faint at the other end but discernable. "Mr. Wilson, this is Dr. Foray at the emergency room of Tulsa Hospital. Your mother is here and has suffered a massive stroke. You'd better get here right away."

Phillip closed his eyes tightly. They all knew that it was only a matter of time. "I'll be there as fast as the traffic allows."

Phillip felt a hand on his shoulder and turned to see the sympathetic eyes of Jonesy. "Faster, Phil. I have a police escort waiting outside."

Phillip reached up and squeezed his friend's hand. "Thanks pal." Jonesy nodded.

Phillip and James rushed out to the car and followed closely behind a Tulsa police cruiser that had lights flashing and siren wailing. They made it to the hospital in five minutes. Phillip pulled the big Chrysler convertible under the emergency room overhang and jumped out with James following. They walked quickly to the check-in window and he said, "I'm Phillip Wilson and you have my mother Sunrise here."

"Yes sir, Mr. Wilson. Follow me." The attending nurse swept out from behind the counter and stepped briskly down the corridor with Phillip and James in tow.

The light was dim as they walked into the room. Samuel was softly chanting as he sat by his wife. His eyes were closed in communion with his Creator. Phillip laid a hand on his father's shoulder and Samuel looked up at his son. "I fear this is the end, young Shouting Crow."

"They can do amazing things these days Father. She could yet live."

"When the Lord calls you Home, who can deny His call?"

Phillip dropped his head and sighed. "Have you heard this call Father?" He raised his head to look Samuel in the eye.

Samuel held his gaze. "I have not heard what He speaks to Sunrise." He laid a hand on his wife. "I have heard what her heart speaks. She is weary of the chair." Samuel nodded toward the corner where Sunrise's custom wheelchair sat. "She wants to walk again. She wants to stand on her feet and run into the arms of Tsisa." Samuel rose to his feet and put a hand on his son's shoulder. "She can never do that here. She yearns to see the sacred tree in bloom with leaves that heal the Nations. She wants to see the hoop forever mended."

"You want to see these things Father."

"As do you, my son. All of the Native nations yearn for this. They express it in different manners and in ways that the Wasichus do not know or understand."

Phillip's eyes sparkled briefly. "You sound like another Grandfather I once knew."

"I think I've passed old Rick by a year or so now."

Phillip's expression grew serious. "Some among the Nations express this apart from the Lord."

Samuel's eyes dropped and he nodded. "Such is true, Phillip, and I do not have an answer for this."

All were silent for a moment and then James spoke. "Grandfather, you speak words of great wisdom. Let's all just pray for Grandmother."

Phillip chuckled at the pragmatic spiritual wisdom of his son. "Yes, let's pray." The family gathered around Sunrise and laid their hands upon her. A symphony of prayer ascended unto heaven in that time that made the angels take note.

Dr. Foray faced Samuel and Phillip with a puzzled expression. "Any serious impact from the stroke seems to be averted. In fact, she is markedly improved. There is an increase in sensitivity to her legs that she has not experienced in years. If it weren't for her advanced age, I would recommend muscle therapy to attempt restoration of the use of her legs."

Phillip laughed out loud and looked at his father whose face was wreathed in a smile. "Doctor," Phillip said, "we will work with her. Just tell us what to do."

"Very well. It will be difficult and you may only have limited success. I will get you with a physical therapist who will assist you." He looked at Phillip and then Samuel. "I do believe your God has heard you."

Samuel nodded. "He Who Is Forever Alive always hears. It is His answers that can sometimes be difficult to discern."

Phillip looked from Samuel to Dr. Foray. "This time we all heard His answer."

1957 AD
SOARING EAGLE, OK

Sunrise pouted and sighed. "Shouting Crow, I am eighty-nine years old. I will be happy just to stand. I don't need to run a marathon too!"

Samuel laughed and leaned back in his chair. "You are just like your grandfather. He used to call me by my Oglala name when he was angry at me too." He leaned forward and grasped his wife's hands tenderly. "I am ninety-two summers and I know we are both blessed with great health by our Creator. I just want our last years here on Turtle Island to be happy for you. Let's take a rest and we can try more later."

Sunrise's face relaxed in the glow of Samuel's gentle words. "Yes my Samuel. Here, help me over to the sofa and I can take a little nap."

Still strong, Samuel lifted his wife to her feet and she leaned heavily against him. "Put your foot forward dear." She haltingly moved one leg and then the other and then they were at the sofa. He gently let her down and she smiled up at him.

"Thank you my husband. Now go away and let me rest."

Samuel stood erect and smiled. "I will catch up on my reading."

The spider knew nothing of safety, only that she had chosen a fine place for her web. It was dim, but lit by one lone flame that had an uncanny way of attracting moths. She had already feasted on two and had a third bound and anesthetized in her web. She would be able to complete her purpose here and she glowed with that knowledge. Soon she could weave her great final egg sac that she would leave as evidence of her existence.

The small flame had gone out and her space was dark but still lit by the daylight that filtered in. She raced across her web to anchor a recalcitrant corner that had come undone. She was in danger of losing her bound moth as it swung perilously close to where the flame had burned.

When she had bound the moth, his struggle was great. In fighting to control him, she had cast her web string wide and it snagged a small sharp piece of loose wire. No matter, she could easily remove it when she was ready to dine.

A gust of breeze swirled in when one of the great beings out there quickly opened and shut the outside door. The bound moth suddenly swung into the spark wheel that was used to relight the pilot. In a freak occurrence, it caused a single spark, which briefly illuminated the area. The spider's multi-faceted eyes reflected the spark dozens of times before the accumulated gas erupted in flame.

Samuel was just closing the kitchen door when the stove exploded. The force of the blast propelled him backwards into the living room where he landed with a bone-crunching jar in front of the couch. His legs lay twisted beneath him at an unnatural angle. He looked up at Sunrise who was up on her elbows with terror on her face. "I cannot move, my wife."

She looked over and said, "Well neither can I Shouting Crow." Flames erupted from the kitchen and quickly advanced upon them.

Samuel closed his eyes briefly in pain. "It is a good day to die."

"Just when I was going to walk again."

"You are going to walk again." He smiled at her and suppressed his natural response to the wave of agony sweeping his body.

She beheld her lifetime lover backlit in red flame. "I love you, Samuel Shouting Crow."

The flames rapidly advanced and enclosed them with a deadly red perimeter. "And I love you more than you can know in this Momentary. We are fortunate Sunrise. We will stand together with the King."

Sunrise nodded as flames licked hungrily at the back of the sofa. She reached for her husband's hand. "We will always stand together, my husband."

"He comes for us with chariots of fire." Samuel tilted his head back and closed his eyes. He began to sing.

"Hey ya, Hey ya, hoka hey, my Grandfather
Hey ya, Hey ya, I will stand with you
Hey ya, Hey ya, I have walked the sacred way
Hey ya, hey ya, I will stand with you
By the Blood of my Lord Tsisa
I am cleansed of all my sins
With my woman here beside me

I am ready for the end..."

The cruel flames consumed the room. The death song of Samuel Shouting Crow was replaced with a roar of fire.

Stuart Blackfox conducted the service that honored Samuel Shouting Crow Wilson and Sunrise Wild Paw Wilson. The Cherokee descendents of the old Arkansas River Band had to remove one wall of the old community hall to accommodate all the people who came for the ceremony. Virtually the entire Sac and Fox settlement in Kansas had come along with almost the whole staff of Oklahoma Air. Cherokees from all over eastern Oklahoma added to the mass of people. Samuel and Sunrise were known and loved by many people.

Phillip had flown out alone to San Francisco in the Mustang. Rosie met him at the terminal and they flew straight back to Oklahoma. It was the first time Rosie had returned to her home since she had left. She appeared in a somber black dress and had a tearful reunion with her sisters.

A large contingent of Sioux from the Pine Ridge reservation also appeared. Walter Mullins commissioned two DC-3's to fly to South Dakota and bring back the friends and relatives of Samuel. Both planes returned with every seat full. The Lakota Sioux honored the deceased by appearing at the funeral in full tribal regalia.

As the flames had engulfed the room, Sunrise must have rolled off the sofa and into her husband's arms. When they were found, each had their face buried in one another's shoulders. Their features were remarkably preserved and there were able to be dressed in their finest clothing and appear one last time together. It took the better part of the day for all to file by the caskets and say farewell to friends. When the viewing was complete, the body of Samuel Shouting Crow was lifted from his coffin on a specially prepared backboard that was already in place. The body was carefully set on a low version of a ritual Sioux death scaffold. Eagle feathers fluttered from the corner posts of the structure as a solemn silence enveloped the assembly.

Blackfox stepped beside the scaffold and stood erect, a black Bible in his hand. He opened it slowly and leafed to a familiar passage. "Behold, I speak a mystery to you; we shall not all fall asleep, but we shall all be changed; in a moment, in a glance of an eye, at the last trumpet." His voice sounded in loud and victorious proclamation. "For a trumpet shall sound, and the dead shall be raised incorruptible, and we shall all be changed." Blackfox looked up over the crowd. He was a medium height Cherokee who wore his hair long and in traditional braids. One eagle feather fluttered from a braid. His face was stern but his eyes were tempered with the softness of wisdom.

Murmured assents filled the community hall and the field beyond. It was as a tribal gathering of old. The field was filled with warriors and chiefs and maidens and matriarchs. He took a breath and spoke. "Shouting Crow was adopted into the family of Soaring Eagle and faithfully lived his life as a Cherokee and a servant of the Lord Tsisa. But he was first an Oglala warrior, a friend of Gray Raven who fought the Bluecoats in another age." He swept his arm wide to embrace the scaffold beside him. "We honor Samuel Shouting Crow with this traditional Sioux death scaffold." He paused with a faint smile. "I doubt the BIA would allow the natural conclusion of this ceremony." Laughter rippled across the field. In Sioux tradition, the body was left to the weather until the platform and body were gone. "George Mountain Bear is a Lakota relative of Samuel Shouting Crow. Mountain Bear, come now and speak."

The old Sioux was as big as his name. He came to stand beside the scaffold as Blackfox stepped out of view. He looked sternly over the crowd as if searching for the perpetrator of this crime. Satisfied that the villain was not present he took a breath and raised his chin. "Shouting Crow was my relative. My father rode with him against Longhair and the Bluecoats in another century when the Oglala were a free and mighty people and the Black Hills were still our ancestral home. He came to you Cherokees bearing the vision of the Ghost Dance. You gave him much greater gifts. You granted him a vision of the Jesus Way. You adopted him as your own in a time when return to South Dakota would have meant almost certain death. You gave him a beautiful wife who was faithful unto death." He swept his arm towards the casket of Sunrise. "She gave him four beautiful children." He swept his arm towards Phillip and his sisters. "You Cherokees have been good to my relative. I say to you that we are friends forever, as long as the sun shall shine and the grass shall grow." He paused with a grim smile. "I say that as an Oglala Lakota, not as a Wasichu." There were murmurs and nods from across the crowd.

Mountain Bear stopped briefly and looked down. When he returned his gaze to the crowd, an Oglala fire smoldered in his eyes. "Today four of the Great Fathers from Washington rule the Black Hills. A Wasichu is building another mountain monument to Crazy Horse, from whom I am descended. Crazy Horse never allowed his picture to be taken and no one alive today has a clear recollection of his face. Whatever is being chiseled into that mountain is not him. Crazy Horse would never have approved of his beloved Black Hills being desecrated in this fashion." He laid his hand on the death scaffold and looked over at the body of Samuel. "Neither would Shouting Crow approve. He was a man who was always true to his people, both Cherokee and Oglala Lakota." He dropped his hand and turned to face the scaffold, bowing his head in prayer as he held his hands extended towards the body. "O great Waken Tanka, I thank You that You have received my brother Shouting Crow into Your Presence. I thank You, Lord that he now sits amidst the true council of elders. I thank You that his faithful wife Sunrise Wild Paw is by his side in Your glorious heaven." He turned towards Phillip and his sisters, hands still extended. "Bless his children and grandchildren that remain and reunite them one day in Your Glory. I speak this to You, oh great Waken Tanka, in the name of Your blessed Son; He whom my Cherokee brothers call the Lord Tsisa. Amen."

There was a great murmuring of "Amen" from across the crowd. Mountain Bear stood for a moment more with a hand on the scaffold, as if saying his last goodbyes. He then turned his back on the crowd and walked away.

The gathering lasted another week after Samuel and Sunrise were laid to rest. The Sioux had come prepared as a tribe of old.

They had packed an entire camp in the DC-3's and they set up tipis in the great field in the traditional circle. There were nightly dances around the great fire at the center of the circle in which Cherokee, Sac and Fox, and more than a few white men participated. It was a slice of life from another century reborn for a brief season in Eastern Oklahoma. One could feel the smiles of Samuel and Sunrise accompanying the festivities in their honor.

Too soon, it was over. The Sioux flew back to South Dakota and the Cherokee rebuilt the wall of the community hall. The Sac and Fox travelled back to Kansas and the children of Shouting Crow were alone again.

The family attorney from Tulsa travelled to Tahlequah and they had a reading of the will. The Wilson children were surprisingly well cared for by a sizable family trust. Apparently, Samuel had made some wise investments over the years. He and Sunrise had hidden the true extent of their wealth in order to present this legacy to their children. He also left them as joint owners of the 160-acre plot on the Arkansas River. In death, Samuel had fully reinstated Rosie as she shared a full portion of the estate.

They sat later in family council to plan the next steps in this new world devoid of their parents. Phillip rubbed his hands together and looked at Rosie. "There's no reason you can't move back here now Rosie."

"Yes," said her older sister. "We would help you build a house and a life here."

Rosie looked down. "There is much I have now in San Francisco. I can't just walk away. Perhaps someday, but not now."

Phillip felt a dark shadow cross his heart and briefly saw again the unknown person of his vision falling into a cavernous black space. He shook his head and sighed. "I wish you'd stay, but I understand. When do you want to go back?"

"In a few days when we're done our business." Rosie smiled. "And when I'm done getting all my hugs. That means you too my not so little Indian."

A much taller James smiled timidly at his aunt. "Not in front of everybody Aunt Rosie." Laughter rippled across the room as all remembered the awkward shyness of youth.

Phillip was leafing through the Washington newspaper that he liked to read. He wanted to keep track of the things that the media thought important. He knew better than most, however, that the media stories were not the most important stories. But he had learned to pay attention to them because they were often signposts that pointed to truly important things.

His eyes were arrested by a headline on page five. "New York Financial Titan Sterling Dies." The name tickled his brain. *Wasn't that Red Beard's boss?* As he scanned the article, he found the signpost for which he was searching. "Hey Dorothy, listen to this," he summoned.

His wife poked her head in from the next room. "Yes master, I sit at your feet and await your profound words of wisdom."

Phillip pouted. "No, you deserted your post. You're in the other room."

Dorothy laughed gaily. "Forgive me, my lord." She sat primly on the ottoman facing her husband. "Your servant awaits."

Phillip sighed dramatically and then broke into a laugh. "Oh my Dove, I love you."

"Flatterer."

"Did it work?" Phillip grinned.

Dorothy reached across and laid a hand on his knee. "Always does."

"Good. Haven't lost my touch."

"Don't push it mister." She looked sternly at Phillip.

He held up a hand. "Okay, truce!" He smiled at her and turned to the paper. "You remember that New York bigwig Sterling?"

"Bartholomew Sterling?"

"That's the one. Red Beard's boss." Dorothy nodded, her eyes widening slightly. "He died. Listen to this: 'The board of directors of Sterling Bank has appointed Galen Monroe to succeed Sterling. Monroe will continue his post with the Council on Foreign Relations, but will move back to New York to take over day to day operations of the bank.'"

"Red Beard sitting on a pile of gold. Sounds appropriate."

"Yes it does, and it sounds like he is positioned to do some real damage now."

Dorothy leaned forward and grasped her husband's hand. "Let's pray about this right now Hawk. You have seen a real danger."

Phillip nodded and the couple bowed in prayer.

16: Distant Thunder

1964 AD
Soaring Eagle, OK

W hile many Cherokee believers had gravitated to the Greco-Roman model of Christian fellowship and worship, the Arkansas River Band had always been different. The legacy of Soaring Eagle kept them operating in their Native expressions of worship. The deeper fellowship of Cherokee relationships made all of them like family and this bond strengthened everyone. Their structure was not hierarchal like the white man's church, but rather a council of peers who gained wisdom one from another.

When James started playing the acoustic guitar, Phillip encouraged him to incorporate it into the very rhythmic worship of the weekly gatherings at the community hall on the Arkansas River property. There were always two or three drummers and sometimes a flute player. James started getting together with these musicians and something unique and new began to happen.

By its nature, Native music often lacks discernable melody. James was able to introduce a completely new melodic thread to the music that had not existed before. They listened to emerging folk music and expanded their musical horizons even further.

Bob Dylan taught them the art of telling a story with a song. Peter, Paul, and Mary exposed them to exquisite vocal harmony. They began to incorporate these ideas into new songs that they wrote together, songs of praise to their Creator. They composed spiritual story songs that captivated the children. Even the elders nodded their heads in approval.

James was in his senior year of high school when something happened that changed everything. The music of the Beatles had already taken over the radio. Their harmonious toe tapping hits had a fresh new sound that was like nothing that came before. Then they came to America.

On a Sunday night, the Wilson family gathered around the black and white console television to watch the Ed Sullivan Show. They all waited with great anticipation until the moment when Sullivan said, "Ladies and gentleman, the Beatles!"

The lads from Liverpool exploded onto the small screen with "All My Loving," a current hit. Phillip leaned forward intensely as he watched. He nudged James and asked, "What are those instruments they're playing?"

James glanced at his father in amusement. "Dad, don't tell me you've never seen an electric guitar!"

Phillip leaned back and exhaled sharply. The instruments were of the same type he had seen James playing in the vision of so many years ago. "Electric guitar, of course."

"What Dad?"

"Nothing son. Hey, these guys sound as good as their records!"

"Aren't they great?"

James had largely learned flying the Indian way; he closely observed his elders. He had flown in the Mustang and the Electra with his father many times. He had flown with Jonesy in a DC-3 and even a Constellation on several occasions. It isn't often that a young man gets to observe two genuine World War II flying aces doing the job that they love best. As he advanced into his teenage years, he had asked his dad to give him formal flying lessons. Phillip said no. He knew that he would be too close to James to be an objective instructor. Instead, he recommended Jonesy.

His old friend gladly stepped into the role of teacher and turned out to be a patient and thorough instructor. James was a fully licensed pilot by the time he was seventeen. Mr. Mullins gladly took him on after he graduated high school, but started him on the ground crew. He wanted to get the measure of the man before he put him in even the co-pilot's seat.

James quickly proved himself a steadfast and reliable worker who could think on his feet. Within a year, he had advanced to crew chief and then to the co-pilot's seat on DC-3 flights. Phillip was pleased with his son's progress and had taken to occasionally allowing him to fly the Mustang on short local courier runs.

The old P-51 was a revelation to James. He stood on the Tulsa tarmac as he and Phillip surveyed the magnificent old fighter. "Dad, I can't believe how responsive that bird is. It makes a DC-3 feel like a bus."

Phillip laughed. "The DC-3 is a bus son. There aren't many larger twin prop planes that could keep up with a Mustang. The old P-38 twin engine could give it a good run but the P-51 still had a higher top speed even with one prop."

"Gosh, I wonder what a new F-4 feels like."

"The Phantom is a whole different animal. I've flown some of the older jets but I'm not qualified on the new fighters. I do know the F-4 will top Mach 2."

James whistled. "That is cooking."

Phillip looked over at his son. "The way things are going in Vietnam, the Great Father in Washington could be asking you to fly a Phantom."

James looked down as his brow knotted. "I dunno Dad. It seems like such a waste. Vietnam, I mean." He kicked at a pebble and looked up at his father. "If my country calls, I'll go."

Phillip put a hand in his son's shoulder and squeezed. No more words were needed.

The conversation turned out to be prophetic. About a month later, a Selective Service notice came ordering James to report for duty. After tearful goodbyes to Phillip and Dorothy, James set off for basic training. After basic, he was assigned to advanced flight school where he found himself learning to fly the F-4 Phantom. Too soon, he found himself flying missions in the skies of Vietnam piloting one of the most advanced aircraft of the day.

It was early December in 1967 that James received his honorable discharge. He had served America with valor, another in a sizeable list of Cherokees who had gone to war for the country. He had also been among the very few Phantom pilots that engaged in aerial combat and he had scored seventeen victories against Soviet MiG's. He joined his father and Jonesy in the elite company of fighter aces. The Christmas celebration that year was extra special as all in the family rejoiced that James had survived a deadly war.

1967 AD
ON THE ROAD TO TULSA

Phillip and James rode together in the big Chrysler that the elder favored. A Christmas shopping trip to Tulsa gave them much needed time alone. The weather had turned cold and a light snow was blowing as they motored up the highway. "They're building the new Muskogee Turnpike over there." He nodded out the window to his left. "It should knock a half hour or more off this trip when it's done."

James nodded but remained silent. Phillip looked over and knew his son's struggle. It was like that for him when he returned from World War II. "It helps to talk about it son."

James sighed and wrung his hands. "Napalm was terribly effective, you know. I lost count of the Vietnamese villages I destroyed with that weapon. They said each was a Viet-Cong stronghold. I just know I sometimes saw children running when I made my approach." He buried his face in his hands for a moment. "It was the hardest thing I ever did."

Phillip inhaled deeply. "One time I flew a mission over Germany. I was close on the tail of a Bf 109 and we were turning to starboard as he tried to lose me."

"A Messerschmitt?"

"Yep. Well, I had him in my sights when he looked at me and waved frantically. He held up a picture. It was a woman standing with two children in a park. He pointed at them and then placed a hand on his heart. I realized that was his family." Phillip gripped the steering wheel tighter. "I took my hand off the trigger and banked away." He looked briefly at James. "I never reported that incident and never told anyone, not even Jonesy or your Mother."

James nodded. "There were several times that I re-directed a strike away from children. I couldn't stand the thought of burning up babies, even if they were Cong."

Phillip was silent for a moment. "The secrets of war are just that. We'll keep this between us son."

"Yunno Dad, I never understood why you were so tight-lipped about the war. Now I know."

Father and son rode the rest of the way to Tulsa in silence.

17: THE ROCK

1968 AD
SAN FRANCISCO, CA

The year 1968 in San Francisco was a time and place like no other in the history of humanity. A confluence of people and events created a strange brew that delighted the young hippies and made the majority of their elders choke. Rebellion, revolution and rock music were laced with powerful chemicals, most of which were not fully understood. The frighteningly potent psychedelic drug LSD was still legal and flowed through the streets of the Haight-Asbury district like floodwater.

Rosie and a younger friend had gone to something called an Acid Test the previous evening. They drank of the free Kool-Aid offered by grinning hippies and had begun to groove on the music of a band named the Warlocks who were playing there. Gradually, Rosie found herself drifting into a world much like that of the peyote trance of the Indian church to which she used to belong. The effect intensified through the evening until she lost track of time and space. It was the middle of the next day before she came to her senses.

Rosie saw a long-haired fellow in a tie-dye shirt walking by and called out, "Excuse me, what time is it?"

He grinned in her direction. "Does anybody really know what time is it?"

Rosie rolled her eyes at the poor temporal humor and raised her chin towards his wristwatch. "Your friend by your hand probably knows."

The man looked in feigned astonishment at his wrist. "Who put that there?" He peered closely at the timepiece. "Hmm, it appears to be 2:00. That is, if you can believe a collection of Japanese gears." He grinned at Rosie. "I'm Wavy Gravy."

"Rosie. Thanks Wavy Gravy."

"It's okay Rosie. Was that your first trip?"

"Is that what happened?"

"Yeah, it was in the Kool-Aid."

Rosie stood and glared at the hippie. "No it was not my first experience, but I didn't ask for it and I was not prepared."

Wavy Gravy blinked in astonishment. "You've grooved on acid before?"

Rosie straightened to imperial height. "No. I am Cherokee and once belonged to the Peyote Church. What you do in jest was a sacrament to us."

"Oh wow."

Rosie shook her head. "You people need to understand the power with which you are playing." She shook her head and walked out of the building on Haight St. She waved down a passing cab and gave the driver her home address.

The great Indian looked down at her from far above. He was impossibly tall. He laughed and said, "Little Cherokee maid, what can you bring to me?" His voice reverberated from the cliffs that surrounded them.

Rosie was terrified but there was nowhere to run. To make matters worse, an insistent ringing noise was driving her crazy. She looked up at the great Indian. "Will you answer that?" He laughed and then reached his great hand down towards her.

Rosie awoke in terror, but the ringing phone quickly brought her to her senses. She reached over to the table next to the sofa where she had fallen asleep and plucked the phone from its cradle. "Hullo?"

"Rosie, were you sleeping?" It was the familiar voice of Debbie Wishflower.

Rosie yawned. "Yeah, but you rescued me from the big Indian."

Debbie was silent for a moment. "Do you still dream of him?"

Rosie sat up and rubbed her eyes with her free hand. "You know, I hadn't even thought of him for years. He was a part of my experience in the Peyote Church, but I left that a long time ago."

"So why now?"

Rosie sighed. "Me and Trish went to something called an Acid Test a few nights ago."

"Oh Rosie, you didn't. The Merry Pranksters put those on just to slip LSD to people in Kool-Aid. They call it Electric Kool-Aid. You didn't drink any, did you?"

Rosie was silent for a moment. "Both me and Trish did." She closed her eyes. "It was wild, Debbie. It is much stronger than peyote. It felt violent and dangerous."

"I've heard other people say that, too."

"I've had several dreams of the big Indian since then."

It was Debbie's turn to be silent for a moment. "Why don't you come down to the Center? There's someone here visiting that might be able to help."

"I'm off today. Might as well. I'll be down in an hour."

"Great, Rosie. See you then." The phone clicked off in Rosie's ear. She reached over and slid it into the cradle while she stared out the window beyond the phone. *I always hated that big Indian.*

"Rosie, this is Adam Fortunate Eagle. He has some ideas you might want to hear." Debbie briefly laid a hand on the arm of Fortunate Eagle. He stretched out his hand towards Rosie.

She grasped it and felt electricity. The young man was dashing with his short black hair and casual dress. He had an essence of concealed power, like a warrior of old. "Hi Rosie. How would you like to help me take Alcatraz for the Indians?"

She squinted closely at the man. He seemed the essence of sincerity. "Why should I do that?"

"To help all your Native brothers and sisters get free of the white man. He sent you here to San Francisco, didn't he?" He crossed his arms and looked her over closely. "I'd say you're from Oklahoma. Kiowa or Cherokee."

"Half Cherokee, half Oglala Sioux. No white blood." Rosie tossed her head imperiously.

Adam's eyebrows shot up in surprise. "You could only be a daughter of Shouting Crow. No other Sioux can claim that lineage."

"You know your genealogy."

"And you know how important my mission is. The Treaty of Fort Laramie from 1868 between the Bluecoats and your father's people..." He paused for emphasis, and then continued, "concedes all retired, abandoned, or out-of-use federal land to the Native people from whom it was acquired. The White Father's plan of acculturation has made us all one people. All of the land belonged to all of us. The Rock is retired and it's time it had a new life."

"And what would you do with such a worthless relic?" Rosie raised her left eyebrow.

"It could become a center for Native studies." Fortunate Eagle's face became animated as he unfolded his vision. "It could be an ecology center; a place where we could teach the white man how to take care of Turtle Island."

Debbie reached over and touched her friend. "This is real Rosie. We can do this thing."

Although she kept her face impassive, Rosie was impressed. There was a certain theatrical flair in turning the words of broken treaties against those who had made them. It sounded like some real good could come from such a venture. Rosie shook her head and looked at Debbie. "I'm getting too old for this sort of thing but, why not. Maybe it will scare the big Indian away."

Rosie and Debbie laughed, as Fortunate Eagle looked puzzled. Rosie turned towards him. "Okay Adam Fortunate Eagle. Meet your new warrior. Where do I start?"

He smiled broadly and reached forth both hands to enfold Rosie's hands. "Welcome aboard Rosie." He dropped her hands and turned. "Follow me," he said as he walked towards the next room. Rosie favored Debbie with a faux surprised face, then turned and followed the leader.

The voice on the phone was electric with excitement. "Aunt Rosie, I'm getting married!"

"Oh James, that is awesome news! This was so fast. Who is she?"

"Her name is Sally. Sally White Deer."

"Cherokee?"

"Nope. Sac and Fox. I learned that trick from my Dad."

Rosie threw back her head and laughed. "When did you meet her, little Indian?"

"It was only two months ago. I've never felt so right about anything."

"You work fast nephew. Congratulations! What do Phillip and Dorothy think?"

"They are totally excited. They love Sally. The best part is that she loves the Lord just like me."

Rosie remained silent. Her new activism had brought her in touch with Native traditions from across Turtle Island that were at distinct odds with the Christianity upon which she had been raised. Her late husband and the Peyote Church had separated her from the stern faith of Shouting Crow and the gulf continued to widen. Rosie took a breath. "That's nice James."

Now there was silence on the other end of the line. Finally James spoke. "Come back, Aunt Rosie. It's never too late, you know. The Lord Tsisa is always ready to hold you once again."

Rosie closed her eyes and sighed softly. James was so sincere and so right. She hated it. "James, I don't even know if there is a Tsisa."

James spoke softly and carefully. "He has always been there Aunt Rosie. He is the Creator's Son, this you know."

"James, I don't know anymore." Rosie tossed her head. "Listen; tell me when the wedding is happening."

"It's going to be in two months. Will you come, Aunt Rosie? I can come and get you in the Mustang."

"That old crate is still flying?"

"It's gonna fly forever. One of the best planes ever built. It's nowhere near as fast as the F4 I flew in 'Nam, but I can cruise going out to San Fran."

"Okay little Indian, I'll come."

"Let me call you when I get a flight time cleared with Dad."

"Okay James. And again, congratulations!"

"Thanks Aunt Rosie. Bye!"

"Bye bye."

Rosie streamed into the Indian Center with a smile on her face. Fortunate Eagle looked up from a planning table where he and a small group were standing. "How was the wedding?"

"It was beautiful, Adam. My brother sure knows how to keep Cherokee traditions alive."

"Isn't your brother a Christian?"

Rosie stopped and looked at him. "My brother and his family all believe in Creator and Tsisa, yes, but they are not a white man's Christian."

Fortunate Eagle nodded. "Okay Rosie." He looked away for a moment and then back at her. "I need your opinion on this plan."

Rosie set down her things by her desk and strode over to the table. They spent the rest of the morning fine-tuning the plan for the occupation of Alcatraz.

1969 AD
SAUSALITO, CA

The midnight fog in Sausalito was thick enough to swallow many dozens of Indians. They drifted unseen towards the city's waterfront. They quietly appeared at a dock in groups of two or three and were swiftly ushered onto waiting vessels. The invasion had begun.

The hair on Rosie's neck stood up as the Natives materialized from the thick mist as if from a distant past age. A gentle hand on her shoulder startled her and broke the illusion. "It's time, Rosie." She turned and followed the young Indian onto the last boat. In a moment, they pushed off and motored out into San Francisco harbor, swallowed in the fog. They held a steady course for about five miles, and then they were there. Alcatraz. Years of planning had finally paid off. The fledgling American Indian Movement had its first taste of victory. It tasted good.

By daybreak, hundreds of Native peoples from an array of different tribes all celebrated on Alcatraz. The tiny island that once housed the most desperate criminals in America was now claimed in the name of all Native Americans.

1969 AD
SOARING EAGLE, OK

The reports from San Francisco swept eastern Oklahoma like a raging wildfire. The occupation of Alcatraz became a top news item replacing the tiring tales of Woodstock that were still circulating through the area. Unlike that hippie festival, Cherokees could instantly understand this cause.

Dorothy picked up the phone after the second ring. "Hello?"

"Hello, is this Dorothy?" The female voice on the line was heavy with excitement.

"Yes it is. Who is this?" The voice sounded familiar but Dorothy couldn't quite place it.

"Dorothy, this is Lori, Lori Tenkiller."

"Lori! I haven't talked to you in years. Are you still in San Francisco?"

"Yes I am, and I'm sure you know what's happening here."

"Alcatraz. Are you responsible for this, Lori?" Dorothy smiled into the phone.

Lori laughed on the other end. "I wish I could say it was all my idea but that's not true. I did help and I'm part of the support team here in the city." Lori stopped and took a breath. "Listen, Dorothy, is Phillip there?"

"No, he's flying to Seattle today. He should be back tomorrow."

"Well, when he gets back, you be sure to tell him that his sister Rosie is on Alcatraz now. She was in the first group to go over."

"Wow, that's amazing! I guess there's no pay phone there for her to call us, huh?"

"There actually were, but nothing was working.."

"I will tell everybody, Lori."

"Thanks Dorothy. Be sure to tell them too that everyone is

welcome to come out to The Rock and join us."

"I will, Lori. Thanks for letting us know."

"Sure thing. Bye."

The greater Wilson family talked over the whole issue. Phillip had immediately felt urgency about the Alcatraz occupation and wanted to take everyone out there. Dorothy couldn't stand the thought of her teenage daughter walking upon such a dangerous island and all agreed that it was not the place for James' very pregnant wife. In the end, they agreed that Phillip and James would fly out for a long weekend and visit Rosie on Alcatraz. They sent her a message through Lori to expect them after New Year's Day.

They had to wait until the second weekend in January before the flight schedule of Oklahoma Air was clear enough to do without them for a few days. Father and son suited up to fly old Soaring Eagle out to San Francisco one more time.

"Just like old times, huh Dad?" James grinned at his father as they strode quickly towards the P-51.

"Yeah, except for one thing." Phillip's eyes twinkled as he looked at his son. "You drive, kid."

James laughed. "You're kidding, Dad! You never let me fly the Mustang when you were in it."

Phillip brushed off the comment with a wave of his arm. "First time for everything."

"Guess so." James grinned at his Dad and then they climbed into the cockpit. A few minutes later, they were airborne.

The flight was uneventful until they reached San Francisco airspace. "Hey Dad, wanna buzz Alcatraz before we land?"

Phillip laughed from the back seat. "We'll never hear the end of it from the flight controllers." He was silent as he gazed out the cockpit. "Go for it, son."

James let out a Cherokee whoop, banked to port, and began his descent towards the harbor. It was only a couple of minutes before a tired voice hailed them. "Tulsa P-51 this is San Francisco control, you are off course. Please adjust your approach."

James cleared his throat, glanced quickly over his shoulder, and winked at his dad. "Uh, roger control, we are experiencing some temporary navigational difficulties."

The radio crackled briefly in their headphones. "Roger Tulsa P-51. Do you require assistance?"

"Negative control. Please stand by. We should have the problem sorted out a couple of minutes." James keyed off the mic. "Just enough time to do a quick buzz around The Rock."

Phillip leaned forward nervously. "Better step on it son before they scramble an F4."

"Roger Dad." James kicked up the airspeed to just over 400 mph. "I know a few tricks to dump an F4 tail."

"Let's hope you don't have to use them." Phillip thought for a moment as the harbor came into view and then quickly shot a prayer into Heaven. It sailed forth on a course as sure as any warrior would have fired. "James, put me on with control."

"Roger Dad, you're on now."

"San Francisco control this is Tulsa P-51, Cherokee craft Soaring Eagle, bringing greetings to the Native population of the island of Alcatraz."

There was silence for a moment, and then the controller came back on. There was an excited babble of voices behind him. "Uh, roger Soaring Eagle, we read you five by five. Give them our best."

"Roger control. We will be setting course for runway five zero in a few minutes."

"Roger, Soaring Eagle."

Both Phillip and James let out Cherokee war whoops. "You read them like a book, Dad!"

"I know the climate here is very sympathetic to the Indians so it occurred to me to take the direct approach. Then I prayed and I felt sure."

James was throttling back as his dad was speaking. "I'm gonna bring her down to just above stall so we can circle the island a few times."

They were passing the dock as Phillip looked down. "James, look, there's Rosie on the dock."

"It is, Dad!" Both men waved at the dock and James waggled the wings briefly. After another circuit they headed back across the harbor.

The plane began a slow low circuit of the island as startled Indians looked up at the strange craft. Rosie happened to be on the dock when the P-51 drifted by. She looked up and screamed in delight. "Everybody look, that's my brother in his P-51." The great eagle head and the name Soaring Eagle were plainly visible. Rosie saw two figures waving from the cockpit. She jumped up and down and waved madly. "Phillip, James, I'm here!" In an uncanny answer, the sleek old warcraft waggled its wings. It made one more circuit and then turned away towards the airport.

1969 AD
ALCATRAZ, CA

Phillip and James stood in the bow of the charter boat that was motoring towards Alcatraz. It was a crisp sunny morning and both men were bundled up against the chill winds of San Francisco harbor. As they neared, they could make out jubilant Indians on the dock waiting to welcome new friends. They also looked ready to repel old enemies. Hastily painted signs proclaimed that this was now "Indian Property."

Rosie was waiting for them as they jumped onto the dock. She ran and gave Phillip a fierce hug. "Thanks for the air show, flyboy."

Phillip held his sister at arms length. "Hey, don't blame me. That nephew of yours was flying today."

Rosie turned and enfolded James in her arms. "Thanks, little Indian." She broke the embrace and looked him in the eye. "You have no idea how great that was for all of us."

"Yeah, we had no idea there was a Cherokee Air Force." A lanky young fellow had just stepped up and favored them with a toothy grin.

"Guys, this is Ron Waterfall," Rosie said. "Ron this is Phillip and his son James."

Ron looked at Phillip. "Son of Shouting Crow who rode with Gray Raven. Your fame precedes you."

Phillip favored him with a tight-lipped smile. "It sounds like my father's fame precedes me."

"Oh Phillip." Rosie pursed her lips at her brother. "We are all excited about heritage out here on The Rock, that's all."

Ron looked genuinely chagrined. "I meant no offense sir. I know that you are a greatly decorated World War II flying ace." He looked over at James. "And you are a decorated Vietnam flying ace."

"You see? He knows who you are." Rosie patted her brother's arm.

"Yeah, that's fine. Hey, why don't you and Ron show us around this miserable place?"

All laughed as they set off for a tour of Alcatraz.

The fire burned high and shot rivers of sparks into the air. The incessant rhythm of the Native drums demanded obedience from around the fire. It compelled each Native heart to synchronize with its sound until every heart beat as one. The dance around the fire followed in the wake of that rhythm like the blood that was pumped by each heart.

Phillip did not feel like dancing but James joined in for an hour or so. Finally, several groups broke off and drifted to the Warden's house where they gathered in the living room. Phillip and James followed. An excited discussion ensued when someone brought up Vince Elliot's book, "What Custer Didn't Tell You."

A young girl spoke up and said, "He writes that we must return to our roots; to our Native traditions. He points to Gray Raven of the Lakota as an example."

Phillip and James looked at each other. Phillip cleared his throat. "My father rode with Gray Raven against the Bluecoats." All eyes turned toward him with serious attention. Phillip looked over at the girl who was speaking. She nodded her assent to him taking the floor. Phillip stood and looked over the group. "I am Phillip Shouting Crow, son of Samuel Shouting Crow of the Oglala Lakota and Sunrise of the Cherokee. My father came to the Cherokee in 1890 to bring them the Ghost Dance." A surprised murmur circled the room. Phillip waited for it to die down before continuing. Out of the corner of his eye, he saw Rosie slip into the room and stand quietly in the shadows.

Phillip took a breath and continued. "While he was there the news of Wounded Knee came. All mourned the loss of Bigfoot's band. My father had nothing left in South Dakota, as all of his family was dead. He was adopted into the Cherokee Nation and lived the rest of his life as a Cherokee." Phillip stopped and looked around. There was total silence in the room as everyone was riveted with the tale. "My great-grandfather was Soaring Eagle. He walked upon The Trail Where They Cried. Before he died, he gave me a gift." Phillip reached down and picked up the small trunk that he had brought with him and straightened, holding it in front of him. "I call it the story trunk, because Grandfather told me to remember the stories of my people." He set the trunk down at his feet and straightened again. "Grandfather gave my father the greatest story that he knew and my father gave it to me. They called it the Jesus Way."

A tough looking young brave stood. "Bah," he said. "That is the way of the Wasichu, not the warrior."

Phillip smiled thinly at his opponent. "And you have learned such bullying from the Wasichu. A true Native in council allows a man to finish and then gives a moment." The young man reddened slightly and sat down.

Phillip used the pause to gather his thoughts before continuing. "Elliot writes of Gray Raven as he was. I knew Gray Raven as Uncle Rick." He spread his arm towards James. "Uncle Rick held my son in his lap before he died." Phillip looked over at James and then stepped forward. His voice rose in presence. "Gray Raven became a believer in the Jesus Way and lived his days in the work of his Lord. Yes, he still honored the ancient ways but he had a way of integrating them into his faith. He knew how to honor the Lord with the pipe." He looked pointedly at the young man who had challenged him. "And so I offer to whoever would hear, the greatest story ever told. If you would hear of this story and of Jesus, who we Cherokee call Tsisa, please speak to me or my son James while we are here on Alcatraz." Phillip looked around one time and then sat down. The room remained silent and contemplative for many minutes.

Phillip and Rosie walked alone on the severe shore of Alcatraz. Seabirds scolded them for their uninvited intrusion. Phillip had his hands thrust into the generous pockets of his parka while Rosie kept her arms wrapped around herself as proof against the cold.

Rosie glanced over at Phillip. "You made me think last night, little brother." She looked over at San Francisco sparkling in the cold sunshine. "Grandfather gave you something pretty special before he died."

"The story trunk?"

"No, his faith in Tsisa." Rosie skipped to avoid treading on a scuttling ghost crab. "It's been so long that I forgot how much this all meant to him. How much it meant to Ma and Pa."

Phillip was silent for a moment. "Do you know what happened when we took off with you for your move here?"

"No, what do you mean?"

"The feather of a crow was blown onto Pa's lapel by the backwash from the Electra. He picked it up and told Ma that they would never see you again in this life. That word was true."

Rosie brushed a tear from her eye. "I never knew that, Phillip."

"The Lord spoke that in his heart, Rosie. He didn't hear it from a Native practitioner."

Rosie nodded. "I know you speak the truth." She was silent for a moment. You know I've been having dreams of the big Indian again."

"It was the LSD, right?"

"Yes Phillip, but I was fooled. I didn't mean to take it." They walked for a long moment before Rosie spoke again. "Phillip, I want to come back to the Lord Tsisa. What do I need to do?"

Phillip stopped and turned. He grabbed his sister's hands and said, "Just pray to Him. You remember how. Pray and ask for forgiveness for your sins. Pray that He restore you to your highest calling. Tell Him you love Him. His ears are always open to your cry, Rosie. The Bible says, 'Draw near to God and He will draw near unto you.' Open your mind and heart to His Voice and expect Him to answer."

Rosie's voice got very small. "Will you pray with me, Phillip?"

Phillip smiled tenderly at his sister. "I have been waiting for years to pray with you sister."

18: Death and Life

"Ron, it's like I found something I lost a long time ago. Something that was precious and real." Rosie made a wide gesture as she faced her friend. "I wanted to bring you here to tell you." They stood on the third level of the main cellblock.

"Why here, Rosie?" Ron's voice echoed through the eerie silence of the storied detention center.

"Because this is what life used to be for me, a prison. I was in lockdown and didn't know that I had the key."

"And you just found the key?" Ron looked puzzled. "You talk in riddles, Rosie."

Rosie reddened and lowered her head briefly. "I didn't have the answers. I didn't know the reason for my life. Indian Relocation and Termination destroyed my sense of purpose." She shook her head. "What's a third generation from the Trail Cherokee doing in San Francisco, anyhow?" Rosie walked up and leaned on the railing. The dimly lit cells marched into distant darkness. Rosie looked out over the first level walkway where some of the most desperate men in American history had once walked. "My parents led me to the Lord Tsisa when I was just five years old. I had that the whole time I was growing up until I got married. My husband fell into the Peyote Church and I willingly followed." Rosie looked over her shoulder at Ron. "Willingly," she emphasized. She looked back into the darkness of Alcatraz. "I was forever estranged from my father after that. Only Phillip tried to stay close to me. Ma would call too from time to time, but Dad never let me back in the house."

"That's pretty cruel, Rosie."

"I had it coming, Ron. I was not nice to Shouting Crow the last time we spoke." Rosie shook her head. "I so regret that. I never said I was sorry and then they died in the fire."

Rosie turned and straightened, leaning back against the railing. "The point is this: the Lord Tsisa holds the keys to everything. As long as I held His hand, I could use those keys. When I willingly let go, I was locked out of the true meaning of life. I got locked out because of my own stupidity, Ron."

"Aren't you being a little hard on yourself?"

Rosie straightened and her voice rose in power and authority. "No, Ron, for the first time in a long time I'm being real with myself." Rosie tossed her head. "I'm telling you this because you can have it too. You and I, all of us here on The Rock, are flawed beings. We all sin; we all fall far short of the glory of the Creator. All we have to do is admit we are wrong, that we have sinned. You see, the Lord Tsisa died on a Cross and rose again to pay the price for all our foolishness. All we have to do is accept that fact as true truth in our own hearts and confess that we have sinned. Then we turn our back on that sin. They call it repentance but it's like doing an about face and walking away from what you were, into what you are supposed to be. Only then can you claim Tsisa as your Lord."

Ron was silent and then they heard approaching footsteps. Phillip appeared out of the shadows. "She speaks the truth even better than I, Ron." He nodded approvingly at his big sister.

Rosie leaned back against the railing again and suddenly, Phillip recognized what he was seeing. It was the vision of years ago, the vision of someone falling to their death. Without warning, the railing screeched loudly and gave way into the gloom. Rosie pitched backwards with a terrible scream.

Phillip saw the whole scene unfold as if in slow motion. He fought against the inertia of dusty centuries to bound forward and reach Rosie. He saw in his right periphery that Ron was also diving in her direction. James had been right behind him and he heard his giant thudding footsteps straining to reach her. Rosie seemed suspended in air just beyond their grasp surrounded by the broken metal piping that had been the railing. Her face was a mask of sudden life-wrenching terror.

Phillip landed on his stomach as he stretched out towards his sister. For the briefest fraction of a second, his fingers touched Rosie's, and then she was gone with a mind-rending scream that was silenced by a sickening thud punctuated by the clanging of the railing piping skittering across the concrete floor. "Rosie, no," Phillip screamed out. "No! No!"

"Dad, let's get down there. Ron, go get some help." James was already bounding down the stairs by the time Phillip and Ron got to their feet. They all made it to the first level in seconds. Ron ran for the exit yelling, "Help! Help! Rosie has fallen, help!" His voice faded into the evening as he ran for the ever-present night fire.

James was already kneeling by his aunt when Phillip skidded to a stop and fell to the floor by his sister. She lay on her back with her limbs at impossible angles. A pool of blood that looked black in the dim light was spreading from her head on the floor. Her eyes were open and a half-smile was on her face. James was already feeling for a pulse. He looked at his father with stricken eyes and shook his head from side to side.

Phillip let his head back and screamed in grief. "Oh Lord Jesus, why?" He broke down into desperate tears and his head fell down onto Rosie's body. James broke into tears and put his arm around his father. The large group of Indians that came running found them this way just a brief moment later.

Rosie saw the faces of Phillip and Ron recede from her like a poorly filmed movie scene. They got so small so fast and she couldn't stop screaming. She briefly felt a blinding pain that vanished instantly, as she seemed to bounce off the floor and float above it. She heard the yells of Phillip and James and then their grief stricken faces were above her. Suddenly they froze in time or timelessness. A diminutive creature materialized beside her. "Your brother is such a good person. If only he would learn to listen."

Rosie found that she could sit up even though suspended in

air. "Who are you?"

"Oh, I have been called many things. Let's just say that I am a messenger."

"A messenger from whom?"

"A messenger from the one you call Tsisa, the Very Son of God."

It seemed to Rosie as if her comprehension were expanding. It was as a great tsunami washing through her entire intellect and unlocking hidden backwaters. "You are of the Little People, the Yvwi Tsunsdi. You have been the guardians of the Cherokee through untold ages."

The small little creature suddenly sparkled with a golden glow and morphed into a huge winged humanoid. "Yes Rosie and I have come to take you Home." He held out his hand and she grasped it with all her strength. The creature smiled at her and then looked up. They suddenly rocketed through the ceiling as if it wasn't there. They flew beyond the sunrise and into shining black space. Rosie looked down and saw the vast Milky Way beneath them.

All at once, they were before a gleaming open portal. A golden glowing figure stood in the shimmering dimensional doorway and spread forth his arms. "My Father has put you into My Hands and no one can snatch you from them. Welcome Home, Rosie."

She fell into the arms of Tsisa and closed her eyes in rapture. When she opened them, she saw over His shoulder the forms of her mother and father waiting with smiles to greet her. "I am Home," she breathed.

The news of Rosie's death rocked San Francisco and mobilized many people into action. Sympathetic mourners came to the island to lay wreaths at the site of her demise. A large contracting firm sent a team to Alcatraz to repair the railing and do a safety inspection of all railings, making additional repairs where needed. A disk jockey set up a memorial fund for Rosie and solicited donations to go to the physical needs of the Indians of Alcatraz.

Phillip was shattered by the death of his sister. He had seen the vision that could have saved her but he never implemented it. He felt responsible for losing her and could see no resolution. He was sick with grief.

He sat on the edge of the dock at Alcatraz and watched the Police boat approach. A team of investigators was coming to the island to reconstruct Rosie's death. They had to be sure there was no foul play and the word of a few Indians was insufficient proof of that. The detective that had visited shortly after the tragedy had asked that all who were involved stay on The Rock until they were questioned. His words had the steel edge of authority.

James walked up and stood by his dad. "They should be here in about ten minutes." Phillip nodded, saying nothing. James sat down next to him. "There was nothing you could do, Dad."

Phillip slowly turned his head and looked darkly at his son. "Nothing I could do? I could have prayed to the Lord for a clear interpretation of my vision. I could have paid attention to my vision and integrated it into my thinking. I could have been looking for a situation that fit its criteria so I could respond before it was too late." Phillip looked back out over the water. The Police boat was noticeably closer. "Instead I just filed it away as a curiosity, an object of wonder but no value."

James was silent as he absorbed the words. When he spoke, his voice was small so that Phillip had to lean over to catch all the words. "Maybe that's the first lesson the Lord wants us both to learn. Maybe that would make this tragedy less senseless."

Phillip dropped his head down and wiped his eyes. James placed a strong hand on his father's shoulder and squeezed. He could feel the vibration of his dad's weeping.

The questioning lasted through the afternoon and in the end all could tell the detectives were satisfied that the death was accidental. Phillip and James immediately prepared to leave the island and head for the airport. As they waited on the dock for their boat, Ron walked over and shook both their hands in a strong two-handed grip. His face was lined with grief as he searched both of their eyes for answers. He sighed deeply and then spoke. "I wanted you both to know that those last things that Rosie said to me made sense. A lot of sense. I've heard

Jesus Way talk all my life but no one explained it in that manner before." He stopped and looked down. "I want to do what she said. You know, repent." He looked back up. "I don't know how. It was like someone didn't want Rosie to tell me the rest." He shook his head.

Phillip and James looked at each other. James eyes widened as he absorbed the impact of Ron's words. Phillip gave a barely perceptible nod to his son, who turned back towards Ron. "God is there and not silent, Ron. His ears are always open to your cry. He sent His Son, the Lord Tsisa, to die for your sins, for my sins." James spread an arm towards his father. "For my Dad's sins." He had to stop for a moment to hold back the tears. "For my Aunt Rosie's sins. If you can believe in your heart that Jesus, the Lord Tsisa, died and rose from the dead to pay the price for you; if you can acknowledge that you have sinned and you repent or turn away from those sins, and if you can tell this all to Him, you can be saved."

"How do I tell Him?"

"Here, I'll get you started. You pray to Him like this..." James laid a hand on Ron's shoulder. "Dear Father in Heaven, my Grandfather, I come to You now and would speak with You. Hear me now Grandfather, for I am poor and lowly. I thank You for Your grace in receiving me and I bring my friend Ron to you now, Lord. He would like to speak with You."

Ron bowed his head instinctively and breathed deeply. "I have heard of You, Grandfather, and of your son whom the Cherokees call Tsisa. I want to believe in You and in Him, Sir. Please show me how." Ron was silent and then raised his head with eyes still closed intently. "Yes, Lord, I believe; help my unbelief." Ron breathed deeply again. "I believe in You, Lord Jesus. I confess that I have sinned. Please clean me up. I turn away from the sin and turn to You. Thank You Lord!" Ron opened his eyes and looked at James in amazement. "He spoke in my heart. I heard Him!"

"Praise God, Ron!" The three men broke into excited laughter. "Ron, there's one thing you can now do. You can be baptized in water to show your obedience to the Lord."

"Go to water?" Ron pointed to the harbor licking at the dock.

"Let's go!" With that, he peeled off his jacket and jumped in the chilly water.

James grinned at his dad as he peeled off his coat. "Never done it this way, but there's a first time for everything." With that, he jumped in beside the treading Ron and came up sputtering with the cold. He swam behind Ron and said, "I'm gonna duck you under once real quick. When you come back up, it's just like Jesus coming forth from the grave. You get it?" Ron nodded. "I immerse you in the Name of Unetlanvhi, the Lord Tsisa, and the Holy Ghost." He reached up, ducked Ron's head under, and brought him back up. "You are a new creation, brother. Now let's get out of this freezing water." Both men laughed as they swam for the ladder.

Some Indians on the docks had run for some towels and came hurrying back with several that they distributed to the wet men. "You better get inside and dry off, guys," said one.

"Go ahead, I'll hold the boat here," Phillip said.

James and Ron laughed and ran into the structure by the dock. They found the men's room, peeled off the wet clothes, and pulled on some traditional Sioux garb that the helpful Indians had handed them. As they dried their hair further with the towels, James looked at the new convert. "Where are you from, Ron?"

"I live in Horton, Kansas."

"Kickapoo?"

"Yep."

"Wow, both me and my Dad married Sac and Fox ladies. Their tribal headquarters are near you in Reserve, Kansas."

"Yeah, I knew that. Rosie told me. She loved to brag on you two fighter aces."

"Listen, Ron, do me a favor when you get back to Kansas. Check out the Sac and Fox Christian Fellowship in Reserve. It's important that you have fellowship with other believers, and those are some of the best. They respect Native traditions and don't try to turn you into a white man."

"I've seen their place when I've been through there. I'll do it."

"Tell them James Shouting Crow sent you."

Ron nodded as they gathered their wet things and returned to the dock. James flagged down the Indian who gave him the clothes. "Where do I send these when I get back, brother?"

He waved his hand and looked him up and down. "They fit you better than they do me. Just save them for the next time you visit Pine Ridge."

Phillip looked closely and finally recognized him as one of the many Lakota he had met in that place. "Yeah, I remember you! George, right?" The Sioux nodded. "Thanks a lot." They exchanged a hearty handshake and then James climbed aboard the waiting boat.

1970 AD
SOARING EAGLE, OK

Phillip remained morose and uncommunicative until Sally gave birth to his first grandson. The night of the birth broke something loose in the man and he wept for a long time in his wife's arms. He alternated between the deep wrenching sorrow over the loss of his sister and the joy over the birth of his grandson.

Dorothy stroked his head as Phillip's shoulders shook. "Oh Hawk, my gentle warrior. What would I do without you?" She raised his tear-stained face gently between her two hands. "Do not worry my husband. The Creator does nothing by accident. This you know." Phillip sniffed and nodded. "He never stopped loving Rosie and He used you to return her to Him. She is now rejoicing with Shouting Crow and Sunrise in a place of no pain and no tears." Dorothy tossed a lock of hair back that had fallen in her eyes. "It could be that there was nothing you could do to save her. Perhaps Creator loved her so much that He brought her Home."

Phillip nodded. "You comfort me, my wife. You soothe me like your name, Running Water."

"And now we have a grandson."

"Yes, and I must hold him upon my knee. Perhaps Unetlanvhi will give me a word for this small Cherokee the way Gray Raven spoke over James."

"And Soaring Eagle spoke over you."

Following what had become family tradition, James and Sally did not tell their elders the name of the baby boy. When he was about a week old, they visited Phillip and Dorothy with the infant. Phillip motioned for Sally to bring him the newborn. Grandfather Phillip held the baby up for a close inspection and then set him in his lap. Sally hovered nearby and Phillip smiled at a distant memory. "Child, I have the little one and I will not drop him. I promise."

Sally chuckled. "Thank you Grandfather. I will sit down now."

Dorothy covered her mouth with her hand to hide her grin. She looked over at Phillip with mirthful eyes. He winked at her.

He turned his attention to the babe and closed his eyes briefly in prayer. His brow furrowed as he communed with his Creator. When his eyes opened, they were filled with thoughtful wonder. "His name is Luke, for he will be a healer. The apostle of the same name was a physician. This Luke will heal with the Song." He looked over at James. "Like his father, he will be a Son of Thunder!"

"Father, that is amazing," Sally said. She brimmed with excitement. "That is the exact name that we had decided upon." She looked over at James with a huge smile. "When James told me how Gray Raven had named him, I couldn't believe it. Now you have done that very thing. Praise the Creator!"

Phillip laughed. "Just be glad we're not out in Oglala country. They would make us act the whole thing out."

They laughed together and began talking of Luke's future. The little guy was passed from lap to lap until he fell asleep in exhaustion.

On July 8, 1970, President Richard M. Nixon addressed Congress in words that showed the Indians of Alcatraz that the Great Father in Washington was listening to them. It told them that their actions had achieved something beyond what they had dreamed.

"The first Americans - the Indians - are the most deprived and most isolated minority group in our nation. On virtually very scale of measurement - employment, income, education, health -

the condition of the Indian people ranks at the bottom.

"This condition is the heritage of centuries of injustice. From the time of their first contact with European settlers, the American Indians have been oppressed and brutalized, deprived of their ancestral lands, and denied the opportunity to control their own destiny. Even the Federal programs which are intended to meet their needs have frequently proved to be ineffective and demeaning.

"But the story of the Indian in America is something more than the record of the white man's frequent aggression, broken agreements, intermittent remorse and prolonged failure. It is a record also of endurance, of survival, of adaptation and creativity in the face of overwhelming obstacles. It is a record of enormous contributions to this country – to its art and culture, to its strength and spirit, to its sense of history and its sense of purpose."

The President was forthright in exposing the Congressional agenda: "As recently as August of 1953, in House Concurrent Resolution 108, the Congress declared that termination was the long-range goal of its Indian policies. This would mean that Indian tribes would eventually lose any special standing they had under Federal law: the tax-exempt status of their lands would be discontinued; Federal responsibility for their economic and social well-being would be repudiated; and the tribes themselves would be effectively dismantled."

Nixon took an opportunity and turned it to the benefit of all Native peoples. The twin deadly policies of Relocation and Termination received a mortal wound that day. The administration went on to introduce twenty-two legislative proposals that supported Indian self-determination. Perhaps President Nixon was atoning for the years he spent as Eisenhower's Vice President in the era when the Termination policy passed into law and Indians from across America were dislocated and separated from their heritage.

If the occupation of Alcatraz did one good thing, this was it. There was still, however, a long dark road ahead for the Natives of Ameliquo and the words of the President could not fully derail the momentum of centuries of hate.

19: BURY MY HEART

1972 AD
NEW YORK, NY

Galen Monroe strode back and forth before the window of the office high atop New York City. Bartholomew Sterling was a distant memory and he now occupied this place of power. A city much larger than Washington lay before him. "Nixon would not listen to me. He felt guilty about abolishing the gold standard so he had to have pity on the poor Indians. He would not understand how both policies were necessary."

"The President will be consumed by his own hubris, sir." The advisor that answered Monroe bore an uncanny resemblance to the chancellor of one Romanian Prince of another century.

The likeness was not lost on Monroe. Indeed, it had been a convincing factor in the man's employ. Although he was clearly a contemporary American, the hint of Romanian ancestry hung over the man like a clinging perfume. "It matters little." Monroe waved dismissively. "The BIA is still in place and its policies are not so easily dismantled." He sat down and faced the man across the desk. "Perhaps you should go and speak with our friends in the Bureau, Warren. Encourage them that our goals have not changed."

"A wise idea, sir. I will travel to Washington in the morning and speak with the Director."

"Excellent," Monroe said. He turned to gaze again over New York as his associate slipped quietly from the room.

The book "Bury My Heart at Wounded Knee" by Dee Brown was published during the Alcatraz occupation. Some saw President Nixon's pro Indian policies as a response not only to Alcatraz but also to this deeply moving and meticulously researched volume. In many ways, it fueled a future action at its namesake. For Natives from across Ameliquo, Wounded Knee had become the center of their struggle to regain what was rightfully theirs.

The great Oglala Teton Sioux Chief Red Cloud had once chased the Wasichus from the Black Hills. In the end, he sat conquered at Pine Ridge where he died in 1907 and is now buried. He said this in his old age of the white men: "They made us many promises, more than I can remember, but they never kept but one; they promised to take our land and they took it."

1973 AD
WOUNDED KNEE, SD

"Nixon's words meant nothing. Look what's happening to him. Liddy and McCord are going to prison and there's more heads on the chopping block." Sporadic gunfire could be heard in the background. "Nixon lied to us just like the Wasichus have always lied."

"George, I think he meant what he said. Legislation was passed into law. It's those who are supposed to uphold that law that are lying." James cradled his forehead in one hand as he held the phone close to his ear with the other. "They are Bluecoats of today and they are acting like it."

"Well, we foxed them this time. We took over Wounded Knee and ran them off without their guns. When they saw our position, they knew they couldn't storm it. The free Oglala Nation reigns at Wounded Knee, South Dakota."

George Gray Feather was a passionate supporter of the American Indian Movement. Ever since he had given his ceremonial clothes to James at Alcatraz, the two had stayed in close touch. George had made another triumphant call to James just last December when AIM had occupied the Bureau of Indian Affairs building in Washington, DC. The new Wounded Knee standoff, however, had a much graver tone. Both sides were heavily armed.

"George, please consider now what I have told you before. Open your heart to your Grandfather and my Grandfather and to His Son."

A few more shots were heard before George spoke. "I know you are right my brother. I do not fear the Wasichu but I do want a sure path across the Milky Way if I must die here." George sighed. "I know what you did with Ron and I know it was real. I don't know how much longer the Bluecoats will allow our phones to stay on, so why don't you teach me how to pray?"

James raised his head and smiled. "I will, brother. You have to talk to the Grandfather and tell him you are sorry…"

Phillip and James stood together as warriors of old on the Pine Ridge Reservation. Phillip wore Cherokee garb and James wore the Oglala Lakota ceremonial clothes that George had given him back on Alcatraz. "George always told me to save this until I visited Pine Ridge." James mouth was set in a grim line. "I never thought it would be in the midst of an armed uprising."

A mile or so away, the sky was lit up in a lurid pink by the flares fired by the government forces. Occasional gunfire announced the earnestness of confrontation. An acrid gunpowder flavored breeze ruffled their hair as approaching headlights flared in their faces.

"James, get off the road now!" Ever since the death of Rosie, Phillip had operated at a heightened perception that bordered on paranoia. This time, however, the warning was real. As they dove for the bushes by the roadside, shots rang out from the passing vehicle.

The car skidded to a halt and doors opened. "There's more of them Injuns. They're over there, c'mon boys."

Phillip and James faded silently into the sparsely wooded plot behind them until they had a hundred yard lead on their pursuers.

"Aw Jake, you sure they went this way? Ain't no sign of Injuns here."

"All right, let's head back. We'll find 'em." The heavy boot treads of the self-appointed executioners backtracked to their car. Doors slammed and the engine revved as they roared away in the night.

Both Phillip and James had enough wartime experience to remain still and silent for some time. After perhaps twenty minutes had passed, James heard the soft call of a whippoorwill. He chuckled softly and whispered, "No whippoorwills in South Dakota, Dad."

Phillip materialized at his side and laid a hand on his shoulder. "I think the locals are out of control, son."

"And I think you were hearing from the Lord, Dad." James felt an answering squeeze on his shoulder. "Are we ready to penetrate the perimeter, Colonel?"

"We're ready now son." Both men wore full packs filled with foodstuffs to smuggle into Wounded Knee. "Let's move out."

They stayed in the brush and crossed the mile that separated them from the government lines. They probed several spots until they found a sleeping sentry and slipped by into free Oglala country.

As they approached the Lakota perimeter, they stopped and lay flat. "Hoka hey," Phillip called out in a stage whisper.

They both suddenly felt gun barrels in the back of their heads. "Hoka hey yourself. Friend or foe?"

Phillip spoke in the Oglala Sioux dialect he had learned from his father. "I am Phillip Shouting Crow and my son James Shouting Crow. We have come from Oklahoma with supplies."

The gun barrels were instantly withdrawn and friendly hands helped them to their feet. "Phillip and James, you are both well known here," a voice replied in English. "Welcome to the Free Oglala Nation. Come on brothers, follow me."

They walked into the center of town and were greeted warmly by Lakota who looked more like freedom fighters than Indians. Many carried guns and wore extra ammunition. They had serious expressions filled with gritty determination.

George suddenly appeared and ran up to James. He enfolded him in a fierce bear hug. "You've come, my brother. It's great to see you!" He held him at arms length. "You're wearing your Sioux skins too." He turned to Phillip and gave him a two handed handshake. "And you, Elder Philip. Welcome."

"Thanks George," Phillip said. His voice rose slightly. "And thank you, all of you. We bring greetings from the Cherokee."

A great chorus of approval went up from the assembled Sioux. "Hoka hey," many of them shouted. They moved into a large building that they used as a meeting place. Phillip and James distributed the goods they were able to smuggle in and they spent hours bringing the occupiers up to date with what the world thought of their struggle.

The morning dawned clear as the sporadic firefights continued between the government forces and the Indians. There were some three hundred armed people surrounding Wounded Knee made up of everything from U.S. armed forces to State Police. They were grimly determined to put an end to this uprising in whatever way they could but the Sioux position was strong. It would require overwhelming force to conquer. The court of public opinion would crucify them for using such force so they bided their time and continued to contain the Sioux.

Behind Oglala lines, the situation was becoming grim. Friends continued to smuggle in a trickle of supplies but the authorities had cut off all power to the town. Campfires and oil lamps were the only proof against the night that was available to them. Phillip and James had a plan, however. They were going to cross the lines back out of Wounded Knee and return to the nearby motel where they had rooms. There they would change into their dress war uniforms and confront the commander of the siege. They would demand physical relief for their friends. The Sioux were enthusiastic with the plan.

That night, they slipped back and made it to the motel without incident. In the morning, Colonel Phillip Wilson and Major James Wilson drove up to the blockade in a rented black sedan. They popped out, demanded to see the commander, and were deferentially led to his presence.

"Colonel, Major, to what do I owe the honor of your

presence?" The commander eyed their decorated chests and missed their Native features. This was part of the plan.

Phillip spoke first. "We are veterans of two wars and we feel this blockade is dishonorable. We would like you to grant food and clothing to those inside your perimeter."

The commander leaned back. "That's a tall order mister. You see, I'm operating directly under the DoD and I don't think you outrank them."

It was James' turn. "We understand. That is why I have asked my friend General Williams to give you a call and explain this to you." James paused dramatically and peered closely at his strict military issue watch. "That should be about now."

A corporal stuck his head in the tent. "Sir, there's a priority call from Washington for you. Should I pipe it in here?"

"Do it," growled the commander as he glared at James. The Cherokee smiled politely in return. The commander grabbed the field telephone. "Yes sir? Yes General sir. I understand. Right away sir." He hung up the instrument and snorted. "Seems like you men have some pull." He stood up and faced them. "I have been ordered to send in supply trucks with food and clothing right away. I have also been instructed to put you two officers in charge of the convoy." He slammed his hand down on the table was not given the satisfaction of a flinch from either man. "For the duration of this operation, you are under my command. Corporal!" The young non-com appeared. "Get these men three trucks."

"Four trucks," Phillip said quietly. "The General said four trucks."

The commander glared at Phillip and was answered with narrowed eyes filling with inherited Oglala fire.

"Make that four trucks Corporal. These... gentlemen... will instruct you what to do from there. That is all." They turned to file out and the commander called out, "Wilson and Wilson, report to me when your operation is complete."

"Yes sir," they chorused.

The convoy rolled into the center of Wounded Knee amid deafening cheers and Oglala war calls. James popped out of the lead truck and called out, "My brothers, come and get your food!" A newsman that Phillip had smuggled in popped out with a camera and began filming the operation.

George called out, "Phillip Shouting Crow, you are a mighty logistical warrior. James Shouting Crow, you are another. You will always be remembered in this place, whatever the outcome." All the Sioux shouted their affirmation. Strong natives quickly emptied the trucks of their valuable supplies.

"George," James called out, "I think you'll find a few camp stoves that accidently fell in with this stuff. Oh, and propane to run them."

"Got 'em my brother," George replied.

"And George..." Phillip's voice was suddenly steely so that all turned to look. "Don't let me hear about any propane bombs, do you understand?"

"Yes sir," George mumbled.

"And the rest of you?" Phillip looked around the group with narrowed eyes.

"Yes sir," came multiple responses.

"Good. Your honor and my honor both rest on that."

The Sioux nodded and returned to their work. The trucks were empty within minutes.

George walked up to the two officers. "Will you share a meal with us from our new bounty?"

"We're under orders on this operation, George." James pushed back his officer's cap. "Gotta get the commander's trucks back to him before he sends a tank in."

George's laugh trailed off nervously. "I hope it don't come to that."

"Let me pray with you brother."

George nodded quietly. James and his father laid hands on George's shoulders and prayed for Creator's wisdom for him and all of the Sioux and then said their goodbyes and detailed the trucks back outside the perimeter.

The voice on the phone cracked with grief and exhaustion. "We lasted seventy-one days and then it was over. Since then, things have gotten worse. The corrupt Tribal Council is working with the BIA and FBI. People are disappearing, James. The GOON squad is terrorizing all of us who were involved."

"George, this is not good. The Guardians of Our Oglala Nation are acting like paid terrorists. GOON squad indeed."

George took a shuddering breath. "James, it's not over. If I have to spend my whole life fighting them, I will."

"I know you will my brother."

20: ANCIENT FIRE

1974 AD
SOARING EAGLE, OK

J ames sat alone at the piano in the old community hall on the Arkansas River. It was early evening and all was quiet there on a Tuesday night. The keyboard had become James' latest musical conquest and he enjoyed exploring different musical forms on its black and white keys. It could be more expressive than the guitar but sometimes less intuitive. It was far more liberating than the old Cherokee flutes that he also played.

He played a slow melancholy progression that mirrored his spirit. The increasing plight of his Oglala friends was a needle in his heart. He feared for George who remained outspoken against the Tribal Council. *Oh Lord, shed Your light upon my Oglala brothers and sisters!*

Sally had unfolded the magic of the keyboard to James. She had played since a young age and had studied under an old master in Wichita. Sally had achieved concert status in her teenage years and even won some competitions. Though easily able to stretch into Liszt and Chopin, she preferred free form improvisational playing.

James began to feel the pull of the Song as he lost himself in the music. A new song began to come forth that naturally began with praise unto the Creator. He went on for some time singing bits of the Psalms that he loved. He could feel the glow of anointing as he sang and played for an audience of One. He naturally moved into intercession in Song for his Oglala brothers. The Song soared on the wings of angels or eagles unto the very Throne Room of the Most High God as a rosy golden glow seemed to envelop James. He cried out for the Sioux for some time in this fashion before the Song swirled into Selah ending.

Unknown to James, both Phillip and James' wife Sally had slipped into the community hall as he played. As he came to an end he heard their expressions of praise and turned to see them both standing with their arms extended towards Heaven. Tears glistened on Phillip's face, as his eyes remained closed. Sally opened her eyes and looked at James in wonder. "Oh my love, that was so beautiful. You were speaking to Creator in your song." Sally shook her head with a smile. "Why haven't we always done this?"

James lowered his head. "Aw, it wasn't that good. Not like you playing Chopin."

Phillip dropped his hands and fixed his gaze on James. "Son, you played from your heart and it was an anointed prayer to God. Chopin is beautiful beyond words but what you just did is different." Phillip lowered his eyes as he was washed with memory. "A Son of Thunder you shall be. I think we heard some of what old Uncle Rick prophesied so long ago here tonight."

Within several months, James and Sally had formed the core of a new band. The still new Jesus Music scene was exploding across America and such groups as 2nd Chapter of Acts and Resurrection Band had come through Tulsa. James recruited two friends into their musical concept. His Alcatraz buddy Ron happened to be an excellent drummer and he gladly joined them. Ron brought a unique integration of Native drums and the more standard drum kit that became part of a signature sound the new band was building. Their Oglala friend George rounded out the lineup on bass. Both Ron and George temporarily relocated to Oklahoma to give the group a good start. They called themselves Ancient Fire.

James (with willing help from Phillip) outfitted the band with the best equipment they could afford. Sally got a huge Hammond organ complete with Leslie. She also got a Mini Moog, one of the new synthesizers that were taking the musical world by storm. James got a Rickenbacker guitar and a big Vox tube amp while George got a big Ampeg bass amp. George had several of his own basses and Ron was well equipped with drums. Phillip did replace all of Ron's aging and cracked cymbals with brand new Zildjians.

Ancient Fire began a rigorous rehearsal schedule. Out of this came a host of new songs. They began to play out in various small venues. The entire band agreed with James that they should not be afraid to play at bars and other darker venues. They were, after all, the places that most needed the Light.

They began to develop a following and were becoming noticed by national promoters. After playing together for a little over six months, they were asked to join a tour as an opening act for Phil Keaggy and 2nd Chapter of Acts. They all felt that this was God's open door for them and agreed.

Before they packed up and left for the tour, Phillip gave his son a special gift. James opened the box and took out a beautiful buckskin shirt. He held it up and saw it was covered with Native symbols, but in the center of the front was a large cross. Phillip looked at his son and said, "This is the shirt that I saw you wearing in my vision of so long ago, son. You wore this and the very Rickenbacker guitar you now own."

James quickly drew in a breath as the import of this magnificent gift hit him. "This is the Holy Ghost Shirt."

"Yes son. The circle is almost complete."

1975 AD
CHICAGO, IL

The crowd in Chicago was huge. The stagehands reckoned around ten thousand, a remarkable turnout for any show. For a group of plainly Christian bands it was astounding. James and Sally peered out from stage left as they prepared to go on. Sally looked at her husband with a knitted brow. "We've never played for a crowd like this, James."

"Aw Sally, they're all here for Phil," George said. "We'll just do our best and make way for the young master."

James grinned. "Yep, just warm up ear candy, that's us."

Suddenly the announcer was heard throughout the great hall. "Ladies and gentlemen, put your hands together for Ancient Fire!"

They ran forth in darkness into the embrace of the applause and took their places. Sally started playing an eerie progression on the organ with a wispy lead from the Mini Moog. George came in with a driving bass line and, on cue, the whole band exploded into their opening number, "Fill Me." The stage lights came on in a bright pulsing pattern that matched the music. James clear tenor took off in the first verse and all joined in tight harmony in the chorus.

The Chicago crowd answered the tune with wild cheering. James looked over at Sally with a stage faux surprise face, she answered with a laughing smile and one finger pointed Heavenward. James nodded and called out the count-in to the next tune. "One, two three, four, five..." The song took off in the 5/4 time signature that he had counted. The crowd roared its approval.

The whole set went off perfectly and they were poised for the last song. James had felt the anointing grow as the evening progressed and knew it was time to do something he had never before tried. He looked down at his Holy Ghost Shirt and shot an arrow prayer heavenward. He then stepped up to the mic and spoke. "I am here by the grace of my Lord Tsisa. That is the name we Cherokee call the Lord Jesus. He is great and gracious with love that abounds unto to each one of you. Many of you know Him already." A roar went up from the crowd as over half raised up the single forefinger One Way sign. James let the crowd settle down and then leaned into the mic. "I have a word for the rest of you in this place." James paused as he felt the electric tingle of destiny. He looked over the crowd again, turned to the left, and held forth his hands. "I say unto you in the Name of the Lord Tsisa, be saved!" He turned to the right and said again, "I say unto you in the Name of the Lord Tsisa, be saved!" He turned again to center and called out the prophetic declaration once more and, as he watched, people all over the great hall began falling down under the power of the Holy Spirit. "Be saved," he called. "Be saved!"

Ancient Fire launched into their last song as James called out, "Let everyone who has been touched by the Lord now come up front. We will be here for you after this song." James took off into the first verse as people touched by the Spirit began to rise and make their way to the stage.

1975 AD
SOARING EAGLE, OK

Phillip sat alone in the room lit by only the comfortable blaze that burned in the fireplace. With his eyes closed, his lips moved in prayer. Each night that Ancient Fire ministered in music, Phillip was here. He was a faithful intercessor and a steward of his son's vision. He knew in his heart that what James was now doing was the beginning of the most important phase of his life and a fulfillment of a decades old prophecy.

As he prayed, a vision unfolded in his consciousness. He saw Ancient Fire on a stage before a vast crowd and he knew it was Chicago. He watched James speak the holy words three times and then saw people fall under the Power of the Lord. He heard Ancient Fire launch into a song and the vision faded.

Phillip's eyes sprang open and he leaned forward. "The circle is complete," he whispered.

21: Flying Free

1979 AD
Tulsa, OK

Walter Mullins looked out of his expansive office window. A Delta Lockheed L-1011 was just starting its take off on the main Tulsa runway. The impossibly huge craft looked as if it would never fly, but sure as daybreak, the nose lifted off and the plane floated skyward. He would miss these spectacles. The old farmer now had jet fuel in his veins and hated the thought of leaving this all behind. A knock on the door jarred him out of his reverie. He was expecting company. His secretary had already called ahead. "Come in men."

The door opened and Phillip walked in with Jonesy trailing behind. "Have a seat, gentlemen. Can I get you some coffee?" Mullins leaned forward with a smile. He had always enjoyed the company of these two. They had been the pillars of his flying business.

"I wouldn't mind a cup of Joe, sir," Jonesy said. "Let me get it for us." Jonesy had already risen and was walking toward the credenza at the side of the office. "Black as usual for you, Mr. Mullins?"

Mullins leaned back with a smile. The get-it-done attitude of the man showed through in everything he did. "Yes Jonesy, black. And I keep telling you to call me Wally."

"Oh, yes sir Mr. Mullins." The three men shared a laugh. "How you want yours, Geronimo?"

"Two sugars today, Jonesy. Thanks." Phillip leaned forward to receive the steaming mug.

The men settled in to a brief moment with their coffee, and then Mullins set his mug down and put crossed arms in front of him on the desk. "Gentlemen, I want to say that you have been the main reason that Oklahoma Air has become what it is. Being a top regional carrier in 1979 is no small feat." Mullins stopped and drew in a deep breath. "The business climate today is miles away from when we started. I remember when we were the only game in town. Today we compete with national carriers increasingly running the local routes. Our small fleet of DC-8's can keep up with them, but just barely." He leaned back and looked up at the ceiling for a moment, then looked both men squarely in the eye. Head shifting from Phillip, then to Jonesy, he said, "I have received an offer from Delta Airlines for Oklahoma Air. It is attractive enough that I can offer substantial separation packages to all senior executives who would rather not stay on with Delta."

Jonesy whistled through his teeth. "What kind of package are you offering, sir?"

Mullins reached for a scrap of paper and jotted down a figure. He folded it and slid the paper across the desk to Jonesy. The old flier picked it up and opened it as if he was fanning out a poker hand. He looked at it without expression and then looked blandly at Mullins.

"That's a total net value." Mullins leaned back and rested his arms on the plush chair. "There's more to the story, but I think you get the picture." Jonesy nodded ever so slightly while maintaining the perfect poker face. Mullins scribbled another figure, folded the paper, and slid it to Phillip. "Same thing applies to you with one addition which we'll talk about."

Phillip was never a poker player. When he saw the six figures on the sheet, his eyebrows shot up. He did know how to retain his cool, however. "Yes sir," was his only reply.

"There is one other thing for you, Phil. I will transfer the title of Soaring Eagle to you personally. I would suggest setting up a small corporation and title the plane to that, thus protecting your asset. My secretary Janice can help you with that. I will also include the parts plane that you and Jonesy found and any other Mustang parts in our inventory."

Phillip looked over at Jonesy and then back to Mullins. "If Jonesy would agree, perhaps he and I could own it together in a partnership. He has been the one that kept the old bird flying all these years. I know he loves to take the plane to the EAA Fly In at Oshkosh every year, and I wouldn't want to deprive him of the pleasure."

Jonesy gave his friend a wry grin. "You just want a cheap mechanic, Geronimo."

"That too," Phillip said as they all laughed.

"Can I take that as a yes from both of you?" Both Phillip and Jonesy nodded. "All right then. I'll have Janice draw up all the papers and give you a detailed overview." Mullins rose and extended his hand to Phillip.

The Cherokee took it and gave a firm shake. "Thank you, sir."

Mullins then shook Jonesy's hand as he stood. "Men," Mullins said, "I won't say farewell because we all are still neighbors down around the Arkansas River. I'll just say, see you soon."

"Yes sir," both Phillip and Jonesy chorused in unison.

1980 AD
ON THE ROAD

With their daughter Sarah grown and out on her own in New York City, Phillip and Dorothy were now free to pursue their own dream. They bought a Winnebago Warrior and took off to find Native America. Phillip liked the RV because he thought that it was the closest they could get to an Indian vehicle. They travelled to Pine Ridge to visit the Sioux. They crossed the Dakotas to see the Arapaho still living in the area. They went and met the Paiute descendants of Wovoka, the man who had originally prophesied of the Ghost Dance. They picked up several new Nez Perce friends in Idaho and took them to visit the great ancestral homeland of the tribe, the Wallowa Valley in Oregon.

As Phillip surveyed the great depression from an overlook, he whistled slowly. "I understand why Chief Joseph and his people did not want to leave this place."

"It is wild and beautiful," Dorothy added.

"Joseph was defeated by the Bluecoats." One of the Nez Perce shaded his eyes with a hand. "If that had not happened, we would still be here." The Indian was named Wind Follower. He and Phillip had been speaking of the Jesus Way and the Nez Perce picked up that thread. "We stand here and look upon my ancestral homeland. In this place, Joseph would never allow a school or a church to be established."

Phillip lifted his head at looked closely at Wind Follower. "This I have heard."

Wind Follower stepped to the edge of the overlook and shook his head. "This is what Joseph spoke when a BIA commissioner asked him why he did not want any schools. He said, 'Because they will teach us to build churches.' The man asked him if he did not want churches." The Nez Perce stepped over to Phillip and gestured, summoning the memory of a Chief so great that he was never personally conquered. "Joseph said he did not want the white man's churches. The commissioner asked why. 'They will teach us to quarrel about God,' Joseph said. 'We do not want to learn that. We may quarrel with men sometimes about things on this earth, but we never quarrel about God. We do not want to learn that.'" Wind Follower dropped his head and stepped to the overlook again. All were silent before the judgment of Joseph. The Nez Perce gazed across the beloved Wallowa Valley. "Joseph died as a prisoner of war. The physician who reported his death said that he died of a broken heart." He turned his head and smiled at Phillip. "Not a very medical diagnosis."

Phillip sighed deeply. "No, it was a true discernment."

The Indians stood together silently on the overlook for some time remembering a great man named Joseph and a Nation the French named Nez Perce. Phillip walked over next to Wind Follower and laid a hand on his shoulder. "I do not want to build any white man's churches either, my friend." The man looked over at Phillip deeply as if searching the truth of the matter. He then nodded once.

Everywhere they travelled, the story trunk came along. Phillip recorded many key conversations with tribal leaders in the Gawonisgi Nvya. He had long ago shared the wonder of the ancient stone with Dorothy and they often spent evenings exploring the stories of past ages. As he had uncovered the lives of former holders of the stone, he discovered that almost all of them had shared the stone's existence with their wives. Only Soaring Eagle had shown it to a child, but he noted that Feather was a special case.

Back in Oklahoma, Wilma Mankiller was now Principal Chief of the Cherokee Nation. As the first woman chief of her people, Mankiller was receiving national attention. She had even received the Woman of the Year award from Ms Magazine. The lot of the Cherokee people as a whole was on the upswing and Phillip felt good for his people.

Yet most everywhere else they visited among the Natives, there was desperate poverty. Their homelands stolen and their entire lifeways stripped away, tribes like the Oglala Sioux experienced terrible squalor. It was true among the majority of others. A bitter rock of anger grew inside Phillip in a way he had never known as he met tyranny's progeny from across Turtle Island. The tribes in Canada fared no better. The free and wide-ranging cultures of the Natives of North America had been totally swallowed by the white European culture. There was nothing left but shadows of greatness.

The vast majority of white men he spoke with knew absolutely nothing of the ongoing plight of the Natives of their land. Cowboys and Indians were a forgotten relic of the nineteenth century, as were the treaties of that time. Many white men were sons of twentieth century immigrants and disavowed any responsibility for the Natives. Such men did not reckon with the brutal policies Relocation and Termination that had been products of their very lifetimes; legislation that a Congress that they and their fathers elected had passed into law. Legislation designed to bring cultural obliteration to a once free people was unknown to them. They did not reckon with the relentless machinery of the BIA that their elected representatives had authorized. They hid their eyes as it continued to oppress Natives of all tribes even after the policy of Termination had been outlawed. It was not their responsibility.

The dark bitter rock inside Phillip continued to grow and he knew not that it was consuming him.

22: NEW THUNDER

1991 AD
CHARLOTTE, NC

In several fellowships across America in the late eighties, a growing recognition of the central importance of prophecy began to expand. In disparate places like Kansas City, Charlotte, and Anaheim the knowledge and practice of prophecy grew. Many felt that it was the beginning of the restoration of the historic office of the prophet to the Christian Church. Many more scoffed at such nonsense.

Indians knew that the Great Spirit was always ready to speak to them. The concept of prophecy had been central to their various faiths. As those Natives embraced Jesus Christ, they carried their notions of prophecy with them. It was only natural that God would want to speak to them. Of course they would then tell those around them what He had said. This was what God had always done, was it not?

Phillip followed this development with interest because it helped him to quantify many of the things that he had heard from the Lord. He and Dorothy visited the Vineyard fellowship several times when in California. Their talk of a faceless generation coming forth to impart the Good News appealed to both of them. They liked it when God received all the glory.

They visited the growing group in Kansas City a number of times when they were home. It wasn't that far away and it gave Phillip a good excuse to roll out Soaring Eagle for a quick flight with his wife. They could fly up to KC for an evening meeting and be back late that night. The style of these gatherings was decidedly flamboyant with much public prophecy.

One young man in Kansas City had once singled out Phillip for a prophetic word. He told him that the Lord had declared that he was an ambassador to the nations. "I know," Phillip replied. The young man walked away with a puzzled expression.

It was 1991 when Phillip and Dorothy visited a small group in Charlotte. They had started just a couple years ago with four couples and now were filling the substantial converted four-car garage in which they met. After the meeting ended that had included stirring music and intense oratory, Phillip browsed the book table. He picked up a recent copy of their magazine and was stunned when he read the contents on the back.

"Dorothy, look at this." Phillip pointed to the title of an article.

Dorothy's mouth got round as she mouthed an oh. "The Sons of Thunder."

"Written by a guy from Boulder, Colorado."

Phillip quickly paid for the magazine and they left. They hopped in the Jeep that always followed the Winnebago on a low trailer and drove back to the RV campgrounds that were in South Carolina just below Charlotte. Dorothy prepared a late meal while Phillip excitedly devoured the article. After they ate and Phillip cleaned up, he read the whole thing to Dorothy. "Listen to this part of his vision," he said excitedly. "This girl stands up in a meeting and begins singing, 'In the name of Jesus Christ the Lord we say unto you, be saved.' Then people start falling down. Does that sound familiar?" Dorothy nodded with round eyes.

The article recounted a series of dreams and visions and went on to interpret their true meaning. This was something that any Indian could understand. That a white man would proclaim them underscored their importance to Phillip. "This is the thunder vision declared to a whole generation! We Natives can learn from this in how we disseminate what the Lord gives us." Phillip poked at the magazine to underscore his point.

"Oh my Hawk, still the mighty warrior." Dorothy smiled tenderly at her husband. Though in his seventies, he was still strong and youthful. The gray invaders had begun to take a toll, but the shiny Cherokee black hairs still held the infidels at bay. "You know, Luke is one of these. You saw that at his naming. Perhaps now is when it begins for our grandson."

"Let's pray for the young thunder beings, my Running Water." The old couple bowed before their Creator and began to intercede for a new generation of musical warriors that the Lord was now ready to bring forth.

1991 AD
CHARLESTON, SC

They decided to stay for another of the unusual Friday night meetings at the Charlotte fellowship. In the intervening week, they took a three-day trip to the beautiful coastal region of South Carolina around Charleston known as the Lowcountry. Only a couple of years ago, Hurricane Hugo had blasted the area with 140 mph winds and there were still signs of devastation.

They walked down historic East Bay St. and Phillip reminded Dorothy of a tale from the Gawonisgi Nvya. "This is the very street where Thunder Walking first met Red Beard. It was here that he gave him that name. The old Indian recorded that meeting."

Dorothy shook her head. "It's too bad he didn't know how to trigger a visual recording."

Phillip laughed. "I would liked to have seen Banica and Red Beard when they first arrived in America."

"I'll bet old Thunder Walking was quite a sight to them."

"I'm sure he was."

The couple walked more of the historic areas of downtown Charleston and came upon the old Customs House, where slaves were bought and sold in another time. Phillip stood and looked at the imposing columned structure. "Did you know that Cherokees once bought and sold slaves on this very spot?" He looked at Dorothy with raised eyebrows.

"I knew there were Cherokee slaveholders, even through the Civil War."

"I don't mean just black men. The Cherokees all but obliterated the Catawba's once long ago. Most of the remainder became part of the Cherokee tribe."

Dorothy nodded. "Isaac Tworiver back in Oklahoma is descended from the Catawba."

"Right. He still has almost half Catawba blood." Phillip glanced across East Bay at a street musician in the corner. He inclined his head in the guitar player's direction. "He's pretty good."

Dorothy looked over. "Yeah, not bad." She looked back at her husband.

Phillip refocused on Dorothy. "Anyhow, the Cherokees took a large group of Catawba captives, some three hundred if I remember correctly. They brought them to the slave market that was here where we stand. They were sold as slaves to land barons in the Caribbean. As far as I know, they were never heard from again."

Dorothy turned to face Phillip. "Aren't there some Catawba in the area south of Charlotte?"

Phillip grinned at his wife. "That's just where I was going. We need to visit them before we leave the Carolinas."

1991 AD
CHARLOTTE, NC

They made it back to Charlotte in time for the next Friday night meeting. The music was wonderful once again, but the man who addressed the crowd afterwards riveted Phillip with new insights. He spoke specifically of the Catawba Nation of that region and the blood debt that was still upon the land. He said that the Bible spoke of such things affecting descendants unto many later generations. He taught that it was up to us to break the cycle that was begun so long ago by recognizing the sins of our forefathers and repenting for those sins. He added when we owned the land, we also owned the debts to that land.

The concept shot through Phillip like an arrow. A Cherokee understood blood debt. Until the law was abolished after the move to Indian Territory, the blood debt was collected brutally. This was why Major Ridge and his two brothers were murdered back then. It was the debt they owed for setting the Cherokees on the course that led to the Trail of Tears. To speak of that debt generationally was a powerful thing. To repent of that sin was even more powerful.

When the meeting ended, Phillip turned to Dorothy. "I know what I must do. I must go the Chief of the Catawba's and repent for the sins of the Cherokee to them from so many hundreds of years ago. I don't know if it will matter, but I must try."

1991 AD
ROCK HILL, SC

The Catawba Chief received Phillip and Dorothy graciously. Phillip had intentionally worn his Cherokee buckskins. The old Chief laughed when he realized Phillip was Cherokee. "Have you come as a war party against us, my brother?" He looked at Phillip with a twinkle in his eye.

"No sir, I come in peace."

"Sit," said the Chief. "I will bring you refreshment." He went into the next room and returned with handmade mugs decorated with Catawba symbols on a similar tray. There were likewise crafted creamer and sugar bowl filling out the tray. "Some genuine Indian mugs filled with good American coffee." They all chuckled as they received his hospitality. You generally didn't have to ask an Indian if they wanted coffee. To this day, they consider it one of the good gifts of the white Europeans.

"I am Phillip Shouting Crow, half Cherokee, half Oglala Sioux, no white."

The chief raised his left eyebrow. "The son of Samuel Shouting Crow. A pleasure to meet you."

Phillip looked over at Dorothy with a pained expression. "All these years and Pa still won't leave me alone." He rolled his eyes as they all laughed. "This is my wife, Dorothy Running Water, full blood Sac and Fox."

The Chief looked at her. "A rare prize indeed, Phillip Shouting Crow." Dorothy smiled sweetly as the Catawba continued. "I am Eugene Fallen Timber. My father was Chief before me and his before that."

Phillip leaned forward. "Chief Fallen Timber, I have come to you on a most serious matter. We both know the history of the Cherokee and the Catawba." Eugene nodded as Phillip continued. "I am a believer in the Most High God and His Son the Lord Tsisa."

"I am too my brother. The Son of Manatou is well known to us. I think that you and I also call Him Jesus."

Phillip nodded. "Yes, the Very Son of God. He has put it in my heart to pay an ancient blood debt. My fathers killed your fathers and sold those left alive into slavery. This was so long ago, yet I feel the debt today. I would do to you the only thing that I am able. I repent to you for the terrible sins of my fathers. I ask your forgiveness, Chief Fallen Timber."

The old Chief had bowed his head as Phillip spoke the words. When he raised it, tears glistened in his eyes. "Friend Phillip, in all the hundreds of years since the wars with the Cherokees, not one Cherokee has done what you just did. It is remembered that no Cherokee spoke again of the wars with us. What you have done is wonderful and it gives me great hope. Yes, I forgive you Phillip, and through you, the Cherokee Nation." The Chief shook his head and looked out the window. "There are a little over a hundred of us left in this place. We are fighting now to be recognized by South Carolina but the signs have not been good." He looked back at Phillip. "Perhaps you have just broken a terrible generational curse between our peoples today, Phillip Shouting Crow. Perhaps this is a sign of better things for our tiny Nation. This I choose to believe."

1991 AD
SOARING EAGLE, OK

Ancient Fire had always operated on the fringes of the popular Christian music scene. Although they had achieved early popular success, their increasingly daring musical explorations into odd time signatures and bizarre instrumentation had placed them somewhere between neo-progressive and avant-garde. A reviewer of their first genuine Compact Disc release "A Day of Weeks" had likened them to "Emerson Lake and Palmer meets Laurie Anderson." While Sally was gratified to be compared with the great Keith Emerson, the CD experienced lackluster sales. The Christian music scene was moving in Alternative circles and Ancient Fire was out of sync. Ever true to the vision entrusted to him, James was not fazed.

Luke had become the fifth man and his blistering lead guitar work moved them all in new directions. Perhaps "A Day of Weeks" was a transition as it was the first album that featured Luke as a full band member. Maybe it was all of them waiting for the next big direction from the Lord.

That came in spades when Phillip and Dorothy returned from Charlotte with the Sons of Thunder article in hand. The band devoured it and experienced a new energizing from the Lord. Phillip ordered the Sons of Thunder video that had the entire message by the pastor from Colorado. James showed it to the band and they began sharing it with other Christian musician friends. The vision that was seen in Colorado and distributed in Charlotte came alive in eastern Oklahoma. Musicians began to gather weekly at the old townhouse and make music unto the Lord well into the night.

New songs came out of this experience and Ancient Fire released a CD called "Rekindled." It was filled with music born in these gatherings. While they still explored the odd time signatures, there was a fresh accessibility to these tunes. One song even did a most surprising thing. "Light of Day" crossed over onto the Billboard Top 100 and began climbing the charts. It peaked out at number seven and stayed in the top ten for five weeks.

The gatherings had kindled new musical vision in Luke. He and a group of Native musical friends formed a new group that they named Redbird. They emulated the dropped D music of such bands of Christians as King's X and Galactic Cowboys. They began opening for Ancient Fire and Luke pulled double duty for both bands. It was exhilarating.

During one of their prayer times together with both bands, Luke had a vision of them walking back along the Trail of Tears. Where they walked, flowers sprang up behind them. A swath of beautiful fragrance remained across America.

James latched onto this immediately and they decided to launch a special event. The "No More Tears" tour would backtrack across the Trail and stop for concerts at significant locations along the way. They would end at Ross's Landing in Chattanooga, Tennessee, which was the main launching place for the many groups that set out on the Trail. They would go on and do a show near New Echota, the old Cherokee capitol in north Georgia, and a final show in Atlanta.

James and Luke met with their promoter who received the idea enthusiastically. The tour was set to begin in the fall and reach Atlanta before Christmas. Unlike their ancient ancestors, they didn't have to walk the whole way.

1992 AD
PORT GIRARDEAU, MO

Phillip went with them when they played at the Trails of Tears Park on the Mississippi River. Just north of Port Girardeau, Missouri, it was remembered as the crossing place of many bands of Cherokees on the Trail. Phillip also knew it was the place of the lost burial site of his relative Feather.

He had watched the scenes of the burial many times that Soaring Eagle had recorded on the Gawonisgi Nvya. It was a brutal snowy winter when she was buried and landmarks were unsure. Still, he wanted to do a search. He slipped off at the start of the show and walked into the woods. He knew it was on a low rise and he found several candidates. He searched each carefully in the afternoon sun and was finally rewarded with a clue. Beneath some fallen leaves, he found a group of stones formed into a circle with a cross in the center. It was the ancient Cherokee symbol for the Sacred Fire. Phillip nodded at the sight. The stones were weathered and windblown and obviously very old. He walked into a copse of trees just down the gentle slope and began to probe the area with the small folding shovel he had brought with him. He hit several rocks, but digging only produced the edges of irregular boulders. Finally, he hit one and dug, finding a flat rock about two feet long and a foot wide. He cleared the surface and brushed it clean with the whisk he carried for this bit of archeology.

On the surface was inscribed in the characters of the Syllabary: "She Who Floats on the Wind, beloved daughter." Phillip felt electric excitement as he read the symbols. He pulled the Gawonisgi Nvya from his great pocket and hit the moving image record sequence.

He looked up at the clear sky as he took a breath. "I have found what my Great Grandfather never could, the grave of his daughter Feather on the Trail of Tears." He reached down and touched the stone. "Hello my Great Aunt. One day soon I will meet you." He closed his eyes in prayer with his hand still on the gravestone. After a moment, he opened them and pressed a stud on the stone. He slipped it back into his pocket and carefully covered the gravestone once again. As only an Indian can, he removed all signs of his presence. The Lord had shown him that this site was to remain secret.

The final show in Atlanta was glorious. There was a vibrant group of Christian musicians in the city so the turnout was huge. Both bands were well received and they played an impromptu final set together of free form music that just praised the Lord. The crowd enthusiastically joined in and they went on for another hour in this fashion. The promoter had to finally shut them down as they were overstaying their allotted time in the venue. Ancient Fire and Redbird bid a fond farewell to the Big Peach.

1995 AD
SOARING EAGLE, OK

The phone rang twice before Phillip picked it up. "Greetings in the Name of the Lord Tsisa!"

"That could only be Phillip Shouting Crow with such a

greeting. How are you my brother?"

The voice was familiar, but he couldn't quite place it. "Yes this is Phillip. With whom do I have the pleasure of speaking?"

"This is Eugene Fallen Timber from Rock Hill, South Carolina."

Phillip's face lit up in a huge smile. "Yes Chief, it's so good to hear you. We haven't spoken in years. How have you been, friend Eugene?"

"Things have been steadily improving since our meeting several years ago. I wanted to be absolutely certain before I called you, but I have great news."

"Tell me, my friend."

"The Catawba Nation has been officially recognized by the State of South Carolina!"

"Praise Tsisa brother! That is great news."

"Yes, we will finally be able to do some things we've talked about for years. Perhaps some of the scattered Catawba's will return, now that there is a home to return to."

"I hope that it will be a blessing to your children's children, Eugene."

"It will. I think what you did several years ago helped to set the stage for this victory."

Phillip nodded and smiled into the phone. "Thank you Eugene."

"I won't keep you friend, but I just wanted you to be blessed with our success."

"I am. Chief Fallen Timber, please send the greetings and blessing of the Cherokee to your people."

"I will, Phillip Shouting Crow. Goodbye."

"Goodbye good friend."

23: ENDINGS AND BEGINNINGS

It was sudden and catastrophic. Dorothy was standing in the kitchen when she collapsed on the floor with a moan. The pan she had been holding clattered to the floor and the lid spun like a top before rolling to the corner. Her chest heaved twice and then was still.

Phillip came running when he heard the noise. "Dorothy, are you okay?" He shot around the corner and saw her lying lifeless on the floor. Phillip cried out in pain. Tears filled his eyes as he quickly knelt beside his wife. "My Dove, what has happened?" He looked for signs of injury but saw none. He held his hand to her mouth and realized she was not breathing. He quickly began CPR on her, the two breaths, then the thirty pumps to the chest, then the two breaths. She was not responding and he desperately needed help. James would be fastest. He finished thirty pumps and then jumped for the kitchen phone, almost yanking it off the wall in his urgency. He dialed James' number. One ring. Two rings. *Come on son!*

Sally answered, "Hello?"

"Sally, this is Phillip. Dorothy is unconscious on the kitchen floor and I am giving her CPR. Get help now!"

Sally let out a choking scream. "James!" Her voice trailed off. "James, Mother is unconscious!"

Phillip heard enough to know that they were moving. He

dropped the phone and returned to give Dorothy two more breaths, then thirty pumps. Two breaths, thirty pumps. His world contracted tightly to those two tasks.

That is how James found him minutes later. "Dad, the paramedics are on the way. They said to keep up CPR until they got here." Phillip nodded grimly. "Do you want me to spell you?" Phillip shook his head violently. This was his Dove!

The paramedics arrived twelve minutes later in what had been a record run from Tahlequah. They quickly loaded her onto the stretcher and rushed back to W.W. Hastings Indian Hospital. Dorothy was pronounced dead on arrival.

1995 AD
ON THE EDGE OF ETERNITY

She floated above the floor where her body lay. Phillip rushed in and fell on her old self in desperation. "Oh my Hawk, we will be together soon. Do not grieve overmuch."

A great angel floated down and faced her. Dorothy found she could stand in the air. "I have no death song. I am a Sac and Fox servant of the Lord Jesus and I await my Creator."

The angel smiled. "Then let us go forth to meet Him." He took her hand and they flew into the deep of outer space. She looked down and gasped as she realized they were crossing the Milky Way. Suddenly they were before a shining portal. The angel held forth his hand. "He awaits."

She stepped through into pure liquid light. She heard a great Voice so filled with Love that it made her bones tremble. "Welcome Home, Dorothy Running Water. Enter into the joy of your Lord."

1995 AD
TAHLEQUAH, OK

The medical team declared that she had died of a catastrophic pulmonary embolism. Her overall health had been so good that no one suspected the formation of a blood clot that usually caused these events. The doctors traced it to deep venous thrombosis, which had remained undetected. If she had reason for a CAT scan, they would have found it. As it was, the clot grew unheralded and dislodged that fateful day. The doctors reckoned that her death was almost instantaneous.

1995 AD
SOARING EAGLE, OK

Phillip had sat grim and silent through the funeral. At the gravesite, he tossed a white rose onto the coffin as it descended. An old-fashioned Sioux medicine bundle was wrapped around the rose. Many Natives nodded solemnly at this last gesture. He did not speak a word.

Phillip remained dark and silent for many months after Dorothy's sudden death. He would not answer the phone and returned no calls. He did not answer his door when concerned friends called. His world contracted to the company of James, Sally and Luke.

Luke spent hours with his grandfather reading scripture to him. He read the entire book of Psalms which expressed the gamut of human experience and emotion like perhaps no other literature in the world. He would look at Phillip from time to time and would often find the old Cherokee regarding him intently, as if taking his measure. He would look back later and Grandfather would be gazing vacantly out the window.

They prepared him meals and saw him to bed. They were there in the morning when he awoke. Perhaps it was this constant sacrifice of love that broke through to Phillip. Luke was alone with him and had just finished reading the book of James.

Phillip leaned forward and licked his lips. "My wife is dead. Did you know her?"

"She was my Grandma. I knew her as only a grandson could." Luke tingled with the moment of breakthrough.

Phillip suddenly focused on his grandson. "Luke you are here. Luke, your grandma is dead." Phillip suddenly broke down into tears. Luke rushed to his side and Phillip put his head down on his shoulder. "She is dead, Luke." The floodgates had finally opened and Phillip wept for a long time, cradled in the arms of his grandson.

The weeping finally subsided and Luke got his grandpa a glass of water. Phillip drained it thirstily. He looked up at Luke. "Is James at his house?"

"He has not left since Grandma went Home, Edudi, except to see you."

Phillip got a distant look in his eyes. "Home, yes." He focused on Luke again and stood. "I would see my son."

"Okay Grandpa, but are you up to walking over there? It's almost a quarter mile."

Phillip adopted a stern expression. "Has something happened to my legs? Of course I am up to it, young man." He made a harrumph sound and turned toward the door.

Luke smiled at his grandpa's back. A walk outside would probably be the best thing in the world for him.

"I don't want the old Warrior any more. It only reminds me of my Dove. Give it to someone who needs it son."

James stood and crossed the room to his desk. He brought up the display on his computer and pressed a few keys. He studied the screen with his back to Phillip. "There are families here that could benefit from an old Winnebago, but there are other families that could use it as a home." He turned and looked at his father.

"In Pine Ridge?" Phillip raised his chin to look his son in the eye.

"Yes, Dad, in Pine Ridge. Let me talk to Uncle Rick's granddaughter."

Phillip nodded and considered the matter settled. "I want to get rid of the Jeep too."

James turned around and crossed his arms. "I can think of a Sac and Fox family that needs a vehicle."

Phillip nodded. Another matter settled. "I will need a new car. I think I will be doing some travelling."

It was James' turn to nod. "I can take you into Tulsa early tomorrow. We can hit the major dealers."

"Just the big Chevrolet dealer. I want a new Chevy."

James scratched his head. "No more Chrysler?"

Phillip laughed. It felt good to laugh. "I don't like that cab forward design they use now. I couldn't even change a spark plug on one of those engines."

James grinned. "C'mon Dad, when's the last time you changed a spark plug?"

Phillip stroked his chin and looked at the ceiling thoughtfully. "Hmm, I think it was 1963 on my old Pacesetter ragtop. Now that was a Chrysler."

James laughed. It was good to have his Dad back. Each day they got further from Mom's death, the better he got. James briefly bowed his head as his eyes welled up with tears. *I still can't believe she's gone.*

"You alright son?"

"Yeah Dad."

Phillip was silent for a moment, then rose, and walked to James. "I still miss her desperately James, but the black days are gone."

James sniffed and nodded, momentarily unable to speak. Phillip patted his son's shoulder and turned to sit down. James turned back to his computer for a few moments until he was able to talk again. "So, a Chevy, huh? An Impala?"

"Nope." Phillip leaned back and crossed his arms. "A Camaro Z28."

James sputtered and spun around. "What? You're kidding!"

"I don't kid." He looked blandly at his son. "With the 5.7 liter engine, the LT1. Black."

"Is that all?"

"No. Six speed tranny."

"Mom would have a cow!"

Phillip looked down with a darkened expression.

"I'm sorry Dad, I shouldn't have said that."

"That's okay son." Phillip chuckled. "Actually, you're wrong. She would have a buffalo." Father and son looked at each other and broke out into laughter.

"Okay Dad, we'll go find your new pony tomorrow."

"It's a deal."

The salesman started talking about financing and Phillip waved him to silence. "What's your best price?"

The salesman consulted his records and scribbled down a figure. He passed it to Phillip. "I'm paying cash," said the old Cherokee. "I will pay two thousand less than that figure."

The young man's eyes opened a little wider and he was silent for a moment. "Let me speak to my manager." He returned a moment later with a counter offer. Phillip replied to that and they finally settled at fourteen hundred discount.

The old man grinned smugly as he walked out to his brand new 1995 Camaro Z28. James walked beside him. "So, did you scalp the white man, Dad?"

"Let's just say he got a close shave." Phillip hopped into his Camaro and was gone before James made it to his car.

Sally rolled her eyes and tapped her foot. "Dad is going to be eighty in just two years. He has no business traipsing off across America all alone." She blew out a breath, briefly puffing up her cheeks. "He could disappear and we would never know."

"Sally honey, he's a warrior. Besides, I've talked Luke into going with him on this first trip. They're going up to Pine Ridge and then over to Washington state and back. A couple of months and they'll be back. Maybe Dad will get it out of his system."

Sally folded her arms. "What about the bands?"

"Everyone's on hiatus now, you know that."

"Luke will call?"

"He said he'll call every few nights." James stepped forward and took his wife's hands. She had long ago owned Phillip as blood kin and her concern was real. "You know that Dad is unstoppable when he makes up his mind. Let's pray for him and our son." She nodded and they lifted their voices and hearts to the King.

1996 AD
ON THE ROAD IN SOUTH DAKOTA

With the glass T-tops stowed in the rear, the shiny Camaro sped north along Interstate 29 towards Sioux Falls. Phillip and Luke had been listening to Ancient Fire earlier on the impressive sound system. Now Luke was driving as his grandfather dozed in the passenger's seat. They both enjoyed the wind in their hair and the bright afternoon sun. Phillip opened his eyes and yawned. "Do you know that the first time I made this trip with my Pa it took us two weeks?"

Luke shot a smile at Phillip. "Yeah Granddad, you told me."

Phillip chuckled. "I'm allowed a little senility, don't you think?"

Luke laughed. "Yeah. Hey, what road are we cutting onto to get to Pine Ridge?"

Phillip consulted the folded map that was lying in his lap. "You know, I used to cut across on Route 20. I still think that's the fastest. The exit is right before Sioux City."

"You'd think the Sioux owned the place, huh?"

Phillip shook his head. "They once did Luke."

They drove in silence for another twenty miles to the turnoff. They headed across country on Route 20 into the heart of Oglala territory.

In two months to the day, Phillip and Luke returned to the Arkansas River homestead. They were sure to stop for a car wash in Tahlequah so the Camaro still looked showroom fresh. The family reunion was joyous and, for Sally, relieving. Perhaps the old man could traipse around the country and find his way home again.

For the next six years, that became the pattern of Phillip's life. He would plan a trip and then execute it like a precision field operation. He always returned on time and he always stayed in touch with his family while he was gone. Phillip visited virtually every tribe he could uncover in North America in that time. From the far reaches of Alaska and northern Canada down to the tip of Florida, he found his Native brothers.

In the back of the Camaro, he always carried the story trunk in a special compartment that he had made. He often used it as a way to share the Good News with young Indians who would ride with him. An ancient Cherokee holy man driving a Z28 and carrying a mysterious trunk always got their complete attention, just the way the Lord Tsisa had showed him it would.

Phillip knew that his time was short. He would have to pass the Gawonisgi Nvya to Luke soon, before it was too late. He was a very old man and sometimes the veil became so thin that he could faintly see the great cloud of witnesses surrounding him, cheering him on. But the vision would fade and he would drive on to the next stop on his holy itinerary.

1998 AD
NEW YORK, NY

Galen Monroe had caught himself a number of times in the last years almost calling the man Thomas. He was not Banica, but he was surely a twentieth century recreation of his old chancellor. His level of thoroughness rivaled Banica's and he had the distinct advantages of the emerging technologies of the day. The Council kept them well equipped with devices that would have made James Bond green with envy. Warren Cole used them to full advantage.

"The 1993 attack on the World Trade Center was a poorly planned and botched operation. Yousef lit a freaking fuse with a flame." Cole shook his head.

"How nineteenth century," Monroe said drily. "I would be most embarrassed if you employed such crude methodology."

Cole grinned at his boss. "Galen, we have satellite detonators at our disposal." He fielded a tight smile. "A fuse."

"Are you suggesting that we destroy the World Trade Center, Warren?"

"Not unless the Director tells us to." He looked innocently at his boss.

"Don't be expecting that order." He looked out over New York. Their proximity to the plaza from which the twin buildings rose allowed those towers to dominate a full third of the view. Monroe had never complained. "But I think that they are still a target."

"Oh, yes sir. One of the terrorists wrote that the World Trade Center would continue to be one of their targets."

"I think America has forgotten that." Monroe was silent as he surveyed the great buildings.

"What would you have us do, sir?"

The President of Sterling Bank looked at his closest aide. "We must accelerate the hardening of this building. We must also recommend contingency plans for the CIA headquarters that are at number five." He again gazed at the great towers. "There are secrets that must remain secret," he said as he looked at his aide. "No matter what the cost."

"Yes sir, I will draw up the appropriate plans."

"Posthaste, Warren. We do not know what tomorrow holds."

"Yes sir." Cole rose and exited the room.

"At least we don't know everything that tomorrow holds," Monroe said softly.

24: THE TOWERS

2001 AD
SOARING EAGLE, OK

"Go with me to New York, Luke. It's late summer and the weather is still beautiful there. We can go to Hunter Island and look for the remains of Joe Two Trees." Phillip leaned back in his easy chair with his hands behind his head. "I know you love New York."

Luke grinned at his granddad. The man was amazing. Eighty-three years old and he had more energy than his grandson did. All these years and all those trips and he was always ready for a new one. The Camaro kept up with him too. The old man made sure the car was in top shape.

Luke liked the idea of seeing New York again. Yeah, he would poke around for a day on Hunter Island with Granddad, but he could spend a week exploring the streets of Manhattan. The place was endlessly fascinating. Especially the girls. "Okay Granddad, but you know I gotta be home by September twelfth."

"Yes, I know son. New sessions with Redbird." Phillip smiled and began planning what he would say to Luke. *The boy has to know about the stone.*

2001 AD
NEW YORK, NY

It was the dawn of a new millennium and the excitement swept the globe. The year 2000 celebrations worldwide were extravagant and beautiful. New York seemed recharged by the transition, as if the already never sleeping city had gone into overdrive, barreling into 2001. Over all of this festive spirit reigned the World Trade Center. The two main towers ruled New York, dwarfing all with their presence. From many miles away they were plainly visible, arguably the most famous skyscrapers in the world and symbols of American prosperity.

Luke spied them while they approached the city on the New Jersey Turnpike. "There they are, Ma and Pa New York."

"That what you call them?" Phillip grinned towards the tall buildings.

"Yep. Wouldn't be New York without them."

Phillip glanced in the mirror and put on the right signal, moving over into the lane for the Goethals Bridge. The Camaro cruised across the grimly named Arthur Kill and onto Staten Island with a brief stop at a toll booth. They continued straight on Interstate 278.

Phillip glanced at his grandson. "We actually have a small piece of business in the North Tower."

Luke looked over. "We do?"

Phillip nodded as he glanced in the side view mirror. "My friend Lucy Redbird is heading up a group of Native consultants doing some translation work. They have temporary offices on the seventy-third floor of Tower One."

"Nice view?"

Phillip smiled. "If they have strong binoculars, they could probably pick us out right now."

Luke glanced to the left to see the Towers glinting in the sun. "No way Granddad."

"Yes way Grandson." The two laughed. "Anyhow, they need help with some sticky Cherokee words. They're from a paper dated in the early nineteenth century."

Luke whistled a low note. "From the dawn of the Syllabary."

Phillip nodded. "Yep, and that's the problem. Not everyone wrote the characters quite the same at first."

"Of course, you were there so you'll know."

Phillip smiled and winked at his grandson. "Of course."

They crossed Staten Island and then the Verrazano Bridge into Brooklyn. They finally arrived at their first destination, The Bronx. They found the motel near Pelham Bay Park where they had reservations and pulled in. Their room was ready.

The next day they took a boat over to Hunter Island. It had once been an island alone but was now connected to Twin Island and Rodman's Neck by landfill. The area was a protected paradise that was remarkably untouched by New York. Seabirds abounded and small critters could be seen skittering through the brush. Now it was a part of Pelham Bay Park.

Phillip chose his venue well. There was no one in the wilds of the island and they slipped unseen into the interior. As they followed a sketchy trail, Phillip spoke over his shoulder. "Do you remember the story of Joe Two Trees?"

"The Last Algonquin? Sure Granddad. You made that book required reading when I was younger, remember?"

"That was then and this is now."

Luke rolled his eyes. "Two Trees lived alone on this very island for over fifty years, virtually under the noses of white men. They never knew he was here."

Phillip stopped and turned. "And he prospered, son."

Luke skidded to a stop. "If you call living in a twig hut and eating fish you spear prospering."

Phillip folded his arms and peered at Luke. "I do and I'll tell you why. He did it with no money and no help from any man. I don't think there's an Indian alive in America today who could make that claim, me included."

"You have a point, Granddad."

Phillip looked in all directions briefly and listened intently. "Come this way, Luke." They walked over a rise and were greeted with a tangled wall of vines and other leafy growth. Phillip stopped again and closed his eyes. He opened them and said, "This is likely." He felt along the growth and found one weak spot. He forced his way inward and found the vines yielding reluctantly. "Follow me Luke." The young man was right behind him as they broke through into a darkened clearing. It was mostly overgrown, but showed signs of ancient cultivation.

"This isn't what I think it is, is it?" Luke looked around with an open mouth.

"I cannot tell for sure, Luke. If not, it is very like it. Yes, like the old camp of Joe Two Trees, the Last Algonquin."

"This is amazing, just like I remember from the book."

"Ah, you did read it."

Luke grinned in the dusky light of the overgrown clearing. "I never told you but I read it twice." He looked up at the cathedral ceiling of vines and branches. "Old Joe was one amazing Indian."

"Indeed he was." Phillip had begun poking through the vines overgrowing the far side of the small area. "Hmm." He pulled a handful back and was rewarded with a low dirt mound. "I wonder what surprises we would find in here." He looked at the mound for a moment and sighed, letting the vines drop back in place. He stood and looked around, searching for something. He strode across the clearing and pulled some vines back, exposing a flat rock. "There's my seat." Phillip made himself comfortable and motioned to Luke to do the same.

Luke searched around for a moment until he found a log. He cleared it of vines and sat, pulling a bottle of Dasani water out of his outer pocket. "Want a drink, Granddad?"

Phillip laughed. "Look at the twenty-first century Indian with his Dasani." The old Cherokee pulled a worn miniature canteen from his voluminous outer pocket. "I filled this from the spring on the Arkansas River before we left." He unscrewed the lid and took a healthy swig. "Didn't want any big city germs." He grinned at his grandson as he screwed on the lid.

Luke pointed his chin at the canteen. "War relic?"

Phillip looked at the old canteen. "In fact it is. Used to carry this on missions in Soaring Eagle." Phillip looked down for a moment, and then raised his head with a look of frightening concentration. "I carried something else on those missions, son." He reached in his pocket and maneuvered an unseen object. A three dimensional image appeared in the air between them. It was a view from the cockpit of a World War II Mustang. Ahead through the canopy was a Messerschmitt Bf 109. The German pilot of the plane was waving frantically.

Luke stood in amazement. "Grandfather, what is this? What are we seeing? How are we seeing it?"

"Shh, grandson. All your questions will be answered, I promise. Just watch." The Mustang pulled ahead and to the side of the German warcraft. The German pilot held up a large photo. On it was a beautiful woman standing with her arms over two children on either side of her. There was a river in the background and trees dotting a lawn. The pilot pointed to the woman and children, and then put his hand on his heart and looked tearfully across the void between the aircraft. He held that for several seconds, and then it was obvious that the Mustang banked away from his adversary. The last glimpse of the German found him holding up a hand, palm outward.

The image faded as Phillip touched something in his pocket again. Luke sat down very slowly with wide eyes. He looked intently at his grandfather. Plainly, there was more to Phillip Shouting Crow than he had ever imagined.

Phillip lifted his chin and surveyed Luke, taking his measure. *He holds his peace. Good.* "Men who go to war live through more life and death moments in a day than most people do in a lifetime. These moments determine not only who lives and who dies, but the character of the man who lives through them." Phillip leaned forward with his forearms on his knees. "The P-51 outclassed the Bf 109 in every area. To a skilled American pilot, it was an overwhelming advantage. Nevertheless, Mustangs were shot down. There was never a certain victory." He straightened his back. "In ancient times when a man yielded in battle, he was given his life. This was part of honorable warfare." Phillip got a distant sad look in his eyes. "In our own history there were a few Bluecoats who were more honorable in this than our own warriors. But that, too, was another time." Phillip took a breath. "This code of honor is forgotten today. There is no honor in war." Phillip stared intently at Luke. "I showed you this first of all to teach you this lesson. You are accountable for the life that Creator puts in your hand, be it friend or foe. Always remember that Luke."

Luke nodded, his eyes round and luminous. He remained speechless, waiting for a cue from his grandfather.

Phillip smiled at his grandson. "And how did the old Indian bring World War II into this secret place?"

Luke sat mesmerized. He couldn't believe what he had seen. It was a moving hologram right out of Star Trek. Technology like this didn't exist. Not yet, anyway. He was afraid to speak a word or break the spell of this moment. Surely, Granddad was playing some Sioux trick on him. He looked around furtively for the hidden accomplice, but there were only branches and vines.

"There's just us grandson. Let me tell you a story. Many years ago, a frightened young boy came home from an Indian Boarding School and saw his family for the first time in years. That night he saw his great grandfather for the last time."

"That was you and Soaring Eagle?"

Phillip nodded. "I am convinced that Creator kept him alive to see me that last time. You see, he had to give me something, something very important. Sequoyah School upset the timetable and there was no time left. No time to mentor me. So with the barest direction, he gave me this."

The old Grandfather pulled out a strange flat stone from his pocket. Luke stared at it in confusion. It looked impossibly ancient and the flat surface was covered with small studs. Each was marked with a legend. Luke looked closer. The legends were in Cherokee, in the characters of the Syllabary. He shook his head. "What is this Granddad?"

"It is called the Gawonisgi Nvya. It is always with me, either in my pocket or more likely in the story trunk."

Luke snorted. "I always thought there was more to that thing than wood and brass."

Phillip chuckled. "There is. It was made at Tulsa Wood Works but had a few, uh, modifications." Phillip stood with the stone in his hand. "Since time before times, this stone was passed through the generations of our people. It was a gift of the Yvwi Tsunsdi to the first of the Anikutani."

"The Little People and the priests? Have you seen a Small One, Edudi?"

"No, but I think I heard them once." Phillip got a momentary faraway look in his eyes, and then refocused on Luke. "The date of the gifting of the stone is uncertain, but, the best I can determine by scanning its records is that it would correspond with the time of Abraham."

Luke was speechless. "The Cherokee were contemporary to Abraham? That would make them an ancient race indeed. Wait a minute, its records?"

"This stone is an ancient recording device of incalculable power." Phillip stepped toward Luke and held it forth cradled in both hands. "In this stone are the stories of my people."

Luke leaned down for a close look and then looked up at his Phillip. "Granddad, this is unbelievable."

With a twinkle in his eye, Phillip pushed a couple of studs and an image appeared of Luke saying, "Granddad, this is unbelievable."

Phillip lowered the stone even with his waist. "The steward of the stone has a solemn charge to pass the object onto his youngest male descendant. It almost always skips a generation. In rare cases like mine, it skips two. It is time to begin your training, for you are to be the new steward of the stone." Phillip put a hand on grandson's shoulder. "Unlike me and Great Grandpa, you and I still have plenty of time."

Luke had wanted to stay in a hotel on Manhattan for their final couple of days there but Phillip vetoed the idea. "Too expensive. I'd pay twenty-five dollars a day just to park the Camaro. We'll stay on Staten Island with my friend Will Openwater."

Early in the morning, they rode on the Staten Island Ferry towards the island that Peter Minuit acquired from the Algonquin Natives of the area for sixty Dutch guilders worth of trinkets. The ferry seemingly had no bow or stern, both ends of the boat were open ramps designed to mate with the docks on Manhattan and Staten Island. Phillip and Luke stood on the ramp facing the storied isle. Several sea gulls paced the boat and swooped low when a passenger would throw a treat in the air. Off to port, the Statue of Liberty tirelessly held her torch of freedom in the air over New York Harbor.

Phillip smiled up at the cloudless sky. "Pilots today call this severe clear," he said to Luke. "Unlimited visibility." He looked at the lower Manhattan skyline. The World Trade Center dominated the view and the Towers sparkled in the early morning sun.

Luke nodded. "A great day to visit Manhattan. If we get up to Times Square by lunchtime, maybe we can have lunch at Hello Deli."

"Oh yeah, Letterman's buddy. Sounds good."

In a few minutes, the great orange craft eased into the dock next to Battery Park. Phillip and Luke followed the herd out into the street. Luke pointed his head at an inviting bistro. "Wanna get a cup of joe, Granddad?"

"Yeah, just what a body needs."

They shambled over and enjoyed a quiet fifteen minutes nursing very strong and overpriced coffee. They then walked out into Battery Park. "The history of this place goes back to the late sixteen hundreds." Phillip pointed to the street where the skyscrapers began. "The British government then controlled New York and they mounted cannons, I think over there. This little park had a part in the Revolutionary War and the War of 1812." He rubbed his nose and looked across the street. "We can't see the Towers from here, let's stroll up Broadway and get a better view."

Luke fell in beside his grandfather as they ambled up the famous avenue. On the sidewalk along the way were thin granite plaques inset in the concrete commemorating the multitude of historic parades that had transpired along that storied street. Each one spanned almost the width of the sidewalk and had a single person or group of people transcribed upon it in stainless steel letters.

"They call this stretch the Canyon of Heroes." Phillip pointed at one of the stones. "That's why. Each one commemorates the person or people honored by a ticker tape parade. I think they've had about two hundred of them since they started doing it in the late eighteen hundreds. They all happen on this stretch of Broadway."

Luke leaned over a plaque and several speeding pedestrians made quick detours around him. "This one is for the astronauts of Apollo Eleven, the ones who first landed on the moon."

"I'll bet they had quite a parade."

The pair walked up to Liberty Street where they made a left. They strolled one more block and found themselves at the corner of Church and Liberty Streets. The twin Towers stood before them like monstrous sentinels. This close, their real size was apparent.

Luke put his hands in his pockets and slowly looked up. "I knew they were big Edudi, but I had no idea." His head leaned all the way back as he peered at the distant top of the stupendous twins. "Utterly amazing."

Phillip chuckled. "I forgot... you've never been in this end of Manhattan before, have you?"

Luke looked over at Phillip and shook his head. "Nope. I've been in Greenwich Village when we played there once with Redbird. The only place we visited then was Times Square."

"This street we're going to cross is interesting. To the left it's Trinity Place, to the right it's Liberty Street." Phillip looked at his watch. "It's about 8:15, we've got about an hour before our meeting with Lucy and her friends. Let's go across the World Trade Center Plaza."

The two Cherokees traversed the street and walked by the massive buildings to the other side of the square. Bearing to the left, they found a walkway that took them over West Street, depositing them near the Winter Garden Atrium. Phillip nodded at the glassy art deco structure. "We'll have to check that out later but now I want to see the river."

They skirted around a building and crossed Pumphouse Park to find themselves at the edge of the great waterway. "Let's sit for a moment Luke."

"Sure thing. How about here? We can see the Towers just fine."

"Yeah, that's the ticket. The edudi needs a break."

It had taken the best part of a half hour to traverse the plaza and wend their way to the Hudson River. In later years, both of them would look back in reverent awe at that last time they were able to walk so close to the twin Towers.

The growing sound of an approaching jetliner intruded on their consciousness. Phillip looked to the left towards midtown

Manhattan. A passenger jet was streaking across the skyline. It was much too low. "That jet jockey is way outside the zone."

Phillip had activated the Gawonisgi Nvya when they started their walk up Broadway. The stone had absolutely unlimited memory so he had no fear of losing images. It was remarkable in its operation. It seemed to know what you wanted and it didn't matter whether it was in the story trunk or his pocket, it always captured things as seen through his eyes. He had learned through decades of operation to be very careful where he looked when the stone was on.

Phillip jumped up and walked forward a few steps with his grandson beside him. "Luke," he barked, "Watch the Towers and be ready for anything."

Luke never had the battle training that his father and grandfather had shared. He did not enlist for the Gulf War, but he had the intensive Cherokee training of all his kin. He shifted his weight immediately to the balls of his feet and prepared for action, keeping his grandfather in his periphery to follow his cue.

The two Cherokees stood at a spot that afforded a view of everything. The jet sound became an immediate roar. The impossible sight of a Boeing 767 screaming just over the buildings of South Manhattan at what appeared to be top speed was seared forever into their memory. The jet took less than two seconds to traverse the space they were seeing, and then it slammed into the North Tower. The aircraft was totally swallowed by the building and a fireball of stupendous proportions exploded from the structure. The shock wave of the explosion rolled across south Manhattan and out into New York Harbor. The ground under their feet shook with the tremendous impact.

People around them were in total panic. There was screaming and crying and folks even falling to the ground. Phillip and Luke stayed rooted where they were and looked around to take stock of the situation. The moment was surreal with terror.

Suddenly the air around them began to sparkle and it seemed that everything outside the glow slowed and stopped. A small creature walked through the luminance and looked up at them. "Keeper of the Stone and his Apprentice, I bring you greetings."

Luke looked at the small person with open mouth, and then at Phillip. "A Yvwi Tsunsdi?"

Phillip nodded silently with large eyes. For once, he was speechless. He glanced up at the North Tower. The fireball hung suspended around it like some unholy halo. He looked back at the creature before them.

The Little One looked up at the young Cherokee. "Yes, Luke Shouting Crow, and it is appointed unto you and your grandfather to know our real worth." The diminutive creature suddenly morphed into a huge angel. A great sword hung at his side and the wings from his back cast a shadow on both of them.

Luke sunk to his knees. "My lord!"

The angel reached for his hand. "Rise, Luke Shouting Crow. I am a servant of the Most High God. Worship Him." The angel looked at both of them intently. "The group of Native Americans of which you know will be trapped in the North Tower in a few seconds. I can free them but you must lead them to safety. This will be a day of terrible tragedy, and you will not be able to save many, only these few. Can you help them?"

Phillip found his voice. "Yes, take us there right away."

The angel grabbed each of their hands and they flew up from the bank of the Hudson River towards the North Tower, surrounded by the yellow glow. Both Phillip and Luke found themselves floating effortlessly by the angel's side. Time again came to life and the great fireball blossomed upwards until it briefly obscured the entire top of the building. Debris from both the plane and the building ejected into the air and fluttered toward the ground in a dance of death.

Phillip looked below him as they rose into the air. People were running and pointing and crying and shouting in confusion. How could this thing be? What flight controller let that pilot fly into the Tower? He looked at the great angel and said, "Who has done this thing?"

The angel looked over with eyes of compassion. "This is many things. On the physical level you are witnessing, it is a revelation of a great evil that is a part of the end of all things. On a spiritual level, it is a prophecy, but few will discern it and fewer still will act upon it. Let he who has ears hear."

Suddenly they were below a terrible ragged hole in the North Tower. It belched forth black smoke as white fire raged inside. The heat that radiated from the fissure was blistering. They flew through the wall about twenty floors below the decimation and landed in front of a blocked door. They heard banging and yelling from inside. The angel looked at them steadfastly and said, "You have just enough time to escape from this building with those behind this door." He touched them both and they each felt a sort of liquid electric jolt that energized them with purpose. "The elevators are useless. Take them downward on the stairs and do not falter. Encourage all you meet to hurry and escape. Go quickly to the south on Trinity Place when you are out and take shelter in Trinity Church until this is over. You will be safe there." He smiled at the men. "Be bold and strong, oh highly favored of Creator." He turned and grasped the debris blocking the door and flung it aside effortlessly. "Farewell," he said, and then became impossibly small and vanished.

Luke sprang to the door and yanked it open. "Osiyo, brothers and sisters. Follow us now and do not stop. We will take you to safety."

An older woman stumbled forward and gazed at them with a stunned expression. "Phillip, is that you?"

"Lucy, I am here." She ran to the old Cherokee and fell into his arms weeping.

"Phillip, what has happened? We heard a terrible explosion and the whole building swayed."

Phillip held her at arm's length. "A jetliner has struck the North Tower. We are in terrible danger. The elevators aren't working; we must walk down, and quickly."

Lucy gasped. "I am an old woman. I don't know if I can do this."

Luke reached out and touched her arm. "Yes you can, I will help you."

"Lucy," Phillip said, "this is my grandson Luke. Take his arm and we must go. Hurry!"

Galen Monroe sat in the penthouse office on Wall Street

receiving his morning briefing from Warren Cole. Feeling restless and unsettled, he stood and looked out the window towards uptown Manhattan. Something tickled his mind, a piece of knowledge he once knew and was now out of reach. It was such a human feeling that he rejected it completely. As a consequence, the unsettledness turned into outright foreboding.

"The building hardening is now complete. All took place under the guise of remodeling and the true purpose of the project was hidden from those who were involved. As always in the time in which we live, there are some that suspect hidden agendas. We have effectively deflected all of this."

"Warren, come here."

Cole looked at Monroe with a puzzled expression. "Sir?"

Monroe glanced over with a steely expression. "Now!" Cole jumped up and shot to the window. Monroe pointed towards mid-Manhattan. "What is that?"

"It looks like an airplane."

"Unusually low, don't you think?"

"It's barely clearing the buildings. In fact, at that altitude it could hit the Towers."

They looked at each other with wide-eyed expressions. Monroe quickly reached into his vest pocket for his satellite phone. The device was extremely compact and totally wireless. It was also voice activated. Monroe spoke to the phone, "The Director."

After two rings, a voice with a faint lisp came on the line. "Yes Galen?"

Monroe wasted no time. "I think it is happening, sir."

"The WTC?"

"That's right."

"I will make the necessary arrangements." The line clicked and was dead. Monroe pocketed the device. He looked up to see a Boeing 767 in the air just several blocks away. It closed the remaining distance in a fraction of a second and flew into the North Tower without slowing. A fantastic fireball exploded from the building. The structure in which they stood swayed ever so slightly, loath to view such outrage. Cole flinched and stepped back. Monroe remained motionless through the whole thing.

"Holy Mother of God," exclaimed Cole.

Monroe turned to him and spoke in a steely quiet voice. "Warren, evacuate this building. Have everyone walk towards the Brooklyn Bridge. Instruct them to get off this island as quickly as possible. Tell them do not try to get cars or taxis or trains. Do you understand?"

Cole's face was whiter than a freshly bleached sheet. "Yes sir." He turned and then stopped. "What about you, Galen?"

Monroe's expression softened. The man was so like Thomas. "I'll be fine, Warren. Go."

Cole looked searchingly at his superior, and then out the window. Fiery debris was raining on New York. "Okay boss." He turned and ran from the room.

Monroe waited until he was gone, and then reached under his desk and pressed a button. The door lock clicked softly, effectively cutting him off from the rest of the building.

Galen Monroe turned toward the window and did something he hadn't done in many centuries. He centered his thinking and entered wholly into a dimension that was beyond mortal humans. He passed through the tempered glass and headed towards the World Trade Center Plaza.

If anyone had been there to witness the transition, they would have seen Monroe turn into a bat-like creature and fly through the window.

25: Live to Forgive

Monroe briefly relished his true form. Huge and deadly, he looked a cross between man and bat. He was a creature from mankind's worst nightmares. He was a warrior from a battlefield that predated Creation itself. He was a dread specter of darkness that had long ago declared him-itself an enemy of all mankind. He flew directly to Five World Trade Center and the secret CIA office that was hidden in that building. Ignoring the terrified humans, he went directly to a huge vault. He simply tore the door off. He walked inside to survey dozens of shelves totally filled with cash. He grabbed one bundle and observed that they were all hundred-dollar bills. His laugh was a sinister rumble. "Twenty-first century gold substitute," he said.

He concentrated and all the cash shimmered and disappeared. "There you will stay until I need you." He turned and flew from the room, taking a trajectory close to the North Tower. A section that was below the hole that was belching black smoke suddenly became transparent. He recognized an old human inside who was looking directly at him with an expression of angry determination.

Phillip Shouting Crow did not know at first what he was seeing. The building was suddenly transparent before him, and outside in the air was a great man-bat hurtling towards him. Time again seemed to slow and stop and only he and the creature continued to move. He glanced over to see Luke helping Lucy, both frozen in mid-step. He turned back and suddenly knew who he was facing.

Phillip stepped forward and found himself standing in air. He was not afraid. "You are Galen Monroe who is known as Red Beard. What are you doing here, foul son of darkness?"

The demon creature laughed. It rumbled like a landslide that threatened to sweep Phillip into oblivion. "Who is this puny Cherokee that questions me?"

The man-bat sprang towards Phillip. Just before he made contact, Phillip cried out, "You are also Galen Mondragon who came to America with Thomas Banica."

The man-bat stopped short before his foe. "Yes, you are a Keeper of the Stone. You have never grasped just what that thing is have you? The Recreated would be most upset if I took it from you. The knowledge hidden in that puny rock could make me invincible against the Emissaries." The one who was Galen laughed hideously. "I think I will kill you and take your little rock."

Phillip leaned his head back and laughed. "Seeing the past would make you invincible?"

The monster thrust his-its face close to Phillip. "How little you know puny Cherokee. The Stone is older than you can possibly imagine." The creature pulled away and floated up to look down on his foe. "I will take it from your crushed body."

Phillip stepped forward and up, his face set like flint. He knew something about using authority over entities such as this. "I have heard you speak with Thunder Walking and Thomas Banica. Answer me, are you Galen Mondragon?"

"Yes, but I am much more than that, puny one. I am Vlad III, king of Romania. My full name there was Vlad Dracul." The demon chuckled deeply. "I was known as Vlad the Impaler."

"Those were all disguises. I see who you really are. What is your true name, being of darkness?"

"My true peers call me Hugor." The creature drifted closer. "But you can call me lord."

Phillip drew up to his fullest stature. His face darkened and a holy fire illuminated his eyes. "I know no Lord but Tsisa, and I declare to you, Tsisa is Lord!" Phillips voice rose in volume and authority until Hugor winced and fell back at the last pronouncement.

Unseen by the demon, the great Emissary who had brought Phillip here appeared behind the one who called him-itself Hugor. Phillip saw the being in his periphery but kept centered on the demonic creature. "You who are Galen, who is Vlad, who is Hugor, I resist you in the Name of the Lord Tsisa, the Very Son of the Most High God."

Another rumbling laugh emanated from Hugor. "Tsisa I know, God I know. Who are you?"

The great Emissary spoke in a voice like liquid light. It was uncompromising pronouncement that could be resisted by no being. "Hugor, Forgotten Son of darkness, turn and face me."

The great man-bat whirled around, his eyes widening as he comprehended who faced him. "Michael, my ancient enemy, are you still using a sword? How quaint." Hugor thrust forth a hand and a bolt of livid energy sprang forth. Michael neatly deflected it with his weapon.

Phillip turned to see the bolt career into the desperate gash in the side of the North Tower. It was harmlessly absorbed. Everything within that smoking hole had already been consumed. The smoke was frozen in time as the supernatural battle continued.

Michael sprang forward at his enemy and Hugor feinted to one side. The Emissary turned in a position that left Phillip fully protected behind him. Hugor sprang back and executed an inside loop, producing a sword of his own in the process. "I still remember how to use one of these." He flew straight at Michael, his sword the dread tip of a fell arrow.

Michael held forth his sword and slashed down at the moment of contact. Hugor was thrust downward beneath Michael and Phillip. He smashed into the side of the doomed building. "So do I," said the Emissary.

The man-bat shrieked in anger and zoomed up to face Michael. He thrust wickedly with his sword as Michael parried the blows. The Emissary began pushing Hugor out away from the building and from Phillip. They thrust and parried until

Hugor suddenly shot skyward and dove at deadly speed towards Phillip. Michael shot over to the airspace above the Cherokee and a huge shield of light appeared on his left arm. Hugor barreled into the obstacle at tremendous speed and was deflected out towards the South Tower by the impact.

Michael glanced down at Phillip. "You okay?" Phillip nodded mutely. Michael looked back up to see Hugor speeding towards him. He moved towards his enemy holding his sword in an offensive attack position.

Sword fighting in three dimensions was infinitely more complicated than swordplay on land. There were increased opportunities for both error and victory. Michael used one of these opportunities to his great advantage.

As Hugor dove straight towards him, the huge angel pulled up just before impact. With one great downward stroke, Michael severed the hand that held his enemy's sword. The weapon fluttered downwards towards the now frozen chaos on Liberty Street. The hand stayed eerily frozen on the hilt as it disappeared. He looked into Hugor's eyes with a burning intensity. "Again you meet your doom, my ancient enemy."

As he finished speaking, the glowing winged being thrust a sword through Hugor. The man-bat stiffened with terror-filled eyes. The great being pulled out his sword and held it vertically in front of him. "This is Liberator, the sword you have met before. Return to the Shadow, o creature of darkness."

The man-bat looked at Phillip with stricken eyes, and then plunged to the ground. A thin trail of black smoke followed him down. The Emissary then flew over to Phillip. "Oh greatly favored of Creator, you have helped vanquish a terrible ancient foe. Your service this day is great." The being again touched Phillip and he felt a jolt of energizing power. Michael withdrew his hand and looked at him with a faint twinkle in his eye. "Remember the stories of your people." The great being suddenly zoomed skyward and was gone.

Phillip stepped back into the building and time resumed. The wall was again solid. He heard his grandson say, "Follow me people. Let's go Granddad." He nodded mutely and followed them down the long stairs.

The body of Galen Monroe was recovered from the rubble of the World Trade Center. In that much, he was fortunate. Thousands were never recovered. Warren Cole related the story of how Monroe had the foresight to evacuate his building and then how he disappeared. He theorized that Monroe made his way to the North Tower to help survivors, and died in the building's collapse. The truth remained elusive for no one had all the facts.

Secretary of Defense Donald Rumsfeld had stated in a press conference shortly before the World Trade Center was destroyed that some 2.3 trillion dollars of Pentagon funds could not be accounted for. He expressed dismay at the shortfall. The story was utterly obliterated by the catastrophic events in New York.

Phillip Shouting Crow was warned by an angel of the Lord in a dream to never speak of the true nature of the one he now knew as Hugor. To the end of his days, he kept this word. Only Phillip knew the one great victory achieved in a day of death and bitter defeat.

For two weeks, life as it was known in America stopped and every eye focused on a great smoking hole in the ground. Many hoped and some prayed that the almost three thousand souls buried there would rise from their grave. But for a mere handful, they did not.

Phillip and Luke stayed as volunteers to help in whatever way they could. Mostly, they manned the food stations that supplied the firemen with sustenance as they desperately labored to recover what they could. Sometimes they stood in the line helping pass debris from a critical location.

As the fact of Al Qaeda's central involvement became clear, Phillip was stunned. This was a desperate act of cowards. People like this would never declare themselves on a real field of battle. The attack was the demented conception of a self styled leader who was so filled with bitter hatred that he no longer would know truth if it met him in the street. This uncovered a danger so pervasive that it rewrote the world's concept of good and evil in a day.

Yet the rock of bitterness within Phillip still had voice in this darkest scenario. There was a distant cold justice in the event that happened on the island taken from Natives for twenty-four dollars worth of baubles. The bitter rock wanted Phillip to feel avenged, but he did not. He could only feel deep grief and sorrow at the senseless loss of so many souls. The war of feelings went on deep within him without a ripple breaking the surface.

Luke was riding with a fire company to help load supplies to bring back to Ground Zero. The food line was well manned for now, so he had a few moments alone. Phillip walked slowly along Church St. looking down into the endless hive of activity. Smoke still rose from the site and the fireman had told him of raging hotspots beneath the rubble still burning at thousands of degrees. The pit was a seething cauldron spewing poison into the air and the lungs of all who struggled within her.

As he stood and beheld this mass grave, the tears again welled up in his eyes. He was doing better now. He could go a couple of hours without weeping. He wiped his eyes with the sleeve of the fire jacket that one company had given him. "Take it, old man," their fire chief had said. "We've got plenty and you need it for this work."

He didn't hear him approach but Phillip could feel the friendly and sympathetic presence beside him. He looked over and saw a young fireman staring into Ground Zero. He glanced up at Phillip and nodded. "Howdy."

"Hello fireman."

"You know, I don't think I will ever get used to this."

Phillip nodded slowly. "I know what you mean."

The fireman turned toward him. "Hey, aren't you the old Cherokee who's here with his grandson?"

"Yeah, just an old Indian in the big city."

The fireman leaned forward earnestly. "No, no, I didn't mean it like that. I mean, I've heard about all you two guys are doing, and, well, I just think it's wonderful."

The old Cherokee looked the white fireman in the eye and saw a spark of earnest life that made him open his eyes a little wider. "Thank you son."

"Well, yes sir." He put forth his hand. "Name's Joe."

Phillip met his handshake firmly. "Phillip. Pleasure to meet you, fireman."

"The pleasure is mine." Joe looked back over the wreckage. "I heard tell that you and your grandson are believers. That so?"

Phillip chuckled. "Believers in what, Joe?"

The fireman looked mildly flustered. "Well, believers in Jesus the Son of God."

Phillip looked sidelong at his new friend. "Well I guess you heard right, Joe. We Cherokee know him as the Lord Tsisa."

"Gee saa? Is that Cherokee for Jesus?"

Phillip nodded. "He has been my Friend and Guide from my youth."

Joe nodded. "Well, praise the Lord. I love Jesus too. Guess that makes us brothers."

Phillip had known the adoption into the family of God, but knew few white believers in other than passing acquaintance. The concept coming from a white man who was a stranger moments ago took him off guard. The bitter rock within told him it could not be so. He decided to nod once and leave it there.

Joe was silent for a moment and then spoke. "There's something real important I need to tell you Phillip." He straightened up and turned toward the Cherokee. "I don't talk about this much, but my great great great grandfather was an Army officer back in the 1830's. He was one of them that drove your people on the Trail of Tears."

Phillip turned and beheld Joe with new interest. *Where is he going with this?* "My great great grandfather walked on that Trail."

Joe nodded and then looked out over the pit towards the Hudson River. "You know, I've always felt bad about that." He sniffed and rubbed his nose. "Wished there was something I could do." He looked back at Phillip. "It's been more recently that the Lord has showed me there is something I can do and that's this. I can repent."

Phillip remembered his Catawba friend Chief Eugene Fallen Timber and his eyes welled up with more tears. *Darn. That's twice in ten minutes.* He wiped them with his sleeve, leaving a sooty streak across his face. He stayed silent, ready to receive Joe's words as he reached into his pocket and pressed a stud on the stone.

Joe took a step closer. "Phillip, I'd like to repent to you for the sins of my fathers in sending your people on the Trail of Tears. I want to repent not just for what my grandfather did as an officer in the Army, but for what America did to your people. I am so sorry for uprooting you from your homeland and sending you to a foreign place. Please forgive me. Please forgive my country. I'm sorry Phillip."

Phillip dropped his head for a moment and then spoke. "My grandfather would be very pleased to hear your words. His name was Soaring Eagle and he walked the Trail from Ross's Landing to Indian Territory. His daughter Feather died on the way but he and his wife made it." Phillip looked up. "I forgive you my brother and on behalf of the Cherokee, I receive your apology." He nodded slowly. "It is a good thing you have done today, Joe the Fireman." Phillip held out his hand and they shook again. The small dark rock of bitterness inside Phillip began to soften.

Joe didn't let go of Phillip's hand. "I also want to repent to you for what America did to all you Indians in the twentieth century. For the Termination Act in the 1950's."

"1953," said Phillip softly. "It was 1953." Phillip dropped Joe's hand while he continued to look into his eyes. "That legislation sent my sister Rosie to San Francisco and she died there."

At this, Joe's eyes welled with tears. "I'm sorry about Rosie, Phillip. How did she die?"

Phillip stared over into Ground Zero. "It was at Alcatraz during the Indian occupation."

"I've heard about that. I was just a baby then."

"She had just come back to the Lord and was sharing the Good News with someone. An old railing gave way and she fell to her death."

Joe was silent for a moment as he absorbed this. "I know we'll see her again, then."

"Oh yes." Phillip remembered again the good words he had received in Charlotte that took him to the Catawba Nation. "Joe, I can speak for myself and the Cherokees in forgiving you for the Termination Act." He reached out his hand and they clasped once again. "Thank you, my friend."

"Just trying to do what the Lord tells me." Joe glanced at his watch. "My break's about up, gotta get back to work. Good meeting you Phillip."

"You too, Joe the Fireman."

Joe started to go, and then turned back. "Do you have another name, you know, an Indian name?"

"I am Phillip Shouting Crow."

"Shouting Crow, I like that."

"It was my father's name before me."

"Well, see you around."

"Goodbye, Joe." Phillip watched the young firefighter walk away. *So many of them died right here trying to save others.* A plume of smoke obscured his new friend and when it blew away, he was gone.

It was as if the Camaro knew the way back to Soaring Eagle, OK. Even in some less remembered areas of the nation, neither Phillip nor Luke consulted a map, yet always knew the next turn. The trip home was somber and quiet. The revelation of the Gawonisgi Nvya to Luke was so massively overshadowed by the events of 9/11 that both of them put it aside for now. This was a time of mourning.

Phillip pondered and prayed deeply about the words he had received from Joe the Fireman. They required a much deeper and more profound response from him, one that he was unsure he could make. The rock was smaller now but had hardened again.

As usual, they stopped at the car wash in Tahlequah to clean up the old Z28. After seven years on the long road, over 200,000 miles, an engine and transmission rebuild, a repaint, and new Recaro seats, she looked, if anything, better than showroom condition. The car still turned heads.

As they made the final approach to the Arkansas River homestead, Phillip was driving. He turned to Luke and said,

"Son, you know to say nothing of the stone to anyone, correct?"

"Yes, Granddad."

"Good." Phillip turned and wheeled up the long driveway to home.

James and Sally greeted them like returning heroes. The tales of their involvement at Ground Zero were all over eastern Oklahoma and many more people were anxious to welcome them home. It was good to be back.

2001 AD
TAHLEQUAH, OK

Phillip drove into Tahlequah alone several weeks later. It was a bright autumn afternoon and the old Cherokee capitol was wearing her fall finery. He pulled in behind the Cherokee Courthouse and wandered across the park around the old building. He stopped for a moment at the monument to Chief John Ross, the great Cherokee who had brought the Nation through the Trail and into their future. *Andrew Jackson got the twenty-dollar bill and all Chief Ross got was this one lousy rock.* The dark place within him throbbed in response.

He wandered out on Muskogee Ave. and walked down toward the University. He stopped and chatted with several acquaintances along the way. He felt hungry so he stopped into Sam and Ella's just before the campus. He looked at the name and chuckled at the play on words. *White man beware.*

Phillip slipped into a booth and in a moment, a pert young Cherokee maid came to wait on him. He ordered one of the personal size pizzas. As the waitress delivered the steaming pie, Phillip confided, "You know, I've eaten the best pizza that New York has to offer and your pies go nose to nose with them any day. My compliments to the chef."

The young girl beamed. "I'll tell him, sir. Thank you very much."

Phillip finished his meal and paid the tab, slipping back out onto the street. Next to Sam and Ella's was an inviting little park with a beautiful creek and some benches. The old Cherokee wandered onto a bench and sat down to watch the water flow.

The recent events appeared before him and he again felt the agonizing loss of almost three thousand souls. He then saw Joe's face, his compassionate pleading eyes. He was so sincere.

Oh Creator, what is wrong with me? I do love the white man as you do, but I can't let go of the blame. They destroyed over five hundred nations to build this land. The legacy of brutal policies still hovers over all of us and there is no escape. What am I to do?

Phillip felt rather than heard the answer. It came as a long exhaled sigh. *Forgive.*

Phillip stood and wandered onto the campus of Northeastern State University. Tahlequah was home to one of three campuses of this great eastern Oklahoma state university. Students walked about at the end of their day, most headed for the dorms. They were so young and eager. They were the future in this place. They were white and black and red and, to them, it didn't seem to matter. Perhaps the sons and daughters of the activists of last century had learned to accept one another. Maybe this was a part of the key for which Phillip was looking.

But wasn't this playing right into the white man's hand? Wasn't this the goal of the acculturation began at Carlisle in 1879? "Kill the Indian and save the man," said Captain Richard Pratt, founder of that first Indian Boarding School. Phillip shook his head. *Oh Creator, are we just supposed to be American stew? How can I be American and Cherokee at the same time?*

The Breath of God came once again. *Forgive.*

The sun was lowering, calling to her brother the moon to come forth. It was the night of the new moon. Brother moon would be very lazy this evening and stay in bed. He would return soon for the Month of the Trading Moon and sister sun would be happy again. The old Storyteller smiled as he remembered the rich legends and stories of his people. They were the tapestry of his life and they were so foreign to so many of the new generation of Cherokees. Like James' sister Sarah, they willingly went away to the Big City and forgot about their people. It was willing participation in the Termination policy of another century. Move them to the city. Dissolve the tribes. Tear up the treaties. It never happened.

O Unetlanvhi! They are achieving their goal. They are killing the Indian. No one cares and white America doesn't even know this is happening. The earnest face of Joe the Fireman swam into his consciousness. "Forgive me," he said. Phillip felt his presumption exposed. *Yes, Lord, there are those who care, like Joe.*

The Breath of God swept across his inner man once more. *Forgive.*

Phillip turned back and walked into town. He approached the old Cherokee Courthouse once again. Dusk had deepened and the streetlights of Tahlequah quietly brightened. Phillip sat down on a bench on the Courthouse square. There was something inexorable about hearing the Lord whisper in your spirit. A still small voice carried a weight of authority that could not be ignored.

There was no one about when one old man bowed his head and began to weep. *Unetlanvhi, I believe! Help my unbelief.* He saw the face of the cruel schoolmistress from Sequoyah School.

Forgive.

Oh Creator, I forgive Miss Stillborn and the other teachers at Sequoyah School.

He saw a photograph of Senator Dawes who had begun the process of Relocation with his census of all Cherokee.

Forgive.

Lord, I forgive Senator Dawes for what he began against our Nation.

Phillip saw ruthless Bluecoats chasing down mothers and children at Wounded Knee. He cringed as they fired.

Forgive.

Phillip hesitated. *That was murder, Lord!*

Forgive.

Phillip took a shuddering breath and cried out in his inner agony. A squirrel hurrying to his rest paused to look at the old man bowed over on the park bench.

Phillip suddenly stood inside a Bluecoat soldier on that horrible day. He felt his stupefying fear and the thought that recurred over and over; *Kill them before they kill us all.*

I understand, Lord! I do forgive the Bluecoats at Wounded Knee.

He saw the ghostly face of Andrew Jackson rise up to float as a specter prepared to exile him forever.

Forgive.

Oh Creator, he is the father of our worst and most lasting pain! He

was a murderous foul man who would have killed us all if he could.
Phillip saw a vision of an aged John Ross walking to the door of
The Hermitage. He saw the even more aged President receive
him cordially. Is that you, my worthy opponent? Is that regret
in Jackson's eyes as he treats Ross like an old friend?

Forgive.

Oh Lord, I see. Yes, I forgive Andrew Jackson. I forgive even him.
Phillip wept freely at the work the Lord was doing within him.
The small black stone had dissolved completely. It was gone.
He felt love for the white man that was no longer tainted by
suspicion. *Thank you Lord!*

Phillip raised his head and took a breath. It had gotten dark
while he was here and an evening chill began to seep through
the town. He stood to return to the Camaro. He felt lighter and
freer than he had ever felt. The darkness was gone.

He smiled as he walked across the lawn towards his car. *I
choose to forgive generations of sin.*

26: HOMECOMING

2009 AD
SOARING EAGLE, OK

"Granddad, the new twin quad processors are incredibly powerful. I think we can do something here that has never been done in the history of the stone."

"That's a long history, son." Phillip looked at Luke from across the table in his grandson's home. His wife and son were out doing Christmas shopping and it gave the two more time to study the ancient device.

Phillip was now ninety-one years old. His mind was clear and not ravaged by great age. He still lived in his old house and Luke had built a new house for his family only a hundred yards away. Phillip's eyesight had become uncertain and Oklahoma had finally taken away his driving privileges. He had given the old Camaro to Luke who only drove it occasionally. Chevrolet no longer made Camaros so it had become quite a collector's piece.

Luke sat in front of his new laptop computer with several strange peripherals hung off the machine. One device attached by Firewire looked decidedly homegrown. "Look again, Granddad. This one stud has the legend that can be interpreted to mean 'face to face.' That's the one."

"You showed me before son." Phillip stamped his foot. "I am not losing my memory, Luke Shouting Crow!"

Luke laughed easily. "Take it easy Granddad. I'm just reviewing the facts." Luke tweaked a knob on the DIY interface and positioned the stone nearby. "Okay, if I'm right, the Yvwi Tsunsdi were thinking way ahead and what this button means is 'interface.' Granddad, say a prayer before I push this stud."

Phillip cleared his throat and closed his eyes. "Oh great Creator, guide us now. I pray that you reveal to Luke what is Your greatest purpose for this strange device that we bear." He opened his eyes and nodded at Luke.

"Come around here so you can watch this, Granddad." As Phillip moved next to him, Luke pressed a series of keys on the computer. A blank window opened on the desktop. "Okay, here goes." Luke pressed the stud on the stone. For several seconds nothing happened, and then the stone began humming slightly.

Phillip leaned forward and inspected it closely. "It has never done that."

A smoky swirl appeared in the waiting window on the computer and it expanded beyond the screen into the air over the computer. "Cool," Luke said.

A three dimensional airborne image was not unusual coming from the stone, but this was different somehow. It has a depth and intensity that was compelling. A green waveform gradually appeared. It started as a plain sine wave but increased in intensity and suddenly moved beyond the loose confines of the projected area to become a vertical green line that went down through the floor and extended out through the ceiling.

Luke jumped to his feet. "Let me check this out, Granddad," he called over his shoulder as he ran out the front door. "Oh wow," he exclaimed from outside. He ran back in and grabbed Phillip's arm. "Granddad, you gotta see this!"

"Patience grandson, don't pull my arm off." Phillip rose and walked out front. He turned to view the house. The green beam poked up through the roof and into the night sky. Phillip leaned his head back. It was visible for as far as he could see. "Son, turn it off. Now."

Luke knew better than to question the old man. He ran inside and pulled the Firewire connection out of the computer. The green line slowly retracted and then the projected screen swirled out of existence. The stone stopped humming and lay quietly.

Phillip followed him in. "Let's hope NORAD didn't scan that beam. That's all we need is to have a truck full of Men in Black crawling over this property."

Luke pushed his hand through his hair. "What was that, Granddad?"

"I don't know son, I don't know."

It was several days later before the two cohorts had a chance to examine the data from the event. Luke had some difficulty isolating what happened as a single story. He had to input a current data range to find the record. He found it once and then was eager for Phillip to see what he had found.

"Okay, the stone remembers it differently than we do. Watch, Granddad." Luke pressed the replay stud and an image expanded around them and enclosed them entirely. They saw only the stone on the table before them in the image. It began to glow a bright violet and everything in the image around it went dark. Then, below the stone appeared the tales of the ages of the Cherokee Nation. It was like a rocket ride through history. Above the stone appeared a golden portal. Through the portal could be seen a figure, but the details would not resolve. The image then faded away. "That must have been when I pulled the plug."

Phillip stroked his chin. "We didn't see that purple color, we heard it. It was extreme ultra-violet, invisible to our eyes."

Luke looked at him with open mouth. "I think you've got it, Edudi."

"The door was the gate of Heaven and our Eldest Brother was standing there."

"A dimensional gateway!"

"I think I said that." Phillip smiled at his grandson. "He was standing there during all of the history of the Cherokee, watching over us. Literally."

Luke whistled. "This is huge, Granddad."

"Yes it is son. The question is, why we have been shown this and what are we to do with it?"

"There's more that I've discovered. This device has access to an infinite data array. As best as I can determine, it stores the data within itself across eleven dimensions. The matrix that forms is inconceivable. It takes string theory physics to even grasp it."

"Sounds perfectly logical." Phillip leaned back and adopted a scholarly air. "It is traversing freely back and forth across the branes and through the higher curled up dimensions. Because of the infinite possibilities of interconnections that represents, the storage would be nearly unending."

Luke's jaw dropped as he listened to his grandfather. "You know theoretical physics too?"

Phillip shrugged. "I saw The Elegant Universe on PBS a few years back. Fascinating stuff." They both laughed.

Luke stabbed the air with a finger as he continued. "The real interesting question is what powers this thing? How can it run for millennia without missing a beat?" He raised his chin and waited for a response. Phillip remained silent. "I have probed it several ways the best I can and this is what I think. There is an infinitesimal black hole in the center of the unit. I mean, it reads null, nothing there, no echo. Only a singularity could do that. And only a singularity could keep running for five thousand years." Luke looked triumphant.

"Sounds like you've got it figured, Luke. Now, why do we have it?"

"Ah, that's a question I still have not answered."

2010 AD
SOARING EAGLE, OK

It was a chilly January day before Phillip and Luke again had a chance to investigate further. Luke's wife and baby had gone to visit her Lakota parents and Luke stayed behind "to watch over Edudi." In truth, he knew their time was short and there was still so much to learn about the stone.

"Keepers of the Stone always tell their wives eventually." Phillip smiled encouragingly at Luke. "You will too. You'll know when the time is right. It will be after I'm gone."

Luke was silent at the prospect. "I'll miss you, Edudi."

Phillip looked out the window. "You will join me one day my son."

Luke considered the prospect. "Yes, but I think Unetlanvhi has a few things for me to do.

Phillip smiled at his grandson. "You begin to sound like another great grandfather I once knew."

"I only hope I can do a tiny bit of what Soaring Eagle accomplished." Luke began fiddling with the stone. "Edudi, the oldest stories I can find don't give a clue about the origin of the Aniyvwiya. Later there are stories, but nothing very early. There are hints of a great voyage, but only that. There are also Flood stories."

"The dog who told his master to make a great vessel for he and his family?" Phillip smiled mysteriously.

"And it rained for forty days and forty nights as the water gushed up out of the ground."

"And the wicked ones drowned." Phillip sat down and faced Luke. "I believe the stories of my people. I grew up knowing the Flood account in Genesis. It was after I received the Gawonisgi Nvya that I learned that story in the Stone. It is exceedingly ancient."

"And totally true."

"Precisely." Phillip folded his hands across his midsection.

Luke squinted at his grandfather. "But I also believe what the Bible says about the origins of man. God created us."

"Yes He did. But what happened after that?"

"Man became wicked. They built the Tower of Babel to become higher than God."

"And God scattered men across the face of the earth." Phillip leaned back. "Where did they all go?"

"I dunno, to Europe, to Russia, to China?"

"Yes, in part."

"Then they were all destroyed in the Flood."

"Were they?"

"That's what the Bible says."

"Genesis 7:21 says, 'And all flesh that moved upon the face of the earth died.' What was the earth?"

"The world, all of it?"

Phillip leaned forward intently. "Could it have been what the Storytellers who transcribed the Word of God knew as the world at that time?"

"Scary thought, Edudi. That's starting to sound like Higher Criticism."

"Perhaps, but consider this. How could the black man, the red man, the yellow man and the white man all spring from the three ruddy middle eastern sons of Noah?"

"Um... evolution?" Luke raised his eyebrows. He then grinned and they both laughed. "Edudi, those are questions that good Christians don't ask."

"I know son."

Luke looked questioningly at Phillip for a moment, and then turned back to the device. "I've been working on this interface and I think I've got it tuned so it won't put out the alien beacon again."

"Good. No Men in Black."

Luke grinned into his project. "Not today. Let's try this, Edudi." Phillip moved beside him as Luke punched a series of keys on the laptop. "Here goes." He pressed the stud on the stone and they were immediately enveloped in a three dimensional field. The stone appeared to be floating in front of them. "Okay, let me try something recent." He punched in a sequence on the stone and an image appeared below them of the World Trade Center with a fireball exploding on the South Tower. Both Phillip and Luke were again gripped with the tragedy. As they looked above, the golden gateway appeared. Scores of angels were issuing forth and descending below to the Towers. One that Phillip recognized as Michael led them.

"We never saw this Edudi. We were descending with the group of Cherokees in the North Tower when the plane hit the South Tower."

Phillip nodded. "Perhaps the stone remembers more than we know." He wondered if the Stone would have a record of the fantastic battle between Michael and Hugor. "I hope not," he muttered under his breath.

"What's that Edudi?"

"Nothing, Luke."

Luke found that he could focus on one thing and his vision would zoom into that area. He saw an angel behind a fireman on Church St. The great being was whispering to him as he rushed people into a restaurant. They barely escaped a jet engine crashing into the ground. Luke pointed. "Granddad, isn't that your friend Joe?"

Phillip followed Luke's pointed finger and found his vision zooming in on Church St. There was Joe pushing people out of harm's way. "Why, yes it is. Isn't that amazing? No Keeper has unlocked these capabilities. You will be great in the annuls of the stone, Luke Shouting Crow."

Luke ignored the compliment. He was feeling confident. "Okay, let's try pushing the forward stud and the interface stud together." Suddenly they floated in air over a vast unending assembly of people of all kinds. All were dressed in white and all Sang together. They stretched beyond the horizon and yet one could still see beyond the horizon. They made a Song that was so powerful and achingly beautiful that it made Luke and Phillip cringe in fear while they wept for joy. Some of these radiant creatures had musical instruments that seemed multidimensional in structure. Parts of them phased in and out of the current dimension as the Song traversed a trans-dimensional space that mere earthly music could not. "What is this place?" Luke looked around with open mouth.

"Look there!" Luke followed his grandfather's finger unerringly and his vision zoomed in on a great warrior. He was obviously Cherokee, but he wore spotless white clothing and bore a white shield on his back.

Phillip jumped to his feet in boyish excitement. "Look! It is the grandfather! He wears the skin of the white buffalo and carries the Shield of Faith. It is my Grandfather!"

"Soaring Eagle?" Luke stood by Phillip and instinctively grasped his hand. "Where is this?"

Phillip turned to Luke with ecstasy on his face. Years had dropped away and the old man looked young and radiant. "This is the future New Earth where the chosen of Creator will gather!"

Suddenly, the Song reached a massive crescendo and above all of their heads, an infant galaxy-universe sprang into being. It spread forth like a precocious child, quickly enveloping the skies. It wavered momentarily like a dimensional rangefinder finding a focus, and then cleared into a swirling array of stars and planets.

Phillip and Luke gasped and huddled together. They were overwhelmed with what they were beholding. Suddenly the image faded and the stone again floated in blackness. Luke took a deep breath. "There is one more, Grandfather. We have come this far." Phillip nodded as they still held tightly to one another. Luke pressed the up and interface studs simultaneously.

The golden doorway appeared and the shrouded figure of One stood in the opening with His arms spread wide. They only saw His shape and not His features. "My precious children," He said, "It is not yet time. No man may see God and live still as a man. There are stories yet to tell. Go forth with the blessings of Unetlanvhi." The image faded and the spatial area around them seemed to contract into the stone and disappear.

Phillip and Luke found themselves standing by the stone and computer with their arms around each other. As they disentangled themselves, Luke gasped. "Grandfather, your gray hair is gone!"

Phillip felt his head. "What do mean? I have my hair."

"Look in a mirror Edudi."

Phillip rushed into the bathroom. "Praise the Lord!" He ran back out. "It's black again!"

2012 AD
SOARING EAGLE, OK

Phillip lay in his bed and was no longer able to rise. Ninety-four years was a long time to be on planet Earth. "Luke, you are more ready than I ever was to take the stewardship of the stone. The time has come for you to carry the stories of our people into the future." His hair still shone black from their experience several years ago, yet the old man was tired, so tired. "The veil grows so thin sometimes that I can see Soaring Eagle in his white buffalo skin beckoning to me." Phillip sighed deeply. "Unetlanvhi has blessed me with a rich life. I have gone from a mule to a Model A to a P-51 to a Z28." Phillip chuckled. "Not many Cherokees did that."

"I think you're the only one, Granddad."

"Luke, take the story trunk. I've shown you how it is rigged for the stone. This will be the cover for our time together alone. I am giving you the trunk. Beyond that, you alone know that I am bequeathing to you the stewardship of the Stone. Remember the stories of my people."

Luke picked the story trunk up off the floor and stowed the old artifact under one arm. He leaned down and put the other around his grandfather. His eyes got misty as he said, "I'm going to miss you so much Edudi. You have been my best friend."

"And now it's time for you to renew your friendship with that James fellow. Help him to be an edudi to your little Pete."

"I will."

Phillip composed himself and then said, "Call them in."

Luke rushed out the door. Phillip heard him in the next room in a loud voice, "Look what Edudi gave me!" There were exclamations of happiness, and then in a moment the room filled up.

Phillip looked tenderly around at the generations of the Eagle. They were a strong family still holding the homestead that Soaring Eagle and Wild Paw had carved from the wilderness of Indian Territory so long ago. They had survived the Dawes Roll, Indian Relocation, and Indian Termination without losing ground. They or their descendents would be here to greet the Lord Tsisa when He returned. "I have run my race and it is complete. Unetlanvhi has blessed me with the best family an old man could have. My cup is full to overflowing." He looked at his son. "James, you have been a faithful servant of the Most High God. You are the eldest; lead our family in peace and safety." He looked at Luke standing by his Lakota bride Debbie True Deer. She held the youngest of the clan. "Little Peter Shouting Crow, you are the future of our clan. We have moved far from the Cherokee clans and now are just our family. You have polluted the Cherokee with more of that wild Lakota blood." The family all chuckled. He motioned to Debbie to bring the child closer. He laid an ancient hand upon his head. (It did not shake.) "You will bring the deepest spirituality of the Lakota unto the Lord Tsisa and thus you will teach your elders wisdom."

He withdrew his hand and turned his head back on the pillow. Phillip Shouting Crow began to sing.

"I have tread the lonely path
As I walked the Narrow Way
My Creator now is calling
'Enter into endless Day'
The story trunk behind me
And Eternity ahead
I walk the final steps
Upon the Word that He has said"

As he watched, the ceiling became transparent and disappeared. He beheld the blackness of space lit by the uncounted stars of the Milky Way. A group of seven horses galloped across that great swath of stars toward him. On the lead horse was the Soaring Eagle himself. Five others held great warrior Natives, three Sioux, two Cherokee. Each was dressed in the white buffalo hide that his grandfather wore. The last horse was empty, awaiting a rider. Phillip held up his arm and pointed. "Behold, they come on white horses! The servants of my Lord come!"

He suddenly felt weightless and so young. He could feel the blood racing in his veins. He could hear the contraction of his muscles. His vision became crystal clear and he had the sudden and full knowledge of his people.

His family was now surrounding him and falling upon him. They were weeping and calling his name. "Do not weep, my children. See, Great Grandfather has come to visit." He felt himself rising above the bed and realized he could stand in the air. He took one last look at his grieving family, and then turned to behold Soaring Eagle. "It is good to see you again Great Grandfather."

"It is good to see you Grandson. Behold, your steed awaits." The magnificent white horse whinnied and pawed the air. He reared up playfully, inviting Phillip to ride. He ran and jumped upon the mount, and then turned toward his family again.

"As I fly to my Creator
The circle is complete
The Nation's hoop is mended
The Sacred Tree replete
With leaves that heal the Nations
And dry the warrior's tears
We become God's new creations
Leave behind the shadow fears"

His family remained bowed over him as he sang his death song, all except Luke. The new Keeper of the Stone looked up in wonder, open-mouthed as he beheld the Eternal Warriors and his grandfather singing his beautiful song. Tears began to stream from his eyes but he never let them waver from the heavenly vision. When Phillip finished singing, he raised his hand high toward his grandson. Phillip raised his in return.

"Hoka hey," the Sioux warriors called out.

"Hoka hey," answered Phillip Shouting Crow.

"Hoka hey," whispered Luke as he kept his hand raised.

Soaring Eagle's stallion reared and whinnied, eager to be Home. He circled and the rest of the Eternal Warriors wheeled around with him. Phillip turned his face towards Home and didn't look back again.

The group stretched out and raced across the Milky Way. Phillip's steed was strong and tireless. They raced as one, traversing light years in a moment. And then they were before a golden portal. "I have seen this before," Phillip said.

Soaring Eagle smiled at him. "Yes, we know." It felt good to see his great grandfather's smile again.

Phillip jumped from his horse and ran towards the Gate. From the other side he saw One running to greet him. All veils fell away and he knew it was the Lord Tsisa. He fell weeping into His arms.

His Voice was low and melodious. "Well done, My faithful

servant."

> *"Eldest Brother runs to greet me*
> *As I melt in His embrace*
> *And I hear the words of blessing*
> *As I look into His Face*
> *'Well done, My faithful servant'*
> *And I feel a holy thrill*
> *'Join the council of the elders*
> *You've achieved My highest will'"*

EPILOGUE: A STORY TO BE TOLD

2016 AD
SOARING EAGLE, OK

T he brand new Camaro was filled with rakish memories of the nineties. It had a look that was straining to reach 2020 a couple of years ahead of time. "Ever since they brought the Camaro back in 2010 I've wanted one. I think Granddad would love it."

Debbie looked skeptically at the decidedly radical vehicle. Peter was jumping up and down at the sight. "Oh Pop, let's go for a ride now!"

Luke chuckled. "We will Pete. I think we should bring your Ma too, don't you?"

Peter looked down and kicked at the ground. "Well, I dunno."

Debbie lookd contrite. "Please Peter?"

He grinned up at his mother. "Well, I suppose just this once."

They all laughed as they piled into the new vehicle. Luke turned around to be sure Peter was properly belted in. Satisfied, he pulled on his own seatbelt harness.

Debbie was looking in the back. "Now that doesn't look like standard equipment on a 2016 Camaro." She pointed to a special cavity behind Luke's seat.

"Oh that. I had them do that special. That's where I'll keep the story trunk."

"Just like Edudi?"

"Just like Edudi."

The Camaro roared to life and took off down the Oklahoma lane, leaving a swirl of bright autumn leaves in its wake. Overhead a great eagle circled once with a keening cry, and followed in the air.

2016 AD
REDMOND, WA

It was a crisp autumn day in Redmond, Washington. The young man pushed through the door into the world headquarters of Microsoft. He approached the security desk. "I have an appointment with Mr. Ballmer."

The security guard looked at him with a bored expression. "Name?"

"Galen Mondor."

The guard searched his schedule. "ID?"

The visitor extracted a Washington state driver's license and handed it to the guard who noted that he was only twenty years old. Kids. This company ran on kids. This guy's red goatee set him apart but it had the aroma of just another gimmick. The guard remembered the kid who was here a couple of days ago with green hair and checkered pants. He wasn't hired either.

The guard handed Mondor a clip-on Microsoft security ID. "Proceed to the elevators, sir. Mr Ballmer is on the top floor. The secretary will direct you."

"Thank you so much." The young man turned and headed for the lifts. His eyes became dark and filled with the eerie light of distant stars and galaxies.

to be continued...

Hear "The Trail of Tears Suite" by Vertical Alignment,
the music behind "Generations of the Eagle."
http://verticalalignment.com
http://thundersongs.com

www.ingramcontent.com/pod-product-compliance
Lightning Source LLC
Chambersburg PA
CBHW030346020726
47493CB00003B/715